Sapphire Secrets

A Contemporary Christian novel

DAWN V. CAHILL

"I am the way, the truth, and the life: no man cometh unto the Father, but by me." John 14:6 KJV

"Did not our heart burn within us, while he talked with us by the way…?" Luke 24:32 KJV

Sapphire Secrets
Copyright © 2016 by Dawn V. Cahill

Cover design by: Dineen Miller
Edited by Brilliant Cut Editing
Formatting by Wild Seas Formatting
(http://www.WildSeasFormatting.com)
ISBN: 978-0-997-45210-5

Published By Spring Mountain Publishing
Gladstone, OR

To my sons – You inspire me in so many ways with your creativity and your passion for music.

Chapter One

As if the graveyard at midnight wasn't eerie enough, Livy's dad boomed out his annual recitation of Edgar Allan Poe. The same recitation she'd heard for twenty years.

"At midnight, in the month of June, I stand beneath the mystic moon—"

Tonight's mystic moon glimmered around a cloud, through the tops of evergreens, trying in vain to cast a beam into the mild June night and Brighton Cemetery.

"Like ghosts the shadows rise and fall—"

Livy clutched a handful of flowers to her chest and focused on keeping her breath steady and even. Her feet snapped twigs as she and her twin, DeeDee, followed Dad's flashlight arc along a row of oaks.

His baritone voice pierced the night. "My love, she sleeps! Oh may her sleep, as it is lasting, so be deep—"

A heavy wind sighed overhead. Branches creaked under the weight of the night. Livy dared not reach over and clasp her twin's hand. If she did, her shaky grip would betray her. Gravel crunched behind her as the groundskeeper trailed them.

"Some sepulcher, remote, alone—"

Most people would never guess famed rocker Declan Decker quoted Edgar Allan Poe. Tonight he was plain old Dad, Howard McCreary, come to pay his respects on the twentieth anniversary of his late wife's sudden passing.

"Oh to think, poor child of sin, It was the dead who groaned within."

She ground her teeth to keep from telling him to shut up, he was spooking her. He'd only tell her twenty-six was far too old to let a midnight cemetery spook her. Still, at each nocturnal visit to Mom's grave, a secret phobia gripped her. Coimetrophobia. Fear of cemeteries. Each year, she feigned indifference to the waving shadows and moaning wind. She forced herself to stroll with nonchalant strides like her no-nonsense twin.

Her foot slammed into something. The flowers flew from her hand, scattering in the dark. She grappled for DeeDee's hand, but missed and tumbled to the ground, gasping at the surge of pain shooting up her leg.

Her eyes flew open. A headstone, washed pale in the moon's gentle glow, hunkered before her like a determined stalker.

The darkness turned deeper, quieter, as if the whole universe held its breath. Livy lay motionless, an invisible weight pressing her down.

Two hands clasped her arms and lifted her as if she were six years old.

"Are you okay?" The man's soft voice seemed out of place in this graveyard of granite and sharp edges. "You took a nasty spill there."

She squelched back whimpers. "I think so." She winced at the throbbing in her knee and reached to knead the spot, but couldn't restrain her groans. "I hope so."

The groundskeeper grasped her elbow in a solid grip. "You're almost there."

Dad shone his flashlight at her feet and helped her gather the strewn flowers. She limped on, around a corner, to her mother's grave. Although she couldn't see the words, Livy had memorized every line years ago.

Luna L. Rickles McCreary
AKA Luna Raquelle
Lover of the Earth
Inhabitant of the Universe
Wife, Mother, Dancer, Poet
b. July 10, 1960, Seattle WA
d. June 5, 1993, Seattle WA
Survived by beloved husband Howard W. McCreary
And daughters Olivia September McCreary and Diana
Sapphire McCreary
"A dirge for her…that she died so young." Edgar Allan Poe

The marble slab dwarfed the others around it. Dad had spent a bundle on it.

He turned to them. "Do either of you have anything you want to say to your mother?"

DeeDee shook her head. "You go first, Dad."

He inclined his head, faced the stone, and tossed down a handful of wildflowers. "Luna Tunes. I hope you're happy, wherever you are. And I hope you're paying attention to what's going on here below. It's not pretty."

A gust of wind whipped Livy's hair into her face, and she flung it back. A raindrop fell on her head. Clouds covered the moon and threatened to dump their moisture. She moved closer to her twin.

"Mom," DeeDee said, "you would be so proud of Livy and me. We're finally opening our own dance school." DeeDee's always calm voice rose in pitch, as close to excited as it would ever get. "Dad bought us a building a few blocks from Green Lake, and we're planning the grand opening for early September, just in time for our birthday. Guess what we're going to call it?" She paused, as if waiting for Mom's reply. "The Saffire School of Dance."

Mom would get the significance. She would remember

telling them their birthstone, the sapphire, was coveted worldwide for its exquisite, brilliant blue hue.

DeeDee knelt and braced her clutch of flowers on Mom's headstone, then moved aside. Livy stepped forward and dropped her handful of blooms in front of the slab.

"Hi, Mom." She rubbed her fingers together. Raindrops fell harder and faster. "I've been trying to remember what happened the day you left us." She swallowed hard. "I'm sorry, but I still can't."

She could imagine Dad's thought process right now. *You've been saying the same thing year after year. Get over it already, kiddo.*

Instead, he asked, "Are you finished?" At her nod, he turned and led the way out.

With her annual ordeal almost over, she drew in a deep breath. A wet woodsy scent filled her lungs, so vivid she could almost taste it. The ache in her knee ebbed away. She trudged along, flanked by DeeDee on her right and the groundskeeper on her left.

The groundskeeper scrutinized her. "You don't remember your mother's death?"

"No. My mind's a complete blank."

"Were you with her when she passed away?"

"Dad says my sister and I found her shortly after she died. DeeDee remembers it well. But I don't."

He regarded her sister, and then glanced back at Livy, keeping his voice low. "It's odd you experienced your mother's death so differently than your twin did."

"I know, right?"

But she'd never forget her mother's burial, and how she screamed when the box with her mother in it sank into the yawning hole. As her wails crescendoed, DeeDee had attempted to soothe her. Their nanny patted her and picked her up, but she kicked and screamed so hard, Miss Joy

4

handed her over to Mommy's best friend, Audria. Finally, Grandma Gaia carried her to the car and let her hide her face in her shoulder. Only then did her screams cease.

Twenty years later, the memory remained strong. And so did the phobia's grip.

They continued in silence to the wrought-iron gate. The groundskeeper removed a set of keys from his jacket pocket, clanging them as he unlocked the gate. After he gestured them through, he relocked the gate.

A streetlight illuminated the wet pavement, the dense woods lining the opposite side, and their limo beneath an evergreen canopy. The rain had subsided, for now.

Dad pumped the groundskeeper's hand. "Thank you for meeting us here. Hope to see you next year, same time, same place."

The man shook his head. "No, I'm afraid you won't. I'm only filling in for today."

Too bad he couldn't climb into the limo and comfort them with his soothing presence. As she turned to follow Dad and DeeDee, he touched her shoulder. She jumped and spun around.

"Before you go, I'd like to tell you something that may help."

"What's that?"

He fixed his compassionate gaze on her. "A famous person once said, 'Ye shall know the truth, and the truth shall make you free.'"

Warmth filled her heart. "I like that. Who said it?"

"Jesus Christ."

The warmth fled, leaving behind a wasteland as desolate as the graveyard. What did an ancient dead man have to do with truth?

He released her arm. "When you find out the truth about your mother's death, it will set you free."

She nodded, humoring him. "Okay. Thank you."

"Something happened to you the day your mother died." Urgency rasped through his voice. "Something that didn't happen to your sister."

Frozen, she stared at the woods across the street, his words ringing in her head. Her heart thumped out a hollow rhythm. Had she truly thought his presence comforting? She needed to get away from this nut job. She forced her stiff legs forward and fled to the limo.

"Seek the truth," he called out behind her.

She joined Dad and DeeDee, buckling her seatbelt, still feeling the man's gaze on her as the car pulled into the street. She shivered.

DeeDee handed her a water bottle. "What'd the guy want?"

She glanced at Dad, who frowned into his beer bottle. "He wanted to talk about Jesus Christ."

DeeDee snorted, but let the matter drop.

Out the tinted windows, darkened houses blurred together, mesmerizing Livy, until Dad's voice knifed through the fog in her head.

"Kiddos, we need to talk."

She sat up, tensing at the worry in his voice.

Dad leaned forward, his face uncharacteristically somber under the dim ceiling lights. "I'm being sued. West Dakota claims I infringed a copyright of theirs. The band members want fifty percent of my royalties and five million in damages." He lifted the beer to his lips with a quick, jerky movement, swallowed deep, and smacked his lips. "Ridiculous! 'Conversate Me' doesn't sound anything like 'Sidetrack'. Okay, a couple of lines have a similar melody. But it's going to be hard for them to prove I plagiarized them."

Livy sought her sister's gaze, but DeeDee was peering at their father, her eyes dark, lids narrowed. "What are you saying, Dad?"

"I'm going to have to back out on the agreement to help you with the dance school."

DeeDee opened her mouth to speak, but Dad continued his narrative. "My attorney says I shouldn't make any new investments until we resolve this. He thinks it's likely we'll reach a settlement. Which means, the chunk of dough I set aside for your business might be going to West Dakota's songwriters."

"But that's absurd." DeeDee punched the seat.

"I agree." Dad scowled. "I want to see this dance school succeed as much as you do. It's supposed to be your mother's legacy." He swallowed another swig. "But you two have the smarts to run your business without capital from me, right?"

They nodded. Livy's dread and uncertainty reflected on DeeDee's face.

"I've already paid the construction company enough to finish the building. If they stay within budget. After that, you're on your own. Unless the lawsuit gets thrown out."

Livy dropped her head into her hands and rubbed her temple. For the first time since Dad landed his debut recording contract, his wealth couldn't buoy them.

He leaned back and rested an ankle over his knee. "I'm not telling you what to do, but it might be a good idea to tell Nils you won't be singing and dancing with his band come September."

Livy scooted forward. "He already knows." Last week they informed Nils they were weary of touring with Free The Defendants. After six years of hotel rooms, screaming audiences, and short-term relationships, they wanted out. They longed to settle down, get some stability, and look for the lifelong kind of love they would never find on the road. They'd stick with Nils for two more months. Then they'd be free.

And now, apparently, broke.

The limo slowed as Boeing Field illuminated the night. Livy squinted against the brightness and let her eyes close, a reminder of how late the night had grown. The car approached the charter jet waiting to fly Dad back to LA. When it jerked to a stop, the driver came around to open the door for Dad. He held out his arms toward them. Livy gave him a quick hug, then lay down on the seat and closed her eyes, shutting out the murmurs floating around her.

The car's hum lulled her to sleep as it drove north to the home she and DeeDee shared. Dreamlike images fought for her attention. Her father's face drifted toward her, his mouth uttering a warning. "You're on your own, kiddo." Her mother's face, translucent in the moonlight, emerged from a marble headstone. "Seek the truth, Olivia," she urged in a voice as deep as the groundskeeper's. "Seek the truth."

Even through a dreamy mist, she felt her forehead knot.

Seek the truth. But whose truth? And where was she supposed to seek it?

Chapter Two

A stark white banner stretched across the flat building, reflecting enough sunlight to attract the attention of every neighbor. DeeDee tugged on the lower left corner, achieving perfect symmetry. *Welcome To Saffire School Of Dance,* blared its message in eye-catching red letters. Last night, DeeDee had added *In Honor Of Our Mother, Luna Raquelle,* against Livy's wishes.

"Why not?" DeeDee thought she and Livy were on the same wavelength. But Livy's strenuous objection to proclaiming Mom's name stymied her.

Livy's excuse? "People will ask questions."

"We don't owe them any explanations." As usual, DeeDee overrode her twin, and the phrase stayed.

The nearby boulevard hummed with vehicles. DeeDee crossed her fingers in hopes some of them were headed to Saffire's grand opening. She and Livy had set up signs, advertised in newspapers, and spread the word on social media. A topnotch techie fashioned them a fancy website. Now, they waited in the September sunshine for their first guests.

DeeDee shivered as a rare sensation rocketed her pulse. She needed to dial down the excite-o-meter. Emotion equaled weakness. At her right stood Livy, all boho-chic in her peacock-print tunic and teal ankle boots, her hair bunched atop her head like a rooster tail. "Why are you so tense?"

Livy shot her a look. "I'm not tense."

"Yes, you are. You're frowning, and your ponytail is

shaking."

"That's the wind, you dork." Livy, pretending their tiff hadn't happened, plastered on a smile and peered at the street. "I think someone's coming." They turned and went inside to watch through tall, narrow windows flanking the front door.

Four months ago, this one-story space had been a hollow cobwebbed shell. But thanks to Dad and his megabucks, new drywall divided the 4,000-plus square feet into three studios, a small office, restrooms, and a storage closet. The hallway walls gleamed pale yellow above teal wainscoting, offsetting the rich cherry-red enamel below.

Her mother's spirit was here. In DeeDee's imagination, Mom floated along the crimson corridor. She danced in midair, beaming.

"Look, Deeds. A whole family just pulled up." Livy propped the door as a car parked at the curb. "In a Mercedes. Mom, Dad, two daughters."

Craning while the family emerged, DeeDee said, "We need something special to give our first visitors."

The four hesitated in the doorway. She smiled and approached them. "Welcome. I'm DeeDee. This is Livy. Since you're our first guests, you're automatically eligible for a fifty percent discount on any of our fall classes. Congratulations."

The woman entered first. "That's very generous." Glamour exuded from every plane of her flawless face, every seam of her designer clothing. "I'm Roxanne Shropshire. This is my husband, Will, and our two daughters, Amity and Katrina."

The others stepped inside. The husband angled his body away from his wife and refused to look at her. Strained lines marred his handsome face. Maybe they'd been fighting.

DeeDee leaned forward, braced her hands on her thighs, and looked the daughters in the eyes. "And how old are you two?"

"Ten."

"Thirteen."

"What kind of dance would you like to learn?" asked Livy.

"Hip-hop." Amity, the thirteen-year-old, clasped her hands above her head and shimmied. "I can move like Iggy Azalea."

"I want to take Tap." Katrina's saddle shoes shuffled, the toes bouncing with an energy of their own.

Roxanne's gaze swiveled from floor to ceiling. "This is beautiful."

The dad breathed deep. "Smells like fresh paint."

"Why don't we show you around?" Livy led the way.

"Wow, killer." Amity pranced along the hall ahead of them, peeking inside every door. Soft music wafted from each studio's state-of-the-art sound system. Mirrors and shiny barres hugged the walls, reflecting fresh-waxed oak floors.

Roxanne plied them with questions—had they taught dance before? No, but they were lifelong dancers and daughters of a professional dancer. Did they offer evening and weekend classes? They did. How much were the fees? One hundred dollars per month.

"What a nice way to honor your mother. Her name sounds familiar." Her voice took on a coaxing, intimate quality. The tone of someone fishing for information she wasn't entitled to.

DeeDee wasn't biting. "It's unlikely you've heard of her."

She felt, more than saw, her sister's outraged glance before Livy segued them back to business.

"Our teaching approach is a little different from the norm." Livy's measured tones smoothed over her discomfort.

"We call it the three Ps—"

"Precision, Posture, and Presentation."

"Dance enriches kids' lives in so many ways." DeeDee spread an arm wide. "We want kids to have fun, but dance is so much more."

Roxanne arched a brow. "You take a holistic approach, then?"

"You could call it that." DeeDee nodded. "Dancing is good for the body and the soul. Did you know kids who learn dance at a young age grow up to be better students?"

Roxanne's accusatory gaze rested on her husband's face. "There, you see, Will? If you hadn't been so stubborn, Max might not have dropped out of school."

Will's face mottled scarlet as though she'd slapped him. Recoiling, he made his getaway toward the door. "Daddy!" the younger daughter screamed, taking off after him.

Tension hung heavy in the air like a low, thick cloud cover. "My fifteen-year-old son is a dropout. Thanks to his stepdad who made him quit his extracurricular activities." Roxanne dabbed the corner of her eye. Her gaze raked Will's retreating back like malevolent claws.

"I'm sorry to hear that." DeeDee waited for Roxanne to face her, then resumed the speech she'd spent hours perfecting. "We believe in encouraging students to work hard in school and be the best they can be in all areas of life."

Livy clasped her hands in front of her like a wise swami and stepped closer. "Our motto is, 'Dance like the whole world is watching,' which we believe applies to anything we do in life."

Roxanne offered a watery smile, her gaze darting between the door and DeeDee. "That sounds wonderful." Clutching her wallet, she followed DeeDee into the office. "Did your mother pass recently?"

"We lost her when we were kids."

"Oh, how sad. Was it cancer?"

"No." She met Livy's gaze, her sister's eyes saying, I told

you so. Maybe Livy had a point. Did they really want people asking how Mom died?

Will and Katrina rejoined them. Amity, leaning against the hallway wall, ignored everyone, her nose buried in her phone. DeeDee tried not to listen to the parents' low, muttering voices hurling accusations at each other. Their precarious marriage was no concern of hers.

They stopped squabbling long enough to register and pay for fall term. Over the parents' bent heads, DeeDee and Livy shared a wink and a thumbs-up. Once the family departed, taking their friction with them, the air seemed to thin and brighten, as though the building itself breathed out a sigh of relief.

For the next hour, a steady stream of visitors kept them busy. When a forty-something man peered in and surveyed the place, DeeDee recognized him. "Hey, don't we know you from JavaJava?"

Nodding, the man stroked his salt-and-pepper goatee. "Yeah, you do. I'm there so much, they all know my favorite drink. Straight-up dark roast, room for cream."

DeeDee laughed. "I'm DeeDee, Hazelnut Cappuccino. This is Livy, Cinnamon Latte."

He put out a hand. "Call me A.J." A plain brown tee stretched over his protruding belly.

"Nice to put a name with a face." DeeDee shook his hand. "Do you have a child who's interested in dance lessons?"

A.J. shook his head. "I have a grown daughter and a teenager. But my five-year-old granddaughter might like this place."

Outside, a sporty engine revved, followed by a squeal of brakes. Every head turned toward the sound. DeeDee grabbed Livy's arm. "That better not be who I think it is."

Livy grimaced. "Afraid so. Bestie and Frenemy."

"Bestie and Beastie, you mean." How dare Vienna show

up today. As Vienna slunk from the red Ferrari, her mother got out of the passenger seat. DeeDee released Livy's arm and stared Vienna down while the new arrivals sailed through the door in a billow of perfume-and-cigarette scent. "Well, well. Look who's here."

"Livy. DeeDee." Audria Lenno held out her arms for a hug. For a classy woman like Audria to produce offspring like Vienna seemed an anomaly. Like rats in an upscale restaurant.

"Audria." DeeDee hugged her friend, and then glared at Vienna. "Livy, look who dared show her face here."

Livy bracketed a restraining arm in front of DeeDee as Vienna Lenno-Nelsson grinned. "You still mad?" she purred in her trademark husky voice.

DeeDee's lip curled. "Shut up, Vee." Livy's steadying grip clenched her arm.

Audria, the platinum streaks in her hair metallic under the ceiling lights, tilted her head back and forth. "This place is *gor*geous."

Unfazed by DeeDee's hostility, Vienna stretched her arms out, as if she were a movie star addressing her fans. "Dudettes. You be all diva now." She'd colored her hair. Strands of *Noir Riche* curved like graceful ribbons down the back of her pink blouse, a perfect match for the hot-pink eyeglasses she modeled. If not for her vast collection of glasses, she'd squint her way through life, just like her father Nils Nelsson.

Audria loosened a paisley scarf around her neck. She collected scarves with the same compulsion her daughter collected spectacles. "Luna would be so impressed. I can't believe she's been gone twenty years. Did your father—"

DeeDee hushed her with a tiny shake of the head.

The tour resumed, and Vienna fell into step beside DeeDee, her stilettos surely damaging the floor. "I took down

14

the photo of you like you said." Her gaze slid upward to DeeDee's face, more ingénue than agitator.

DeeDee seized Vienna by the shoulders and pushed her off to the side, her face inches from Vienna's. "Don't you *ever* post your party photos of me again."

The ingénue vanished. "Chill." She flung DeeDee's arms away. "You gotta admit it was funny. You were so pie-eyed." She doubled over, shaking with muffled laughter.

"Look who's talking. You've got so much snow going up your nose, it's coming out your ears."

Vienna clutched her middle and shook her petite frame even harder. "You be all comedienne today."

"You be all ghetto today."

Vienna eyed DeeDee's leopard-skin leggings and gasped. "Look at you, girlfriend. You got beastified." She fingered DeeDee's jacket. "And leatherized. Where'd you get 'em?"

"Nordstrom," DeeDee snapped. "And don't call me girlfriend."

"I *so* want me some. Let's go shopping."

"Look. You need to get out of here." Before she jabbed Vienna's eye with a lime-green lacquered fingernail. "I'm going to give you thirty seconds. When I turn around, you'd better be gone." She pivoted and stalked to the other end of the hallway, where framed photos in all shapes and sizes covered most of the wall—photos of Luna Raquelle leaping, bending, pirouetting. Her mother's bright smile and joy-filled poses belied the tragedy of her final years.

A.J. had left the others and now stood inches from the photos. DeeDee made her way to his side. "That's my mother."

He gave a start when she spoke. "Oh. A pink dress. Of course."

"Her favorite color."

Silence ensued as he studied the photos. Then he checked his watch and turned toward the door, saying as he went, "You've got a nice place here. Thanks for the tour."

"Wait a minute." She tapped his shoulder. "Did you want to sign up your granddaughter for a class?"

He darted another glance at his watch. "Oh, I'll let her mother make the decision. I need to get home. The Husky game's about to start." He nodded a quick goodbye, retraced his steps to the exit, and tailed Vienna out the door.

DeeDee returned to the group coming out of Studio B. "Wait up, guys. Sorry—I got waylaid." When Livy cast her a worried look, DeeDee mustered a smile and a shrug. And they thought Vienna had been a drama queen *before* her degree from Cornish College in dance and theater.

Audria pulled her close and spoke into her ear. "I'm sorry about your altercation with my daughter."

Your rich spoiled brat daughter. DeeDee squelched the urge to retort.

Audria sighed. "When she was tiny, I believed if I met all her needs, she'd turn out all right."

She'd created a monster. "Don't blame yourself, Audria."

"Well, you know how we mothers are. We always blame ourselves."

"In that case, I'm never going to be one." She laughed and patted Audria. "Speaking of which, where's Fleming?" An image of Vienna's tow-headed, seven-year-old son flitted across her mind.

"Oh, you didn't hear?" Audria lowered her voice. "Vienna lost custody of him after her drug bust, and Fleming is now living with his father."

"No kidding? You still get to see him, right?"

"Sure." Her mouth tightened. "But I have to drive to eastern Washington now."

"Maybe we'll get lucky and Vee will land a TV role."

DeeDee glared in the direction of the Ferrari. "Then she'll have to move to LA."

Livy gave Audria a hug, rocking her back and forth. "Thanks so much for coming, Aunt Bestie."

"Your mother is out there in the universe smiling. I can feel it." Audria stepped back and smiled into Livy's face, then planted a kiss on her cheek. She turned to DeeDee and did the same. Blowing more kisses, she floated out the door.

As the Ferrari roared away, a blonde woman rushed through the door, breathing hard, miniature clones on each hand.

"Hi," the woman gasped. "Did I get here in time for a tour?"

DeeDee glanced at the wall clock. "Yes. We'll be doing tours for another hour."

"Good, good. I'm Shari. Shari Lorenzo." Shari scrutinized the hallway walls. "What a creative color scheme you came up with." She glanced at the little girls. "These are my daughters, Kinzie and Lacie. They're seven and five. They've never had dance before, and they're begging to start lessons."

The little girls regarded DeeDee with big, solemn eyes then turned their heads when Livy appeared at her side.

"We'll show you around." DeeDee beckoned. In the ballet studio, "Swan Lake" played over the sound system. She stopped in the middle of the room, closed her eyes, and let the opulent music soak her spirit.

When she opened her eyes, Livy was circling the room in a *pas marche*, and the little girls trailed her in a stiff-legged ballet walk. Shari and DeeDee shared a grin.

Then Shari chuckled. "Look how anxious they are to get started." Her eyes widened as she scanned the room. Then she approached the sound system for a closer look. "My husband would love this mixer. Are these wireless speakers?"

"Yes." DeeDee nodded. "We'll be moving them around the room during class to enhance the dynamic we're going for."

Shari eyed the speaker across the room. "My husband is an inventor — well, I guess I should call him my soon-to-be-ex-husband — and he rigged up something like this for us when we were first married. You couldn't find wireless speakers in the store back then. I loved them. I could carry them from room to room — "

DeeDee tuned out and visualized the woman's inventor husband, who, in her mind, bore a strong resemblance to Mr. Szalinski in *Honey, I Shrunk The Kids*.

She came to when Shari asked, "How do I sign my girls up for classes?"

"You can fill out registration forms here or sign up online. If you pay today, we can guarantee them a spot."

Shari shook her head, sending layered hair swishing across her shoulders. "I'll fill out the forms, but I'll have to bring you the payment after I get it from Scott."

DeeDee refrained from asking why she was divorcing him if he was so clever. "Come on in and sit down." She gestured toward the office. "Livy will keep an eye on the girls while you and I talk business."

***

DeeDee locked the front door. Then she followed Livy to their earth-friendly office, savoring anew the peaceful sage-green walls offsetting a simple desk made with recycled materials. A matching credenza, topped with coffee maker and silver tea set, sat against the back wall next to a fireproof cabinet.

"I told you people would ask questions."

"It's no one's business but ours."

"But you made it their business when you put up that

sign." Livy plopped into the green-tweed swivel chair, fingering the leaves on the potted ficus. Her action drew DeeDee's eye to the plants hanging beside it—a long leafy philodendron and a String of Pearls, its puffy strands draping halfway to the floor like a bead curtain. Beyond it, a sculpture of a woman pouring water over rocks graced a corner, churning recycled water twenty-four seven like a mountain stream.

"Point taken, okay?" DeeDee sank into a black leather chair. Silence hummed between them, broken only by the water's rhythmic music. Even when they disagreed, their quiet moments buzzed with camaraderie.

DeeDee thumbed through the half-inch stack of cash and caressed a one hundred dollar bill. "Ten new students, ten maybes. Coolness."

"Sweetness."

"But where are all our boy dancer wannabes?"

"I know, right? We'll have to work on that."

Outside, the daylight waned. The sepia-framed window afforded a view of the orange sky behind the distant Olympic Mountains, draped in their snowy winter blankets.

DeeDee picked up the bankcard receipts, shuffled them, and tucked them securely in the desk drawer. "Thank you for keeping me from punching you-know-who."

"You're welcome."

She cracked open a bottle of champagne and filled two goblets. They lifted a reverent toast to the heavens. Then their gazes lowered from the plaster ceiling and met, their voices blending, "Here's to you, Mom!"

Chapter Three

When Scott Lorenzo's boss ambushed him in the R&D lab, he knew his day was about to crash and burn.

"Scott!" On the other side of the Plexiglas cubicle wall, Stuart glared at him like a drill sergeant. His three team members kept clanking their keyboards and pretended not to notice.

"Change of plans!" Scott flinched at Stuart's roar. "Boeing wants the prototype by Friday!"

Flexibility was an unspoken requirement at ENFO's Research and Development Department.

"Not a problem, sir." Scott peered at the schematic on the screen. *Big problem, sir.* Two days? Seriously? The team desperately needed another week of tweaking and debugging the design. He wouldn't be the only engineer grinding his teeth today.

Of course, he didn't mind bending over backward for his team. But he drew the line at backflips.

He nodded to his boss. "We're on it. It'll be done by Friday."

Stuart gave him one last doubtful glare, and then stalked out.

Scott sighed. Another hour until he got out of here and —

What? Commute to his empty house? His silent abode?

He drove home slower than usual, the now-familiar hole in his heart gaping even wider.

The doorbell rang fifteen minutes after he stepped inside. Heart leaping, he strode to the door, hope in every step.

Maybe Shari had come to her senses.

"Mr. Lorenzo?" A diminutive gentleman stood at his doorstep and held out a thick envelope.

"What's this?" His throat and stomach tightened. "Is someone suing me?"

"Sign here." The man handed him a pen, and Scott signed. "Have a good evening," the gentleman called over his shoulder as he sprinted toward his ancient VW Beetle, the mindless platitude not escaping Scott's notice.

He tore open the envelope containing his worst fears— divorce papers. After ten years of marriage, his estranged wife had taken the plunge into the wrong end of the pool.

"Doggonit." He flung the papers down and clutched his shaved head in both hands. What had he done to deserve such a no-good day?

The week started in high gear last Sunday when the Seahawks beat the Forty-Niners. And while sunny, cloud-free days rarely visited Seattle in November, today's cheerful blue sky couldn't erase the ache plaguing him since Shari took his two little girls.

"Dear Lord." He launched a mumbled prayer. "If this is Your idea of a trial, You picked a good one."

Tossing the papers aside, he wandered into the kitchen. He needed to load the dishwasher, then eat and work on his side project. But with brain cells shocked into numbness like a slapped face, there would be no tinkering with his invention tonight.

His aimless steps carried him back to the living room, its silence always shouting at him now, unless the TV blared. He picked up his phone and texted Shari. *Got the divorce papers.*

Their wedding picture graced an end table, and he moved closer. Lately he hadn't done more than glance at the ten-year-old photo of them in happier times, beaming toothy smiles at the photographer. How young they looked. And what a contrast—her sunny beauty next to his darker Mediterranean looks. Although Shari and others complimented his supposed handsomeness, he had never been able to see what they saw.

He slammed the photo face down on the table. Then he grabbed his wallet and keys and marched toward the dusky street, passing the mailbox at the end of the driveway—7005 Rosemary Drive. Shari's hankering for this house landed him on a street with a girly name instead of a good old Southern one like Scrub Oak Avenue. Or Swamp Thistle Lane.

A thumping thundered closer as his next-door neighbor, Jamie McRabb, roared home in his beater, subwoofer maxed out. As always, Jamie threw Scott a jack-o-lantern grin, and Scott threw Jamie a glare, the exchange now a regular ritual.

Clutching his phone, he touched the screenshot, a family photo representative of the life that ended the night he cursed at Shari after another overdraft hit their bank account. He cringed over the names he'd called her. If he'd known she would stomp out of the house and out of his life, he would've curbed his tongue. "The tongue is a fire," wrote the Apostle James. His had set fire to the things most precious to him— his marriage, his family. So much more important than an overdrawn bank account.

Two right turns brought him to a quiet residential street lined with steep-roofed clapboard homes. In spring, the yards flaunted colorful rhododendrons, except widowed Mrs. Langley's. Her yellowed lawn was dying a slow death. But what her yard lacked in color, her flamingo-pink cottage made up for.

Next to Mrs. Langley, Big Doby and Little Doby ruled the Richardsons' yard with jaws of steel. "Good doggies!" he called to Boss and Sergeant as they bounded alongside the fence. Big Doby, Boss, never barked—he gruffed. And Little Doby, Sergeant, never barked either—he yipped. Together, they generated enough noise to awaken Mrs. Langley's dead husband.

Stopping to let a young couple and their dog pass by, he gave a friendly wave. Instead of returning his wave, they smirked.

No wonder with his whistling "Hound Dog" in a desperate attempt to keep despair at bay. If he were the blushing type, he'd be as pink as Mrs. Langley's house.

Two houses down, he reached the Townsends, their rear yard back-to-back with the McRabbs, his next-door neighbors. He rapped the knocker once, then twice, on the red front door.

The Townsends' faces lit with welcoming smiles as though they'd expected him. Paula hugged him and led him into her comfortable living room. He sniffed the mouth-watering aroma of steaks grilling in barbecue sauce. He hadn't eaten, and now, his stomach growled like an angry pit bull.

"Scott?" Rick, his voice as soothing as a doctor with an impeccable bedside manner, gestured toward the immaculate suede sofa. "Here, sit down. Why the long face, bro?"

"Shari." Scott traced the toe of his Rockport shoe along the hardwood floor. "She served divorce papers on me today."

Paula clucked like a mother hen. "I'm so sorry." She patted the cushion beside her. "Now I understand why you look rumpled tonight. You usually look so spiffy."

"If it weren't for my job, I'd wear sweats and keep a five o'clock shadow."

"Are you going to contest the divorce?"

"Nope. The last thing I want is a complicated mess. She already has custody and child support. Now she wants alimony. And the court's giving me a year to either sell the house or buy out her half."

A frown crossed Rick's face. "Bro, when's your accountability group meet?"

"Friday morning, breakfast at Elmer's."

"Great. How's the grief book I loaned you?"

"Really good. Telling me to wait at least a year before dating again."

"Good advice. Give yourself time to heal."

"Except I know it's God's will for us to be a family again. And that's how I'm praying."

"Let's pray for it right now."

Scott nodded and moved to the cushion between them. They placed hands on him as Rick began to pray. The grandfather clock in the corner ticked off the minutes.

"Father God, we bring our brother Scott to you. We know he's hurting—"

"Yes, Lord," whispered Paula.

"We know Kinzie and Lacie are hurting. They don't understand why their parents don't live together anymore."

A lump rose in Scott's throat, and he clenched his lips.

The prayer continued until his despondency lifted. "Thank you, Lord," he murmured.

The familiar reverberation of Jamie McRabb's car stereo thrummed from beyond the back fence, sending faint shudders through the house. "And, Lord," Paula prayed, "please bless Jamie Mac. Help us to reach out to him with Christ's love even though we don't feel like it. Please bless James Sr. and Nancy, too, Lord, and the rest of the family."

"Amen." Rick's tone signaled the end of prayer time. "Speaking of our friend Jamie, Scott, have you had a chance to talk to his parents again?"

"I have." Scott dug his fists into his thighs. "James Sr. said he'd talk to him, and then he said Jamie was doing it to get a rise out of us."

"Oh, for Pete's sake." Paula tossed her head.

"Then Nancy told me if Jamie knew it bothered us, he'd do it even more."

Rick and Paula rolled their eyes. "There's a name for that." Rick grinned. "I don't want to say it out loud, but it means the same thing as 'donkey's backside.'" He slapped his leg, accompanied by a whoop of laughter.

"Honey." Paula, giggling, backhanded his arm.

Once the snickers died down, Scott rubbed his hands together. "Next time I see Jamie, I'm going to tell him he's a little donkey's backside."

They laughed again.

"It's crazy how people change." Scott nodded in the direction of the McRabb home. "Remember when he won MVP on his Little League team? Two years in a row? I was sure he'd turn out well." He examined his intertwined fingers. "Anyway, thanks for your prayers. They helped."

"You know we're always here for you." Rick clapped a hand on Scott's shoulder.

"Why don't you stay for dinner?" Paula offered. "Sometimes there's nothing better than a hearty home-cooked meal to soothe the soul."

The scents teased his nostrils, hunger pangs responding.

"Sounds perfect." But it wouldn't bring his family back.

***

On most afternoons, Scott's I-5 commute from Boeing Field to Green Lake turned into a white-knuckled, jaw-clenching test of patience. But today, his cheery whistle accompanied Christian artist Chris Tomlin's smooth voice soaring from the stereo. To the east, Lake Washington sparkled in the sun like a sheet of glass. Behind him, an oversized Hummer tailed him. To his left, a semi boxed him, and a second semi slowed in front of him.

He spiked the volume and resumed whistling. He'd

declined his teammates' invitation to happy hour to celebrate their project's successful completion, preferring instead to see his precious angels, who'd be arriving soon, and staying for the entire weekend.

He was still whistling when he reached home and settled at the kitchen table. Retrieving pencil and paper, he tapped the wooden surface, envisioning his list of must-dos. His engineer mind couldn't function without its ever-present lists.

Number One. Tonight: Take girls to see *Monsters University*. Come home; make popcorn.

That would save him several dollars.

Number Two. Tomorrow: Girls' dance lesson, eleven a.m. Saffire School of Dance.

He still needed the address from Shari. He sent her a quick text. *Where is the dance place again?*

Number Three. Afterward: Lunch at Kidd Valley, Northgate Mall—Kinzie and Lacie's favorite burger place.

His phone dinged. *The dance place is off Ravenna. Here's the website.*

Number Four. Sat night: Go with girls to street ministry downtown? He double-underlined the question mark, doubting a five- and seven-year-old could get anything out of serving spaghetti to the homeless. On the other hand, perhaps he should give them a chance to experience it. Maybe they would enjoy it—especially if he reminded them they were doing it for Jesus.

Glancing at item Number Two, he opened his iPad and pulled up the website. The golden words—*We teach your child to dance as if the whole world is watching. Because it is.*—flashed over a purple banner. A map filled the lower right corner, and photos of dancers in various degrees of movement created a slideshow over the center. White lettering marched across the screen: And those who were seen dancing were thought to be insane by those who could not hear the music. — Friedrich Wilhelm Nietzsche.

Two attractive young women — their arresting blue eyes, high cheekbones, and thick dark brows virtually identical — smiled at him. The left one displayed a sweet, engaging face, the right a confident smirk. Although familiar, he couldn't recall if or when he'd ever met them.

Olivia and Diana McCreary. A layer of cosmetics thick as pancake batter obscured Diana's face, and tattoos covered the skin below her neck. Her hair matched the color of the cayenne pepper growing old in his cupboard. He angled his head to the side to make sense of her asymmetrical hairdo. Wild curls on one side, flat braids on the other. In contrast, the angelic-faced Olivia's hair shone as though lit from within — a glossy river of honey flowing over her shoulders.

Still curious, he clicked their bio. "Hi there, thank you for visiting our website. We are twin sisters whose passion is dance, and we are here to spread the magick." Magick with a K. Pagan terminology. Shari must have enrolled his daughters in one of those New-Age type dance studios. The type that talked about spirit guides and seeking one's inner godhood. The type tolerant of all beliefs except the Christ of the Bible.

"We grew up here in Seattle and have been dancing as long as we can remember. We dedicated our school to our mother, Luna Raquelle, dancer and poet extraordinaire. May you rest in peace, Mama. We love you."

Luna Raquelle. He'd heard the name somewhere. And, if he wasn't mistaken, Luna was the name of a Roman goddess.

But no matter how hard he wracked his brain, he couldn't remember ever meeting a Luna Raquelle. He pulled up a search engine and keyed in her name. A chill shivered up his spine.

LUNA RAQUELLE DEAD FROM HEROIN OVERDOSE. He clicked the twenty-year-old headline.

"Luna Raquelle, Seattle dancer and wife of local rocker Declan Decker, was found dead this morning in her Lake Washington home, apparently the victim of a heroin overdose...."

He'd been in grade school. Never a fan of Decker's band, The FireAnts, nor the rest of the era's grunge bands, he and his friends had preferred Mariah Carey and New Kids. He would only recognize the name Luna Raquelle if it had been in the national news.

"Luna battled heroin addiction for several years and sought rehab at least twice. Mr. Decker refused any interviews and requested he and his daughters, Olivia and Diana, be left alone to grieve in private."

He returned to the website. The twins did resemble Declan Decker. No wonder they looked so familiar. Was their relationship to the rocker common knowledge? He grabbed his to-do list and added "check out dance class tomorrow" next to item Number Two.

He jerked when the ringing doorbell reverberated through the house. Then he rushed to the door. Opening it, he froze for a moment, his heart twisting, his gaze soaking in the heavenly sight of two little angels looking up at him with eager eyes. Shari stood behind them, a hand on each back.

He ignored his estranged wife. "Kinzie. Lacie. Ready to go see *Monsters University*?"

They squealed, and tears burned his eyes as he knelt and scooped them into his arms.

***

In Studio C, DeeDee cued ten soft-rock songs for her Saturday morning Lyrical class. She shuddered as she added Justin Beiber's "Baby". Every week, her students begged for it.

Voices hummed as the students formed a multihued

cluster in the center. Small arms and legs stretched, posed, and imitated J Lo's isolation moves. Miniature divas admired themselves in the wall-to-wall mirror. Parents found seats at the back.

"Ahem." Someone cleared his throat. "Are you Miss Dee?" A faint Southern drawl tinged the voice.

She spun around toward a well-built man in a Mariners sweatshirt. Deep frown lines pinched between his eyes. Close-cropped dark hair formed a shadow on his oblong head. She held out her hand. "I am."

He gripped her hand, gave it a quick shake, and she glanced at the two little girls flanking him. Kinzie and Lacie.

So this was Shari's inventor husband. He was no Mr. Szalinski. He was Channing Tatum with a dash of Vin Diesel.

She snapped her jaw shut and offered her brightest smile. "Oh, you're Dad."

"Scott Lorenzo. Glad to meet you."

"And you. I've chitchatted with your wife a few times."

A shadow passed across his face. "She won't be my wife much longer. We're divorcing."

"She mentioned that." Did he have a new woman in his life? Channing Tatum lookalikes didn't come around here often.

He patted his daughters and aimed them toward the cluster of students, then turned to her. "Do y'all have a particular philosophy which influences your teaching?" He kneaded his fingers into his palm, his frown deepening.

DeeDee wrinkled her brow. None of the other parents ever asked that particular question.

"Well." She shuffled through several possible replies. "Our motto is, Dance like the whole world is watching. Is that what you mean?"

He shook his head. "I mean, do you include spiritual or metaphysical ideas in your teaching?"

"Oh, I see what you're saying. Right now, we're primarily focusing on teaching dance. If that sort of thing is important to you as a parent, we can certainly incorporate-"

"No, no." Scott pointed at his girls with emphasis. "They get their spiritual training at home, and I believe it should stay that way."

She gave him a polite smile, wincing from his mild rebuke. "Of course."

"What about music? What kind do y'all use in your classes?"

She bit back a retort. Patience. "Lyrical is a slower-paced style of dance, so for this class, I tend to go with a softer rock sound. Or I may go with reggae or Celtic or New Age."

"New Age?"

"Yes. Mainly Enya. I like her music. The relaxed pace works well for beginners."

Scott's worry lines relaxed as well. "Okay, thanks for bearing with me." A sudden smile brightened his face, and he checked the clock on the wall. "Looks like I kept you too long. I'll go on back there with the other parents."

DeeDee tried for a kind expression. "After class, I'll introduce you to my business partner and twin, Livy."

Chapter Four

On the first Saturday of Saffire's winter term, the ever-present winter gloom blanketed the city, and the smell of impending snow hovered in the air.

In the hip-hop studio, Livy greeted each parent and child filing in. Amity Shropshire rushed in, her brows in their usual frown. Instead of her mother, her father trailed her. Will scanned the room, his steps hesitant, then caught Livy's eye. Wanting to make him feel welcome, she smiled.

He returned her smile, added a nod, and moved to the side of the classroom for a seat. He brushed his left hand through his hair. The hand was bare, with no glint of a wedding ring.

Had he and Roxanne finally split?

Time to start class. Reaching high, she stretched her warmed-up limbs. "Welcome, kids. I'm glad you're all here. Can we say our motto together?" She raised her hand like a conductor.

"Dance like the whole world is watching!" yelled seven voices in unison.

"Because why?" She spun her arms in circles, amping up the energy.

"Because they *are*!"

She caught Will's eye. For a moment, she faltered, the planned words fleeing like frightened rabbits.

She smoothed her hands on her tights and tried again. "And parents, thank you for bringing your kids." She sought safe territory, her focus settling on Chloe's mom on the other end of the row from Will. "We had a lot of fun last term, and they learned a lot. In April, DeeDee and I plan to host our first showcase."

Will applauded. Soon the rest of the parents joined him.

"And we need some boys in this class. You know how those boys are—you get them anywhere near a dance studio, and they run for the hills."

Tessa bobbed her head.

"But hip-hop ain't for sissies. So send some boys our way. Please and thank you."

Embarrassed giggles ensued.

She grinned. "Who remembers the lion dance?"

Cheers sprung from seven attentive faces. The hopeful expectancy in their eyes made all her hard work worthwhile.

Soon Nicki Minaj's rhythmic chants filled the room. "Okay, on the count of one, crouch like you're a lion about to attack. Show some claws." The girls struck threatening poses. "Remember what we learned? Seventy-five percent of hip-hop is attitude; the rest is precision." Her gaze wandered toward Will, then slid back to her students. "See? Like this. Crouch, two, three, four, pivot—pivot. Stay low, gangsterettes." Will's chuckle nearly interrupted her focus again.

Her seven students ranged in age from ten to fifteen, their abilities as varied as their ages. Chloe tried, but failed, to move with street smarts. She stayed on the beat, but went high when she should go low and stiff when she should be loose. She had precision but not attitude, and precise steps lacking attitude was not hip-hop.

Tessa, however, was fun to watch. She oozed attitude. Although she always lagged a beat or two behind, she moved like a gangsterette wannabe. If she had a better sense of timing, she'd be awesome.

Amity's moves presented a hip-hop master in the

making — precision and attitude.

By the end of class, the seven young students puffed for air. "Wow." Livy applauded. "Pure magicness, girls. Practice every day this week, okay? And I'll see you on Wednesday." She exhaled and focused on the mixer to keep from watching Will.

"You looked like you were enjoying yourself today." A deep voice startled her.

She whirled to Will, feet away, his even teeth appearing, and then disappearing, in an uncertain smile. A jolt raced through her, leaving her heart thudding, but she managed a nonchalant expression. "So did your daughter." With trembling fingers, she readjusted her ponytail, flipping her hair and cinching it just so. "Where's Roxanne today?"

His eyes followed her movement as if attached to invisible strings, but his face darkened. "We split up."

"Oh. I'm sorry."

"Don't be. It was inevitable."

"Still." She patted her hair for stray strands. "It's always sad when a marriage ends."

He nodded. "True, that. By the way, I like your motto, 'Dance like the whole world is watching.'"

"Thanks." She rested her hand on the barre. "You know the old saying, dance like nobody is watching? Well, what good is the joy and wonder and magic of dance if we don't share it with the world?"

"I completely agree."

"I can see Amity performing someday. I think she has potential." Livy dropped her voice. "Which is probably true of only a handful of our students. The rest, well — " She thrust out her hands, palms up. "They're the ones who will someday dance like nobody's watching."

"I never thought of it that way." He glanced at Amity, who hovered near the door practicing new moves, then met her eyes. "You hear the saying all the time, but you've given it new meaning."

Warmth crept through her. "Tell Amity if she keeps at it, she could do great things someday."

He eyed his gyrating daughter. "Did you hear her, Amity? You could do great things someday."

"I know, Dad. Hey, you were gonna take me to the mall, remember?"

"Sorry." Will leaned toward Livy. "She's having *issues*. We need to leave now, but we'll see you next week. Great job." He finished with a wave, and then grabbed his daughter by the hand. But Amity, who'd transformed from a precocious child to a chilly quasi-adult in only three months, yanked her hand away and strutted chin first out the door.

***

The last class of the day had ended. The half-light of dusk slowly faded outside Saffire's office window. Livy, munching a sandwich, peered at the crate next to her where her new puppy curled up like a snowball. His whiffling snores assured her he was fast asleep. Her heart swelled.

"I can't believe how many parents don't stay and watch their kids' classes," DeeDee huffed. "They must think we're a babysitting service."

"One hundred bucks a month is a pretty expensive babysitter," Livy replied, still eyeing the crate. She swung her soft-shoed feet to the top of the desk. "But Will isn't like that. I can tell he's engaged in what's going on with Amity."

"When it comes to dads, he's one of the good ones."

"Speaking of Will—" Livy paused for dramatic effect. "He and Roxanne finally split up."

"Thus, that goofy grin on your face."

"No, the goofy grin is due to cute little Murf. Not Will."

"Yeah, right."

"But Will's cute too, isn't he?"

DeeDee fixed her with a knowing smile and bit into her own sandwich.

"Then again, so is Kinzie and Lacie's dad," said Livy. "Maybe if you give him a little encouragement, he'd ask you out."

"Scott 'Mr. Hotness' Lorenzo?"

"He *is* the epitome of hot. He's got a quiet intensity about him like he's pondering how to solve the world's problems." Livy snickered. "*And* a cute Southern accent."

"He seems a little uptight." DeeDee tossed her sandwich wrapper in the recycling bin.

"I read his vibe as intense." Livy wiped her fingers. "Not uptight."

"Whatev."

"Anyway, keep your paws off Will." Livy kept her tone light but firm. "I've got dibs."

A plaintive whimper drifted toward her. The ten-week-old puppy had awakened and was sniffing around for food.

"Ah, Murf." She stepped to the crate and picked up the fluffy white bundle, snuggling him next to her cheek. She'd bought the tiny Samoyed from a breeder last week, and soon he would be ready to stay home alone. Until then, he'd scarcely left her side.

She kissed his soft head, nestled him back in his crate, and then refilled his food bowl. Between bites, the pup yelped in the same manner he did when DeeDee's big yellow tabby took a swipe at him, as she so often did at home. Livy stroked his back with her finger. "Don't cry, baby boy. Miss Piggy isn't here. I know you hate her killer paws, but on the inside she's a very sweet kitty."

Murf searched her face with opaque black eyes, clearly unconvinced.

Chapter Five

Saturday's weather report forecast a mere thirty-five degrees for the high, yet the blue December sky glowing outside Saffire's windows conveyed a false impression of warmth. So did the high-energy dance tunes thumping through the hip-hop studio.

Livy kept her gaze on her bouncing students instead of the parents' bench where Will sat. Would he talk to her again? Was he truly interested or merely friendly?

Class ended and the seven future superstars reverted to a bevy of giggling tweens. After fifty minutes of trying not to watch Will, Livy let herself relax. As she waved goodbye to the girls, he stood and strode in her direction.

Just like last week, her pulse sped up. "Hi, Will."

A slight crease between his brows replaced the easy smile from last week. His gaze darted from her eyes to the lotus flower tattooed on her right bicep, then back to her face. His thumbs twiddled at forty miles per hour. "Great class today."

"Thanks." She leaned against the barre. "I thought it went well. Amity looked awesome."

"Yeah, she did. She's been dancing since eight, but she told me this was her favorite class ever."

"That's nice to know." To give her hands something to do, Livy wrestled with the stick holding her hair in place.

"What age did you start dancing?" His gaze wandered to the hair wadded on top of her head.

"DeeDee and I learned to chasse as soon as we could walk. Our mom taught us simple steps early on. She enrolled us in dance classes when we were five, and we've been learning ever since."

"Da-ad," Amity called from across the room as Livy propped her leg over the back of a chair. Will's eyes again followed her movements as she bent toward her knee and sighed in pleasure at the release of muscle tension.

"I'd love to talk more." He frowned. "But Amity is in a big rush."

Amity swung on the barre near the door and eyed her father with lowered brows.

"Can I buy you coffee tomorrow?" His gaze sharpened. One brow lifted. "Then we can talk without interruption."

Livy flashed her sweetest smile. "Sure. Where should I meet you?"

"Your choice."

She couldn't wait to tell Deeds.

***

Rain streamed down the windows when Livy breezed into JavaJava the next morning. The brightly lit interior and white Formica tables belied the gray day. Soft jazz played over the speakers, blending well with the pervasive coffee aroma.

Several familiar patrons sipped drinks and ate pastries, including A.J., who sat at a corner booth reading the Sunday paper. The young Goth couple by the window sat there every weekend morning with their baby. The same web surfers, the same faces hidden behind newspapers and smart phones — nothing ever changed at JavaJava, her warm, relaxing home away from home.

Will waited near the front door, tense lines twisting his face. He wore a blue tee and plaid-shirt combination with his jeans, topped with a black jacket. Livy's hooded parka dripped moisture while they put in their orders, and her boots left soggy footprints as they approached a small booth. She tugged her knit cap off and let her hair spill over her shoulders and down her back. Will moved behind her and helped her remove her jacket. Although she couldn't see him, his proximity, his musky cologne, filled her senses.

They settled in, and Will gave her a little crooked grin as he slid his hands up and down the coffee cup. She mustered her most disarming smile to put him at ease. With his nervous body language, this date must be his first after splitting with his wife. He'd made her his first choice.

He held her gaze. "How are you?"

"Really good. And yourself?"

"Not bad." His upturned mouth always crooked on the verge of a smile, casting good cheer to his well-sculpted features. Laugh lines creased the sides of his eyes. His hair—black, smooth, chin-length—tempted her to lean across the table and run her fingers through it.

"So tell me something." His voice pulled her to the moment. "How did you come up with the name Saffire?"

She stirred her latte. "DeeDee and I were born in September, and the sapphire is our birthstone."

"Ah."

"My parents named me Olivia September, and her Diana Sapphire."

"Very cool."

"Thank you. When we were young, we were known as Liv and Di. But we got laughed at so much, we switched to Livy and DeeDee."

"Your parents were interesting people."

"Yes, they were. My mom was into rhymes. Edgar Allen Poe, Ogden Nash, you name it."

"Good thing you two weren't boys then. What if she'd named you Edgar and Ogden?"

"No doubt she would've called us Ed and Og."

Their chuckles drew attention from a couple at a nearby table, who bestowed curious smiles on them.

Nostalgic memories loosened her muscles. "But limericks were her passion. She could make up a limerick or a rhyme on the spot."

"You could call her a limericks-and-leotards kind of woman, then."

"Precisely." She had to laugh. "My dad fell in love with her the day they met because she wrote him a limerick."

"That's a creative way to meet a soul mate."

"I know, right? And they were true soul mates." She paused for a long sip of latte, savoring its warmth all the way down.

"Do you remember any of her rhymes?" He leaned forward, his eyes lit as if the answer were of utmost importance.

"I remember a couple."

"Tell me."

"Okay. Here's one she used to tell us at bedtime:
'Dreams are magical, sweet, and bright,
The moon is a happy, glowing sight.
The fairy is dancing,
The unicorn's prancing,
While little girls slumber so deep tonight.'"

Will clapped. "Very charming."

"Indeed."

"How old were you when she passed away?"

"I was six."

"Aw." The sympathy in his tone started to crumble the wall inside her. "That's too bad. If you don't mind my asking, how did she die?"

For a moment, she said nothing. Her compulsion to confide turned to regret over bringing up the subject.

Finally, the words came. "She had a fatal reaction to a

drug."

He grimaced. "It must have been rough on you."

Livy focused on her coffee and gripped her knee. A hard knot lodged in her chest. She lifted her head. "It was. I went into shock and don't remember a thing."

His forehead crinkled. "Really? Did the same thing happen to your sister?"

"No, she remembers everything."

Will shook his head. "I don't know much about identical twins. Was it unusual for the two of you to react so differently to the same event?"

At her pause, he held up his palms as if in appeal. "Not trying to be nosy, just interested in how twins tick."

He scrutinized her with a guileless, waiting expression. Behind him, damp daylight filtered through the window. Rain blasted the glass with tiny rat-a-tats.

"Usually we were on the same wavelength, especially as kids."

"But that particular day, you went into shock, and she didn't."

"Correct." A slight tremor in her hand jostled her latte.

"Have you ever wondered why?"

"What do you mean?"

"I mean, your reaction suggests trauma. Maybe you saw or heard something that frightened you."

"I saw my mom dead on the floor. What could be worse to a six-year-old?"

"Well…" He studied his twiddling thumbs. "Was it an accident?"

She rocked back. "Why wouldn't it be? Are you suggesting suicide? Or…or—"

His face turned stricken. "My sincerest apologies." He reached toward her, gazing at her like a guilty puppy. "It was none of my business. Please don't leave."

He gestured to the purse in her hand. She'd grabbed it without realizing it. "I broke a cardinal rule of first dates," he said. "'Don't ask nosy questions about your date's family.' My bad."

His winsome manner dissolved her anxiety.

"Can I get a do-over?"

Her heart rate settled into its normal laidback pace, and she set her purse down. She'd been about to violate her own first-date rule: Be willing to give a guy a second chance.

"No worries. It just frustrates me that I can't remember anything. I'm starting to think the odds I'll ever remember are about the same as—as—finding magic orange leprechauns in my garden."

"Magic orange leprechauns? There's one I haven't heard before."

"It's something my grandma used to say."

"Magic orange leprechauns. Hmm. I'll put that one in my hat." He took a sip of coffee. "Thank you for sharing your story with me. Even though you didn't have an easy childhood, it's one of the things which makes you so interesting."

"I like your positive spin on things."

"Life's too short to be negative all the time." He smiled into her eyes. "Were you raised around here?"

"A lifelong Seattleite. DeeDee and I were born in Redmond, across the freeway from the Microsoft campus, although it wasn't much then."

"Still, a claim to fame."

If he only knew her real claim to fame.

"You know what they say, don't you? The best things in life come in pairs."

Livy laughed. "You just made that up."

He grinned back. "I admit it. I did."

A comfortable silence wrapped around them like a

blanket fresh from the dryer. A draft of warm air stroked Livy's arms. "Now tell me about you."

"Where shall I begin?" He moved his head side to side as if trying to decide between two alternatives. "In a nutshell, I'm an actor-slash-tour guide. Or a tour-guide-slash-actor, depending on how you look at it."

"You mean, one feeds the body, the other feeds the spirit?"

"You're right on the money." He leaned forward again, an interested gleam in his eye. "You know what the experts say. Do what you love and the money will follow. Unfortunately, here in the Northwest, it's difficult to make a decent living as an actor. So I opened a tour company five years ago. It's done pretty well, so I can't complain."

"What kind of acting?"

"A lot of community theater." He drummed his fingers on the table. "Occasionally I'll land a part when a TV movie or Broadway musical comes to town, but competition for those roles is fierce. And I don't want to move to LA. So, at this point, I don't see myself ever becoming a paparazzi magnet."

Livy could tell him a thing or two about being a paparazzi magnet. "What was your favorite role ever?"

"Great question." He studied his interlaced hands. "Last year I got cast as the murderer in an Agatha Christie play. Playing the 'who' of the whodunit is my all-time favorite role. Nobody knew I was the murderer until the end."

Livy couldn't pull her gaze away from his animated face. She'd made the right choice by staying.

"But Roxanne thinks I'm chasing a pipe dream."

Livy snapped to attention.

"She's a real estate agent and quite successful." Will rested his chin on his hands. "But she's hardly ever home—one more reason we don't get along."

Livy soon learned what she had been eager to know but didn't want to ask: he and Roxanne were battling over custody issues and assets, not to mention the home she didn't want to sell. "I call it inconsolable differences," he qualified with a smile. Judging from recent interactions with his sullen daughter, the inconsolable part also applied to Amity.

They ordered a second round of coffee. Finally Will glanced at his phone. "It's almost lunchtime. We've been here close to two hours. Do you want something to eat?"

The rain had eased while they talked, bringing patches of sunshine. "Now that you mention it, I do." Later they went for a walk. Hours passed in a dreamlike haze.

"Do you have anything you have to do today?" he asked as they strolled along Green Lake. "I don't want to presume on your time."

"You're not presuming." She hopped over a wide puddle reflecting sponge-painted clouds. "I don't have anything else going on today."

"I want to take you out for dinner." He grasped her hand. "There's a great little hole in the wall two blocks away. They serve awesome food."

A giddy wave hit Livy. Her coffee date was turning into an all-day date. She wondered if DeeDee was curious over her whereabouts, but Livy had silenced her phone and left it in the bottom of her bag.

"Have you heard of Purple Tomato?"

"I've heard of it. Italian or Greek or something."

"It's a smorgasbord of various Mediterranean cuisines. I go there a lot for lunch." Appeal gleamed in his eyes. "You'll love it."

"Seeing as how purple's my favorite color…" She gave him a sidelong smile. "How can I say no?"

Will craned his neck, peering at the darkening, cloud-studded sky. "I'm glad it stopped raining." He grinned at her.

"My dad used to say Seattle's weather is as changeable as a woman's mind."

Livy rolled her eyes and gave him a playful punch.

"I hope I didn't offend you."

"Not really. I can take a joke. But he could just as easily say Seattle's weather is as changeable as Hugh Hefner's girlfriends."

"Touché." He nodded his approval, then placed his right hand on her back and pointed with his left. "Here we are. Welcome to Purple Tomato."

He led her inside a small and dark restaurant with white stucco walls and tiny wooden tables scattered around inside and on the sidewalk. Night had fallen, but traffic, both human and automotive, still hummed along on the boulevard.

They found a table in the corner, and Will opened a menu. "I recommend the lamb kebobs."

Livy, her stomach growling, didn't waste time reading a menu. "Sounds perfect."

A clean-cut young waiter paused at their table, and Will ordered for both of them. The pulsating beat of Stevie Nicks's "Edge of Seventeen" played over the speaker, and Livy hummed along, pausing long enough to say, "I feel like we're in a scene in *School of Rock*."

"Same here. We must look like Jack Black and Joan Cusack grooving to this song."

"I loved that movie." She closed her eyes and became one with the song.

When she opened her eyes, Will was watching her. "You have an amazing voice."

A shiver vibrated through her. "Thanks." She stopped herself from telling him her father taught her to sing. Their kebobs arrived, and she picked up a knife and fork to cut the meat into small pieces instead of eating it off the stick. Grandma used to warn them not to stuff too much food in their mouths on a first date.

Finally he spoke. "This must seem strange to you."

"What must seem strange?"

"I never intended for this to be more than a get-together over coffee." He set his half-eaten kebob on his plate. "But I'm having such a good time, I don't want it to end."

"I feel the same way."

"We keep finding more things to talk about."

"And more fun things to do—"

"And nothing to rush home for." Something sizzled in the air between them. They sat, mesmerized, until a waiter approached and broke the spell by asking if their dinners were okay.

"Fine," said Livy, still looking at Will.

"Very good," said Will, eyes on Livy.

By the time he walked her home, nine p.m. had come and gone. On her porch, he embraced her and caressed her back. "Cute house."

"Thanks. I love it here." She nestled her chin on his shoulder. "You can't tell in the dark, but it's gypsy red with white shutters." Rhododendron bushes marched along the front of the house. In spring, they made her yard the most colorful on the block.

"How long have you lived here?" His breath jostled her hair like a gentle breeze. His body rested lightly against hers.

"Going on six years." Dad bought it for her and DeeDee on their twenty-first birthday.

Will released her and took her hands, his thumb's caress as light as cotton. "Just so you know, I wasn't planning to ask this, but since we've spent the entire day together, I'm thinking a goodnight kiss is in order."

Livy, leaning in, smiled into his eyes. His lips pressed hers as he reached behind her head and grasped her hair, the minty flavor of his mouth tingling.

When he pulled away, she sucked in a breath. His face stayed inches from hers, and a wide smile crinkled the edges of his eyes. "That was nice."

"Yeah." A croak emerged from her throat.

"I had such a good day."

"I did too. Thank you for a great time."

He paused, his silence dense with expectation. She waited for the make-or-break moment when he realized she wasn't going to invite him in for a drink, and then some.

"Can I see you again tomorrow?"

She exhaled. He wasn't a rush-her-into-bed kind of guy. So far, he was a keeper.

"Yeah," she purred as he brushed a feathery kiss on her forehead. "I'm looking forward to it."

***

A ghostly figure visited Livy in a dream that night. Swathed in a black cape and boots, the apparition warbled "Edge of Seventeen" in a high, off-key voice. Stevie Nicks's face came into focus, but the flowery scent said it was Mom.

"Mommy." Livy inhaled as the figure floated into Saffire's cherry-red hallway, which towered several floors high, each floor filled with mirrored, empty dance studios.

"This looks so lovely, bebby gulls." The sweet voice pulsated all around. "Look, the walls are orange. Like magic leprechauns." As if on cue, the cherry transformed into fluorescent orange. DeeDee appeared at Livy's side, and Mom gathered them in her arms. They swayed inside her bone-bending embrace.

"Mommy?" Livy said. "I thought you were dead."

"You did?" Her mother's chalk-white face elongated, eyes wide and unblinking. "I'm not dead. It was all a misunderstanding."

Overjoyed, Livy started to cry. Soon DeeDee's sobs

joined hers. Livy woke with moisture all over her face. Then reality hit, and she wept real tears.

As a child, she'd often dreamed of her mother. The dreams followed a common theme, with varying details. Always her mother appeared and told Livy she wasn't dead after all. There had been a mistake. And Livy would cry. But the dreams ceased in middle school. Until the graveyard visit last summer.

She sniffed and checked the digital display on her bedside clock, 4:47 a.m. As the last tear trickled down her cheek, she patted her face with the sheet. She needed DeeDee. She needed to lie beside her twin and hold hands like they used to.

Livy threw off the floral comforter, swung her feet to the nubby jute rug, and checked in Murf's crate to ensure he was still sleeping. His white mass of fur nearly glowed in the dark, undulating with his breathing. Satisfied, she tiptoed to the bedroom across the hall, turned the handle without a squeak, and crept inside. DeeDee wouldn't mind if she climbed in next to her.

She elbowed Miss Piggy away from the center of the queen-sized bed, resulting in a yowl from the animal. DeeDee didn't stir. After crawling under the sheet, Livy found her twin's hand, allowing her mind to wander back, to the early years when Mom was still alive. To her fifth birthday when she realized something wasn't right with Mom.

Chapter Six

Liv woke up forgetting she was a whole year older than yesterday. But then she remembered. Today she and Di were five.

A high-pitched chant poured from her mouth. "To-day is our birf-day." It floated into the quiet bedroom. "We're gonna have a fun time."

If she sang the words over and over, maybe they would come true.

"Gonna have a fun time. Gonna have a fun time."

She pressed on her tummy to shush the loud growly bear inside her. He was squeezing her tummy so hard, it hurt.

"Today is our birf-day." She leaped from the bed, ran to Di's dresser where the candy was hidden, and opened the bottom drawer. Only four itty-bitty Snicker bars remained. They had eaten most of them yesterday after running home from the corner store with their pockets full. Grabbing the candy after the fat man went to the back was so easy. Then, while the tall boy helped a lady buying Coke, they stuffed their pockets and fled for home.

Liv scooped up the candy and jumped onto her twin's bed. "Di."

Di mumbled, so Liv jostled her. "Wake up. It's our birfday. Mommy and Daddy are giving us a party."

Di bounded up, nearly knocking Liv off the bed. Pike thumped his tail on the floor and looked at them with wide brown eyes.

"Oh yeah," Di whispered because Mommy and Daddy

made them be quiet when they got up. Her tummy's growls echoed Liv's as she swung her legs to the floor. "Is it waining?"

If it wasn't, they could play outside. She swept the curtains aside. Rays of sunlight bounced off the Space Needle. "Yay! It's sunny."

Liv stared at the fat, round Space Needle. Mommy and Daddy kept promising to take them to the restaurant at the top. Daddy said you could see clear to the end of Seattle and beyond, to the mountains and even forever.

If she begged hard enough, maybe Mommy and Daddy would take them tomorrow. Daddy said tomorrow was Labor Day, a special day because everybody got to stay home from work.

Liv tore open two tiny candy bars and stuffed them into her mouth. Di devoured the other two. Clad in their red pajamas, they snuck into the hall and crept toward the living room. If there were no strangers in the house, they could turn on the TV.

A pair of feet poked around the edge of the couch. She and Di crept closer. A strange man snored on the couch, and a woman lay bundled up in a blanket on the floor.

Liv hesitated and stared at the man. Di stepped around the pop cans all over the floor, and Liv followed, careful not to knock against the overflowing ashtrays on the couch arm. A pizza box on a table held two half-eaten slices in a bed of crumbs.

Dropping her blanket, Liv rushed to the pizza. She grabbed one slice, Di the other, and they bit into greasy sausage and cheese, as hard as cardboard. Liv liked her pizza fresh and hot, but when she was hungry, she'd eat it any way she could get it.

The bear in her tummy quieted after she finished the slice. Now she needed something to drink. Spying an opened

Coke can, she peered inside and shook it. Liquid sloshed, so she poured it into her mouth, then grimaced at the lukewarm, fizz-less soda.

Di found a dark brown bottle and gulped a long drink. "Yucky!" She sputtered, spitting the drink onto the floor. "Ew, ew."

"Quiet, you two." The person on the floor sat up. Mommy's friend Audria gaped at the bottle in Di's hand. "Put that down, Diana. Why are you drinking beer, you little silly?"

Di hung her head. "It's woot beer. Mommy and Daddy let me dwink it."

"That is not root beer." Audria swiped at her hair, a mess of tangles as she sat among the twisted blankets on the carpet. "It's beer. Put it down and go get some pop if you're thirsty."

Di pouted and set the bottle on the table, then picked up a can of Sprite. Liv looked around the room for Audria's daughter, but didn't see her anywhere.

"Where is Vienna?"

"She's at a neighbor's house." Audria lay down, her back to them. "Now be quiet."

Liv swiveled to the couch. She couldn't resist eyeing the strange man. He was scary with his long brown beard, and he growled as he slept. Pictures of big-eyed monsters were all over his chest and arms. Jolting, she stepped back, grabbed her blanket, and hugged it to herself. Yet, despite her fear, she had to take one more peek. She shivered at the nails stuck all over his face. What a lot of owies. Even though it wasn't Halloween, he was dressed like a monster.

The man opened one eye and looked straight at them. Liv shrunk back, heart pounding, and she clasped her twin's hand. Comforting warmth spread from Di's hand to hers and chased away the frights.

Deep silence vibrated as they stared at each other. Di

broke it first. "Who are you?"

"Rolf." He talked like he had sandpaper in his throat. "Who are you?"

"Di."

"Liv."

His eyes opened wide as he chuckled. "Die and Live? Live and Die?" He laughed so hard he coughed.

Liv stared at the man. What was so funny?

"I must still be drunk, man. I'm seein' double." Another rattly laugh erupted from his mouth. "Just pullin' your leg. You must be Declan Decker's daughters."

They shook their heads in unison. "No, we aren't." Di's voice stayed firm.

"You aren't?" His mouth opened wide, revealing broken teeth. "The guy with long black hair ain't your daddy? The one who sleeps in the bedroom back there?" The man lifted a shaky finger toward the back of the house.

Liv frowned at Di. It sounded like Daddy, but his name wasn't Declan. "Our daddy's name is Howard. Howard Mc-Crear-y."

The man no longer seemed scary. When he smiled and laughed, he looked like Santa Claus, only much younger.

"Hey, pipe down over there," Audria snapped. "I'm trying to sleep."

Liv faced Audria, her hands on her hips. "But we wanna watch TV. We wanna watch cartoons."

Audria made the funny clicking sound she did when they were "getting on her nerves." Whatever that meant. "Go back to bed, girls. Nobody is going to be up for hours."

Di stomped her foot. "But it's our birthday, and we s'posed to have a party."

"Your party isn't till tonight." Audria wrinkled her forehead and peered at them. "Have you two been eating candy?"

Liv licked her lips. "No." If she told the truth, Audria would scold them.

Di crossed her arms. "Huh uh."

"Sure looks like chocolate smears on your mouths."

Di rubbed her lower lip. "No, it's not."

Liv nodded and wiped her mouth. "We didn't eat some chocolate."

"Conniving little liars." Audria snorted and stretched back out on the floor. "By the way, happy birthday."

Liv stared at the spotty carpet, unable to say thank you, because Audria had called them a bad word.

The man on the couch shifted to his side, his growls almost as loud as Liv's tummy. She grabbed Di's hand and pulled her into the kitchen.

With Mommy sick so much and Daddy gone a lot, no one fixed meals for them.

They checked the cupboard with the missing doors. As Liv feared, it contained only two boxes of instant oatmeal and a box of Saltine crackers. She and Di didn't like oatmeal so she climbed onto the counter and pulled out a package of crackers, then slid down, landing on her feet with a thud.

If Katie still lived next door, they would be going to Sunday school. She missed Katie's Sunday school. She missed the cookies and the fun songs about sunbeams and the stories about Jesus, who was always kind to children. She wished Katie hadn't moved away.

She clutched the crackers to her chest. "Do you know where the Jesus storybook is?" It had been so long since she'd seen it.

"Huh uh. I don't know where it is." Di opened the refrigerator. A six-pack of 7-Up rested on the bottom shelf of the mostly empty refrigerator. Di grabbed two and handed one to Liv, and they crept back to the hall so they wouldn't wake Audria and the man.

They were almost to their room when Daddy came out of his bedroom, wearing big square underwear and rubbing his eyes.

Liv jumped up and down. Maybe Daddy would take them to McDonald's for breakfast. "Daddy, you're up."

"Can we have our party now?"

Daddy was cross-eyed. "Huh? What party? We just had one last night."

They exchanged puzzled looks. Last night Daddy told them he and Mommy were having company, and let them have one slice of pizza before he sent them to bed. Twice Liv awakened in the night to singing and loud laughter. If she'd known it was a birthday party, she would have begged to stay up. "Whose birfday was it?"

Daddy shook his head. "Kiddos, give me a minute, why don't you?" He went into the bathroom, and they waited outside the door, stuffing their mouths with crackers, followed by big gulps of 7-Up. While they chewed and swallowed, they practiced the ballet steps Mommy taught them. Deep knee bends in second position, tushies tucked. Releves stretched high and held for ten seconds. Ronde jambes on the hardwood floor.

After the toilet flushed and water splashed, Daddy came out. They each grabbed one of his long legs. "Daddy." Di's tone was insistent. "Come to our woom. Please?"

He sighed and slid one foot after the other as they clung to him, their feet dragging behind. He lifted them and deposited them on Di's bed.

"How are my kiddos this morning?" His voice rumbled like a distant semi-truck.

Liv poked his skinny arm. "Daddy, did you forget? It's our birfday."

His eyes opened wide, just like his mouth. "Of course I remember! Happy birthday, lil' punkins." He grabbed their noses and tweaked them side to side until they giggled. Plopping down beside them, he pulled Liv onto his knee. "Today's your birth-day," he sang, his voice a soft rasp. He picked up Di and set her on his other knee, grinning big. "It's your birthday too-oo."

Liv bounced on his knee. "Today is our birfda-a-a-ay! We gonna have a fun time!" She made sure she outshouted Di, who stuck out her tongue.

Grinning in triumph, Liv leaned on Daddy's shoulder and sniffed. He smelled funny, sort of like cold medicine. She wrinkled her nose and reached behind his head to pat his thick hair. Di patted the scratchy mass of dark whiskers all over his cheeks and jaw. "Daddy, why is that man on the couch?"

"He's my buddy Rolf. He stayed here last night so he wouldn't have to drive home drunk."

Liv searched Di's puzzled face. Di didn't know what "drunk" meant either. "He called you a funny name."

"You mean he called me a—" Daddy uttered a long word Liv had heard many times before, but still sounded like the most scary word in the world.

"No, not that name. He called you a declan."

Daddy laughed hard and squeezed her around the middle.

"Why did he call you that?" Di asked.

"Declan Decker's my stage name." He rubbed his hands gently on her and Di's backs. His kind daddy face leaned in.

"What's a stage name?"

"It's the name my fans call me."

"Your fans?" Liv scrunched her nose, picturing a roomful of whirring fans calling out "Declan" to her daddy.

"I'm in a rock band, punkins."

"What's a wock band?" They had never seen Daddy playing with rocks.

"It's a bunch of us guys who get together to play music and sing."

"Oh! Like when you play your guitar wif Nils and those other men?"

"Yeah, exactly. But people pay lots of money to hear us play. You know what that means?"

Their heads moved as one, side to side.

"We're gonna be rich, that's what."

Liv wasn't sure what "rich" meant, but from the look on Daddy's face, it must be something great. His smile stretched tight across his teeth like a thick rubber band. Pinpricks of light danced in his eyes. "And you know what else?"

"What?"

"We'll move out of this little dump and into a great big house."

"When?"

"Real soon, kiddos. Real soon. And we'll get a big car too, like Nils."

They whooped.

He poked their tummies until they squealed. "You want to hear the song that's gonna make us rich?"

They nodded, still giggling. Daddy broke into a soft song with funny words. "'She's an oxymoron, yeah, an oxymoron, uh huh—'" Liv loved Daddy's singing voice—deep and kind of mournful, the way cows sounded in the old Western movies he watched. And when he sang to them at bedtime, his voice never failed to carry her away to Dreamland.

But sometimes his voice came out rough. Like now. "'Sweetly cruel, a real pretender, she loves me, yeah, she hates me tender—'"

A knock interrupted. Daddy stopped singing and cocked his head. "That you, Luna Tunes?"

The door opened, and Mommy peeked in. "It's me." Wrapped in her fuzzy pink robe, Mommy stepped into the room, all smiles. "Look at my pretty birthday girls. Happy birthday, lovies."

When Mommy got sick, she never smiled, and she stayed in bed for a long, long time. But today, Mommy's smile shone like a toothpaste commercial, her teeth like tiny, perfect marshmallows.

She tilted her head. "My baby girls' hair looks so pretty this morning. It sparkles like brown sugar."

"Mommy, did you make a poem fo' us?" asked Di.

"Of course I did." She sat next to Daddy. "Do you want to hear it now, or later at the party?"

Di bounced up and down. "Now!"

"Tell us now!"

"Okay, then." Mommy set one hand on Liv's head and one on Di's. Her hands shook as she recited:

"Today my twin and I are five —
Can't wait until the gifts arrive.
To be a twin is oh so nice,
We get to open presents twice."

Liv giggled. Di smiled big. Mommy had a poem for everything.

Mommy scratched her arms hard and looked at Daddy. "Did you tell them, hun?"

"Oh yeah, punkins, guess what?" Daddy tugged on their hair. "We're taking you to breakfast for your birthday. How does Clown Palace sound?"

"Yay!" Clown Palace had everything—a humongous play area, yummy food like pancakes and waffles, and funny clowns on unicycles.

"Then get dressed."

Liv danced over to her dresser in a haze of joy and pulled on leggings and a shirt. The hungry bear in her tummy had stopped growling. He must be happy she was going to Clown Palace.

By the time they stood dressed and ready to go, Daddy came in. The look on his face sent tremors through Liv. "Hey, kiddos." He knelt and looked each of them in the eye. "Mommy won't be going. She's feeling sick to her stomach, so she went back to bed."

Liv's heart fell to her feet. Mommy always got sick whenever she and Daddy planned to take them anywhere.

Desperate, she pleaded her case. "Daddy, take us anyway." She jumped up and down. "Please, please?"

"All right, fine. Go get in the car."

Still motionless, they stared at him, until Di spoke the question nagging at Liv. "Daddy? Is something wong with Mommy?"

He didn't reply, merely grasped their hands, and led them through the living room, past Audria and the man on the couch.

Once in the car, Liv repeated Di's question. "Is something wrong wif Mommy?"

Daddy tilted his head to meet her gaze, his face tight. "You let me worry about your mother, Olivia. This is your time to be a carefree kid, okay?" He started the car and backed out. Liv sought Di's gaze and, despite Daddy's words, saw her fears reflected on her sister's face.

Chapter Seven

"Hey." DeeDee's slurry voice broke through Livy's haze of sleep. "Did you have a bad dream?"

Livy opened her eyes to her mirror image looming over her. She yawned, her mind clearing. "I had a dream about Mom. She was alive."

"Freakishness. Just like when you were little."

"I know, right?" Livy bunched the sheet under her chin, jostling Miss Piggy at the foot of the bed. The cat meowed, arched her back, and pranced across Livy's legs.

DeeDee propped her cheek on her hand. "You haven't dreamed about Mom for years."

"I think it came from something Will said."

"What'd he say?" DeeDee's voice hardened as if Will committed a bad deed.

Livy repeated the conversation, leaving out her mention of the weirdo at the graveyard. Weird coincidence. "He implied it was suicide. Or worse — " She couldn't bring herself to utter the word she feared.

DeeDee flung a strand of hair out of her eyes. "I think most kids would freak out if their mom OD'd. Besides, Mom wasn't the suicidal type. And why would anyone want to kill her?"

"But he has a point. You didn't go into shock like I did, Deeds." Her voice lifted a few decibels. "Neither of us ever tried to figure out why."

"Why what?"

"Why I lost my memory and you didn't after we both

witnessed our mother's dead body. Think about it. We've been told a certain story all our lives. But what if there's more to it?"

"I remember it." DeeDee's emphatic tone discouraged argument. "The story they told us agrees with what I remember."

"But that was you, not me. And Will is the second person to suggest a different scenario."

"The second person? Who was the first?"

Too late to slam shut the door she'd inadvertently opened. She and DeeDee never kept secrets from each other. She shrugged. "Remember the guy at the cemetery on our last visit?"

"The Jesus freak?"

"Yes." Livy stared at the plaster ceiling, swirled and pockmarked like the moon's surface. "After you and Dad got into the limo, he grabbed my arm and told me something happened to me the day Mom died. He seemed totally convinced. He goes, 'Seek the truth,' and something about being set free. But I don't know what truth he was talking about. And then yesterday Will says something along the same lines. It's starting to make me wonder."

"You're scarin' me, sister."

"I know. It's trippy." She turned on her side, and DeeDee plopped down next to her, eye-to-eye. "Next thing I know, Mom comes to visit me in a dream. Why would she?"

Instead of answering, DeeDee puckered her face. "You ought to go talk to the guy from the cemetery, find out why he said what he did."

"I'm not sure I want to talk to him again. The whole thing creeped me out."

DeeDee threw up her shoulders in a shrug. "We should call Grandma." She lay back and closed her eyes. "After we sleep some more."

Livy rolled over, her mind and heart settled. Grandma would offer words of wisdom. Grandma had been the rock of her childhood whenever life threatened to crumble around her. Especially during Mom's rehab trips.

***

Grandma Gaia was the best grandma ever. Whenever she saw Liv and Di, her whole face grinned. Her hair rippled down her back in a long silvery stream, and she always smelled like flowers. Too bad she lived so far away.

Her house in Portland perched on the side of a mountain—coolest house ever. A steep set of stairs angled into a dark, spooky basement Liv feared venturing into. An even steeper set beckoned her and Di to the attic bedroom, their special haven. The slant of the V-shaped ceiling reached the floor like a fairy-tale cottage. From the window, high wooded hills dwarfed the downtown skyscrapers, making them look like a toy city.

Grandma had a man living with her, and she told them to call him Grandpa Phil. He was a smiling man with long gray hair like Grandma's, except he pulled it back in a ponytail.

According to Grandma, Mommy was sick, but had gone into the hospital for a month so she could get well. At once, Liv's fears evaporated. If Grandma said Mommy would be all well in a month, it must be true.

After dinner, when their tummies were full and happy, Grandma tucked them into their little attic bed as they begged her to tell them stories about the land with the funny name.

"Oh, you must mean the land of Oggawogga," said Grandma in her lullaby voice. "Where all the homes are filled with loveness. Where magic orange leprechauns live, and baby quidgilas float in the air—"

"What's a quidgila?" Liv asked with a sputtering giggle.

"A quidgila? Why, it's a funny-looking creature like a duck but with paws like a kitten. They are all over the land of Oggawogga. And a little girl lives there. Can you guess her name?"

"Olivia?"

"Diana?"

"Her name is Liviana. Isn't that a lovely name?"

Liv chuckled. "It's *our* name." She felt for Di's hand under the covers and grabbed it. Di squeezed back.

"One day Liviana and her quidgila friend went to visit the magic man." Drowsy waves gently rocked Liv's head. "The magic man lived in a warm little house painted blue and pink and green, filled with the softest of pillows—"

She heaved a warm and comfortable sigh and made believe she was cuddled in the magic man's house.

"The magic man led them into a dark forest of huge soft yurvels big enough to sleep on—"

Liv was too sleepy to ask what yurvels were. She gave into the irresistible lure of Dreamland and let her eyes drift shut.

"Liviana and the quidgila curled up on a big soft yurvel and soon fell fast asleep."

And so did Liv. She fell all the way into Dreamland and snuggled there all night.

***

Livy awoke with a jerk. DeeDee's bedroom was cold, so she nestled closer to her twin. She needed to get up and turn on the furnace, but the bed was so warm and comfortable. Just like the magic man's house.

She eased out of bed, donned DeeDee's robe and slippers, and then shuffled to the hall thermostat. Fifty-eight degrees. Shivering, she turned the setting up ten degrees.

Wandering into the kitchen, she glanced at the

microwave clock—8:25 a.m. Monday morning. Grandma would be sitting at her kitchen table in Portland sipping coffee.

She prepared a pot and returned to her own room, leaving the light off. Right now, she welcomed the shadowy dimness. It fit her mood and hid the tranquil pink walls, the delicate violets and mauves in the comforter and pillows.

Murf's whine greeted her, so she retrieved the pup and stroked him as she perched on her big pink balance ball. He burrowed into her lap and settled in. Cinnamon scent from the diffuser sent warm waves through the room.

Rocking gently, she picked up her phone and pulled up Grandma's number. "Hi, Grandma."

"Lambie. What's new with you?"

"Well." Livy sucked in a deep breath, unwilling to waste time on small talk. "I had a vivid dream about Mom last night. For the first time since I was a kid."

"How odd. Tell me about it."

After Livy relayed the details, Grandma replied in an almost reverent hush. "I'm really surprised Luna visited you last night. I thought she had finally achieved peace. Alistair told me she had a beautiful soul, and she'd been reborn into a family in India where she is cared for and loved."

"Then why would she appear in my dream?"

"Tell you what, Alistair and I will walk to the top of Mt. Tabor tonight and invoke prayers to the universe. If I hear anything from beyond, I'll call you right away."

"Wait. I've been wondering something else."

"What?"

Livy stopped rocking and planted her spine against the wall. "Why did I go into shock the day Mom died?"

Grandma's pause stretched for breathless seconds. Livy swung her foot, waiting.

"What makes you ask such a question after all these

years?"

"I've had two people recently point out how it's odd DeeDee and I had such different reactions."

"Why, you were a little girl who had just seen her mother lifeless on the floor."

"Then why didn't DeeDee go into shock, too? From what you've always told me, she was right there beside me."

A deep sigh huffed on the other end. "I don't really know, lambie. We don't know what triggers these things. But Alistair and I will pray about that tonight as well. Perhaps the universe knows some secrets we don't know yet."

"Okay, Grandma. Thanks."

Livy ended the call, her shoulders drooping. If Grandma didn't have answers, then who did?

Chapter Eight

After two weeks of dating Will, Livy still hadn't told him her father's identity. She needed to soon, but quaked each time she thought about it. Would he consider it a deal breaker? Or would he latch on to her even tighter, hoping to exploit the connection?

The morning sun cast cheery beams into the breakfast nook and mingled with the aroma of fresh-baked pastries, lifting her spirits. DeeDee tried to give her a helping of courage. "Just do it. You'll know by his reaction whether he's a keeper."

"Easy for you to say. I'll be heartbroken if he's not a keeper." Livy bit into a raspberry scone from the batch cooling on the counter. "He's such an awesome guy. I haven't liked anyone this much for ages."

"Yeah, but if he's a cad, better to find out now than later."

Livy clutched the edge of the table. "I'll tell him tonight. After we drop off the girls."

After breakfast, DeeDee put a movie on, and Livy got ready to meet Will, who'd be here with his daughters in less than an hour. Her hands shook as she flat ironed her hair. The bathroom's subtle sea blues and greens calmed her nerves, until steam from the iron sizzled too close to her fingers, and she dropped it. Wincing, she jumped back, then knelt and retrieved it. As she worked the iron through her hair, her stiff face stared at her from the bronze-framed mirror.

When Will arrived, his hug and kiss settled her. *It'll be okay. He's a good man, and he'll be cool about it.* But on the drive to the water park, Amity whined so frequently, Livy had to cling to the car's armrest a couple of times to keep herself from whirling around and slapping the girl.

If Will would take a firm stand with Amity, their outings would be far more pleasant.

When he finally dropped off the girls at Roxanne's, Livy unclenched herself, welcoming the absence of conflict. Roxanne could deal with the little shrew.

Streetlights blinked on during the drive to her house. DeeDee was gone—no doubt out with friends. She led Will into her living room, where he glanced around at framed prints of dancers in action livening the place up. An eclectic mix of plaid throws, paisley pillows, and geometric area rugs added sparks of color contrasting the dove gray walls.

Will relaxed on the corduroy sectional, leaning his head against the plush back as if the day exhausted him. In the kitchen, she crossed to the embedded sound system and clicked it on. Gentle jazz piped through the speakers and into the living room. She selected a bottle of Zinfandel from the wine rack, filled two goblets, and carried them to the teakwood coffee table.

She placed her hand on his knee. "Give me one more minute."

He nodded, and before she lost her nerve, she hurried to the white shelves built into the wall next to the kitchen. Three shelves held objets d'art they'd picked up while touring—cloth dolls from Brazil dressed in native attire, hand-painted terra cotta pots from Mexico, religious figurines from Asia. On the bottom shelf sat DVDs of their favorite movies. She knelt to the single white drawer below the shelves, opened it, and wrested out an old photo album. Rejoining Will, she tucked a puffy pillow behind her back and snuggled closer to him as he wrapped his arm around her. Murf, curled at her feet, wheezed as she kneaded her bare toes in his baby-soft fur.

"I have something uber-important to tell you about myself." She set the album on his lap and opened it, then sought his gaze. "This is huge. It's taken me awhile to feel ready."

Will widened his eyes at her. "You used to be a man?"

A snort erupted from her mouth and she punched him twice. "You silly guy." She laughed again. "It's nothing like that. It's my father." She fingered a photo. "Are you ready?"

Will squinted at the album and nodded.

She turned the page. "He's Declan Decker."

His mouth gaped like a cavern. His brows rose nearly to his hairline.

"What?" Livy nudged him. "Say something."

"Surprise, surprise." An edge of sarcasm crackled in his voice. "I'm dating Declan Decker's daughter and didn't even know it."

Her heart accelerated. "Are you mad?"

"No, I'm not mad." His voice rose. "Just wishing you'd been upfront with me from the get-go."

"I'm sorry. I needed to wait until I had a sense where things were going with us." She leaned away from his arm as unwelcome tears filled her eyes. "I wasn't trying to deceive you."

"What *were* you trying to do?"

"I rarely tell people who my father is." She met his hard gaze. "I only want people in my life who like me for me."

Will blew out a breath. "I do like you for you."

Then why was his tone flat?

"Will, this doesn't have to change anything between us."

He returned to the photos. She held her breath, waiting, wishing she could read his thoughts. Had she sprung a deal breaker on him?

After ten seconds of awkward silence, he pulled her to

his side and studied her face. "You do look like him." He tapped her nose. "But you're prettier."

A relieved giggle broke through her clenched lips. After a second, he grinned back. She burst into snuffling laughs, and he joined in, baffled delight brightening his face.

"Well, whaddya know," he said, still grinning. "I think we survived our first fight."

She laid her head on his shoulder, her mouth to his ear. "There is an upside to this, you know. Getting to meet him."

"True, that. I'll be sure to tell him what an awesome daughter he raised. And that I like his song 'Nothin' But Roadkill'."

Livy lifted her head and began to sing, but her smile put a lilt in the song that would make Dad cringe. "'I'm nothin' but roadkill — to you, Nothin' but roadkill — oh yeah —'"

"You sound great, rock chick."

"Except I never could get his angry growl down." She brought her face close to his. "C'mon, sing with me."

"'Some — daaaay, you're gonna beee — Nothin' but roadkill — to *me* — Nothin' but *roadkill*!'"

Their faces were inches apart, so close Livy could see the individual whiskers on his jawline. They stared into each other's eyes. Will pressed his lips hard on hers. "That was fun." His voice was a murmur as he planted more kisses over her face. "You're a woman of many talents, you know?"

"Aw, thank you —"

His kiss cut off her words. Then he released her with a lingering sigh. "Let's save this for later." He winked at her. "I want to see the rest of your photos."

Livy shifted the album and showed him a photo of a platinum disc mounted on a wall. "He named his album 'Lunatunes' after my mom."

"What a great album. 'White Cobra.' 'She's An Oxymoron.' Awesome songs."

"The songs that made us rich."

"What a trip it must have been, having a rock star for a dad."

"Trippy doesn't even come close. When fame finally caught up to him, it turned our lives upside down."

***

Before Liv knew it, moving day arrived. Mommy marked the day on the calendar with a big red circle: October 15, 1991.

"Guess what, bebby girls?" Mommy flashed a smile as they climbed into their new black truck. "Grandma Gaia is driving up to help us unpack. She'll be at our new house this afternoon."

Di leaped into the back seat and landed on her knees. "Hooway!"

Pike settled at their feet as the truck roared, and Daddy, watching the rearview mirror, backed out of the little garage for the last time. With a curse, he hit the brakes.

Di jerked forward. "What, Daddy?"

He cursed again, so Liv hopped up on her knees and swiveled to see what Daddy was so mad about.

On the opposite curb, a large crowd had gathered, yelling and holding cameras. Three big men in uniforms stood in front of the crowd to keep them back. When Daddy honked, another big guy came running. Daddy got out and shouted at the man.

Liv gawked. "Who are those people, Mommy?"

"Those are your daddy's fans. They want to follow us to our new house."

"How come?"

But Daddy hopped in the car before Mommy could reply. He slid on a pair of big black glasses and a baseball cap, and wrapped a scarf around the lower part of his face, hiding his beard.

Mommy laid a hand on his arm. "Hun, don't flip them off as you drive by. Those people made you the rock star you are today."

"Told you we should've done this in the middle of the night."

"This is what you've always wanted, isn't it?" Mommy's voice came out shrill.

Liv understood now what "rock star" meant. Daddy had helped her understand. He said so many people liked his songs, they paid money to hear him sing and play with his band, The FireAnts.

"Daddy, what about the kitties?" Mike and Ike had crawled under the house this morning and couldn't be lured out even with food, as if they knew something big was happening. The cats hadn't hidden since last year when Ike had her kittens.

"The cats will be fine." Daddy scowled as he backed out the drive. Even though Di pouted and Liv begged, Daddy wouldn't get out and search for Mike and Ike. "We got a crisis, kiddos. The cats will have to stay."

Mommy reached back and patted their legs. "I'll drive back in a few days and get the kitties, okay?"

Di sniffed away her grief and set Big Bird next to her on the seat. The big men kept forcing the crowd back while Daddy rolled the truck onto the street. The crowd's shouts punched through the closed windows. As the truck lurched, someone slammed into the back.

"Get away!" Daddy yelled. He glared at Mommy. "Did ya see that? One of those losers tried to jump on the bumper."

Di waved through the rear window as they drove away from the excited crowd. "Bye, kitties. Bye, Daddy's fans. Bye, old house."

Liv waved at the corner store. "Bye, candy store. Bye, fat man. Bye, tall boy." They didn't wave to Apollo the dog, because he always snarled at them. "Bye, Katie's house." Liv waved goodbye as they rolled along Fourteenth Street to their new home. Their new life. Sadness and excitement played tug-o'-war.

Daddy squealed the truck around the corner onto the boulevard. "Bye, old stweet," said Di. They waved and waved, hands rippling like flags in the wind.

A long red car roared up behind them and stayed almost bumper-to-bumper to the next red light. Daddy lurched to a stop and glanced at Mommy. "Babe, we got a paparazzi behind us."

She and Di waved and smiled at the man in the passenger seat as he lifted a camera to his face. "Cheese!"

"Kiddos, turn around!" Daddy's sharp tone startled Liv. "Don't even look at those dudes."

Liv plopped to the seat. "Why not? He was takin' our pitcher."

"I know he was. Do you want your face to end up in a tabloid?"

Baffled, Liv scrunched her nose at Di. Daddy jerked the gearshift. "Watch me lose that dude." He swerved into the outside lane, and the truck leaped forward. Liv couldn't resist another peek at the red car. It stayed behind them until Daddy stopped at a red light.

She caught Daddy watching her in the rearview mirror. He thrummed his fingers on the wheel, lips edging upward. Mommy peered through the back window, her eyes alight, a smile dancing on her lips. The light switched to green, and Daddy punched the gas pedal. Wrenching the wheel to the right, he spun around a corner and onto a rutted dirt lane. Di fell sideways onto Liv, and then bounced over and over as Daddy yelled, "Yeah, baby! That old beater's gonna fall to pieces if he tries to follow me now."

Mommy laughed. "Looks like he gave up on us."

Daddy let out a shout and patted the dashboard. "Way to go, Land Rover." He swung onto a paved street and headed back to the boulevard. Liv grinned at Di, recognizing the sparkle in Di's eyes as her own.

Di giggled. "That was like a carnival wide."

Daddy laughed again. "Getting mobbed and followed is just one of fame's many perks, kiddos. When you're famous, everybody wants a piece of you."

Di leaned forward. "We're famous?"

"*I'm* famous." Daddy flipped his blinker and moved into the other lane.

Mommy shifted and smiled. "Your daddy's lifelong dream was to be famous. And now he is."

Liv still wasn't sure what famous meant. Maybe it was like being rich. "Famous people get mobbed and followed?"

"Yep." Daddy nodded. "You wouldn't believe how many times I've had to break the law to get away from people following me." He tapped the side of his glasses. "So I have to wear a disguise now."

Then Liv never wanted to be famous. She would hate to wear ugly glasses and hide her face behind a scarf. "Do rich people get mobbed and followed too?"

"Yeah, if they're famous."

Liv sighed. It must be a bad thing to be famous.

Mommy reached to the floor in front of her seat, then held out a stack of magazines. The one on top had a picture of Daddy on it.

"See, baby girls, there's your daddy on the cover of *Rolling Stone.*"

Liv took it and studied Daddy's face staring at her like he was mad. She shrunk back and handed it to Di. He didn't look like her kind, smiling Daddy.

Mommy showed her another magazine with some photos of Daddy and Nils inside. "And look, *People* magazine interviewed him. Here's a whole article about him. It even mentions us." Mommy brought the magazine close to her face. "'Decker and Luna have been married for seven years. They make their home in Seattle with their five-year-old twin daughters, Olivia and Diana.'"

Liv grinned big at Di. Their names were in a magazine she'd seen in the store.

This feeling—part-embarrassed, part-proud—must be what "famous" meant.

***

As Livy finished her story, she checked Will's expression. His wide-eyed gaze stayed riveted on her. "Amazing. Shockingly amazing."

"It wasn't your ordinary upbringing." She shrugged. "No structure. Very few rules. We all pretty much did our own thing."

Will squeezed her shoulders. "You seem to have turned out all right."

"Little do you know." She chuckled. "Just kidding. Dad always told DeeDee and me two things: Don't do anything to land yourself in jail, and treat others the way you want to be treated."

"Good words to live by."

"We managed to grow up without ever landing in jail, or getting addicted to drugs, thanks to our nanny, Miss Joy." Livy indicated another photo. "My dad hooked up with her after my mother died, and they're still together."

"He hooked up with the nanny after your mom died? Sounds like soap opera material."

Livy elbowed him. "It wasn't like you make it sound. He waited a long time before he even thought about dating. Then, one day Dad told us Miss Joy was now our stepmom and told us to call her Joy, not Miss Joy. She and our Grandma

Gaia pretty much raised us."

"Your family fascinates me. How often do you see your dad and the nanny these days?"

"We saw them at Christmas. They've never married. They claim they don't believe in marriage. Which is weird, because my dad married my mom." Livy studied the photo of Joy, her red head gleaming under the Christmas tree lights, Dad's arm over her shoulders as Livy and DeeDee said cheese for the camera. "So he must have believed in marriage at one time."

"A long time ago, I believed in marriage too." Will's tone was wistful. He caught her eye. "What about you? Do you believe in marriage?"

"I'm not sure." Her toes tightened on Murf's fur, and the pup shifted. "I do know I would never marry anyone unless we were together for at least two years."

"Same here." Will nodded. "Although Roxanne and I lived together two years before we got married, and it still didn't work. Which is why I don't believe in it."

"Dad and Joy seem happy, even though they never married. They had two more kids together, so I have a couple of little brothers in Cali right now."

She flipped the page where she, DeeDee, and a very pregnant Joy celebrated their twelfth birthday. Two-year-old August clutched Grandma's hand, pouting because he hadn't gotten any presents. Dad was missing from the photos, off on a long world tour.

"I remember when I first noticed Miss Joy had moved into my father's bedroom. Surprise!"

Will chuckled. "Not very nanny-like, was it?"

Livy grinned. "Not nanny-like at all. But she was a great stepmom. I'm convinced we wouldn't have survived childhood without her."

"Thank God for the Miss Joys of the world." Will leaned

in for another long kiss, then pulled away and searched her eyes. "You're so full of surprises, Livy. This is one more reason I'm enjoying getting to know you."

Chapter Nine

Scott shifted. He always felt conspicuously out of place in Saffire's corridor. The scarcity of males, the girly colors. A romantic song by some boy band drifted from Studio A, and two swaying preteen dancers lip-synced in the doorway. Kinzie tugged his hand. "Lookit, Daddy. There's two men holding hands."

His gaze followed Kinzie's pointing finger to a gay couple and a young girl walking toward them. The little girl was probably a student in Miss Livy's hip-hop class, which ended ten minutes ago.

As the trio neared, Lacie giggled, and soon Kinzie joined in. Livy stood near the office door, close enough to hear them, but deep in conversation with a student's father. They leaned their heads intimately close like a dating couple.

After the father and his sour-faced daughter exited the building, Livy raised her brows at Scott. "I take it your daughters aren't used to seeing same-sex couples?"

An opportunity knocking. He touched his daughter's shoulders and gestured them forward. "Girls, go on to class, and I'll be there in a few minutes." They obeyed. The two chattering men passed, fingers waving at Livy. One of them eyed Scott with frank curiosity. He turned away, fighting a distasteful sensation in his stomach.

Feeling like he needed fresh air, he inhaled a deep breath and caught a whiff of a light, sweet scent. "Something smells good."

Livy moved to the back of the office. "Believe it or not,

it's an herbal tea called Foxtrot. I found it at a teashop near Pike Place. Want some?"

"No thanks, I'm not much of a tea drinker."

Livy lifted a silver pot and poured light-brown liquid into a cup. The room, with all its greenery and its fake babbling brook, reminded him of The Garden Center. Yet it suited Livy. He leaned on the doorframe, enjoying the graceful way she moved, and her well-shaped legs in those striped tights. The braided bun on her head emphasized her long neck. "I'm more of a coffee guy, myself. I like to experiment by grinding two different kinds of beans together to see what I get. Komodo Dragon with Ethiopian Roast, for instance."

She lifted the cup to her lips and sipped. "I like to do the same with tea. How does English Rose with Jasmine sound?"

"Like the time my wife hauled me into Bath And Body Works."

Livy laughed — a musical wind chime sound — and glided around the desk. "I like coffee too, but today I happened to be in the mood for tea." She pointed to a chair. "Want to sit down?" She eased into the chair on the other side of the desk.

"Sure." He settled himself in a smallish chair, the wooden arms squeezing him around the middle. "Most of the time my coffee experiments work, but every now and then I end up with some strange brew."

"I know what you mean." She took another sip. "Usually my tea concoctions work, but like you said, some have flopped."

Scott hadn't pegged Livy as a woman with whom he'd have anything in common, much less something as trivial as mixing coffees and teas. Yet here he sat, wondering if she'd felt the same split-second surge of connection. A tiny stud in her right nostril flashed a spark every time she turned her head. A red and pink flower tattoo covered her upper arm.

Despite the trappings, he sensed she might be the kind of woman a man would be eager to come home to, a calming presence after a hard day's work.

"Did you have something on your mind?" Her face puzzled, she swiveled her chair back and forth.

He reined in runaway thoughts. "I wanted to answer your question about my daughters." He sent silent prayers heavenward. "No, they're not used to seeing same-sex couples. They haven't been exposed to that type thing much."

"I see." She pursed her mouth. "Well, the couple your daughters were giggling over is Queen David and his boyfriend, Darrell."

Queen David? Apt name. He chuckled. "Is the girl a relative of theirs?"

Livy tilted her chair back, still rocking. "She's their adopted daughter, Tessa."

"Their daughter?"

"They're great parents." Her tone turned defensive. "They adore her."

He kept his even. "She has two fathers?"

"She does."

"But no mother?"

Livy shrugged and sipped again. "I guess not."

"Poor girl."

Livy gave a light laugh. "Are you kidding me? David and Darrell own a big house on Magnolia, and she's living the high life. I'd call her a lucky girl."

"What good does all that stuff do when she'll never know what it's like to have a mother lovin' on her?"

She stared at him through narrowed eyes. "Lots of kids grow up without mothers, including myself. Most of them turn out fine. And a lot of kids *with* mothers turn out all messed up."

"It's one thing to lose a mother through death, divorce,

or some other factor." He rested his hands on the desk. "But when adults deprive a child of a mother or a father because of their own preferences, I think it's selfish."

Her face radiated skepticism. "Selfish? What about mothers who deprive their children of a relationship with their father, or vice versa—"

"That's selfish, too," he cut in, thinking of Shari.

"What if the father is abusive or a crook?"

"Nobody is advocating for that kind of father." He grasped a nearby pen and tapped it on his palm with hard rapid beats. "I'm just sayin' kids need both parents."

Livy's head moved back and forth as she regarded him in dismay. He didn't let it stop him.

"Poor little ol' Tessa doesn't have a mom." He worked the lever on the pen up and down. "How will she know what kind of woman she should be? What about when she starts dating?"

"I—"

"How will she recognize a man worth keeping when she probably doesn't have a lot of contact with straight men?"

A veil seemed to have dropped over Livy's face. "I don't know." The earlier connection fizzled. "Is it even any of your concern? Or mine?"

Ouch. He mentally launched a series of kicks to his backside. As Shari often reminded him, he needed to curb his tendency to preach.

Livy eased off the chair and gave him a cold smile. From her vantage point, she towered over him, although she wasn't any taller than his five-foot-six ex-wife. "I guess we can agree to disagree, Scott. You made some good points, but I honestly don't see anything wrong with same-sex couples raising children." She shrugged again. "I feel this world is big enough for all shapes and sizes of families to coexist."

He nodded, heart heavy. "Okay. Well, I think I'll get on

over to class now. Nice chatting with you." He set the pen back in the cup.

"You, too," she said.

He pushed out of the confining chair, strode across the hall, and joined the other parents at the back of the Lyrical class. He locked his gaze on his dancing girls, the heaviness in his heart growing stronger. How should he explain the same-sex couple to his daughters?

***

DeeDee tried to ignore Scott's presence in her class as John Mayer crooned over the sound system and five girls moved in hesitant synchronicity. But he overshadowed all else. And John Mayer's voice stirred her romantic urges.

Scott didn't even glance her way. Instead, his face held a slight smile as he watched his daughters perform awkward plies and releves.

DeeDee pivoted, surveying the girls herself. "Good job, Abby. Nice presentation."

Life was so not fair. Her twin had found a man who made her happy. Why did men always consider Livy, not her, keeper material? And here was handsome, newly divorced Scott less than twelve feet away.

She and Livy had agreed on a rule. No chasing the single men. But she could certainly encourage them to chase her.

John Mayer ended, and she switched to a snappier song—Bruno Mars's "Locked Out of Heaven."

She did her best to look cheerful for the kids. "Let's practice your *pas de bourrees*, starting on your right foot. Good job, Lacie." Little Lacie beamed. "Right, left, right. Left, right, left. Remember to twist!"

She may not be Scott's cup of chai, but he was, from all outward appearances, most decidedly hers. Chiseled jaw. Firm mouth. Eyes the color of warm green tea. What she wouldn't give to know what brought about his divorce. If only she could ask such an intrusive question.

She inhaled. Focus.

"Okay, little ladies, let's do jazz walks across the room." A sharp edge heightened her tone. She tempered it. "Remember, your arms are an upside-down *V*. Kinzie, your turn to lead out."

Scott wasn't in a relationship. One of the moms dared ask him if he was dating. "I'm hoping to reconcile with my wife," he'd informed the woman.

Talk about chasing a fantasy. Shari showed no sign of hoping to reconcile. So he was up for grabs.

The song ended. Five panting girls waited for her to speak. "Let's try those *chaine* turns again. They're tricky, but you can do them. Go!"

They performed a halting series of spins until the clock hit the fifty-minute mark. DeeDee applauded. "Nice job, little ladies. On Wednesday, we'll put it all together. See you next week."

And now, time to get out her man-magnet toolbox. She situated herself near the door as parents and students exited, making eye contact with Scott when he neared. She offered a friendly smile meant to announce, I'm approachable. "Scott, thanks for staying and watching the class. The kids always perform better when their parents are there."

"You're welcome." His probing green eyes studied her, sending a quiver through her. "I didn't realize it made a difference."

She tilted her head. "It must be why Kinzie and Lacie are two of my best students."

"That's great." His daughters played tug-o'-war with his arms. "I know they enjoy the class." He swayed right then left as the girls pulled and pushed.

Other parents swarmed past them, leaving them alone in

the hall. She needed a meaningful topic. Something to keep him there for a few more minutes. "Most of the other parents drop off their kids and leave. They're missing an important part of their kids' development. Don't you agree?"

He nodded, but didn't reply. Something flickered in his eyes. Impatience?

Kinzie tugged his hand. "Daddy, can we go now?"

He glanced at Kinzie, and then offered DeeDee a polite nod. "We'll see you next week, DeeDee," he drawled. "Thanks for investing in my daughters."

Her spirits deflated like air seeping from a balloon. She might as well be an eighty-year-old grandma.

She needed to cry on her sister's shoulder.

The afternoon dragged with more classes, then errands. Her first chance to confide in Livy presented itself at home after she'd finished her dinner of Kung Pao chicken, and Livy ended her phone call with Will.

They laid paisley yoga pads on the sunroom's hardwood floor, then stretched and maneuvered their limbs, while ethereal music wafted through the speakers, curling, and then dissipating, like the incense burner's fragrant smoke.

"I'm sorry," Livy said after DeeDee related the details of the conversation. Not that there was much to relate.

"Scott has a sign around his neck saying, No Trespassing." DeeDee arranged her legs in the lotus position. "He's obviously not interested in me. You know what I have to say, don't you?" She pressed her knees to the floor. "Go jump in Green Lake, Mr. Lorenzo."

"I don't think he's your type after all." Livy's muffled voice emerged from the vicinity of her feet. "You were right about him. Wait until you hear the conversation *I* had with him today."

After Livy shared every detail, DeeDee rocked back. "Yikes!" She drew her bent knees to her chest. "He sounds like a homophobe."

"A real caveman."

"A Mr. Neanderthal."

Livy snickered. "You've been spared a horrible future with a man who likes his woman barefoot and preggers."

"Well, then. As far as I'm concerned, he can crawl back in his cave." DeeDee extended her legs and reached for her toes. "Next," she announced, bending low, the word their mantra. They used it each time a relationship, real or potential, proved a dead end—closure and moving on all wrapped up in one little word.

***

Scott knelt next to his bed in the darkened bedroom. Across the hall, his little girls slept like babies after a Saturday full of dance and fun. A narrow sliver of hallway light shone in under his door and threw a glittering beam across the carpet.

Instead of praying, his thoughts wandered to two young women—Livy and DeeDee, who had been on his mind and heart in recent days. Surely, the Lord wanted him to pray for them. They seemed so lost, especially DeeDee. Her hard desperation perplexed and repelled him. When she spoke, her voice sounded exactly like Livy's, except hers held an edge of steel. Like a razor blade inside angel-food cake.

From the outside, most folks probably couldn't tell them apart. On the inside, Livy and DeeDee were as alike as a rose and a cactus.

No doubt they'd had a privileged childhood, and he suspected their father foot the bill for the dance school. He'd half expected to see fat, grinning Buddhas or paintings of Hindu temples. So far, he'd seen no Eastern religious symbols. His daughters weren't being taught to think of themselves as goddesses. DeeDee recited to them after each class, "Remember, the world is watching you. Be the best dancer, the best student, the best person, you can be." He'd explained to his daughters that Miss Dee was partly right. But it was Christ who watched them, and Christ who gave them the power to do their best and be the person He wanted them to be.

"Father God," he prayed, "thank you for the open door to Livy today. I pray you'll take those seeds and make them fruitful, even though my delivery could've been better. I pray for more open doors to share You with them.

"And Father," he whispered, "my precious daughters are hurting. Please, Lord, comfort their broken hearts. I pray Shari will give me another chance to be the husband you intended me to be."

He stayed on his knees, waiting for a settled peace. It never came. The clock read ten thirty, but his brain wouldn't be winding down anytime soon. Now would be the perfect time to tinker on his project, a little device promising to make his world a happier place. If he could get it to work.

Already his mood had brightened. Anchoring his laptop under his arm, he carried it to his garage workbench and opened the schematic he needed. Next, he found the microscope and examined the tiny circuit board, fingering the scattered components. His head swiveled between schematic and circuit board as he worked out how to reconnect and reconfigure. Retrieving a tiny tool, he set to work.

He whistled, until it dawned on him he was whistling Lady Gaga's "Bad Romance". He chuckled. He'd been thinking about Shari.

Background music would cure his mindless whistling. He clicked a music website, and soon soft Christian hip-hop streamed from the speakers.

Then Jamie McRabb's Celica, its subwoofer cranked, sped into the driveway not twenty feet away. Sighing, Scott set his tools down and headed for the outside door.

Jamie bounced his head like a rock star and flashed a jubilant grin. When Scott rapped a knuckle on the resonating driver's side, Jamie lowered the window. The blast almost flung Scott backward.

"Yeah?" Jamie snapped.

"My daughters are sleeping," yelled Scott. "Can you turn it down, please?"

"Yeah, okay." The words rushed out as Jamie cranked the window closed. The volume dropped a notch, if even.

Scott gritted his teeth until they hurt. "Donkey's backside," he muttered, returning to his workbench. "Dear Lord." He squeezed alongside his silver Chevy Avalanche. "I need grace to put up with Jamie."

A full ten minutes later, the booming ceased. Scott peeked out the side window. Jamie's car formed a dark, silent hulk in the McRabb driveway, and Scott resumed his project. After another hour of meticulous work, his eyelids drooped, and he trudged to bed.

Chapter Ten

Livy kissed Will goodbye in Saffire's office. "See ya, sweetheart." She playfully batted her eyes. "You and the girls have fun without me today."

"You know it's not as fun without you, babe." He clutched her waist and kissed her again. "See you tonight."

After Livy wrapped up her hip-hop class moments ago, she and Will shut the office door in Amity's face so he could give her a proper kiss. Now Livy meant to spend the next hour updating the books. The CPA had been pestering her for their year-end records.

When they emerged, Katrina was swinging her feet from the bench. Amity glared and sulked. "Sorry, sweeties, your dad and I had to talk for a minute."

"You mean, play sucky-mouth for a minute," Amity muttered.

Livy clenched her lips to stifle a smile, then waved goodbye to father and daughters. She returned to the chair and logged onto her laptop. Perching reading glasses on her nose, she opened the bank statement and began downloading numbers.

Bean counting—the most boring part of owning a business and a task all too easy to procrastinate. A little energetic music would help keep her brain alert. She clicked a music app and selected a hip-hop playlist, adjusting the volume to stimulate her analytical juices but not impel her to get up and dance.

She bounced her knees as she posted deposits. When she

finished, she compared the total to the estimated revenue. Too low. But some parents paid in cash. She and DeeDee used part of the cash for expenses and stored the remainder in the lockbox.

Livy rummaged in a drawer for the lockbox key. DeeDee explained a way to lower the revenue on their tax return without the IRS being able to trace it. Cash revenue would never show up on the bank statement and left no trail for the IRS. Livy unlocked the fireproof cabinet, lugged the lockbox to the desk, and began counting.

She gave a low whistle. Their actual revenue totaled nearly two thousand dollars higher than their stated revenue. She formed a fist and punched the air, her elbow jostling the coffee cup in front of her. It tipped and spilled muddy brown fluid.

With a curse, she shot up and knocked the chair over. "I did not need this." A three-rag mess, no doubt. Jamming her glasses on her head, she marched to the storage closet for cleaning supplies.

As she returned to the office, her hands full, a book on the bench caught her eye. Maybe a parent had forgotten it. She moved closer. Bold green letters flashed the title: *Religion Or Christ? Your Choice.*

Why would someone bring a religious book to dance class?

On the other side of the hall, a door opened, and Scott Lorenzo stepped from one of the bathrooms.

"Hi, Scott. Is this your book?"

He glanced at the book. "Yes, thanks. I'm waiting for Lacie to finish using the commode." He crossed over and picked up the book. She turned to the office, but his voice stopped her. "Sounds like you chose some fine mood music."

She cocked her head. Percussive chanting echoed from the office. "You mean the rap on my computer?"

He nodded.

She blinked at him. "Are you being sarcastic?"

"Not at all. I like the beat." He rubbed his jaw. "Don't tell anyone, okay? It'll ruin my reputation." A twinkle flickered in his eyes.

She laughed. "Your secret's safe with me." She eyed the book in his hand. How did a love for rap and religion coexist in a person?

He held up the thin paperback. Geometric designs crisscrossed the cover. "This is a great book. You ought to read it sometime."

"Sorry, not my thing."

"What? Religion or reading?"

"I mean, religion isn't my thing. Nobody in my family is religious except my grandma—Wiccan to the core."

Something flickered in Scott's eyes. "Really?" His tone suggested he held as negative an opinion of Wicca as he did of same-sex relationships. "Well, this book isn't necessarily pro-religion—"

"Daddy!" Scott's head jerked toward the shrill call.

A little face peeked out the bathroom door.

"What, Lacie?"

"I can't reach the sink."

Livy set the rags and cleaners on the bench. "I'll help you." She hurried to the bathroom. With a gentle boost, she lifted Lacie. The little girl flailed her yellow-clad legs and stuck her hands under the faucet, giggling when a stream of water landed on her Miley Cyrus tee shirt. Livy grabbed a handful of paper towels and did her best to wipe it off.

She and Lacie returned to Scott studying the book, his brow creased, his mouth a firm hyphen. He nudged Lacie back to class, and his gaze followed her down the hall, and then switched to Livy.

Why was he just standing there? She edged toward the

office. Last week, their conversation had started out so well. They'd even laughed together. Then he got dogmatic, and it ended so awkwardly. Maybe she needed to get back to the office before it happened this time.

"Like I was saying." He faced her again, stopping her progress. "This book isn't pro-religion; it's pro-Jesus Christ."

"How is that not religion?" A frown pinched her lips.

"Because Jesus Christ is a person, not a creed. And not a swear word, either." The corners of his mouth lifted.

"In my home it was."

"That's true of a lot of homes. However, he claimed to be God."

"He did?" Had she been told that when she went to Sunday school?

"Have you ever wondered why people use Christ's name as a swear word, but not Mohammed or Buddha? Have you ever heard anyone say, 'Oh Zeus!' when they're frustrated?"

She pursed her mouth. "You have a point. I guess I never thought about it before." Her parents and their friends so often uttered the name of Christ like a dirty word. She and DeeDee had continued the habit.

Scott tapped the book's cover. "A former atheist wrote this book. He was determined to disprove God's existence. Instead, he ended up converting to Christianity."

"Why?"

"Because he concluded there was no way Christ wasn't who he claimed to be."

"You mean…God?"

Scott's eyes gleamed with righteous fervor as though he'd switched on his high beams. "Jesus Christ told the religious folks of his day 'I am He', meaning God."

She stepped back. Time to find a polite way out of this conversation. Scott didn't look like a religious fanatic — too good-looking, too polished. He didn't look like a homophobe, either. His black button-down shirt, tailored to perfection, paired with flawless khakis, conveyed GQ Man.

Scott, giving meaning to the phrase *looks are deceiving,* wasn't finished. "He actually claimed to be one with the Supreme Being of the universe." Awe edged his tone. "What would *you* do if I said, 'Hey, guess what? I'm God.'"

Her laughter bubbled out. "I'd say, 'Oh, God, where have you been all my life?'" She grinned to show she was kidding, and he chuckled, proving a sense of humor lurked underneath all his intensity.

Her smile wobbled. "To be honest, if someone came up to me and told me he was God, I would either tell him, 'You're crazy,' or 'Get in line.' My grandma says there are a lot of gods, big ones and little ones. What's one more?"

"Jesus didn't claim to be *a* god. He claimed to be the one and only God."

She needed strength not to back up from the way he leaned toward her. When she took another step back, he seemed to snap out of his fervor, straightening up and offering a heartfelt smile, which erased five years from his face.

A whir of yellow sped past and slammed into Scott's legs. Lacie clung to him and buried her face in his thigh.

"What is it, Lacie?"

"Class is done," she said, her voice muffled.

He patted her head as a swarm of girls and parents passed in colorful chaos. Kinzie strode with sedate grace. He sat and pulled both daughters close.

"Miss Livy and I are talking. If y'all can stay quiet for a minute, we'll go get ice cream, okay?"

They nodded. Lacie bounced against her daddy's knee, back and forth, in complete silence. Kinzie stared at Livy, her blue eyes grave, while she braced against Scott's other knee.

"Here." He handed Livy the book. "Why don't you take

it and read it for yourself? I can get another copy."

Livy grasped it. Polite excuses whirred through her mind. She didn't want to appear as reluctant as she felt. Besides, next time she sold books online, maybe she could get a few bucks for this. She tucked it under her arm. Problem solved.

Lacie turned to her. "Is Daddy giving you a book about Jesus?"

"Yes, he is." Livy rubbed Lacie's soft, bright head. "Isn't that nice of him?" The next minute, she exclaimed, "Oh no, I forgot all about the spilled coffee." She gathered up the cleaning supplies and ran, wincing. She'd be facing a mud-like, congealed mess when she walked through the office door.

Chapter Eleven

Livy awoke Monday to another clammy, foggy February morning. A long johns and fur-lined parka kind of morning. The chill had kept its grip on the city all week, a burrowing kind that stung her face and soaked into her bones.

She and DeeDee, scarved and gloved, strode along Woodlawn Avenue, opting, as usual, to walk the ten blocks to Saffire rather than drive. Stick-figure trees stretched twisting tentacles toward the hidden sky. Clouds of breath became one with the fog—fog which would dissipate by afternoon to reveal crisp sunshine.

As they passed JavaJava's distinctive kelly-green door, Livy's phone rang, displaying Audria's number.

"Good morning, Aunt Bestie."

Sniffing and weeping vibrated through the other end. Putting the phone on speaker, she stopped on the sidewalk and held it up so DeeDee could hear. "Audria? Is something wrong?"

Audria gasped. "Nils—"

"Nils? Is he okay?" Although Audria and Nils's relationship ended when Vienna was a toddler, they'd remained good friends.

Audria let out a wail. "He's dead!"

"Dead?" Livy and DeeDee nearly shouted in unison.

"Brittany found him and called me right away. I got there in time to see them take him away. To the morgue." Her sobs came through so loud, Livy lowered the phone's volume.

DeeDee cursed. "Was it heroin?"

"I think so. He kept promising to go to rehab, but he never did."

"Does Vienna know?" DeeDee clipped her words, no doubt to hide emotion.

"She was with me."

Livy moved the phone closer and lowered her voice. "How about Dad? Does he know?"

"I haven't told anyone yet. I'm about to send a message to everyone, including the media, since Brittany's a basket case and can't manage it right now." Audria's sobs had diminished, but a remnant of tears shook her voice. "Do you two want to let your father know?"

"Sure." Livy nodded, even though Audria couldn't see her. "We'll call him right now."

"Thanks."

"Audria? Promise to call if you need to talk?"

"I will." Her sigh, feathery and light as the fog, drifted through the phone. "I'd better go now. I've got a lot to do."

Livy ended the call and stood frozen with DeeDee. Someone brushed by muttering about all the blankety-blank tourists who block sidewalks. Livy didn't bother correcting him. She stayed planted in place, peering at the phone as though it held clues to Nils's death. Nils Nelsson's drug use had never been a secret to his hometown or fans. Still, a shockwave coursed through her.

DeeDee shook her head over and over, her face tight. "He wasn't my favorite person in the world, but I'm still sad he's gone."

Livy moved closer and reached an arm around DeeDee's waist, tears hiding behind her eyes. "It is sad." She sniffed. "I'll never forget his drunken rants on tour. They were kind of funny, weren't they?"

"Sometimes, yeah." A tear fell from DeeDee's cheek. "We'd better call Dad now."

Livy pulled up his number. A click sounded, then a pause.

"Kiddo." His raspy voice suggested either she had woken him from a deep sleep, or he'd sung his heart out last night.

"Dad." She and DeeDee turned toward Seventieth Street. "We have news about Nils."

"What about him?"

"He died last night. Audria's pretty sure it was a heroin overdose." Livy kept her voice low and an eye out for passersby.

A string of expletives burst over the line. "I told that no-good junkie he would end up like Luna Tunes if he didn't knock it off."

"Well, he did, Dad." Livy paused, letting this sink in. She could sense his brain cells on the other end awakening at the news, awed he was still alive and kicking, and thankful for it. Due in large measure to Joy, Dad had beaten heroin before it beat him. Kudos to both of them. How tragic if both her parents had died of drug overdoses.

Too bad Dad's best friend couldn't, in the end, join his journey to clean living. Too bad Luna Raquelle—

She stopped. The royal blue letters spelling out Saffire School of Dance shimmered through the fog across the street, but she was reluctant to end the conversation. DeeDee waited, hands on hips, eyes impatient, so Livy motioned her to go on, mouthing that she would meet her over there.

"I'll talk to Morton about a memorial service," Dad was saying, sounding surprisingly calm for someone who'd just lost his best friend. "I wonder if—"

"Dad," Livy blurted. She stood on the sidewalk, the phone to her ear, seeing, but not seeing, the cars careen around the corner in front of her.

"Yeah?"

"I've been thinking about the day Mom died."

She could imagine him reluctantly shifting gears. Her statement must have surprised him. "Why? It was twenty years ago."

"I know. But my new boyfriend—his name's Will—asked why I went into shock and DeeDee didn't."

After a five-second pause, Dad replied, "The doctors said it was from witnessing your mother's dead body."

"I know, but DeeDee found Mom and didn't lose *her* memory."

"Trauma doesn't affect everyone the same way."

"We're twins. Stuff always affected us the same." She took a deep breath, regretting it when exhaust filled her nose. "Dad, listen. I need to know everything you can remember from that day. Besides the fact that DeeDee and I were getting ready for our recital and we had a few extra people over."

"Well, your Grandma Gaia and Vienna were there. I think Audria came over later."

Joy's voice intruded in the background. Then Dad rumbled something in reply.

"Give Joy a hug for me." Livy shifted, antsy to resume the conversation.

Another muffled conversation. "Joy says hug back. Look, I need to go." The line crackled. "Joy's made plans. But we will see you at Nils's funeral, or whatever they do for him."

"Wait, Dad—"

"I'll call you back later. Ciao."

She jammed the phone into her coat pocket, muttering over his lack of concern, and stepped off the curb.

A massive object slammed into her. She flew to the pavement. Then searing, bone-crunching pain unlike any she'd ever known slammed even harder into her body.

All she heard were her screams.

Chapter Twelve

DeeDee heard a faraway scream through the office window. Her head snapped up. Empathetic twinging cramped her legs.

"Livy!" she gasped. An unfamiliar panic seized her as she ran out of Saffire. Through the thinning fog, she saw a small white car in the middle of the street and a couple of people huddled nearby. The island spanning the center of the street blocked her view of the pavement, so she stepped into the crosswalk, heart pounding, limbs trembling.

Her sister, still and silent, lay face down on the asphalt. Tire marks smeared Livy's quilted tan jacket, and her legs lay hidden next to the front tire. DeeDee's heart lurched. Was her sister alive? She dropped to her knees and felt for a pulse. Livy's heart put out a feeble beat.

"What happened?" she asked the two people gaping at Livy.

"She stepped out in front of me!" cried a wild-eyed teenage girl, skinny as a stick. Another girl stood next to her, frozen.

"Don't just stand there," DeeDee snapped. "Call 911." She shook her head and picked up Livy's limp hand. "Livy," she hissed. "It's me. Can you hear me?"

Livy didn't respond, but her head moved the tiniest bit. She was probably barely conscious.

DeeDee glanced at the hunched-over driver to ensure she contacted emergency services. She could hear the girl's panicked voice, so she turned back to her sister, who suddenly gripped her hand so hard she thought it might snap in two.

"Hurts," Livy whispered. Under the car, her left leg splayed outward at an awkward angle.

"How's your head? Did you hit it?"

She only groaned. Rage bubbled up in DeeDee. If she had a sledgehammer, she'd pound the white heap of junk into the pavement.

The young driver materialized next to them. "The ambulance is on its way." The girl's voice came out a gasping squeak. A faint siren echoed far off, getting louder.

Livy kept squeezing DeeDee's hand and groaning, as though she were in labor. More pedestrians had stopped to gawk.

DeeDee glared at the girl. "Don't you go anywhere, you little —" The girl shrunk back, her face a mask of fright. "This is my sister you knocked over. You're going to have some explaining to do to the cops."

The girl gave a little whimper. "Sorry! I'm so, *so* sorry. I didn't mean to do it."

DeeDee paid no attention to the feeble apologies. "Also, I'm going to need your insurance and contact info. Write it down for me." The girl scurried to the car, emerging with a piece of paper.

"Here." She thrust it forward.

DeeDee pocketed it. The wail of two sirens drowned out all else. An ambulance and cop car screamed around the corner.

Emergency personnel leaped from their vehicles. The paramedics examined Livy and loaded her on a stretcher. DeeDee made sure the cop interviewed the trembling driver and her passenger. Afterward, she climbed into the back of the ambulance and held Livy's hand all the way to the hospital.

***

Voices through the fog—muffled voices, deep ones and soft ones—called to her. Livy kept trying to reach them. But a black wall blocked her, and she wanted to stay cuddled next to it.

Warmth spread through her, a sweet river free of pain, and she slid into it.

***

"Your sister is going to need surgery."

DeeDee tried to listen to the orthopedic surgeon. The badge on his white smock said Dr. Nausherwani, but he'd said she could call him Dr. Nosh. Even his competent air did little to reassure her.

X-rays of Livy's broken body filled the computer screen on the cluttered desk. DeeDee leaned forward, gripping the metal chair arms.

"She has two fractured ribs, and her chest wall has extensive bruising. Her left hip is dislocated, and her left tibia and fibula are shattered. Those rib fractures will be painful, but they should heal with time. If they were her only injuries, she'd be a fortunate young lady. The hip dislocation and tib-fib fractures are another matter. You can see from the X-ray"—Dr. Nosh tapped the screen—"there's gravel around the bone. It's an open fracture, and the gravel and dirt in the wound put her at high risk for infection. She's going to need surgery and antibiotics."

DeeDee, her breath threatening to erupt in a scream, swallowed her fear and voiced *the* question. "How long will it be before she's able to dance again?"

"Dance?" Dr. Nosh gaped at her as if addressing a child who hadn't been listening. "It's going to be several months before she can walk normally again."

She moaned. When she'd called Will earlier, she'd shared the hopeful news that Livy's head hadn't been injured—only her legs—and the doctor felt he could fix her up good as new. But that was before the X-rays. Now Livy's future looked as bleak as the wispy fog floating outside the window.

"I hope the little idiot driver's parents have good insurance," she muttered under her breath. If Livy could never dance again... DeeDee might as well tell her she could never *breathe* again.

She returned to the room where Livy still slept, her expression peaceful. The doctor entered followed by two orderlies with a stretcher. "We're going to take her to surgery now." Dr. Nosh tucked the blanket around Livy. "I don't know if you want to stay here, or go home and wait for a call. I expect this will take several hours."

"I'll stay." She followed Livy's stretcher to the elevator, up one floor, down a long corridor, and into a room filled with impressive equipment.

"You can wait in the sitting area down the hall," a sweet-faced nurse pointed her along.

DeeDee entered the family waiting room, where children played with toys on the floor and two worried parents buried their noses in magazines. She sat across the way from them and took out her smart phone, prepared to wait until Dad and his family arrived.

The hours dragged before she heard his familiar resonant voice. She swiveled. He entered first, followed by Joy, their somber-faced sons on either side of her, and two imposing bodyguards trailing close behind. She rushed to them, and Dad enfolded her in a long, tight hug. He'd hidden Declan Decker behind a blond toupee, fake beard, and nerdy black eyeglasses. Although his face showed every one of his fifty-three years, his eyes shone brighter than they had in a long time—still drug-free and taking better care of himself.

In truth, he and Joy looked like any middle-aged couple. Joy's bright hair had faded, but not her smile, still white and shining. DeeDee had often wondered about the dynamics of her father's relationship with Joy. Did his feelings for her match his level of devotion for Mom? Or was their relationship one of convenience?

Her two redheaded half-brothers, ages sixteen and fourteen, shifted from side to side, their gazes darting around the room. Having only seen them once or twice a year since they'd moved away, she didn't know them as well as she wished.

"Got your license yet, August?"

He nodded. "Yep. Want to see?" He pulled out his wallet and flourished a brand-new California driver's license.

"Very cool." She gave him a hug. "Congratulations." She shifted to Dominic and hugged him. "You're growing into a chick magnet, my bro." A shy grin crossed his face as she patted his head.

The boys hesitated and glanced around until she led them to a row of seats, where they settled in with electronic devices, their drooping jaws betraying boredom. Dad and Joy found seats on either side of DeeDee. Already, bright afternoon sunlight poured through the windows. Livy's accident seemed as long ago as yesterday.

A teenage couple, who likely weren't born when The FireAnts debuted, had replaced the worried family from earlier. The teens surveyed the new arrivals with distinct disinterest. When they noticed the bodyguards, they received cold stares in return. The couple quickly moved their attention to the blaring TV.

"How's our Livy doing?" asked Dad.

"Our Livy may never dance again."

Joy gave a strangled cry.

Dad clutched his head, his eyes popping with distress. "I

blame myself."

"You blame yourself?" Her voice rose nearly to a shriek. When the teenagers glanced over, she cupped her hand over her mouth. "Whatever for?"

"The accident happened right after she and I talked on the phone this morning, right?"

"Yes—"

"Well, she wanted to talk about you guys' mother, and she sounded upset. I cut it short."

"I didn't know that. What did she say about Mom?"

"She wanted to talk about the day Luna Tunes died." His face softened as he whispered Mom's name. "Livy wondered what happened to make her go into shock, but not you."

"She and I had the same conversation. Her new boyfriend put the idea in her head."

"Yeah, she told me." Dad wrung his hands. "But I couldn't help her. I don't know if anything happened to her we don't know about."

Joy nodded. "I think your dad is right. Trauma does different things to different people."

Most unlikely. She and Livy occupied the same wavelength. Now and as children. Livy's suspicions sounded more and more plausible. "It's not your fault, Dad. The little twerp who ran her over didn't watch where she was going. Livy needs to take her to court." She stopped and continued in an undertone, "That reminds me. Livy and I have been wondering whatever happened to your lawsuit."

"Oh, the West Dakota thing?" He scowled. "We settled." He glanced at the other occupants, as if worried they might overhear, but they sat fixated on the TV. "They wanted half the royalties, which they got, but they also wanted five mil, and only got two."

"They were able to prove the plagiarism?"

He shook his head. "No, the problem was I couldn't

prove I didn't. The choruses of the two songs were similar enough the judge wasn't convinced. Exactly what I feared would happen."

She opened her mouth to ask if he'd start lending financial assistance again. Then stopped. She loved the feeling of achieving success on her own. She didn't need Dad's money.

For the first time all day, her spirits lifted.

Her phone beeped. A text from Will flashed. "Speaking of Livy's boyfriend," she said, "here's a message from him."

Any news yet?

No, we're still waiting. The rest of the family just got here. Do you want to come over and meet them?

Will didn't reply for several minutes. Then he texted: *I'll swing by in about half an hour.*

She'd been here over five hours. The surgery ought to be over.

As though someone read her mind, a nurse rounded the corner. "Surgery is done," she said as DeeDee approached. "And your sister is resting. She's doing great. We're waiting for the anesthesia to wear off, but in the meantime, Dr. Nausherwani will be ready to have a consultation with you in about fifteen minutes."

Ten minutes later, the nurse beckoned them. "Dr. Nosh can see you now."

DeeDee and the others followed her to a cramped consultation room, but due to privacy laws, only DeeDee and Dad were allowed inside.

An expectant hush descended as they stared at the doctor's grim face. "To be brutally honest, Olivia's in a world of hurt," Dr. Nosh told them. "We were able to reduce the hip dislocation and repair the torn ligaments. I had to put five screws and three wires in the bone to reconnect the shattered pieces, but it will take time to heal completely. She'll have a cast on her left lower leg for about six weeks. I want her to be completely non-weight bearing to give the bone time to heal. No weight at all on her left leg for at least three weeks. I'll X-ray after that and see how the bone has progressed. She'll need a splint after we remove the cast. Once the bone is healed, she'll need physical therapy. She's looking at months of therapy. It's going to be a while before she can dance again. If ever."

DeeDee's heart ached. Poor, poor Livy. How grateful she was right now to be in her own shoes and not Livy's.

Dr. Nosh peered at Dad. "Do I know you?"

Dad stared back, his gaze equally intent. "I don't think we've met before." He thrust a hand forward, and the doctor gave it a vigorous shake. "I'm Howard McCreary. Those three waiting outside are my wife, Joy, and our two sons."

DeeDee added, "People always say he looks familiar."

"I have one of those faces, you know."

The doctor nodded. "Glad you could come up from California on such short notice. Did you charter a flight or something?" Dr. Nosh chuckled as if to say he was only joking.

Dad merely smiled. No need to set the doctor straight. Best to let him think of them as an ordinary family.

DeeDee's phone vibrated. Will had arrived and waited downstairs.

"Can you excuse me? Livy's boyfriend is here and wants to meet everyone."

She found Will in the ground floor lobby and updated him on Livy. His face froze in an expression of horror, and his eyes stayed glazed all the way up to the third floor where the rest of the family waited. When he shook hands with Dad, a tinge of awe cracked through his tightly pinched features, though he obviously tried hard not to show it.

Chapter Thirteen

Livy, floating in semi-consciousness, sensed someone standing next to her and chanting. It sounded like he chanted to the Heavenly Father, to God, and to Jesus. She tried to ask him, Was Jesus God? but couldn't form the words. Something held her mouth shut. And something heavy weighed her down, making her feel a thousand pounds. She sunk deeper into the softness surrounding her and surrendered to sleep.

She dreamed about her mother again. "What happened to you, bebby gull?" Mom said, her lips blood-red, her blue eyes wide and horrified.

"Mommy. You're alive."

"Of course I'm alive, you silly. I didn't mean I was literally dead."

Livy started crying tears of joy. Maybe Mommy would know if Jesus was God.

"Mommy? Was Jesus God?"

Her mother reared back, her expression fierce. "Jesus is not God, Olivia," she growled. "You are god and I am god."

The bleakest of darkness flooded Livy. Writhing figures snatched at her mother and pulled her away. Livy shrunk back and screamed. "Mommy! Don't leave!"

She woke up, sweaty and terrified, in an unfamiliar setting. Her heart pounded a furious rhythm. Where was she? Why couldn't she move? Was she dreaming or awake? The room took on a surreal feel, and she heard herself moan.

Someone rushed to her side, shushing her and telling her she was all right.

"Did you have a nightmare?" the woman asked, her voice a well of sympathy.

Livy nodded. A nightmare indeed. Like a scene out of *Ghost*.

"The morphine can do that to you." The woman wore a baby-blue smock. Comfort flowed from her. "We can cut your dosage."

"Where am I?"

"Northwest Hospital."

Then she must still be dreaming. She tilted her head to the side and closed her eyes. "What happened?"

The nurse placed her hand over Livy's and patted it. "You got hit by a car this morning."

Hit by a car—

Now she remembered. Squealing car brakes. Pavement as hard as a brick wall. All-consuming pain.

"But you'll be all right," the nurse added. "The doctor fixed you all up today, and you'll be able to go home in a few days."

Home. Where Deeds was. "Deeds," she pleaded.

"What?"

"I want Deeds."

"I'm sorry. What do you mean?"

"Sister Deeds."

"Your sister? You want your sister?"

"Mmmm—And Will."

"Who is Will?"

"Boyfriend," she garbled.

The nurse patted her again. "I'll see what I can do. You rest now."

Tipping her face to the side, Livy closed her eyes and soon fell asleep again.

Sometime later, Livy opened her eyes to Will's distraught face. He gripped her right hand as if it might run away. His forehead furrowed as though someone plowed a field through it.

Her head flopped to the left toward DeeDee, who frowned and clasped her other hand. "Finally you're awake. Look who came to see you."

Her whole family circled her hospital bed — Dad, Joy, and her two brothers, their faces solemn. As if she were on her deathbed.

She managed to ask, "What you all doin' 'ere?"

"We heard about your accident," Joy answered. "And wanted to be with you."

"We planned to come up anyway for Nils's service," said Dad. "So we decided to come early."

Nils's service — Right. Nils's death. Seventieth Street.

"Dad." Her tongue felt heavy and thick, as though drowning in maple syrup.

"Don't feel like you have to talk," said Joy. "If you're not up to it, don't."

"'Kay." She plopped her head to the side again. Will leaned down and kissed her cheek. She longed to feel his arms around her, yearned for his intense kisses to send thrills up her spine.

"Will." Holding his gaze with her own, she tried to lift her arms. "Hug?"

He obliged, held her for at least a minute, all while dropping soft little smooches over her face in plain view of her family's scrutiny. "Ah, babe," he whispered, and a warm feeling crept over her. Her family's soft murmurs surrounded her, and an undercurrent of something else shifted through the room.

When Will released her, Livy gazed deep into DeeDee's eyes, her own sudden unease there. "What?" she mouthed, her distress growing.

"Dr. Nosh'll be here in a few minutes." DeeDee turned

away.

A dark-skinned man in a smock strolled into the room. "Did I hear my name?"

When the family cleared a way for his approach, he studied Livy, his face grave. "Hi there, young lady, I'm Dr. Nosh." The letters in his nametag blurred together. "I came to give you an update and a prognosis."

He studied his clipboard. "Do you remember much of the accident?"

"Mm hmm…"

"You've probably already noticed the cast on your left leg."

The reason for the heavy sensation.

"I will be sending you to physical therapy as soon as the cast is off," he continued, "since you'll need to learn how to walk again."

In the ensuing silence, a machine hummed and a female voice intruded over the loudspeaker.

Livy tried to shake her head. "No," she mumbled. When that didn't work, she pled with him with her eyes. "I-I—"

"I know this is a shock." Compassion softened his voice.

Will took her hand, and she latched on tight.

"But you have to understand your leg was shattered. You're going to undergo extensive physical therapy to rebuild close to normal again. Even then, you'll have no guarantees."

Livy shook her head more insistently this time. This doctor didn't seem to understand. Dancing was her livelihood. If she couldn't dance…

She latched onto DeeDee for reassurance, but saw only raw fear in her twin's eyes.

Nothing ever scared Deeds. A wave of panic slammed into her. She snapped her head to the doctor, Will, Dad. Unmistakable naked truth in their eyes shredded her last denial.

Her head lurched forward, and she heard loud wails. A whirlwind of voices and activity swirled around her bedside. The wails were her own.

Chapter Fourteen

DeeDee stayed with Livy all night and into the next day. The hospital provided her a cot.

Most of the time, Livy remained sedated, weak, and uncommunicative. But DeeDee could tell her mere presence comforted Livy after Will and the family departed. It had taken a while for them to calm and soothe her, and finally a nurse gave Livy a happy shot.

Throughout much of Tuesday, Livy stared dull-eyed at the TV. DeeDee took a taxi home to the frantic animals, who clearly sensed something wrong. Miss Piggy eyed her. Poor Murf whined and pawed at her. After ten minutes of feeding and consoling him, she returned to the hospital with her little yellow Miata, her laptop, some overnight supplies, and Livy's scent diffuser. Lavender would keep her calm.

To pass the time, she led Livy in their favorite game of Remember When. Although Livy didn't respond much, DeeDee narrated vivid childhood memories, hoping for a flicker of recognition, a smile of nostalgia.

"Remember when we went looking for those million piggy banks?" she began. "It was the first day in our big new house, right before Mom went into rehab for the second time...."

Livy's eyes stayed closed. But her mouth lifted, and she raised her chin in a feeble nod.

***

Daddy revved onto a curvy street lined with the biggest

houses Di had ever seen, so big their old home and Katie's old house and the corner store could all fit into one.

He braked at a driveway wide enough for ten cars. "You can stop bouncing around like clowns, punkins." He grinned at them. "Look, we're here. Our new mansion." A grand building towered through the trees. A perfect green lawn carpeting the front went on just *forever*.

The rest of the white and yellow house burst into view. Daddy pressed a button above his head, and one of the four garage doors lifted — by itself. Daddy drove into the garage, parking between his new yellow car and his old blue one.

Mommy smiled at Daddy. "You've arrived, babes. You did it."

He grinned again and pulled Mommy in for a hug and kiss. "Go ahead and take the girls inside. I need to inspect all the equipment, make sure the movers didn't wreck anything."

Mommy twisted to face them. Her blue eyes sparkled like they had specks of glitter in them. "Want to go check out your room, bebby girls? The movers brought all your stuff over this morning."

Di reached for Big Bird, yanked open the door, and leaped out, searching for a way into the new house, then stopped, overwhelmed.

Trembling, she hurried to Mommy, who was emerging from the front seat, and buried her face in Mommy's tummy. Mommy rubbed her back with shaky hands. "What's wrong, baby?"

Di snuggled closer. "What if I get lost?" Mommy's blue sweater muffled her voice.

Liv joined her, twining their fingers.

Mommy knelt down and clasped onto their hands. "We won't let you get lost, baby girls."

Reassured, Di allowed Mommy to lead her to a door at

the far side. Di, hand-in-hand with Liv, entered a shiny, high-ceilinged room with a sink and an oven, and finally emerged in a hallway so long, she wasn't sure how far the end was.

Mommy steered them up wide stairs and around a corner, into a bedroom twice as big as their old one. All their boxed-up stuff sat on the floor waiting to be unpacked and put away in new closets and dressers.

"My bed!" Di, awestruck, cheered and jumped onto her unmade bed, hurtling up and down in sheer glee.

"Get down, Di." Mommy made a fierce face, but broke into a smile, pulling open a door. "Look, your very own bathroom." A black and white tile floor shone like a brand-new keyboard. "Come look out your windows. You can see Lake Washington."

They obeyed, gaping. Boats of all sizes and shapes bobbed across the lake — big ones with sails, little motorboats, skinny canoes. Mt. Rainier peeked over the distant treetops, like a fat vanilla ice cream cone, the kind Mommy bought them at Dairy Queen. The tall kind you could lick and lick until only a shiny round dome remained.

Di's stomach growled. Hours ago, they'd devoured the breakfast sandwiches Mommy bought. "Mommy, I'm hungwy. Can we have something to eat?"

When Mommy didn't reply, Di whirled around. Mommy had left. Di grabbed Big Bird by his claw. "I want some Os." She beckoned to Liv. "C'mon." She ran into the hallway and hurried the opposite direction from the way they'd come. Liv trotted alongside.

Three more doors lined the hallway. They couldn't help glancing inside each empty room. At the end, Di stopped and pointed. "Look, more stairs."

"Awesome!"

Their old house didn't have any stairs. So far this house had two flights. Liv giggled as they slid down the stairs on their bottoms. "One, two, free, four—" They bounced down *sixteen* stairs, interrupted by one landing. In the downstairs hallway, tiny rooms on each wall contained little tables with flower vases.

Di stopped and examined the square holes in the walls. "What are these?"

Liv shrugged. "Little hidey-holes."

They continued around a corner, nearing the living room on their left. To the right, Mommy and Daddy's bedroom door stood open. Far away on the other end of the room, Mommy stood next to a doorway leading into the back hallway. She hunched over a box, her golden hair tied back with white flowers.

Di hesitated at the door. "Mommy?"

Mommy stood and ran her wrist across her brow. Deep creases slashed across her forehead.

Di hugged Big Bird to her chest. "What are those holes in the walls?"

"What holes in the walls?"

Di pointed. "Over there."

"In the hallway," Liv said.

Mommy chuckled. "Those are alcoves." She rummaged through the box again.

Di wandered into the bedroom, Liv beside her. Another doorway led into a golden, shiny bathroom with a round tub big enough to fit five grownups. She gawked at the closet, roomy enough for a bed of its own. Mommy and Daddy's bed was high and square, and she and Liv knelt to see how much hiding room it had underneath—easily enough room for ten kids.

Di got to her feet and watched Mommy reach into a box. "Mommy?"

Mommy frowned and dropped the garment in her hand. "What, Di?"

"Are we wich now?"

Mommy's frown vanished, and a smile lit her face. "We're stinkin', filthy rich, baby girls."

Confused, Di scanned the grand room. It didn't smell stinky or look filthy. She checked herself, then Liv. Neither of them looked any dirtier than usual.

"Do we hafta take more baths now?"

Mommy gasped out a laugh. "I didn't mean literally filthy, you silly."

"What does rich mean, Mommy?" Liv's voice was small. Mommy and Daddy used the word *rich* a lot, but she still didn't understand it.

"It means having lots of money, honey."

"You mean, like the money you give us for our piggy banks?"

"Mmm hmm, but lots and lots of it. We have a million piggy banks' worth of money now."

A *million* piggy banks. Di gaped at Liv. Her feet danced. Her fingers itched to find all those piggy banks.

Signaling Liv with her eyes, she ran from the big room and found a door at the end of the hall leading to the back yard. There they examined the glass-paned gazebo and peeked underneath the wide deck. Finding no piggy banks, they rushed back inside and found another set of stairs leading into a basement. Daddy and Nils hauled instruments and recording equipment into a little room next to a big open area filled with couches and armchairs. Di opened her mouth to ask Daddy where the piggy banks were, but Liv tugged her arm and whispered, "Daddy has his mad face on."

Di backed away. "I wonder who he's mad at." They headed upstairs to hunt some more. The second floor had crawl spaces behind the bedroom closets, perfect for hiding piggy banks. They searched, hunted, poked, prodded, but didn't find any piggy banks, much less a million.

"Maybe they're hidden someplace else." Liv's brow wrinkled.

They gave up the hunt and drooped down the stairs, intent on asking Mommy.

But she lay sprawled on the living room floor, asleep, surrounded by unpacked boxes. Di hated Mommy getting sick again, because she would sleep until almost dinnertime, and Di would be starved from having nothing to eat all day except cold cereal.

Pike, his tail wagging, sniffed Mommy and ran away, whining and sniffing all the new furniture—long couches with fat cushions, shiny new tables, big chairs with thick fuzzy throws.

Di's tummy growled again, reminding her why they came downstairs. In the kitchen, a mass of unpacked boxes greeted them. Di started to count them, but gave up at ten. "Hey, somebody cut the tape. Let's look for the ceweal." She started at one end, and Liv at the other. Sticky tape tangled Di's fingers as she yanked open the first box, packed with brand-new, solid-black dishes. Huffing, she moved on to the next, her desperation growing. When she spied green and red pots and pans in the next two boxes, her tummy growled louder.

Liv whooped, and Di's heart leaped. Liv grinned as she pulled out two unopened boxes of Cheerios. Di grabbed one and ripped it open.

"Yoo hoo, Lu!"

Di froze.

"Grandma?" Livy squealed.

Grandma Gaia's voice echoed somewhere in the house.

Di, clutching the box of Cheerios, ran toward the sound, trailed by Liv. "Gwandma!"

Grandma Gaia stood by the front door, a big white smile on her face. Even her blue eyes smiled. She wore jeans and a purple blouse. A colorful scarf wrapped around her hair, and strings of chunky beads clattered around her neck. "How are my lambies?"

Liv clung to Grandma's legs. "Come see our new room." Di grabbed her hand and pulled her toward the stairs.

"Yes, I heard it's nice and big. In fact, you two could each have your own room now, couldn't you?"

Di nodded. Mommy said so too, but she and Liv didn't want to split up. Neither of them could imagine being all alone in her very own room.

Di's hunger gave way to anticipation as they led Grandma up the stairs. Hers and Liv's was the biggest bedroom on the second floor and had the best view. Grandma gasped when she saw it. "This is so nice. Oh, you lucky lambies. Now that your dad's a rock star, you get to have all nice things now, huh? I'll bet you get lots of good food to eat too, right?"

Di nodded, but inside she screamed, "No, we don't! We eat ceweal all day!"

Grandma frowned at the box in Di's hand. "Well, now. I think we can find something better than cereal, don't you think?"

"Hooway!" Di jumped down the stairs two at a time.

"Where's your mommy?" Grandma paused on the top step.

"She's asleep." Di jumped to the floor.

"Asleep? At three in the afternoon?"

Liv's voice echoed Di's thoughts. "Mm hmm, she's sleeping in the living room."

Grandma Gaia made a funny sound. She hurried down the stairs and stomped into the living room, then rushed to Mommy and jostled her. "Luna! Get your butt off the floor right now."

Di had never heard sweet-voiced Grandma yell. She

clutched Liv and edged to the doorway.

"Huh?" Mommy stirred and blinked puffy eyes.

"Lu." Grandma stood with hands on hips. "You have two hungry little girls who need to eat and a houseful of boxes to unpack. Come on, now. I raised you better than this."

"I was tired," Mommy mumbled, her eyes bleary like she'd been sleeping all night.

"Look, I promised to help you unpack." Grandma softened her voice. "But I'm not going to do it for you." She caught Di and Liv watching them. "Girls, go upstairs. Your mother and I need to talk."

Di, stuffing Cheerios in her mouth, started up the stairs. On the landing, she whispered, "Let's go down the other stairs. I bet we can hear Gwandma and Mommy if we hide in the hidey-holes."

They ran the length of the upstairs hall to the stairs at the other end. Downstairs on the first floor, Di placed her finger over her mouth, beckoned Liv to the alcoves, and crawled behind a little table. Liv tucked herself behind the other. Grandma's voice floated from the living room.

"Every time I see the girls they're hungry." Her words hissed like a snake. "And you and Howie spend all your time getting high. It has to stop, or I'm suing for custody."

Mommy mumbled something Di couldn't hear.

"I am serious, Lu. I had a feeling something like this was going on."

Mommy spoke again, but Grandma interrupted. "I'll take the girls off your hands for a month, and while they're gone, I expect you to go to rehab again. If you still can't handle parenthood, hire a nanny."

Di's heart pounded. Grandma planned to take them away from this house, from Mommy, from Pike. A month sounded like a long time. Beside her, Liv's face scrunched, her eyes bulged.

Maybe a month at Grandma Gaia's house wouldn't be so bad. She had a big yard with lots of trees to climb and sweet-smelling candles all over her house. And she cooked the yummiest meals.

She and Liv crept out of the alcoves and up the back stairs again. As soon as they'd settled on their beds, Grandma peeked in the doorway, her face drawn into a frown.

"Lambies, pack your bags. You're coming to live with me for a while."

Chapter Fifteen

While DeeDee reminisced, Livy had fully awakened. Her mind whirled with memories. Some as sweet as the Honey Os they munched on as kids; others as bitter as the medicine Mommy made them swallow when they were sick.

"I remember it well." Her voice sounded as weak as she felt. "Do you remember who was waiting for us when we got back from Grandma's?"

A faraway look passed over DeeDee's eyes. "Miss Joy. Our new nanny."

***

From the instant she met Miss Joy, Liv liked her. Miss Joy's red hair curled into ringlets, the kind that went boing if you tugged on them. Her teeth, white as paper, glistened whenever she smiled. And she smiled a lot. Even better, freckles dotted her cheeks, as if some kid had taken a magic marker and made polkadots all over her face.

She began teaching them to read. All week she drove them to tap dance classes and doctor appointments. She went grocery shopping and cooked meals — real meals. She hugged them before she went home for the day. She always arrived six a.m. and left at six p.m. after making sure they had a decent dinner.

Life got a whole lot better. She and Di never went hungry anymore. They always had a ride wherever they needed to go. Mommy and Miss Joy took them shopping for clothes and toys. A new swing set, complete with a bumpy slide, showed up in the back yard. On dry days, Miss Joy played Uncle Wiggily and Candy Land with them in the gazebo.

Daddy started taking Mommy with him when he went on tour, and sometimes Liv wouldn't see her parents for weeks. When Mommy and Daddy were gone, Miss Joy and her boyfriend stayed overnight in the room across the hall. Miss Joy read bedtime stories and giggled like a kid. Her boyfriend stayed in the other room and played tapes of Daddy's band so loudly, she yelled at him.

Sometimes during the day when Miss Joy turned on the TV, Daddy appeared on the screen, either sitting and talking to some people or performing with his band. Liv would screech and leap off the couch. She and Di got as close as they could to the screen and pumped up the volume high enough to scare Pike, who'd slink out of the room.

When fall came and they began first grade, Miss Joy chauffeured them to and from Elmhurst Academy. Vienna also attended Elmhurst, along with other children of famous parents. She and Di met sons and daughters of professional athletes, CEOs, and actors fleeing Hollywood. Liv came to understand how fame affected people's lives. She met other kids whose parents had to either stay inside or go out in a disguise. She met kids jaded by fame, who acted like her father being Declan Decker was no big deal. Liv liked their attitude far better.

By the time their first grade year at Elmhurst ended, Mommy looked sick and pale again. Liv heard Daddy yelling at Mommy for the first time *ever*. Now, whenever Mommy got sick and had to stay in bed a long time, Daddy yelled at her.

***

Liv stood before the master bedroom door, her fist poised to knock. "Mommy?" No answer. Daddy was in his basement recording studio. Miss Joy was off today, like every Sunday.

Di was upstairs with Vienna trying on new clothes, but Liv had grown tired of playing dress-up and wanted to go to Clown Palace.

"Mommy?" She knocked and counted to ten. Nothing. The door was unlatched, so she pushed it open and stepped inside. Rumpled bedding covered the empty bed. Mommy's white bathrobe lay next to it on the floor. Liv peeked in the bathroom, in the closet. No Mommy. Then she noticed the door to the back hallway standing open.

Liv ran from the room to the back door and spied Mommy's golden head in the gazebo. Rain poured hard as she skipped across the deck. Her ballet shoes didn't make a sound, and Mommy didn't look up. Liv stopped at the entrance, her mouth open to speak.

A startled gasp burst from her mouth.

Mommy, sitting on the edge of the gazebo bench, gripped a fat needle. The needle slid into her arm. At Liv's gasp, Mommy's head snapped up.

"Why are you spying on me, Olivia?" She wheezed. "Go away."

"Wha-what's that?" A quaver broke her voice.

"It's my medicine." Mommy winced. "Now leave."

Liv stared, the horror ebbing. Mommy gave her medicine when she was sick, except Mommy made her drink it. And she knew what shots were. She and Di had had many.

"Why are you giving yourself a shot?" Didn't only doctors and nurses give shots? "Are you a nurse?"

"No, I'm not a nurse. I told you to leave." Mommy took the needle out of her arm and sprang to her feet, inches from Liv.

She smacked Liv hard across the face. Gasping and grasping her cheek, Liv recoiled like a kicked puppy.

"Don't you dare tell anyone, you hear?" Mommy's white face was scary and angry. "Some people have to take medicine every day. But you're not to talk about it with others. I mean it."

Wailing, Liv bolted into the house and up the stairs. Her face stung from Mommy's slap. She rubbed the spot hard, but the stinging didn't go away.

She needed Di. Mommy couldn't have meant not to tell Di. After all, there was nothing wrong with taking medicine.

Unless she was so sick she could die.

Between sobs, she managed to tell Di and Vienna. Di's eyes bugged. "She must be really sick."

Vienna thrust her face close to Liv's. "Your mommy takes bad medicine, like my daddy."

Liv stepped back. "She does not!"

"She does so. My mommy said so."

"What's bad medicine?" Di's voice wobbled.

"It's what ad—ad-dics do."

"What's that?"

"Mommy says they always die young."

Even though Liv didn't understand, at Vienna's tone her face crumpled with more tears, which made Di cry too. They plopped on Liv's bed and held each other, sobbing, while Vienna tried on clothes.

Her tears spent, she felt calmer, stronger. "Let's ask Miss Joy tomorrow if Vienna is right." She patted Di's shoulder and, squaring hers, brushed damp hair back from her own face.

Liv pounced on Miss Joy the moment she walked in the door the next morning.

"Good morning, little ladies." Miss Joy offered her usual kneeling hug. "What do you want for breakfast?"

Liv, silent, tugged on her right hand. Di yanked her left. Miss Joy's curls bounced as she turned from one to the other. "What is it?"

"Miss Joy?" Liv whispered since they were standing next

to Mommy's bedroom door.

"What?" Miss Joy's voice bounced off the high ceiling.

Di put her finger on her mouth. "Come to our room."

Joy, her mouth open, followed up the stairs. Once behind closed doors, Liv told her what she'd seen in the gazebo. Miss Joy's eyes grew big, and her mouth twisted.

"Miss Joy, does Mommy take bad medicine?"

Miss Joy choked out a funny noise, a laugh mixed with a cry. "Let me explain something. Here, come sit down." They followed her to Di's bed, and she laid gentle hands on theirs, giving them light squeezes. Her eyes grew ever so serious. "Your mother's medicine is something she shouldn't be taking."

"But..." Liv's face scrunched. Her head hurt. "Why does she take it?"

"Some people, like your mother, use it because it makes them feel good. But only a doctor should give medicine."

"But..." How could bad medicine make a person feel good?

"Is..." Di's voice trembled. "Is bad medicine like poison?"

Liv's heart rate surged. "Is she going to die?"

Miss Joy's mouth puckered as though she'd watched a sad movie, and her curls shook. "As long as she doesn't take too much, she won't die."

Liv stared at Miss Joy and slid her free hand around Di's waist.

"Your mother needs to go a place where they can help her. But your father says she won't go."

"Is that why he yells at her?" asked Di.

"Yes." Miss Joy nodded. "Although he takes it himself."

"Daddy takes bad medicine, too?" Di screeched.

Miss Joy bit her lip. "I've already told you more than I should have."

The fear in Liv's heart built to something close to terror. If Mommy could die from too much bad medicine, then Daddy could, too.

Miss Joy placed a finger under their chins and leaned down to study them. "Don't tell your mom we had this conversation, okay? She doesn't want you to worry about her."

What a strange house. Both Mommy and Miss Joy kept secrets from each other. She and Di were caught in the middle like a game of tug-o-war.

Chapter Sixteen

After she'd tended to Livy for two days, DeeDee's nerve endings jumped, antsy from forced inactivity. She needed to exercise her muscles.

On Wednesday morning, Livy still slept, so DeeDee threw off the blanket, covered her sleep shirt with a hospital robe, and sought a nurse. But she lurched when a man and woman strode into the room and nearly sideswiped her. She gave them a quick once-over. Wide-open, guileless faces. No tattoos or piercings. A vibe as wholesome as vanilla ice cream.

The man peered at Livy's bed, then at DeeDee. "I'm Ron. This is my wife, Melody."

DeeDee held up a blocking hand. "Can I help you?"

"We're here to minister to patients." Ignoring DeeDee's hand, he and the woman moved to Livy's bedside, placed their hands on her head, and chanted a prayer.

DeeDee balled her fists and jutted out her chin, like she did in high school when bullies got in her face. But this time she couldn't do a thing to stop them.

"Heavenly Father," the man intoned. "Please heal this woman in the mighty name of Jesus. Restore her to health, Lord."

Livy's eyes jerked open. Her lips expelled the faintest of sighs. "Was Jesus God?"

DeeDee jolted. Surely, she'd imagined it.

The man stopped chanting. He and the woman looked at each other, and the woman spoke first. "Did you ask if Jesus was God?"

Livy nodded.

Gasping, DeeDee flipped on the overhead light, her heart thudding, brain whirring, something fermenting in the pit of her stomach. Was she dreaming? She moved closer. The bright light over Livy's drawn face clarified reality.

"Yes, dear. Jesus was God. Is God," the woman replied in a Sunday-school teacher voice. "What's your name?"

"Livy."

The man spoke next. "We're glad to meet you, Livy. I'm Ron, and this is my wife, Melody. We head the hospital ministry at Green Lake Baptist Church."

"We're here to pray for and encourage you." Melody fluffed back her bobbed, streaked hair. "How long will you be here?"

DeeDee intervened. "She might get to go home today. If not, tomorrow."

"Are you her sister?" Melody cast her a wide-mouthed smile. DeeDee couldn't picture this woman ever allowing a frown to trespass on her unlined face.

She should curse just to see her reaction. Instead, DeeDee muttered, "Yeah, I'm DeeDee." Grandma Gaia said organized religion was responsible for most of the wars throughout history. No reason these people should be any different.

"Do you two already have a church home?" asked Ron.

"Nope."

"You're welcome to visit ours."

"No thanks. Not our thing."

"If Jesus was God—" Livy pushed the soft words out, and then gave a light sigh.

"Yes?" Melody prompted.

"How come—how come—people don't know about it?"

Livy was challenging them. DeeDee smirked. Judging by the look the couple exchanged, they thought her question legitimate.

"Oh, Livy," Melody's eyes shone, "lots of people know about Jesus."

"Livy, I have a Scripture passage for you." Ron opened a thick book. "Have you ever heard of the Gospel of John?"

Livy shifted her head side to side.

"It was written by Jesus' best friend."

As if Livy cared whether Jesus had a best friend who wrote part of the Bible.

"This is the passage John wrote about Jesus." Ron's voice took on a preacher-man quality. "John 1:1 — 'In the beginning was the Word, and the Word was with God, and the Word was God. The same was in the beginning with God. All things were made by him; and without him was not anything made that was made.'"

Livy lay there, her eyes closed. Was she listening or not? DeeDee approached the couple like a protective mother bear.

"It was nice of you guys to drop by." Her sharp tone sent a firm message. "I'm sure you mean well, but" — She refrained from saying, you can take your religion and shove it — "Livy needs to rest now."

The two backed away, questions all over their faces. As they stepped through the door, Ron stuck out his hand and offered a Jim Carrey smile. She forced her own and shook his hand.

"God bless you two." The man had to get in the last word.

A curse hovered on her lips again. But they turned and disappeared.

"Whoosh." DeeDee plunked in the stiff vinyl armchair the color of vomit. "Just what we don't need — religious freaknuts."

Livy let out a sigh. "Scott said…" She drew in a breath. "He told me Jesus…was God."

"Scott did?"

"Mmm hmm."

"That explains a lot."

"I know — right?"

They shared a chuckle, a soft one from Livy, a hearty one from DeeDee.

***

In ENFO System's R & D lab, an occasional voice rose over the clacking of keys. Scott, ready to pound his computer screen, dropped his hand when his Smartphone vibrated. Normally, he'd ignore it, but today had been exasperating. Software imploded, simulations refused to produce desired results, and the help desk ignored assistance pleas. He needed a mental pause, so he pulled the phone from his pocket and read the e-mail from DeeDee McCreary.

> Dear Parents,
> I regret to inform you my sister, Livy, was in a serious accident Monday morning, resulting in a broken leg. We will be canceling all classes for the rest of the week. Livy is currently recuperating in the hospital and expects to go home tomorrow....

"Holy smokes." He spoke under his breath to keep his coworkers from hearing. "What kind of accident?"

> ...Until further notice, starting next week, I will be teaching Livy's classes. Please keep Livy in your thoughts.

He whispered a quick prayer for Livy, hit Reply, and keyed,

> *Was it a car accident?*

Returning to his computer, he struggled with the coordinates for his team's prototype and waited for the phone to chime. Five minutes later it did.

DeeDee's email read:

> Yes. A car hit her as she was crossing the street and crushed her leg. She'll be in a cast for a couple of months.

Scott winced.

> Tell her I'll be praying for her.

He hit Send and opened up a new e-mail, addressing it to the leader of his church's prayer chain.

> Please pray for my friend Livy who got hit by a car Monday. She has a broken leg and will be in a cast for a while.

He faced his computer, but not before glancing heavenward and asking God if Livy's accident was His interesting way of answering prayer.

Chapter Seventeen

"I know it's awkward." The nurse's aide hovered as Livy wrestled with the crutches. "If you keep practicing, you'll get the hang of it."

Today Livy would go home, but first she had to learn to walk with two aluminum contraptions jammed under her arms. Awkward didn't begin to describe it. Manipulating crutches reminded her of the first time she used chopsticks, multiplied by one hundred.

Her spirit felt like a wasteland every time she contemplated the possibility of never dancing again. DeeDee had tried reassuring her. "You know Dad will pay for whatever the insurance won't cover," she'd reminded Livy. "He'll do what he can to help you get back to normal."

True. But the doctor said there were no guarantees.

How would Will adjust to her injury? He'd been so attentive since Monday. Would he lose patience with her soon? Anyone would.

The rest of the family, who'd been staying at Four Seasons, came to see Livy home. Thoughtful DeeDee drove her Miata home and returned with Livy's roomier Jaguar XJ. Still, maneuvering her stiff-legged self into the front seat proved a beastly chore. DeeDee tossed the oversized chopsticks into the back and slid behind the wheel. Promising to meet up at the house, Dad and the family whizzed away in a rented car.

Rain began spattering the windshield. Livy reclined the seat as DeeDee sped south on Highway 99. They had two stops to make first. Livy shifted left, then right, trying to balance her weight. At least she was going home. She missed Murf and his permanent smile. She missed her queen-sized bed and its mattress contoured with her shape, its abundance of soft pillows. Her back ached from the hospital bed, an unyielding slab of granite she'd slept on for three nights.

DeeDee stopped in front of Saffire. "My tote bag is under the desk," Livy told her, unable to face the building or her dismal future as a non-dancer. She stared at the bleak sky until DeeDee reappeared, lugging Livy's paisley bag. Livy dug through her personal belongings, grasping the solid reminders of a carefree life. A box of chai—her conversation with Scott. A borrowed CD of Josh Groban—her opera-loving frenemy, Vienna. A spray bottle of sweet pea scent—Will.

A few books and magazines rounded out the contents. Livy peeked at the cover of the smaller of the two books, the book about Christ Scott gave her. She'd meant to sell it online. Yesterday, the preacher couple in the hospital had piqued her curiosity. She couldn't forget hearing them chanting. A sensation like warm incense had filled her. While Ron read the Scriptures, the sweet fragrance spilled over, as unlike a drug high as one could get.

When DeeDee chased them away, the warm incense fled.

But her mother told her in a dream Jesus was not God. Her mother wouldn't deceive her about something so important. Not intentionally. So who was right? And *why* did it suddenly matter?

DeeDee stopped at Walgreens's to pick up Livy's painkiller prescription. Waiting for her, Livy flipped to the religious book's table of contents. Chapter names could point her toward the most meaningful sections. She slid her finger down the list, stopping at "Who was 'The Word'?" Hadn't the preacher man read the same phrase at her bedside?

She flipped toward the section, but DeeDee emerged

from the store. Livy shoved the book into her bag, gripped by a strange sensation.

"I almost forgot, I have some news for you." DeeDee opened the driver-side door.

"What?" Livy dropped the bag next to her feet.

DeeDee cranked the ignition. "The insurance agent called this morning."

"Which reminds me, thank you for taking care of the claim for me. What'd the agent say?"

"The little idiot who hit you is claiming no-fault." DeeDee peeled onto the street. "She claims you stepped right in front of her, and she couldn't stop in time. The witness is backing her up."

"Actually, that *is* what happened."

"Seriously?" DeeDee gaped at her. "You're not going to tell the insurance company, are you?"

"I don't know what I'll tell them."

"Why would you step in front of a moving car?"

"I didn't pay attention." The cast dug into Livy's knee. She shifted. "I'd been thinking about the day Mom died."

DeeDee clicked her tongue. "Livs, you've got to get your head together." She switched the wipers to high. "Look what it's done to you. And Dad blames himself for your accident because he didn't have any answers."

"He shouldn't blame himself." A waterfall of rain deluged the windshield. "Maybe there aren't any answers."

"Maybe you need to see a counselor." DeeDee wrenched the Jag onto their cul-de-sac.

"I wouldn't even know where to begin."

"I'll help you."

Her spacious red-and-white house buoyed her mood, and her family's rental car waited at the curb. DeeDee drove into the garage, and then helped Livy haul herself out of the car, nestle the crutches under her arms, and propel herself over the threshold while tilting to the right to compensate for the extra weight.

Thus began her gawky process of learning how to be an invalid.

***

Livy snuggled beneath the covers and snuck the book from under her pillow. She eagerly flipped to the chapter about The Word.

DeeDee had helped her undress and slip into a sleep shirt, got her into bed, and then tucked five of her softest throw pillows around her body. Will had offered to stay and hold her, but she'd told him she would doubtless thrash a lot and he might not sleep well. He'd agreed with obvious reluctance and gone home.

She shifted, sighed, and found page fifty. "In the beginning was the Word," she read, "and the Word was with God, and the Word was God. And the Word became flesh and dwelt among us."

What was that supposed to mean? She read on. The author seemed to be saying the term *The Word* would have been understood by people then to mean either God or the governing principle of the universe.

But was Jesus Christ the Word?

She kept running into the phrase, *The Word became flesh and dwelt among us.* The author asserted the entire Gospel of John was about Jesus Christ, John's best friend.

"John is not saying that the Word was *a* god," she read, "or that God is the Word. He's saying, all that God is and was, the Word is and was."

A shiver slithered down her spine like a trickle of cold water. She returned to the table of contents. The title "What Difference Does It Make?" caught her eye. The pages fanned her as she moved toward the book's middle.

The doorknob squeaked, and the door slowly slid open.

Jolting, Livy stowed the book under her pillow. Deeds would never understand.

DeeDee stepped in. "Do you need me to stay in here tonight?"

"I think I'll be all right."

She approached the bed. "You reading?"

"I just finished." Livy tried in vain to reach the switch.

"Here, let me do it." DeeDee bent over the magenta ceramic lamp and clicked it off. "Goodnight."

"'Night." She'd finish tomorrow.

***

Shari's presence still permeated Scott's living room. When she lived here, the pinky-beige walls felt right. So did the checkered chairs and floral area rugs.

Thursday evening, as he led Rick and Paula past paintings of picket-fenced farmhouses and old rustic barns, colorful birds and flower vases, a sense of purpose filled him. He needed to remove all the countrified art and repaint the walls off-white, then hang the framed photos of Seattle scenes he'd picked up at Pike Place Market last year.

His friends joined him on the pink sofa, which Shari insisted was actually dusky rose. Balancing the five-year-old, flip-top cell phone on his palm, he told them about Livy. "I've been praying for her and her twin sister." He studied the old phone. "But when I heard she got hit by a car, my first thought was, 'Lord, what are you up to?'"

"That would've been my first thought, too," said Paula.

"I hope my prayers didn't bring this on." He braced his elbows on his knees. "I didn't ask the Lord to injure her."

Rick cleared his throat. "Unless it's the only way He could get her attention."

"Sometimes this is what it takes." Paula rubbed her

knees, the fabric of her blue slacks bunching under her fingers.

"The way I see it," Scott lowered the phone, "if God can do anything, He can get someone's attention without hurting them. Can't He?"

"Sure He can." Rick scratched his ear, wrinkling his nose as though the simple movement took great effort. "But it might not have the same impact."

"Why should people seek God," added Paula, "if they already have heaven here on earth?"

"Good point." Scott stretched his legs in front of him. "But when God found me, life was pretty doggone fine. I had just graduated from CalPoly. Shari and I were fixin' to get married. I thought I had a bright future ahead."

Paula placed a light hand on his arm. "What brought about your conversion?"

"At CalPoly, I met some born-again Christians. I considered myself a Christian, too. Growing up in Dallas, we were devout Catholics. Went to Mass and confession religiously." He chuckled. "No pun intended."

Paula smiled.

"When I told those kids I was a Christian, they invited me to their fellowship group." He flipped the phone open. "The speaker talked about what it meant to have a personal relationship with God. It didn't sound like anything I'd ever experienced. So I went up afterward and talked to him. He explained all about what being born again meant and why religion isn't enough."

"Right on." Rick raised his hand in a high five.

Scott snapped the phone shut and clapped Rick's hand. "But it took a few more years before I got it."

"You've never told us your testimony." Paula's eager voice encouraged him to continue.

"My first job out of college was in the Bay Area. A

coworker kept a stack of religious books in his desk and kept trying to get me to read them. One day I took one. Turned out I'd picked up a book about Christ's crucifixion and its meaning to us. I always accepted Christ's crucifixion as fact, but never let it impact my life."

His friends nodded.

"The book got me thinking. For the first time in my life, I began to question the things I'd been taught."

They chatted for a few more minutes until the time arrived to test the gadget. Scott stood, stretching his arms high overhead. "I think it'll work best in the garage."

Once in the garage, he raised the door and breathed a quick prayer for success. Three heads bent over the phone as he pushed Send.

"Doggonit." He pushed Send again, then groaned and palmed his forehead. "I must not have used the right coordinates when I recalibrated."

"That's okay, bro. We'll keep praying. If anyone can do it, you can."

"Thanks." Scott exhaled. "Guess it's back to the drawing board for me."

Chapter Eighteen

Livy's chiming phone woke her from a deep sleep Friday morning.

She squinted at the display—8:17—and smiled at Grandma's headshot. "Grandma," she croaked into the phone as she reclined on her back.

"How are you doing, lamb?" Her compassionate voice jolted Livy into full wakefulness.

"Ugh, I've been better. I hurt all over, and this itch under my cast is driving me crazy."

"Oh, Livy. I was appalled when DeeDee told me what happened. I'm so sorry I couldn't make it up there."

"No worries. DeeDee said your car was in the shop."

"As soon as it's ready, I'm coming up to see you."

"Awesomeness." Livy, yawning, rubbed her eyes and blinked away the moisture.

"Don't forget," Grandma reminded her, "karma will see that little girl gets what's coming to her."

"Actually, Grandma, it was my fault." Livy sighed.

"Your fault? How so?"

She tightened her grip on the phone and relayed Monday morning's events, the news of Nils's death and her absent-minded stupor when she stepped off the curb.

"You were thinking about your mother again?" Grandma's level tone veered into curiosity.

"Yeah. Trippy, huh? Plus, I dreamed about her in the hospital."

"I wonder what your mother is trying to tell you."

Grandma gave a little gasp. "Oh, I forgot to call you back! But I can tell you I didn't hear anything from the universe—"

"Grandma, I'm convinced there's more to her death than I've been told. The things people have said—the dreams—Is there *anything* you guys didn't tell me?"

Silence thrummed on the other end. Then came a soft, "I don't think so."

"You should've seen how fast Dad tried to get off the phone when I brought up the subject." Livy's gaze tracked the ceiling fan's lazy rotation. "Was it suicide and nobody wanted me to know?"

"Suicide?" Grandma's screech resounded through the word. "No one even entertained the possibility. Your mother was the last person who would do such a thing."

"Then why all the secrecy?"

"What secrecy?"

Livy sighed again. "Never mind. Just tell me every detail you remember."

"Well…" Grandma went into her singsong voice. "I was in the kitchen making breakfast when I heard screams and commotion in the master bedroom. I went to see what was going on, and everybody was standing over your mother lying on the floor. Your father told me she was dead, and I nearly fell over dead myself. I couldn't believe heroin finally won."

"Who all was there?" Livy cringed. Did she have to sound so sharp, demanding?

"DeeDee and your dad, of course. You were on the floor in a dead faint, adding to the commotion. You were out for several minutes. Joy and Vienna wandered in…everyone carrying on so. Someone—Joy, I think?—covered your mother with a blanket. I called 911, and the paramedics arrived. But they were too late." Grandma clicked her tongue. "I remember smelling burning. Turns out I left the pancakes, but nobody wanted to eat anyway."

"What was I doing?"

"Well, like I said, you fainted. After you came to you didn't say a word for two days. Hardly ate a thing. You mostly sat on the couch in front of the TV, clutching your blanket and sucking your thumb. Freaked us out. You finally spoke the day before your mother's funeral. You told us you were hungry and went to find her. When we reminded you she was dead, you didn't believe us. You went all through the house looking for her."

A sliver of sunshine pushed through the window slats and briefly brightened the room. "I hoped you could think of something I didn't already know."

"You know, Livy, you ought to try hypnosis. Maybe it'll help you remember."

She blinked back tears over Grandma's lack of answers. Perhaps Will and the groundskeeper had been wrong, and the fateful day happened as she'd been told.

"In fact," Grandma rustled, "I'll give you the names of a couple of trustworthy people in your area."

Livy scowled at her damaged body. DeeDee was right. Look what this obsession had done to her. How dare Will and the groundskeeper feed her such ideas?

"You don't want to go to just anybody. These are people I know and respect. You wouldn't have to worry about anything underhanded or fishy."

Maybe she needed to let this go. Maybe events from so long ago no longer mattered.

"Okay, Grandma. You can give me the names when you visit."

In the ensuing pause, Livy opened her mouth to say goodbye, but...one more thing. "Grandma."

"Hmm?"

"Change of subject, but can I get your take on

something?"

"Of course."

"I've met a couple people recently who claim Jesus was God, so I wondered if Jesus is one of the gods you pray to."

In the distance, someone shouted. A car revved.

After several seconds, Grandma spoke. "Livy, you *can't* be serious."

Grandma's vehemence startled her. "Why not?"

"Don't be listening to religious extremists." Her voice rose. "Those people brought about most of the suffering in the world. Why do you think we have poverty? Or wars? Religious intolerance, that's why."

Not from Ron and Melody. "Well, the Jesus people I've met seem different. Like kind, caring people, not warmongers."

"Don't be fooled. The Holocaust was perpetrated by the Germans, a Christian people. Western imperialism by *Christian* nations caused widespread poverty all over the world."

Livy tugged on her hair, her brain swirling as if drowning in a sea of confusion. Grandma spouted these claims over the years, yet they contradicted what she'd seen in Ron and Melody.

What would Scott say?

"Okay. Thanks for your input. I'll be looking forward to seeing you when you visit."

"Me too. Love you, lambie."

"Love you too."

Livy placed the phone next to her and groped under her pillow until she found the paperback's solid bulk. She shifted onto her side and opened it.

The chapter heading blared at her: "What Difference Does It Make?" She soon learned the answer. Jesus came to earth to forgive sins and make a way for people to know God.

"He that hath seen me," he told his disciples, "hath seen the Father." Her brow knotted. Did this mean Jesus was the Father?

Maybe she should start at the beginning. She shifted to her other side, flipped to the first chapter, and dug in.

Chapter Nineteen

Scott's kitchen hadn't changed much since Shari left. He swept aside the rooster-print curtains which still framed the window overlooking the arborvitae. This morning, the weather couldn't decide whether to rain or shine. Gray-edged clouds wandered the sky, one moment hiding the sun, the next setting it free.

"What do you want to do today, girls?" He poured a cup of Columbian coffee blended with Jamaica Blue Mountain. He tried a sip, and then smacked his lips at the rich tropical taste overlaid with mild acidity. For coffee, and marriage, compatibility was key. "There's no dance class today, so you can pick anything you want."

"The zoo, Daddy." Kinzie leaped from her chair and pressed her palms together. "Please?"

"Yeah, the zoo." Lacie squealed, following suit.

"Okay. Zoo it is."

"I hope the monkeys are out playing today." Kinzie clasped her hands and swung them side to side.

"I hope we get to see polar bears."

"Daddy, can we get candy?"

He chuckled, grabbed his coffee cup, and propelled the girls to the car. Once inside, they bounced so much, he had to put on his "mean daddy" voice.

"Stop bouncing, Lacie. This isn't a trampoline."

"Daddy?" Kinzie's angelic blonde hair framed pleading blue eyes and quivering lips.

"What, Kinzie?"

Her little mouth slanted down at the corners. "I want my Hello Kitty jacket."

"What's wrong with the jacket you're wearing?"

"I want Hello Kitty."

He sighed. If he tried to dissuade Kinzie from her single-minded yearning, he was in for a long pouting session. Apparently, he'd be stopping by Shari's mother's house, where his ex and the girls now lived.

Pacing the garage, he pulled up Shari's number.

"Shari? I'm fixin' to run by for a sec."

"What for?" His ex emphasized each syllable. "I'm leaving real soon."

"Can you hold on for a few? I'm only five minutes away. Kinzie wants her Hello Kitty jacket. Can you find it and have it ready?"

Shari muttered something unintelligible. Scott tensed and waited for the explosion. Instead, the line went silent.

He pocketed the phone and poked his head in the car. "Okay, let's go get your jacket."

"Yay!" Kinzie's eyes lit up.

He backed out the driveway and glanced at Jamie's Toyota, sitting like a tame pet in the McRabb driveway, innocent of boorish behavior.

He turned away from his usual route and headed through curving residential streets toward Shari's place, each twist invoking memories from their early years together.

Shari had been thrilled when he'd gotten the job offer eight years ago from ENFO Systems in Seattle, her hometown. They'd settled in the Green Lake neighborhood, less than a mile from her family home. Baby Kinzie came along then baby Lacie. Scott had fallen in love at first sight. Not once, but twice. A man couldn't have asked for a better life.

They'd been brand-new, baby Christians with a hunger

for fellowship and God's Word. They'd found Ravenna Bible Chapel, a small but growing church. Spiritually speaking, they'd stayed in sync. At least for a while.

In year four, their marriage started deteriorating. Their money arguments accelerated. Shari, frustrated over her thirty extra pounds of baby weight, signed up with some diet-product company, began receiving monthly shipments of bottled concoctions the appearance and consistency of burnt coffee. He assured her she looked fine the way she was, but still, each month the money came out of their checking account, whether it was there or not. Their line of credit maxed out.

He'd encouraged her to take a finance management course with him, but she couldn't be bothered. Finally, she said if this was marriage, she'd rather be single, he was always on her case and she was tired of it. He'd choked out, Is there someone else? She'd denied it, and he apologized for his part. But it always happened again.

Until she left.

A familiar figure hobbling along the sidewalk interrupted his musings. "Hey, girls, isn't that Miss Livy?" He craned his head. Livy, her profile toward them, proceeded on crutches. Will snail-paced alongside her, a protective hand on her back.

Kinzie squealed. "Miss Livy."

Scott pulled over and lowered the passenger-side window. "Hey, y'all."

They looked over at him, and their faces relaxed.

"How are you doing?" he greeted.

"Managing." Livy's teeth flashed in a wry smile.

"She's obeying doctor's orders." Will offered a nod.

"Your recovery must be going well. You're out and about already."

"I was going stir-crazy. Had to get some fresh air."

"What happened to Miss Livy, Daddy?" Lacie's voice echoed from the back seat.

Livy poked her head in the car. "Hi, girls. Do you miss dance class?"

Still staring, Kinzie and Lacie nodded.

"I know Miss Dee is missing you, too."

No bruises mottled her face, no cuts, no scars. For someone hit by a car a week ago, she looked pretty good. "Do you live around here?"

Livy nodded. "I do." She pointed to the cul-de-sac behind her. "Right back there on Laurel Court."

"So we're neighbors." He thrust a thumb behind him. "I live on Rosemary."

"Cool."

"Lived here long?"

"About six years."

He glanced at Will, whose friendly expression showed signs of slipping, then at Livy. "Eight for me."

Will, tugging on Livy's shoulder, offered Scott a clearly dismissive wave. "Nice running into you. Have a good one."

Scott waved, and the couple hobbled down the sidewalk. He slid the stick in drive and rolled on down the street. Will behaved as though Scott invaded his territory by having a friendly conversation with Livy.

When he pulled up to Shari's house, an unfamiliar, blazing-red BMW with Idaho plates sat in the driveway like a well-dressed intruder. Who did Shari know from Idaho? He wrenched the door handle then stopped.

Shari emerged from the house dressed in hiking clothes, a little pink jacket tucked under her arm. Her fair hair bounced with each step, contradicting the stoic face.

He rolled down the passenger-side window. "Got company?"

Shari opened the rear door and handed Kinzie the jacket,

then slammed the door shut.

"Mommy!" Kinzie called.

Instead of answering Scott's question, Shari spun on her heel and stalked up the driveway. In ten years of marriage, he'd never grown tired of her blonde beauty. Man, it was hard to transition from married man to single man. Worse, Dan, Scott's accountability group leader, kept reminding him of Jesus' teaching—anyone who divorces his wife and marries another woman commits adultery. Easy for Dan, happily married to a solid Christian lady, to say.

If Dan's take on Scripture was correct, Shari put Scott in a no-win situation—danged if he remarried, at least in God's eyes, and danged if he didn't, if it meant inhabiting an empty bed for the rest of his life.

Chapter Twenty

"**I** hope Nils appreciates what we're doing for him, wherever he is." DeeDee stood with Audria in the middle of the Four Seasons' Ballroom, chosen for its impressive proportions and equally impressive view. Today, however, a thick downpour obscured the floor-to-ceiling windows' panorama of sea and sky. The hotel staff set up tables to seat five hundred. She and Audria planned to distribute the programs, display all the Nils memorabilia, and cue up Power Point.

The live band—several of Nils's old friends and band mates—warmed up on stage, humming with dissonance. None of them appeared to be a day under forty-five. Except the hunky blond bass player who only had eyes for his Fender. Where *had* they found such a hottie? She looked around for Dad, who was supposed to be on stage with the band.

She and Audria walked to the cars for another load. "Aunt Bestie? Who's the blond guy? The bassist?"

Audria quickened her pace as they braved the pouring rain. "I don't know. But he is fine."

"Wonder if he's taken?" She eyed her friend. "So you noticed him, too."

"Of course. I'm not dead and buried yet."

"No issues between you and Jake? Twenty years together seems like forever. What's the secret to your longevity, anyway?"

"We're willing to do the hard work necessary to stay together." Audria shrugged. "Don't worry. You'll find yourself a keeper one of these days."

"Oh, I have no problem finding keepers," DeeDee snapped. "But it's Livy who snags them."

"Well, then." Audria popped the latch on her Jetta trunk. "Emulate Livy and snag one."

DeeDee clenched a fist. If anyone else talked to her that way, she would've punched them. Audria tugged on a wooden stand, and DeeDee grabbed the other end. "Livy makes men work for her attention." Audria slammed the trunk. "Did she hop into bed with Will on their first date? No? I didn't think so."

DeeDee cringed and balanced the easel between them.

"Did she offer him her phone number?"

No.

Audria wasn't through. "Men like Livy's soft side. Wouldn't hurt you to be softer around the edges."

"Ouch, Audria." DeeDee hoisted the awkward stand through the doorway. "She is she, and I am I. The older we get, the less alike we get."

"Don't look at him as we walk by."

DeeDee signaled her friend to lower her voice as they approached the stage where the cutie was plucking guitar strings—did he pluck women's heartstrings as skillfully? Casting a critical eye over her little black dress, paired with black tights and four-inch heels, she relaxed. No wardrobe malfunctions.

"Don't approach him," Audria hissed. "Let him approach you."

Still, she yearned to do what she'd always done when an attractive man crossed her path: stand up straight, look him in the eye, and offer her most enticing smile.

Instead, she gave the guy a three-second glance, cocked an eyebrow, and allowed a tiny smile she hoped conveyed friendly, not forward. He smiled back. Returning to her task, she placed a large mounted photo on the easel—a photo of Nils flailing drumsticks like a boss, hair flying, mouth agape. She took her time, adjusting and readjusting just so, feeling the blond's gaze on her.

By now, she should be over there striking up a conversation. And she would if not for Audria, the beady-eyed mother hen. She should be telling him he looked like Sting and watching a flattered smile dart across his face. Men loved being told they looked like someone famous. It made them all hers—at least for one night.

The caterers soon arrived and began setting up a splendid array at the back. Security guards lined the doorways and corridors. Morton, Nils's manager and the mastermind behind all this, had been firm: No media.

She spied Dad at the entrance and beckoned him over. "Can we talk?" she whispered when he neared.

"Sure." He raised his brows.

"Not here."

"Come on up to our suite."

DeeDee told Audria she'd be back, then followed Dad up the elevator to a top floor suite—his and Joy's home for the past five days.

The scent of luxury hit her the moment she crossed the threshold. The marble countertops, fat, gold-plated lamps, striped Turkish rugs brought back memories of her touring days. Supersized, Picasso-style artwork overlaid beige walls, and a wall-mounted TV hung above an electric fireplace. She wandered to the sliding glass door to the deck. If not for the drenching rain, she would've had a clear vista of the city. Instead, she faced gray-shrouded humps of hills to the north. Only the Space Needle's spire shimmered through the gloom.

"Where are the others?" Traces of her brothers' presence littered the place—game consoles, smart phones, dirty clothes and dishes mingled with textbooks and school papers.

"They went swimming. What's on your mind?"

"Well, um—" Why did she feel hesitant to confide in him?

"What, kiddo?" He settled on the charcoal sofa and patted the cushion next to him.

"Who's the blond bass player?" She plunked beside him and ran her fingers along the supple Italian leather. "I don't recognize him."

Dad barked out a laugh. "Well, well… You got a thing for Nick, huh?"

"Dad!" She flicked a hand at him. "Nick who?"

"Nick Rush. Cool name, yeah?"

"Very cool. Is it seriously his name?"

Dad shrugged. "It could be his professional name. I don't know." He crossed his legs, ankle on knee. "Want me to tell him you got an eye on him?"

"No, not this time. I don't even know if he's taken."

"He's not. He just ended a long-term engagement. Lucky you."

"How do you know him?"

"Never met him before. Morton hired him when the bassist couldn't make it."

"Nice." She tossed a handful of curls over her shoulder. "Way to go, Morton." A looker with the name of Nick Rush was available. Must be her lucky day.

**

Guests began arriving as early as six, although the caterers wouldn't start serving until six thirty. A crush of bodies surrounded the full-service bar by the time DeeDee and Audria got there. Competing fragrances hammered her senses like Nordstrom's perfume counter. Beside her, someone's black sequined dress twinkled in the bar lights. The forty-something lady smiled at DeeDee as though she knew her, and DeeDee smiled back, trying to place her.

"Aren't you Nils's third wife?" The woman's tight bun stretched the skin around her eyes like a face-lift.

DeeDee gaped and nearly swore. "No," she snapped. "I'm DeeDee McCreary. I used to sing in Nils's band."

Shamefaced, the woman shifted her gaze, but DeeDee was already turning her back. True, Meaghan had curly red hair too, but she was at least ten years older than DeeDee, and looked it.

Bodies kept pushing her closer to the bar. Two stiff-haired bartenders rushed to fill orders, their smooth, practiced movements making it look easy. How long before the bartender on the right noticed his tie was askew?

The cacophony of voices made normal conversation difficult. "He was always a druggie and a womanizer." A childlike voice behind her pierced through the din, and DeeDee whirled. It came from a fortyish woman weighing at least two fifty. Artificially black hair. Navy blue dress, enough bling to bring her weight to two seventy. The crowd jostled her sideways into her companion.

The incongruous voice continued. "That's why he couldn't stay married to anyone."

DeeDee bit back a swear word. "You mean Nils?"

Blue Dress nodded, her eyes wary.

"Why are you here celebrating someone you have such a low opinion of?"

"I-I..." Blue Dress tried to step back, but the crowd prevented her. Her companion, a thin, frail blonde in a black Chanel pantsuit, spoke in a forceful voice. "Don't mind her. She and Nils used to date a long time ago."

DeeDee's gaze bounced between the two women. Had they somehow traded voices?

The larger woman, blushing deep crimson, elbowed the smaller one, her eyes shooting sparks. The surging crowd shoved DeeDee into the edge of the bar.

"What would you like, ma'am?" The bartender had straightened his tie, seemingly untroubled by the chaos.

"Martini, please." Audria stepped forward and ordered the same. Then, drinks in hand, they slithered their way to the hors d'oeuvres table.

A small blond-haired boy stood near the entrance, clad in a black suit and bowtie like a miniature James Bond. Vienna's son Fleming, clutching his father's hand. Zach's hooded gaze scanned the room. No doubt he hoped to avoid his ex-wife. DeeDee smiled and waved, but they didn't see her. She had caught glimpses of Vienna through the crowd, but now craned to see Nick Rush. Or Livy. Surely, she would show up soon.

The band wouldn't start playing until after the speeches, and DeeDee couldn't think of any good reason not to finagle a seat at Nick Rush's table.

The din roared in DeeDee's head as she and Audria carried their drinks and plates among the round tables. About half the seats were filled now. Some of the guests had traveled from New York, some from LA. Movers and shakers of show business. She nodded a greeting to those she recognized.

Nils's family sat near the stage with Morton and his wife and Nils's tear-splotched widow, Brittany. Dad had reserved the table beside it. Royal blue linen displayed fine crystal and gold-rimmed china. In the center, daisies floated in a squat round vase.

Audria slipped away to the Nelssons' table and claimed the last remaining seat next to Vienna. Fleming, chortling, bolted out of his father's grasp, hopped on Audria's lap, and covered her face with kisses. Audria beamed and darted little kisses in return. Zach hovered nearby like a vigilante, casting cautious glances at Vienna.

DeeDee's paternal grandmother, who had known Nils

from his childhood, shuffled in moments later. Dad, resplendent in a black tuxedo, escorted his mother to the table. The creases around Grandma Alice's mouth deepened in a smile when she saw DeeDee. Her new life in Arizona hadn't been kind to her seventy-year-old skin. DeeDee rushed to her and wrapped her arms around her bony shoulders, then stood back to study her. DeeDee's two grandmas couldn't be less alike. Grandma Gaia's smooth, healthy complexion and upright posture contrasted with Grandma Alice's leathery face and stooped shoulders. Grandma Alice still wore the same Clinique Happy perfume, bringing with it a rush of nostalgia, memories of childhood Christmases and road trips to Grandma's house.

While she and Grandma chatted, Dad beckoned to someone. Then hunky Nick Rush came into view, a frothing mug of beer in his hand.

Dad, you're so bad. Catching Dad's wink, she smirked in reply, her face aglow.

"Hey, kiddo." He gestured for her to sit next to Nick, who pulled out a chair for her, and she tossed him a grateful smile.

Dad performed the introductions. "Nick, this is my daughter DeeDee. DeeDee, meet Nick Rush, the band's newest member."

"Hey." Nick stuck out a hand, and she clasped his long, well-shaped fingers. Musician fingers. She almost forgot to muster a casual but friendly shake.

"Hi, Nick." Her voice came out husky as she admired his orbs of speckled green and blue. "Glad to meet you." She released his hand and lifted the martini glass to her mouth.

"Likewise." His head inclined slightly. DeeDee vaguely sensed Joy, August, and Dominic seating themselves on her other side.

DeeDee couldn't help herself. "I bet all the girls tell you that you look like Sting, don't they?"

He chuckled. "Thanks," he said in a clipped British accent. "Actually, you're the first."

"No way."

He nodded. "But I'll take it as a compliment. Better Sting than Mr. Bean, eh?"

"You would never be mistaken for Mr. Bean."

"Nor would you."

At her burst of laughter, his face crinkled. He took a sip of beer and regarded her over the rim of the mug, and her heart went into a gallop.

Such a promising start, but now she couldn't think of anything to say. She needed to think of something. And quick.

"Did you know Nils?" Lame. Very lame question.

He shook his head and lowered his mug. "I knew of him, although we never met. But you must have known him well, from his connection to your father."

"For as long as I can remember." DeeDee sipped her martini. "Until last summer, my sister and I were backup singers in his band."

"Ah." His eyes gleamed. "And what do you do now?"

She smiled and ran her tongue over her lips. "Livy and I own a dance school."

He angled closer, his smile mirroring hers. "I'm intrigued. What kind of dance?"

She set her glass down and arranged her face in solemn lines. "Anything but the Macarena."

As they shared a laugh, she tried to keep her mind and heart from wandering too far into the future. Yet if she ever were to settle down and share her life with someone, he'd look exactly like Nick Rush.

Chapter Twenty-One

Livy wailed inside, longing to throw these crutches in the lake. She peeked at Will, obviously still irritated since he refused to look at her. He did, however, bestow an awed glance at the security guards holding back a crush of shouting journalists.

Inside, she crept through the vast ballroom while voices echoed as noisy as a food court. Working her way around tables and chairs, she felt like a giraffe blundering through a shopping mall. Everyone must be watching her. Out of the corners of her eyes, she saw them nudging each other. They must be saying, there's poor Declan Decker's girl with a messed-up leg.

She spotted DeeDee and the family a mile away near the stage. Exhaling, she stared at the floor, and concentrated on the patterned carpet muffling her crutches' thud and her knee-length black skirt swirling above her ruined leg.

DeeDee sipped a martini and chatted with a good-looking blond man in a black dress shirt. His eyes caressed DeeDee. She flashed a distracted smile when they approached and Will helped Livy settle into a plaid-cushioned chair.

"Livs." DeeDee's voice barely rose above the clamor. "What took so long?"

Livy shifted, trying to get comfortable on the unyielding chair. "It takes me four times as long now to do everything. If not for my hero," Livy forced a smile at Will, "I couldn't have managed."

Will, his face still tense, claimed the chair beside her.

DeeDee nodded. "Let's get you some food." She whispered something to the blond guy. He dipped his head, his eyes never leaving her face.

"Will, follow me." DeeDee beckoned.

Will huffed and padded after DeeDee, and Livy waved at the rest of her family, trying to check out DeeDee's companion. DeeDee hadn't mentioned bringing a date. Perhaps he was a recent pick-up.

Joy leaned in from two chairs over. "Livy." She patted her mouth with a napkin. "Do you want to give a tribute tonight?"

Livy's mouth jerked in a frown. "No way. Sorry."

Joy stretched her arm and massaged Livy's shoulder. "If I could make this all go away, you know I would." Worry lines sprouted from the corners of her eyes, her black and white blouse leaching the color from her already pale face.

"I'll be all right, Joy."

Dad craned his neck toward the neighboring table and shouted a conversation with an LA music producer. Her brothers ignored everyone as they stuffed appetizers in their mouths and slurped Pepsi. The blond man studied her, brow arched.

"You must be Livy," he said in a cultured accent, half-standing as he held out his hand, his blue houndstooth tie brushing over his plate. "DeeDee's twin."

Livy grasped his hand. "Yes."

"I'm Nick Rush." He gave her hand a firm shake, emitting a whiff of musky scent.

"How do you know DeeDee?"

"I met her tonight." He settled in his chair. "Your father as well. He invited me to sit with you folks. I'm filling in on bass in lieu of John Kloberdanz."

"Oh."

He picked up a half-full mug of dark beer. "I understand you and DeeDee opened a dance school."

"Yes."

"Sounds like fun." He lifted the mug to his lips in a drawn-out sip.

"It is." Livy shrunk down, feeling monosyllabic. Today had been ghastly. Will had tried to be understanding, but this cast and those crutches—she was so ready to be done with them. The prospect of another five weeks of this horrified her, and poor Will took the brunt of it.

This afternoon he'd teased her while she'd struggled with her skirt and bemoaned her plight. "Where's the happy Livy I know and love?"

"She's buried inside a two-inch-thick cast!" she had snapped, followed by a curse. Will had lurched back like she'd slapped him. Despite her instant apology, the tension remained as dense as midnight fog.

Will and DeeDee returned with plates and wineglasses. As Will and Joy conversed on her left, and DeeDee and Nick chatted to her right, Livy twisted the silver wrap ring on her index finger round and round and studied the appetizers Will had brought her, hoping to work up an appetite. Stuffed pita pinwheels lined her plate, almost too symmetrical to eat. Butter pooled beneath bacon-wrapped asparagus. Yet her mouth remained dry.

She hated Will being mad at her.

Livy nudged him. "Hey, babe."

He turned. "Yeah?"

"Sorry again for being such a pain today." She pressed her lips into her sweetest smile. "You're a real trouper."

Will surveyed her from hooded eyes.

"I know you didn't deserve it." Was there a tiny crack piercing the ice between them? "C'mon, don't be mad." She brought her face inches from his. "I love you. You know that, right?" She batted her eyes, leaving butterfly kisses on his cheek.

The crack widened, and the ice fell away. "I love you too, babe." He reached across her shoulders to give her a squeeze. His mouth nuzzled her ear. "And I miss waking up next to you. Must be why I'm cranky."

She laughed and wrapped her arms around his shoulders and squeezed him back.

Morton bounded up the stage steps and hoisted the microphone. "Good evening, everyone." Beams of light bounced off his businesslike black glasses. "Thank you all for coming to pay tribute to our dear friend Nils Nelsson—"

Livy tuned him out. While guests came up and shared memories of Nils, some funny, some bittersweet, she picked at her food and sipped wine.

When Vienna grabbed the mike, Livy sat up. Vee's mile-high platform boots elevated her height to somewhere around five-foot-six, and her knee-length, black wrap dress just brushed their tops. Black hair perched high on her head while rhinestone cat-eye spectacles rested on her nose. She could have been a time-traveler from the sixties.

"Hey." She boomed into the mike, then jerked back and gave it a wary look. "Good evening, ladies and gentlemen! I am so pleased you came to pay your respects to my father. I have so many great memories of my dad. I want to share one very special story." Hand on heart, head cocked, she dropped her voice to a raspy whisper. "You all know my dad was talented. And smart. But most of all"—she threw out a dramatic hand—"my dad was really, really rich."

Chuckles resounded throughout the room. "Hi, Mommy!" Fleming's high voice squeaked from the next table.

Vienna stopped, her face pensive, mike sliding idle to her side as she paced. DeeDee pursed her lips to squelch laughter and scrunched her face as if leery of Vienna's next move.

Audria kept a firm arm around her suddenly restless grandson.

Livy held her breath. Hadn't Vienna heard her son over the laughter?

Vienna thrust her chin up, her face puckered with emotion. "I'll never forget the year I spent in Switzerland at a finishing school," she rasped in a dramatic whisper.

Livy and DeeDee grinned. Vienna never attended school anywhere but Seattle.

"True story, ladies and gentlemen, true story! At Christmas break, I said to my father, 'Dad—I feel so bad whenever I drive to school in the Ferrari you shipped over there. My classmates take buses and trains everywhere they go.'

"My dad said to me, 'I understand exactly how you feel, tiger. And I have the solution.' He took me into his office and wrote me a check for two million dollars. 'What's this for?' I asked. And then he said..." Vienna cocked her head, a faraway look in her eyes. "'Can't you guess? Now you can go buy your own bus and train.'"

Laughter rang out while Vienna grinned and bowed. "True story!" She stuck the mike in the stand and raised her hands with an ear-to-ear smile, soaking in the applause.

Audria's hands cupped her face. Laughter hid beneath her shaking shoulders. Fleming took the opportunity to bolt from Audria's lap and run to the stage. But Zach scooped him up and hugged the whining, wiggling boy against his chest. When Fleming wouldn't calm down, Zach spun to the exit, but not before glowering at Vienna, who glared back as she stormed down the steps.

Livy could almost see flaming darts flying through the air. Vienna stalked after Zach, but with security so tight, no way would she get very far. Livy wished she could see the altercation that must surely be taking place in the lobby.

The crowd sat through several more speeches before Dad bounced up to the stage with the energy of a twenty-year-old. "C'mon up, band," he yelled into the mike. "Time to rock this town!"

Nick Rush and four other guys jumped up and ran onto the stage. "We're gonna be covering my best buddy Nils's favorite band — third favorite, that is, after The FireAnts! And Free The Defendants!" He waited for the chuckles to die down. "Ladies and gentlemen — AC! DC!" Applause burst forth as the chainsaw riffs of "Thunderstruck" vibrated the room. Dad swung the mike stand in a wide arc and belted with vigor. His Bon Scott growl was infectious. Soon the crowd chanted along.

"*Thunder! Thunder!*" Will looked as alive as she'd ever seen him. He grabbed her shoulder. "This is great," he yelled into her ear.

The song ended. The band mates crouched before taking a final leap and punching their fists in the air.

"And now, friends," Dad shouted. "Nils's favorite ACDC song — 'Highway to Hell'!"

The guitarist thrummed the opening measures. The drummer pounded sticks at a punishing pace. Dad and his scratchy whine wailed into the mike.

The room rocked with cheers and claps, but Livy barely noticed. Dad kept screaming about the highway to Hell until she wanted to clap her hands over her ears.

Livy wished she'd never laid eyes on that book. For if it were true, they were in a heap of trouble, far worse than any of them could imagine. If the book were true, they shouldn't be here celebrating Nils's life. They should be mourning and weeping the fact that he was cut off from God.

Despair dragged at her like a sack of weights. Did the lyrics' implication strike anyone else? DeeDee swayed, eyes closed. Audria smiled serenely and sang along. Will tapped his foot and clapped. August and Dominic bobbed with the beat.

The descriptions of Hell she'd read pulsed through her. Outer darkness. Weeping and gnashing of teeth. Like the stuff of horror movies. Grandma always assured them Hell was a myth. Yet Livy couldn't shake her dream, and the dark, frightening place she'd seen.

Panic bubbled inside her like poison-laced soda. She pounded DeeDee's arm. Startled, her twin whipped around.

"Bathroom break?" Livy mouthed.

DeeDee scowled. "Right at the good part."

"Sorry," Livy muttered as DeeDee and Will helped her rise. At her turtle pace, it took forever to escape the room, those lyrics. The words kept assaulting her ears. She pictured Bon Scott screaming them. He died years ago of alcohol poisoning. Where was he now?

"Liv, you don't look good." DeeDee frowned as she helped Livy maneuver onto the toilet. "Are you feeling okay?"

"I've had an awful, dreadful day," Livy moaned. "I kept snapping at poor Will, and I'm feeling weighed down, not like myself at all."

"Those nasty pain pills—"

"I know, right? But I can't go off them yet. I still hurt a lot."

"Repeat after me: This is only temporary."

"This is only temporary. This. Is. Only. Temporary." Soon Livy giggled, her panic eased, and DeeDee chuckled and helped her to the sink.

"You're so right. It is only temporary." The warm water soothed her. She needed to get her mind off her panic attack. "So tell me about Nick," she said, her voice bright, the trembles subsiding. "You two seem to be hitting it off."

"Oh, he's so cool," DeeDee gushed. "I've found out all

kinds of interesting things about him. He's from Victoria, BC, and he knows all the members of the band Rush."

"That's awesome, Deeds." Livy wiped her hands on a paper towel. "You seem different tonight. You've had one, maybe two drinks all night. What's up?" She tossed the towel in the bronze-plated receptacle.

"Oh." DeeDee shrugged. "Audria gave me a talking-to about the way I behave with men. I figured I ought to stay clear-eyed if I want to get anywhere with the Nick Rushes of the world."

"Well, he seems to like what he sees."

DeeDee's smug grin betrayed her pleasure. "I definitely like what *I* see." She flung her handbag over her shoulder. "Ready?"

They made their ponderous way to the table. Livy mulled over the pesky book. "I am the way, the truth, and the life," Jesus told his friends. "No man cometh unto the Father but by Me."

Chapter Twenty-Two

Livy started her Sunday morning in her favorite spot in the house — the sunroom's Papasan wicker chair from Pier One Imports. She loved the wall-to-wall windows that kept the room in perpetual daylight until sundown, even on the dreariest of days. The potted bamboo trees in the corner and the tropical-print futon evoked memories of trips to Hawaii. They'd set aside the spacious open area on the south wall for dancing, Pilates, or yoga.

She opened her e-mail. "Hi, **Scott**," she typed. She snuck a glance at the door, though she knew DeeDee still slept. Her thick robe wrapped her in warmth as she basked inside a solar beam. Dust particles danced in midair around her. She shifted the laptop from the glare and adjusted her reading glasses. Her fingers flew across the keyboard like a master pianist.

When she finished, she picked up the list of parents' contact information from Saffire and double-checked the e-mail address. Then she hit Send.

***

Scott had dropped his daughters off at their Sunday school class when their teacher Claire, a plump, chestnut-haired woman in her twenties, laid a hand on his arm.

"Scott." Her eyes were eager, her smile fixed.

He waited politely.

"Are you going to the singles' meeting tonight? We're having pizza."

"No, probably not." He sounded terse, but he didn't want to encourage Claire. His vibrating cell phone rescued him. Exhaling, he patted his pocket. "I think someone is messaging me. I need to see who."

"Okay." She retreated.

He lifted his phone. A new e-mail awaited. He leaned against the wall.

> Hi Scott, this is Livy.

Livy? The last person he expected.

> I've been reading that book, *Religion or Christ*. It's very interesting, but I don't know anyone, besides you, who believes Jesus was more than an awesome dude who walked the earth a couple thousand years ago. I picture him a bit like the prophet Mohammed. I don't understand why there's so much disagreement over who he was.
> Question. Some people claim religion has been responsible for a lot of the suffering in the world, such as poverty and wars. What is your take?
> Thanks. I appreciate your taking time to answer me.—Livy.

A mixture of sensations stirred his heart—flattered Livy sought his input, humbled and honored. He found a seat in the sanctuary next to Rick and Paula. "Hey, guess what. God's answering our prayers."

***

While Livy waited for Scott's reply, she exchanged texts with Will and caught up on social media. Anxious to know what Scott had to say, she checked her e-mail every fifteen minutes.

> Hi Livy,
> I told your sister to tell you I'm praying for you. I trust she passed along my message. How are you doing? I hope your injury hasn't been too tough on you. Life's hard enough with two good legs. I'm glad you're reading the book. It's yours to keep.
> I did some research, and here are some links to help answer your question. What struck me was atheists, not Christians, instigated many of the wars and mass killings. As for poverty, political corruption, not religion, causes much of it. I hope you'll find them helpful.
> My question for you is: do you believe the message of the book? If so, what will you do with it?
> Blessings—Scott.

***

DeeDee was surfing the web Sunday morning when her phone rang. She grabbed it and read an unfamiliar number. If it proved to be who she hoped it was, then two things were true: Her behavior modifications worked, and Nick Rush was a keeper.

"Hello?"

"Hey, DeeDee?" A sexy accented male voice greeted her. "This is Nick. How are you?"

"Hi, Nick." *Do not* gush, girl. "Really good. And you?"

"Good, good. Still feeling last night's party."

DeeDee laughed. "In a good way, I hope."

"A very good way."

Good this, and good that. They must sound like parrots. Was he as nervous as she?

"The band sounded amazing." She stood and paced.

"Thanks. We enjoyed it too. I also enjoyed getting to know *you*." His pause stretched, thick with meaning. "Can I buy you dinner tonight?"

"That's so nice of you, Nick." Time to lay some sweet lines on him. "I would love to have dinner with you." She eased into her puffy recliner and nestled in for a long conversation.

***

Hi, Scott.

Livy hunched at her bedroom desk and squinted at the keyboard, her purple velvet pillow tucked securely behind her back. After several false starts, she settled into a rhythm.

Thanks for replying and praying. I could use prayer right now. This cast is annoying. I don't know yet what I think about the book's message. Christianity still confuses me. Can you clarify something? I understand the Holocaust took place on the Christians' watch. Wasn't Nazi Germany a strong Christian nation with lots of churchgoers? Why did the church allow it? I don't mean to sound hostile, but the book never addressed that issue.
Thanks—Livy.

***

Livy—You didn't sound hostile at all. A lot of people have the same concerns. Christianity started as allegiance to Christ.

The very first Christians were Jesus' disciples and their converts. But when Constantine made Christianity an official religion, it was no longer about Christ. It was about the church, money, and politics. Being a Christian in name only won't get a person to heaven. In Nazi Germany, the people may have attended church, but true Christ-followers sheltered Jews from the Nazis. It might interest you to know Hitler was an atheist. He courted the church for political purposes, not because he was a believer.

I encourage you to keep thinking about the claims of Christ. Your eternal future is at stake.

Take care of yourself, okay?

Blessings and prayers—Scott.

PS—Do you have a Bible? I have an extra one lying around here if you want it.

Livy read the links he'd sent. Why hadn't she known Christianity had done so much good in the world? After satisfying herself that the articles were well researched and impartial, she read about Christians' role in abolishing slavery in England and the US. She'd assumed the American slave owners were Christians, and the Abolitionists were social justice activists like Grandma and her friends. This article said most of them were strong churchgoing Christians who knew slavery was wrong.

Why didn't her family and friends know that? Who was right?

Chapter Twenty-Three

DeeDee awoke and stretched, proud of her restraint last night. How unusual for the other side of her bed to be vacant following a hot date. When Nick kissed her goodnight, he'd promised a phone call and another date the following weekend, even though she didn't invite him in. Maybe he was an old-fashioned, chivalrous type. She could get used to such a man.

Bunching her yellow-striped comforter under her chin, she reached for her phone and pulled up Audria's number to thank her for the motherly advice.

"Hey, Aunt Bestie—"

"DeeDee, I'm *so* glad you called." Words tripped off her friend's tongue. "I have a huge, *huge* favor to ask of you."

DeeDee went still. "What kind of favor?"

"How would you feel about hiring Vienna to teach Livy's classes?"

The imaginary punch to DeeDee's gut nearly flung her off the bed. Grasping for her nightstand to steady herself, she knocked her water bottle over. "You have to be kidding me," she hissed, watching the water pool and spread on the hardwood floor. "Huh uh. Not a chance. Not going to happen."

"It would mean so much to her."

DeeDee bounded out of bed and wove her way around several pairs of boots she couldn't decide among last night. "You know I don't trust your druggie daughter." She grabbed a burgundy towel lying on the walk-in closet floor. "She thinks I'm going to let her anywhere near the studio? She's insane."

"It's just that…"

DeeDee flung the towel over the puddle and stomped on it. "What?"

"She needs something productive to do."

"Why is this so important to you, Audria?" The waterlogged towel darkened two shades. DeeDee knelt and scrubbed the floorboards, circling the towel over and over, digging it into the cracks as if they were intentionally hoarding moisture. "It's not like she needs money."

"Her probation officer suggested she get a job."

"I don't give a flying flip what her PO suggested. It's her own fault she got busted."

"Please, DeeDee?"

She scooped up the towel and carried it to the bathroom to dry. "I can handle teaching all six classes for a while. And if I can't, I'll hire someone. *Not* Vienna."

"You're the only person I know who's tough enough to handle her." Audria's final arrow broke DeeDee's resolve. "You know why this is important to me?" A faint noise—a sniffle?—carried over the line. "Seeing Fleming Saturday made me realize how much I miss him. It hurts that he's so far away." Her voice cracked. "But if Vienna can get her act together, maybe she could regain custody of Fleming, and I could see my grandson again."

DeeDee uttered an oath and flung a hand in the air. "All right then. But I'm consulting an attorney first."

"Thank you, my friend. You won't regret it."

"I regret it already." Where had she heard that line? *Fiddler On The Roof.* She and Tevye, in solidarity. Imagine that.

She dropped the phone into her bag. She must be crazy. Time to reopen Saffire and seek out a human resources attorney with the name of Attila the Hun.

She tap-tapped on Livy's door and peered in. Livy's fingers were flying over her laptop. She whirled around, wide-eyed, secrecy cloaking her face.

"Whatcha doing?" DeeDee stepped inside.

"Catching up on e-mails." Effort lurked behind her casual tone. "What are you up to?"

"You aren't going to believe what I let Audria talk me into."

Livy minimized her screen and gave DeeDee her full attention.

***

Once DeeDee enclosed herself in Saffire's office, she pulled up Livy's e-mail. Yep, the password automatically filled in. A finger of guilt needled her, but greedy curiosity drove her on. She had to know why Livy acted so secretive this morning—which wasn't the first time she recently acted like she had something to hide.

They never kept secrets. If Livy did something behind DeeDee's back, it must be terribly shameful.

Or she was planning a surprise.

It wasn't the second option. She felt it.

She scanned the inbox, skipped over solicitations, and stopped—Scott Lorenzo. Her heart plummeted to her toes. How could Livy two-time Will, much less with someone like Scott?

DeeDee clicked the most recent one and read the exchange. She pressed her fingers to her cheeks, unable to stop a horrified gasp. Worse than two-timing, her sister was being indoctrinated by a religious freak. After all Grandma's warnings, Livy dared turn her back on the values she'd been raised with—tolerance, peace, justice. No wonder she hadn't wanted DeeDee to know.

DeeDee sunk lower in the chair and read the entire

conversation. This was huge. She couldn't let Livy know she'd spied on her. She couldn't tell anyone.

She opened the sent box to a message sent to Scott less than an hour ago—right when DeeDee walked in on her.

> Hi Scott,
> No, I don't have a bible. I've never owned one. But it might be nice. I'll be at the dance studio off and on this week. Do you want to stop by one of these evenings? I'll try to be there. Thanks—Livy.

DeeDee dropped her head on her arms and waited for the desolate betrayal to subside.

***

"Deeds." Livy pulled a red plaid throw over her legs as she reclined on the sectional while waiting for Will. "I want to start getting in some time at the office. I'm going stir-crazy. Can you take me with you this week?" Adjusting the paisley pillow more firmly behind her neck, she arranged her face in its most beseeching expression.

DeeDee, her booted feet resting on the teakwood coffee table, gave her a strange look. "I don't think you're ready."

She'd been putting out an odd vibe all day. "What do you mean, I'm not ready? Why do you get to decide?"

"You still need to rest," said DeeDee in a soothing tone. "The doctor didn't say you could go to work yet."

Livy snorted. "Well, obviously, I'm not going to teach dance. But I don't see why I can't get the books caught up."

DeeDee's eyes shifted away. "We'll see."

The doorbell rang. Murf yipped and ran toward the door, his toenails clattering on the wood floor.

"My honey's here. Come in!" Livy called out, and Will

entered, bearing pizza and beer, his eyes alight. Murf uttered a couple of unconvincing barks, and then plopped to the floor wagging his tail, ears pointed to the ceiling, his eyes alert and watchful.

Livy lifted the lever and raised herself to a sitting position. Will plunked beside her. She sniffed. "That smells so good."

Will squeezed her in a one-armed hug. "So do you." DeeDee hastily removed her feet when he set the pizza and six-pack on the coffee table. He folded Livy into a proper hug, and then planted an enthusiastic kiss on her lips. It felt so good. Saturday's spat long forgotten, he felt like her Cuddleman again.

Murf yipped and lunged for the box. "No, Murf." Thankfully, DeeDee scooped the wriggling puppy into her firm grasp. Will opened the pizza box and held it in front of her.

She eyed the bubbling cheese and embedded veggies, smelled the overpowering essence of sausage. Her mouth watered as she mentally calculated the calories in one piece. *Just one piece.* Considering her sudden drop in physical activity, she couldn't be a carefree eater anymore. She slid out the smallest slice.

DeeDee's phone chimed, and her face lit when she checked the display. It must be Nick. DeeDee and her big white smile left the room, Murf tucked under her arm.

Will stared after her. "Hard to believe you two are twins."

"I know, right? We're so different."

He eased out a slice of sausage-and-onion. "You might already know this." He scooped up dripping cheese. "But she's a boss lady. Whereas you're a sweet thing."

"Some people say we don't look much alike." She nibbled the crust first.

"No." He scrutinized her. "You're easier on the eyes."

Livy laughed. "How can that be? We're identical."

Will shrugged. "I don't know." His tone hardened. "All the makeup she wears makes her look overcooked."

Livy laughed harder. "Overcooked? Then am I undercooked?"

"No, you're just right." With a sudden movement, he tossed the pizza aside and grabbed her around the waist. She let out a soft sigh. "Ah, Livy." His eyes held hers for a moment as he fingered a strand of her hair.

DeeDee wandered back in, sans Murf, breaking the spell.

He cast her a resentful glance, then picked up the remote. "Anything good on TV tonight?"

Every three seconds, he flipped the channel. Livy, warmed by Will's presence, tossed the pillow and throw aside and finished off her pizza slice. A pompadoured preacher appeared on the screen and disappeared amid a burst of laughter. Livy flapped her hand. "Wait. Go back. I want to see that preacher guy."

Will crinkled his face as he flipped to the religious station. "Why would you want to watch this?"

"Those guys amuse me." Would the preacher talk about Jesus? If so, would she get a burning feeling inside again?

DeeDee wandered out again. Livy found Will's hand and sat mesmerized by the interview. Instead of preaching, the big-haired man turned to someone seated next to him. Livy pointed. "Hey. My dad knows him."

Will's eyes lit up. "His band is incredible."

The long-haired singer gazed at the preacher. "I had millions of dollars, but no joy, no contentment. Now that I have Jesus, I have joy I never found in drugs."

The host pasted a beatific smile on his face. "Praise God, praise God."

The singer looked directly at the camera. His gaze latched

on her through miles of cyberspace. "My friends, whether you're young or old, rich or poor, you'll never find contentment except in Jesus Christ."

She shivered.

Will peeked at her. "You want to keep watching?"

She nodded without speaking.

He gave a baffled chuckle. "I didn't think this was your type of show."

"Shh. I want to hear what he's saying."

The singer talked about the almighty love of God for mankind. "How can anyone reject such a huge love?" he asked the host.

Her heart skipped, shifted into slow motion. Maybe Dad should be watching this, too. She picked up her phone and texted. He replied in less than a minute. *Heard his story several times. Thx anyway.*

The interview ended, and she faced Will. "We've never talked about our religious beliefs, have we, sweets?"

"Maybe because neither of us is religious?"

She propped her elbow against the sofa back and rested her head on her palm. "Did you go to church as a kid?"

"I did." He nodded, eyeing her. "A church down the street. Went to Sunday school until sometime in middle school."

"We pretty much never went." She tousled his hair. "My family didn't have a very high opinion of organized religion."

"My family was Anglican. Handed down from my Grandpa Shropshire, of the Cumbrian Shropshires. Northwest England, you know." His eyes took on a faraway look, as though squinting fifty years into the past. "He immigrated here in 1950. My father was born soon after, but the religion thing never caught on with him."

Livy raked her fingers through his hair. "But you believe in God, don't you?"

"I'm not sure." An uneasy note echoed between them. "I'm one of those people who figure if God is up there somewhere, He'll tell me. So far I haven't heard a word."

"I think I'm starting to believe in God."

Will grasped her hand. "I don't want to talk about religion." He lifted her palm, planting on it the softest of kisses. Clicking off the TV, he wrapped his arms around her in a koala-bear hug. "Right now," he whispered, "I want to talk about us."

Chapter Twenty-Four

Wednesday morning, DeeDee shuffled a stack of papers and shoved the first one across the desk in front of Vienna's stoic face. Keeping her eyes on the paper, DeeDee recited, "This is an I9. Put your number of withholdings right here—"

"Wait a sec," Vienna interrupted. "I thought you were paying me under the table."

"Nope. We're a legitimate business. We don't do 'under the table.' Fill in the top part and sign here."

Vienna eyed the paper, then the second form in DeeDee's hand.

"This is our drug and alcohol policy." DeeDee palmed the sheet. "'Any employee who reports to work under the influence of drugs or alcohol is subject to immediate termination.'" She scratched a big X at the bottom of the form. "Sign here."

"Dude. Why you be all businesslike?"

"These are the standard HR forms most businesses use. If you don't want to sign them," she jabbed her thumb, "there's the door."

Vienna rolled her eyes, muttering expletives.

"Now, that'll get you fired, missy." DeeDee thrust an index finger at Vienna's face. "Especially if you do it in front of the kids. Got it? No swearing or dirty jokes."

"It's not like you don't do it, too."

"Not in front of kids, I don't. If you think you're above the rules, then get up and go home right now."

Vienna shook her head and stared at the next form.

"This is our absentee policy," droned DeeDee. "'Any employee who is unable to report to work due to illness must inform his or her supervisor prior to his or her regularly scheduled time. Three sick days in a row require a doctor's note in order to return to work. Employees who fail to report to work without notifying supervisor are subject to termination.'" DeeDee slapped the form on the desk and looked Vee full in the eye. "Any questions?"

"Yeah," Vienna rasped. "Fifteen bucks an hour ain't much."

"I'm sorry. Would you rather I pay you the going rate of ten?"

Vienna slumped.

"Oh, there's one more." DeeDee plucked a final form off the printer. "Our confidentiality agreement. What happens here, stays here. And that includes no talking about our fathers." She smacked the pen down. "Sign, please."

Vienna picked up the pen, eyed it, rolled it in her fingers. DeeDee crossed her arms. What would she do if Vienna refused to sign?

After a moment's hesitation, Vienna flipped to the first sheet and began scrawling. The silence amplified the gurgling fountain, saturating the room with forest music.

"Done." Vienna flipped the last sheet face down. "Now what?"

DeeDee reached in the drawer for one more printed sheet. "Your schedule. You'll be teaching my classes, and I'll teach Livy's. Your first class is this afternoon at four. The lyrical class. Be back here by three so I can get you up to speed."

She shoved the stack of signed forms into the copier. The machine whirred. Vienna watched in silence.

When the whirring stopped, DeeDee handed Vienna the warm stack of photocopies. "These are for you to show your probation officer. You're free to go. See you at three." Vienna slunk out of the room, and DeeDee checked the text she knew waited for her. It was from Livy.

Can you drive me to the studio tonight at 7?

DeeDee sucked in a breath. Yeah right, just so Livy could meet Scott and get a Bible.

Sorry, no. I'll be busy. It's V's first day. She sniffed, mystified by the sudden prickling sensation in her nose, behind her eyes.

Livy's reply came seconds later. *You're acting weird lately.*

So are you. She couldn't stop an errant tear from sneaking down her cheek.

***

Livy's eyes burned when she read DeeDee's text. All week, DeeDee had been short with her. Now DeeDee accused *her* of acting weird.

Was Deeds bothered because Livy had been less than friendly to Nick at Nils's service? Maybe Nick didn't like her now. But no, that couldn't be it. DeeDee would never choose a man over her twin.

After all, Will didn't like DeeDee. And Livy knew where her loyalty would lie if forced to choose. The old song "Sisters" said it best. Like the Haynes sisters in *White Christmas*, she'd never let a man come between her and DeeDee.

Up until this week, she'd been confident DeeDee's answer would be the same.

Livy sucked in a sob. If DeeDee was going to be a shrew, she'd go with Plan B. She removed her phone and texted Scott. *I don't have transpo to Saffire tonight. Do you mind coming here?*

***

The doorbell rang, and Livy hobbled over. Murf, barking, beat her to it.

"Murf! Go sit." The dog cast her a reproachful look and plopped on his haunches.

"Come in!" she called. Murf yipped and lurched forward.

"Murf! Stay!" The pup retreated with his tail curled between his legs.

Scott, stiff-faced, pushed the door open, holding a thick book. His gaze flicked over her, then settled on Murf.

She leaned against the arched entryway. "Come on in."

He entered and closed the door. "How are you feeling?"

Like I got hit by a car. She gave a half-smile. "Better, thanks."

Murf approached with a grin and a wag, his little body vibrating excitedly. Scott's face relaxed a few degrees. "What a fine-looking puppy."

"Thanks." She held out her sock-covered foot to Murf, who licked her toes. "This is Murf."

"I'm partial to sled dogs, too. How old is he?"

"Just a few months. He is a lovable thing." She adjusted her crutches and gestured with her head. "Why don't you come sit down? Murf won't mind. Will you, Murf?" she crooned.

Scott bent to pat the dog's head. Murf danced around and licked his hand.

She chuckled. "As far as he's concerned, my buds are his buds." She led the way into the sunroom, Murf pattering after them. "Let's sit in here. If DeeDee comes home early, you can slip out this door." She indicated the side porch exit. "I wouldn't want her to get the wrong idea." Her nervous laugh echoed in her ears. When she saw Scott's face, she wished she could grab the words back. The poor guy resembled a high schooler on his first date.

"What about your boyfriend?" He ran his hand over his

head and glanced around uneasily, as though Will were hiding in wait.

"He's at his daughter's school play tonight." She perched on the futon's tropical print cushion and propped her injured leg on the matching ottoman. "Amity has the fitting role of Medusa."

Murf seemed content to box with Miss Piggy. Livy hoped his yelps wouldn't distract them. Miss Piggy solved the problem by charging out the door, Murf hard on her heels.

She laughed as Scott settled on the green suede flip chair. "Those two fight like a couple of kids."

He smiled. "Makes me miss my dog. I had a Malamute until last year."

"What happened to him?"

"We had to put him down. Cancer."

"I'm sorry."

"Not to worry. I have nothing but good memories of him."

"I almost got a Malamute puppy. He was so cute. But something about Murf made me fall in love with him. He was just a little white fur ball with eyes."

Scott laughed, and the tension dissolved. "You made a good choice. Samoyeds make awesome pets. They're pretty low-maintenance. Except their fur."

He handed her the heavy book, covered in rich, blue leather. "Anyway, I could talk dogs all night. Here's the Bible I promised you."

Livy grasped the book. "Thank you. I don't think I've ever seen one before." She eyed it with reverence. "How do you read one of these? Start at the beginning?" She quaked at its thickness.

"I'd say start at the Gospel of John." Scott held out his hand. "Here, let me help get you familiar with it."

He moved to her right and took the Bible, then opened it

to the table of contents. Frail pages rustled beneath his larger fingers. She winced at each flip, afraid they'd rip at the slightest tug. She peered at the list of ancient-sounding names.

Scott's finger stopped halfway down. "Here's your starting point." He handed it back. "See if you can find it yourself."

She thumbed to the spot, the name John jumping off the page. A jolt of recognition coursed over her. *In the beginning was the Word—*

"—and the Word was with God," she whispered as she met Scott's eyes, "and the Word was God."

"Do you believe that?" His gaze probed hers.

"I'm not sure. I'm struggling to wrap my mind around the one God, three persons thing."

"I know. I've never been able to wrap my brain around it, either. I don't know anyone who can."

She blinked, jerked away. "Then how can you believe it?"

He shifted against the futon's cushioned back. "Can you wrap your brain around the universe?"

She cocked her head. "What do you mean?"

"You believe it exists, but do you understand how the universe can be three components in one?"

"I've never heard anything about the universe being three components in one."

"You probably learned it in school." He angled to face her. "The universe consists of space, time, and matter. Yet it's one universe."

"Oh, right."

"Take any one of those away, and there's no universe."

"Hmm—"

"The universe is so vast—nobody knows where it ends or what's on the other side."

"Trippy."

He chuckled. "Yeah, trippy." He nodded at the Bible. "Like God Himself."

A sense of something huge and unfathomable gripped her.

"Imagine if time didn't exist. The universe itself couldn't exist. Time is one of those intangible concepts ready to boggle the mind if you think about it too long. What is time, anyway? And what would the absence of time look like?"

Livy laughed to mask her uneasiness. "Reminds me of old song lyrics from the sixties."

Scott smiled. "I'm getting philosophical, aren't I? My point is, I can't justify rejecting the concept of God being three persons in one when the universe itself is so far beyond my comprehension, yet I can believe in it."

"I think I'm starting to get it."

"So now what?"

"What do you mean?"

"When you truly believe in something, you put your faith in it."

Something inside her resisted. "What about all those gods and goddesses my Grandma Gaia believes in? What are they?"

Scott's brows gathered in a frown. "They're no gods at all. They're—" He stopped, seeming to shift gears. "The God of the Bible is high above all other gods. He's the ultimate God. Maybe you could ask your grandma why she worships inferior beings when she could be worshiping the Supreme Being."

Livy shook her head. "No, I—"

"What did you say her name was?"

"Gaia." Livy lowered her injured leg to the floor and twisted back and forth, trying to ease the kink in her side. "She legally changed her name from Gail to Gaia while in college. She named herself after the Greek earth goddess."

Scott's face went taut. "I'd say that's a real clear message."

"Of what?"

"Of where she's at spiritually."

"She's very spiritual."

He glanced at the Bible. "The book you're holding is God's handbook for all things spiritual."

Livy squinted at the tiny words. "I doubt my grandma would agree."

"Maybe not. But if God is speaking to your heart, Livy…" Scott tapped his chest. "If you're truly convinced Christ is who He says He is, it's time to tell Him so."

Livy stared with unseeing eyes at the page. The persistent glow filled her chest again, like a steady campfire. Something pulled at her, but she didn't know what.

"I don't know," she murmured. "I just don't know."

Hadn't she always sensed something big out there, just beyond her grasp? Even as a child, she'd known there had to be more to life than enduring a meaningless sequence of events, and then dying.

"For most of my life," Livy said in a near whisper, "I've been told we get reborn into a different life after we die." She leaned toward him and searched his face. "I was told our bodies are garments we shed, but our souls live on, and we get a new change of clothes with each lifecycle."

"Reincarnation, you mean?" His tone was gentle, understanding.

"Yes."

"Who's in charge of the reincarnation process?"

"Karma, I suppose."

"So Karma gets to decide how you'll be reborn in the next life?"

"Well, it all depends on how I live *this* life."

"Do you trust Karma with your life? Are you confident

Karma has your best interests at heart? Did Karma die for you?"

Despite the relentless tone, a twinkle shimmered in his eye. She responded with a soft laugh. "Sounds like you're saying God is better than Karma."

His laugh echoed hers. "Exactly." He reached for the Bible. "Can I show you something?"

She nodded and passed him the book. He flipped to another page, pointing. "Read this."

Livy squinted. "'It is appointed unto men once to die, but after this the judgment.'"

She whipped her head around.

A tiny smile creased his face. "There's your answer."

They sat in comfortable silence. New ideas and sensations whirled through her mind and heart. If she were to believe in Christ, what would it do to her relationship with DeeDee? With Will?

"I want to believe," she burst out. "But my family and Will would never understand."

He nodded. "'Now is the accepted time; behold, now is the day of salvation,'" he quoted, his voice soft. "Second Corinthians 6:2."

Livy gave a little cry. "I need to sleep on this."

He opened his mouth, but clamped it shut.

She closed the Bible, set it gently on the cushion, and started to rise, but her stockinged foot slipped sideways on the slick floor, sending her flailing off balance. A swift pain knifed through her left calf, and she stifled a cry. Before she could stop herself, she splayed across Scott's knees, her shoulder digging into his thigh.

For a long moment, she couldn't move. What a klutz. Dare she look at him? What must he think of her?

She peeped upward. His eyes were round, his mouth twisted in amusement.

She sputtered. He laughed. She giggled and tried to rise. "What just happened?"

He gripped her shoulders and lifted her with ease. "Looked to me like you lost your balance." He set her back against the futon cushion as if she were a limp ragdoll.

She giggled again, and then burst into loud snuffles. He laughed with her. "Oh, I'm so sorry." Her laughter escalated, and their hilarity rippled through the room, bounced off the windows.

A pair of headlights swept the room. "Oh no!" Livy screeched. "Someone turned into the driveway." She tried to rise again.

Scott held out an arm. "Don't get up." His tone was firm. "I'll leave right now." He strode to the side door. "I'll text you tomorrow." Waving, he slipped out. Livy grabbed the Bible and stuck it underneath the cushion as footsteps pattered through the living room.

"Livy?" a deep voice called.

She had no sooner lay down than Will peeked in. "Baby," he said, his eyes wide and worried. "Why didn't you answer my texts?"

"Will," she cried. "I'm so glad you're here. I left my phone in my room. Sorry." She reached for him, and he came over and snuggled inside her embrace. "How was the play?"

"My daughter stole the show." He beamed. They lay face to face, sharing soft and intimate words, while Livy's heart throbbed in relief over the near miss. Maybe it *was* true God cared personally for her. She sighed, basking in the warmth filling her heart, and pondered the possibility of a personal God existing, a God powerful enough to orchestrate even the little things.

***

Scott's heart raced as he strode along the side of Livy's

house, out to the street where he'd parked. He looked sidelong at the house and saw, in the beam of the porch light, the front door closing. He inhaled a deep breath, unnerved. Not that he and Livy had been doing anything wrong. But what if the person walked in with Livy sprawled on his lap?

He sequestered himself in his car. "Thanks, Lord, for making sure that didn't happen. And, Lord, I pray you'll bring Livy all the way into the Kingdom tonight."

His heart burst with something he couldn't name. Before he started the engine, he texted Paula. *Pray for Livy. She's got one foot in the Kingdom.*

Seconds later the phone rang. "Hello?" He cranked the ignition.

Paula's voice shook though the speakers. "Scott. How did it go with Livy?"

"I get the feeling she's right on the verge."

"Praise the Lord. How huge would that be? The daughter of a famous rocker gets saved."

"It could have a ripple effect."

"It sure could." Paula paused. "Did you get a chance to mention our potluck tomorrow?"

"No, I didn't. Someone drove up, so I left." He cranked the wheel toward Rosemary Drive. "I'll tell her tomorrow. If she does come, I don't think we should say anything about her father."

"I won't. And I'll tell Rick not to." She sighed. "I sure hope she can make it. Be sure to tell her I'll be happy to pick her up."

"I will." He hooked a left onto his street. "Thanks. I don't think I ought to spend time alone with a good-looking single woman."

"I don't mind at all."

Pulling into his driveway, he pressed the remote on the sunshade, and the garage door slid open. "By the way, I think

I'll be ready to test the device tomorrow. I'm pretty sure it'll work this time. How about after the potluck we give it a whirl?"

Paula agreed, and they said goodbye. Scott rolled into the garage and sat, deep in thought. What about Livy tugged his heart? Was it her intense blue eyes seemingly latching onto his whenever they talked? Her belly laugh somehow sounding like a tree full of happy birds? Maybe the way she reminded him of a flower garden — her scent, flowing clothes, silky hair.

He picked up his water bottle and swigged as though to wash thoughts of her away. He'd better not fall for someone else's girl.

Yanking on the door handle, he punched the garage door remote, waited as the door slid closed, and then stomped into his empty house.

Chapter Twenty-Five

Livy stood in her sister's bedroom doorway. "Deeds, can we talk?"

With a disinterested glance, DeeDee patted the bed next to her, and then sat silent and cross-legged on the yellow satin comforter.

"I want to talk about the texts today." Livy carefully propped herself on the edge and leaned the crutches next to her.

"What about 'em?"

"You've been so detached with me all week." Livy winced. She sounded like a whiny child. "Can you tell me why?"

"No, you're the one who's been detached." DeeDee reached for a bottle of tangerine nail polish and shook it.

Livy reared back, nearly lurching off the bed. "I have not!"

"You sneak around like you have something to hide—"

"What?" She gripped the comforter to hold herself in place. She would've jumped off the bed if she'd been capable of it.

"Why don't you tell me what you're hiding?"

"I'm not hiding anything."

She knows. Livy's heart knotted.

"Don't lie." DeeDee shook the nail polish harder, as though trying to shake sense into Livy. "You know I can read you like a book."

Livy fingered the comforter. What should she say? "Well,

then," she chewed her lip, "if you can read me like a book, *you* tell *me* what I'm hiding."

DeeDee crossed her arms. "Okay, I will." Her chin lifted. Disdain glittered in her suddenly hard eyes. "I had an interesting conversation with Grandma on Monday. She said you asked if she prays to Jesus. I think you're on a little religious kick, and you're afraid to tell me."

Livy gasped. Granted, their closeness sometimes made them think as one, but for DeeDee to guess the truth so easily…

"See?" DeeDee pointed the polish at Livy's face. "By looking at you, I can tell I'm right."

"Okay." Tears prickled her eyes. "I'm on a religious kick. But I didn't want to share it because I knew we couldn't go there together." She tried for a casual shrug. "Ever since my accident, I've been thinking about Jesus and God. Why don't you let me figure things out for myself without being mad I'm not sharing with you?"

"You've been thinking about Jesus and God." Contempt rang in her echo.

With her finger, Livy traced the comforter's swirls of threads, twisting the loose ones.

"Grandma says there's no way to know if the Christian God exists."

Livy's head snapped up. "Sure there is. If He came to earth as one of us, we *can* know."

DeeDee's face twisted. "Grandma says Jesus was a great teacher, not God."

Livy twined her hands and kept her voice steady. "If He were nothing more than a great teacher, He wouldn't have gone around telling everyone He was God, would He?"

"He would if he was a narcissist."

"You've never read His words, or you would know He was no narcissist. Anything but."

DeeDee, mirroring Livy, yanked on a loose thread in the comforter, and then wrapped it around her finger. Despite the rift, apparently her subconscious couldn't undo their lifelong symbiosis. "I'm not interested in reading His words."

Livy groped for her crutches. "I don't want to fight about this, Deeds. Can you let it go and not let it affect our relationship?"

"Problem is, Livs, if you turn into a religious freak, it can't help but affect our relationship." DeeDee's round, grim eyes bored holes into her.

"I'm not a religious freak." Livy faced her twin, crutches planted, fists clenched around the handles. "If God is real, I have a right to know."

DeeDee started to chuckle. "Wait'll I tell Grandma."

"Grandma worships inferior gods," Livy shot back. And the truth crashed over her like hail from heaven.

She *was* convinced.

She did believe.

Livy pivoted as swiftly as her crutches allowed and hobbled back to the sunroom where she'd hidden the Bible. Shaken by her epiphany, her limbs trembling, she struggled to keep the crutches under control. She managed to get to the futon without damaging anything, then groped under the cushion and touched the comforting leather. Tucking it beneath her arm, she carried it to her bedroom and glanced at her bedside clock. Ten after ten. She hoped it wasn't too late to text Scott.

She picked up her phone and found his number. *Guess what. I believe.*

***

Livy awoke with a new, overpowering sensation. An awareness of the presence of God filled her to bursting.

Eager to see Scott's reply, she opened his text. *I'm so happy to hear it. Let's talk later. Would you like to meet some other believers? My neighbors are having a potluck tonight with some church folks. Let me know if you'd like to go.*

She pursed her lips. Surely, he wasn't asking her to be his date. Although curious to meet other believers, she rarely did anything without DeeDee or a date. She needed to think about it and told him so.

Throughout the day, she saw God everywhere. DeeDee helped her bathe with her cast wrapped in plastic and propped on the tub's side. The comfort of the warm water made her think of God. As she struggled into her clothes, His presence filled her room. As she plodded along in the chilly winter sunshine, the majesty of the trees, the green of the grass, the jagged outline of the mountains all shouted of a Creator. The sky itself spilled over with God. She could almost see Him superimposed over the blue backdrop. Yet nobody marveled over it. The people she passed on the sidewalk appeared oblivious.

Feeling an intense need to commune with Him, she sat outside in the sun with her new Bible, basking in His presence and slurping up Scriptures like a thirsty woman at an oasis.

She avoided DeeDee, knowing her twin couldn't possibly understand the things going on in her heart. She would assume, since she hadn't experienced God for herself, He must not be real.

Livy's favorite Friedrich Nietzsche quote kept running through her head. "Those who were seen dancing were thought to be insane by those who could not hear the music." A simple paraphrase showed her a profound new truth: Those who were seen worshiping God were thought to be insane by those who could not see Him.

Chapter Twenty-Six

Livy teetered on her crutches as Paula, her hostess, worked her way around her dining room table filling a plate with food for Livy. Steaming entrees, crisp green salads laden with extras, bags of snacks, covered every inch of Paula's table. Laughter and murmuring voices drifted from the living room. Soft music reverberated in the background, shrouding everything with a soothing blanket of sound.

Paula, a warmhearted, touchy-feely woman, treated Livy like an honored guest as she introduced her. Rick, Paula's husband, was a laugh-loud-and-often kind of man.

When Paula showed up at Livy's door and offered a ride to her home, her engaging smile won Livy over. She'd made the right choice, despite her trepidation. She wasn't sure what she expected Christians to be like, Scott being the first one she'd met. But everyone seemed like perfectly normal, everyday folks, not at all worthy of the "extremist" brush Grandma painted them with.

Livy met two married couples, an engaged couple, and two single women. A preschooler and a toddler played with blocks at the feet of a blonde woman, presumably their mother. The single women's attentive behavior toward Scott amused her. Clearly, he was the finest catch around as far as they were concerned.

At this time of year, late February, darkness fell around five thirty, so the group hung out in the ample living room. Livy caught Paula scrutinizing her a fourth time and shifted. What had Scott told her?

Eventually Paula came to sit beside her. "Do you have kids?" Livy asked as she chewed someone's homemade lasagna.

"A son and a daughter." Paula's smile revealed a small gap between her front teeth. "Both attend University of Washington."

"Go, Huskies," replied one of the single women, a young lady named Claire sitting cross-legged on the floor at Livy's feet. "How do you and Paula know each other?"

"We met for the first time tonight. Turns out we're neighbors."

"Did you grow up around here?"

"I did. Born and raised in Seattle."

"Me too." Claire's small brown eyes pierced her. "I went to Roosevelt. Where did you attend high school?"

Maybe coming here had been a mistake. Her answer would be a dead giveaway. "Elmhurst Academy."

"Wow." Claire's face jolted. Her eyes narrowed, her scrutiny intense. "I'm in awe."

Livy squirmed. Paula chatted with the woman next to her, and Scott stood deep in conversation with Rick across the room.

Livy wanted to haul herself onto her crutches, away from Claire's curious stare and questions. Her leg ached, and she needed to use the bathroom. But she still required so much assistance. She closed her eyes as the weight of her helplessness mocked her.

God, help me. Her gaze darted around the room, then caught Scott's eye. He flashed his now-familiar smile, easing the desolation in her heart. She waved him over and patted the seat next to her.

He came to her rescue just in time. Leaning against the armrest, he gave her a quizzical look.

She put on a brave face. "Thank you for inviting me."

"Not a problem. Your text made my day. What great news."

She nodded. "Today has been amazing. I've sensed God everywhere. But DeeDee's turned into this hostile stranger. If she could only experience God herself, she'd understand. But she's so closed-minded about it."

"Yeah, Jesus warned His disciples this would happen." With his hair grown out and flopping onto his forehead, he'd lost the austerity the buzz cut gave him.

She flipped her hair out of her face. "I think I remember reading that last night."

"What part did you read?"

"I got through half of John before I grew too sleepy."

"That's a lot of reading."

"Then I picked it back up this morning and read the rest of it."

His smile brightened. "You know, it's so cool to see such hunger for the Word in new believers."

"I thought the Bible would be dull, but it's really compelling." Livy swung her right foot back and forth like a pendulum. "I feel like I'm at a feast with a never-ending supply of food."

"I remember what that's like. Before I knew Christ, reading the Bible was like reading a textbook. After I found Him, it came alive."

"I never read the Bible before yesterday."

"What's your boyfriend think of all this?"

"I haven't said anything yet. I'm not quite sure how." Especially after their earlier conversation and his dismay when he discovered her plans tonight didn't include him. She winced. She'd fibbed and said it was a girls' night out.

"If you ask God for the right words and the right time, He'll work it out."

"Which reminds me, I feel kind of awkward when I

pray." She faltered. "Do I—I mean, am I supposed to address Jesus or God?"

"Prayer's just talking to God. Just tell Him whatever's on your heart. You'll get the hang of it."

"Thanks." She glanced at the corner, where the tall grandfather clock poised to strike nine p.m.

Scott stood and stretched. "Time to head home." He assisted her to her feet before crossing the living room to Rick. Paula found Livy and placed a hand on her arm. "Livy, do you have to be home at a certain time?"

"No, anytime is fine."

"Good." She moved her hand to Livy's back. "Rick and I are going to swing by Scott's house for a few minutes. He lives one street over." She pointed to the east. "He's planning to test a device he's been working on. It's supposed to—well, it's kind of a long story. Anyway, you're welcome to tag along and see it for yourself. Afterward I'll drive you home."

Scott and Rick walked to Scott's house, and Paula helped Livy into her car.

"You said Scott's been working on a device?" Livy asked as they rolled down the drive.

"Yes." Paula glanced over her shoulder.

"What kind of device? Is it an invention?"

"Sort of. More like a modification." Paula switched on the blinker. "Did you know Scott is an electronic engineer?"

"I knew he was an inventor."

"He's been working at ENFO since he moved here." She swung the wheel to the left.

"The place designing aircraft instruments?"

Paula nodded.

"Cool."

"Here we are." Paula pulled up to a brick-facade house, which even in the dark, appeared to be at least 2,500 square feet. Livy made out Paula's steep roof catty-corner from the rear fence.

Rick and Scott lagged several feet from the driveway as Paula helped Livy out of the car. "Y'all wait here." Scott neared. "I'll go open the garage." Soon it slid open, and the four of them huddled next to Scott's Avalanche. Electronic equipment pieces littered the workbench. Garden tools propped against the wall. Car parts stacked in precise rows on the shelves.

Scott brought her a canvas lawn chair, and she plunked into it with a sigh. He studied a cell phone in his hand, his mouth puckered. Rick and Paula stood next to her, talking in low voices, their feet shifting. What they were supposed to be waiting for?

"Any minute now." Rick checked his watch. "Scott, got any more chairs? We should look like we're sitting here relaxing."

"Yes." Paula nodded. "Let's pretend we're checking out something on your phone."

Huh? "What is it exactly we're supposed to be doing?"

Scott held out the phone as Rick retrieved more chairs. He leaned toward her. "This phone, Livy, is not really a phone."

"What is it?"

The others unfolded the chairs and sat in a small circle.

"It works like a remote—"

A distant pulsating roar grew louder as it neared. Then a small blue car crawled by and stopped at the driveway next door. The floor under Livy's feet vibrated from the subwoofer's force.

Rick and Paula hunched over the phone as Scott flipped it open. His finger hovered over the Send key.

"Now," they yelled in unison.

Scott pressed Send.

The blue car pulled into the next-door driveway,

suddenly silent. Paula whooped. "Shush," Rick warned her in an undertone. "If you whoop, he'll get suspicious."

What in the world? The car's loud vibrations pulsed again.

"I'll let him enjoy it for ten seconds," Scott drawled, triumphant glee transforming his face as he hit Send.

Again, the car fell silent.

Ha. Scott's "phone" remotely muted the car stereo without the driver having a clue.

The others leaned over the phone. Broad smiles curved all three faces. She peeked at the car. Floodlights illuminated the driver's silhouette. His mouth gaped, and his arms moved in thrusting motions.

The stereo blared. Scott hit Send. The roar ceased.

The young man flung open his door, tossed a brief glance their way, and stomped toward the house. "Dad!" A door slammed.

"Take that, Jamie Mac." Paula chortled. Then whooped. Soon Rick joined in, and their hollers echoed off the walls.

Livy had to applaud. "Absolutely ingenious. How'd you do it?"

His grin stretched as wide as an Olympic gold medalist's. "I took the innards out of this thing and replaced them with a master remote. As long as it's within fifty meters, it hijacks the stereo and disables it."

"I'm impressed." She couldn't stop grinning. Neither could Rick or Paula.

Scott gestured next door. "Their kid has menaced the neighborhood for months. His parents wouldn't do anything, and he wouldn't stop even after I asked nicely. So..." He gestured to the device, his grin ginormous.

***

On the drive home, Livy shifted to Paula. "Scott's so

brilliant, but he comes across as just a regular guy."

Paula smiled. "True. He's a very humble young man."

"I wish my boyfriend could do stuff like that."

Most of the homes they passed were dark, their occupants no doubt readying for another workday, another school day.

"Have you two been dating long?"

"Almost two months, but lately we've been talking about moving in together."

"I see." Shadows covered half of Paula's face. The streetlamps' light undulated over her features.

"But I'll need to wait until I'm fully recovered before I can even think about moving."

Livy's street neared. An odd sensation snaked up her spine, similar to the twinge when as a kid she stole candy. This time, not only did it unsettle her, it also chased away the newfound glow in her heart.

While she tried to work through her battling emotions, the car reached her driveway. Paula braked, put the car in park, and faced her. "Livy, I have an idea."

"What is it?"

"Would you like to learn more about what it means to be a believer in Christ?"

"What would it involve?"

"I thought we could get together once a week and study the Bible. I know you're brand new at this, and I'd be happy to help you grow in your walk with God."

So far, Livy liked what she'd seen of Paula. And she could use help in getting familiar with the Bible and learning how to pray.

"Sure. I would enjoy that."

Paula squeezed her hand. "How about we meet for coffee Saturday morning?"

"I'll let you know. I might be going into work."

"Okay. I'll wait to hear from you. Also, if you're interested, I wanted to invite you to our church on Sunday morning."

"I haven't set foot in one of those since childhood."

"You'll like ours."

"Oh, I do want to go." Livy laid her hands on the dash. "Although I'm sure it will feel strange." She'd do whatever it took to keep the God-light burning in her heart.

Chapter Twenty-Seven

DeeDee lingered in Saffire's hallway, observing the bustle in Studio C before Saturday's Lyrical class. Parents filled the bench in back, and five little girls talked and giggled in the center. Next to her stood Vienna, sleek in tie-dyed tights, gathered purple tee, and mauve triangular glasses.

Vienna nudged DeeDee. "Who's the hot dude?"

She followed Vienna's gaze, then cupped her hand over her mouth to keep the others from hearing. "If you're talking about the guy in the blue shirt, don't waste your time. That's Scott, religious zealot. He even got Livy on a religious kick."

Vienna's eyes widened, and her jaw dropped.

"Besides, he's still hung up on his ex-wife."

Vienna uttered her throaty laugh. "Bet I can make him forget his religion. *And* his ex-wife."

DeeDee tossed her hair, giving it a firm shake. "Oh, no, you won't. And don't even try." She pointed into the studio. "Now get in there and break a leg."

Vienna sashayed into the room. DeeDee, heaving a sigh, returned to the office and allowed herself the luxury of reliving her amazing day with Nick yesterday.

Sure beat reliving the disaster of losing her twin.

Half an hour later, DeeDee finished brewing coffee and peeked in Studio C as Vienna made her closing announcements. "If any of you want to stick around and chat, we have freshly-brewed coffee in Studio A." She aimed a flirtatious smile at Scott. "I don't know about you, but I like mine hot and steamy."

DeeDee clenched her lips. Scott appeared unfazed by the innuendo, although a couple of parents snickered. At least the remark would sail right over the kids' heads.

Several parents took Vienna up on her offer and filed across the hall. While DeeDee poured coffee, Vienna went straight for Scott. DeeDee hovered nearby and joined in conversation with two of the moms while keeping one ear and eye cocked Vienna's way.

Scott leaned against the wall sipping coffee and studying two CDs. His daughters swung on a portable barre.

Vienna faced him and eyed the CDs. "Whatcha lookin' at, mister?"

His head popped up, and he smiled. "These are Christian hip-hop-slash-rap CDs."

DeeDee sipped coffee and raised a brow. Christian hip-hop? Quite the oxymoron.

"Say what?" Vienna stepped back.

"Hip-hop and rap by Christian artists. You know. Anti-gangsta rap."

Vienna inspected the cover. "So you're sayin' these dudes be like, 'We don't hang with Eminem and Jay-Z, man.'"

Scott laughed. "Good way to put it."

She appraised him with hooded lids. "You ain't as straitlaced as you look."

"No, I'm pretty straitlaced." Amusement crinkled his eyes. "But rap can be energizing. Every now and then, if I need a lift, I'll listen to these guys."

Vienna cackled. "I hear ya, dude. Opera does that to me."

"Opera?" Scott's brow arched. "I'd never guess you were an opera person."

"Ha." Gravel filled Vienna's laugh. "It's my guilty pleasure. Gets me in touch with my inner fat lady. Like rap gets you in touch with your inner gangsta."

At Scott's roar of laughter, DeeDee jerked back, knocking

her ankle against the table leg. When had he gotten such a fun-loving side to his personality?

"Hey, we should switch bodies, y'know?" Vienna waved her hand back and forth. "Since you be all, Opera Man. And I be all, Rap Chick."

"Oh, I don't know." Scott's drawl deepened. "I always thought I'd make a pretty ugly girl."

"Naw. You'd make a real good-lookin' dudette."

He gave another hearty laugh. "Trust me, I wouldn't."

DeeDee turned to Haley's mom, who wanted to talk about Livy's accident. "Excuse me please, Anna." In five steps, she reached Vienna and grasped her arm. "Vee, can I see you a minute?"

Vienna narrowed her eyes and pulled her Rouge Allure mouth into a frown, but refrained from making a scene. DeeDee escorted her out of the room. "You realize, don't you, his opinion of you would change fast if he found out the reason you're here."

"Dude."

"I doubt he'd be impressed to know you're on probation."

"You threatening me?"

"Just saying." DeeDee fastened a firm stare on Vienna. "You can't be doing anything which might be interpreted as flirting. You were getting way too friendly."

"He was gettin' pretty loosey-goosey, too."

DeeDee clicked her tongue. "Don't you get it? No shenanigans with the parents."

"Livy did shenanigans with Will."

"Wro-ong. She didn't come on to him, missy."

Vienna's stubborn jaw hardened like concrete baking in the sun.

"This is a business." The words hissed past DeeDee's clenched teeth. "If you start treating it like your personal playground, you'll be out of here faster than you can bat your fake eyelashes."

DeeDee released her and stalked into the room. Vienna flounced in moments later, avoiding DeeDee's warning gaze.

"Morning, DeeDee," Scott drawled.

She turned. "Morning, Scott."

"I was wondering if Livy would be dropping by today."

She bristled inside. Scott and Livy might as well be best buds now. Baring her teeth in a polite smile, she shook her head.

He held out the CDs. "I thought she might like to borrow these."

Her clenched teeth loosened a mere fraction. "I don't think so."

He searched her face a moment and shrugged. "Okay." He gestured to Kinzie and Lacie. "We'll see you next week."

As father and daughters left the room, Vienna appeared beside DeeDee. "A man like that is catnip to a girl like me, baby." From the tilt of her chin, to the slant of her lids — a spot-on Halle Berry impression.

DeeDee landed a soft punch on Vee's arm. "That's enough, Catwoman."

***

Livy sat with Paula in JavaJava, her crutches propped against the booth behind her, the booth where she and Will sat on their first date. So naturally, Will was the subject of conversation.

Paula sipped a green tea smoothie. "Have you two discussed marriage at all?"

Livy fought down her annoyance. Why was that Paula's business? "No, other than the fact neither of us believes in it." She leaned toward Paula, feeling the strain in her face. "I think it's way too soon, to be honest. Plus, due to some technicalities, Will is still married."

"He is?" Paula's smile froze.

"His marriage is over." Livy drew her shoulders back, her voice tight. "But they're still fighting over the division of assets. Since Washington is a community property state, he owns half the house. But she doesn't want to sell it, and she can't afford to pay him off."

Paula didn't reply. Livy, the glow in her heart sputtering like a dying engine, wrapped her arms around herself. Something about the words she'd uttered felt wrong. Paula thought so, too, judging by her expression.

Livy stared into her cup, picturing Will's face, as dear as family. His sunny demeanor could shatter the foggiest of glooms. "I wonder if I could persuade him to believe in Christ." Buoyed by the prospect, she sat up straight and gave Paula a hopeful smile.

"What will you do if he doesn't go along?"

"I don't know."

"It's something to pray about. I've known couples where one of them comes to know Christ, and shortly after, the other does too. So don't give up hope."

"He might never though."

"Then you'd be faced with a hard decision." Paula picked up the Bible next to her and thumbed through the pages. "There's a verse for that. Here it is—Second Corinthians 6:14. Do you want to read it?"

She handed Livy the Bible. Livy read the words aloud, "'Be ye not unequally yoked together with unbelievers: for what fellowship hath righteousness with unrighteousness? And what communion hath light with darkness?'" She swirled her hair around her finger in anxious circles. "But Will isn't a bad guy. He's a decent, loving man."

Paula showed Livy verses on God's view of unrighteousness, until Livy jerked back, words bursting from her. "He demands perfect righteousness? Impossible. How can any of us please Him?"

Paula reached to take her hand. "Livy, that's why Christ died. He died and rose to life to take your sin on Himself, and Will's too. In exchange, He granted you His perfect righteousness the moment you believed."

Tears burned her eyes. Christ's death on her behalf felt like the most loving, caring gesture in the world. Far more than she deserved. As the love of God swelled every crevice of her heart and seeped out her pores, her tears fell with abandon. Paula moved next to her and embraced her with the arms of a mother. Livy sobbed on Paula's shoulder, not caring if the other customers noticed.

"Are those tears of joy?" Paula whispered.

Livy hiccupped. "Yeah," she whispered back. "I can't believe He'd do such an incredible thing."

"His love is amazing, isn't it?" Paula held her until her sobs came to a shuddering halt.

Livy wiped her eyes with a napkin, calmer now. Straightening, she met A.J.'s intent gaze across the room. Suddenly self-conscious, she turned and stared out the window.

She needed to get a grip before calling further attention to herself. With a deep breath, she shifted her body and focus, and over the next hour, shared the events leading to her accident. Paula's face twitched when Livy mentioned hypnosis. "In fact," Livy said, "Grandma's driving up tomorrow to spend a few days with DeeDee and me. I don't know how to tell her I don't want to do hypnosis."

"I have a couple of thoughts," Paula said. "First, I agree hypnosis would not be a good thing. But you don't have to tell her so. Second, if your obsession with your mother's death was so consuming it did this to you"—she gestured toward Livy's leg—"then, in my humble opinion, you need to unlock those memories."

"But how?" Livy's heart lurched like a skittish cat. "You said I shouldn't do hypnosis."

"There is another way." Paula held her gaze. "But before I explain, I should tell you I'm a licensed clinical social worker, although I'm not currently practicing. Anyway, a new technique has been effective in treating post-traumatic stress disorder."

"PTSD? You think I have that?" Livy gripped her empty cup so hard, it crumpled beneath her fingers.

"I couldn't give you an official diagnosis unless I did some testing on you. But it sounds like it caused your memory loss." Paula gave Livy's hand a reassuring pat. "This procedure has effectively relieved all kinds of repressed trauma from people's pasts, not just PTSD."

"But it's not hypnosis?"

"I assure you it's not. I think it would be perfect for you. I can give you names of practitioners in this area, if you decide you want to do this."

Livy shivered. Hope and dread warred inside her. Perhaps Paula was right and she could reawaken the events from that long ago day. But... did she really want to know? What if the knowledge proved too terrible to bear?

***

Silence greeted Livy inside Saffire's deserted hallway. Paula, one hand under Livy's arm, complimented her on the royal blue front door and its matching sign, proclaiming both swanky.

Livy swung along the hall, Paula at her side. Two competing sets of music vibrated through the studio walls. How amazing—she'd only met Paula last week, yet Paula had already supplanted DeeDee—something she'd never dreamed could happen. Had God purposely brought it about?

They peeked in on Vienna's Tap I class. Twelve shuffling, out-of-sync feet nearly drowned out the techno music. Vee, absorbed in her task, didn't see them.

She stood for a moment, watching. How she missed all this — the kids' eager enthusiasm, the spark in a student's eye when something finally clicked. Even their unruly giggling. Before the accident, she'd taken her strong, capable body for granted, her easy movements, never thinking twice about it. How long before she could perform even the simplest steps?

She felt like Scarlett O'Hara at the ball, stuck on the outside watching everyone else dance.

What if her bones healed stiff and crooked and she never danced again?

The question dragged on her spirit, as heavy as the cast weighing her down.

In the Tap II studio, the kids were tapping out an Irish pattern when DeeDee met Livy's eyes in the mirror. She did a double-take, and again when she saw Paula. Livy waved and pasted on a smile as though no rift existed, but DeeDee slid her gaze away and kept counting.

"I don't think she expected me." Livy's voice cracked as she closed the door. She gulped. Had Paula noticed anything? "But hey, what better time to get the books done?"

"See you in the morning for church." Paula cupped Livy's face in her hands. "I'll pick you up at nine thirty."

After Paula left, Livy tottered to the desk chair and plopped down, her body tilting awkwardly. As the computer booted up, she angled toward the drawer containing her reading glasses and December's remaining paperwork. If all went well, she'd be sending last year's completed records to the tax accountant today.

As she posted expenses, an old saying ran through her mind — Nothing is certain except death and taxes. Even Christ taught about death and taxes. With her fingers on autopilot, she cast her mind back — what had He said about taxes? She'd read it in the Gospel of Matthew. "Render to Caesar the things that are Caesar's, and to God the things that are God's." The study note for the verse explained how Jesus expected His followers to pay taxes and give to God's work as well.

Jesus was so full of surprises. He always had the perfect comeback for the Pharisees. Amazing she'd never known how clever Jesus was. How sad most people had no clue who He was. But how could they, when popular culture only mocked Him?

His message on taxes flitted through her mind, over and over, like a warped CD. *Give to Caesar what is Caesar's.* Why was this nagging at her?

She kept typing, entering figure after figure, her fingers working on their own. Until she jerked them back. Her last bookkeeping session on this machine! The day she'd found Scott's book and ended up with a copy of *Religion or Christ.*

She'd spilled coffee and gotten up to fetch rags, right after she'd counted the cash in the lockbox. One thousand, nine hundred, and fourteen dollars of untraceable cash.

Cash she'd planned to hide from Caesar.

Give to Caesar what is Caesar's —

God was trying to tell her something.

Her breath came in ragged bursts, and a groan erupted from somewhere behind her throat.

Give to Caesar what is Caesar's —

"Okay, God." She bit out the words. "I'll report it." Her fingers trembled as she scrolled back through the deposits. Her nostrils flared as she added 1,914 to the revenue column.

There. Done.

A profound sense of peace flooded her. If only she could get up and dance. She tipped her head back and smiled at the ceiling, basking in the presence of her Lord and Savior.

***

"I got everything sent off to the CPA, Deeds," Livy said on the ride home, a two-minute ride filled with chilly silence.

"Great."

Nothing less than a sledgehammer could crack the iceberg floating between them.

"How's it going with Nick?"

"We're going out tonight." DeeDee stared at the road. "Then we'll see." A reluctant smile played at the corners of her mouth.

"I'm happy for you."

DeeDee said nothing as she pulled into the driveway, and stayed silent as she parked and helped Livy out of the car.

Why won't you talk to me? Livy whimpered inside. Her face crumpled like a tinfoil mask. Her throat ached from the effort of holding back tears. For the first time in her life, she couldn't let DeeDee see her cry.

Chapter Twenty-Eight

"You feel up to staying with me tonight?" Will's eyes gleamed as he and Livy enjoyed shish kebabs at Purple Tomato. "The girls won't be there. They're overnighting with their cousins."

"I don't know." The dreaded moment of reckoning was imminent.

"We don't have to do anything if you're not ready. I only want to hold you. I miss snuggling with you all night."

"I miss it too." Very true. But she needed to explain her heart.

"I know it'll be awhile before we can go back to the way things used to be." Will took her hands in his and ignored his half-full plate. "But I'm willing to wait."

A deep sadness weighed her heart. She looked at Will, remembering the way things used to be. Her gaze explored the fine, chiseled planes of his face, and she yearned to share an intimate night with him. Just one night. What could it hurt?

Something inside her resisted. What had *Religion or Christ* said? "If any man be in Christ, he is a new creature...."

And she had an out.

"I can't tonight, sweets." She infused as much regret into her tone as possible. "I have plans for in the morning."

The corners of Will's mouth tightened. "Plans which don't include me, I take it?"

"Well, it's church. And I don't see why you couldn't come along if you wanted."

"Church?" He lifted a brow, his grip slackened. "You're

going to church? With who?"

"My neighbor Paula." She attempted a casual laugh. "You know how long it's been since I've stepped foot in a church?"

He shook his head, staring at her, his brow wrinkling. "You've really changed, you know that?" he burst out. "You talk about God and church and all that stuff now. You never did before the accident."

Her heart thumpety-thumped. "I hope I've changed for the better."

He whipped his hands away. "You didn't need to change at all."

She jumped at his vehemence. "Will. The accident could have killed me, you know. I think it's normal for people who've had a brush with death to give more thought to things like God and —"

"Yeah, probably so." He picked up his kebab and stuffed a wad of meat into his mouth. His face softened as he chewed. Then he swallowed. "I understand. I really do. It's probably just a phase you're going through."

"It doesn't feel like 'just a phase.'" She eyed the remaining chunks on her plate, her appetite having vanished along with the daylight outside.

"I hope you have a nice time at church tomorrow." Will's tone lent tolerance and goodwill to his words.

"Will." She grabbed his free hand. "Come with me. Please?"

"Babe, I'm going to pass this time." A shroud turned his eyes opaque, unreadable. "But maybe someday. Okay?"

***

Livy clasped Paula's hand tighter as Paula and Rick helped her out of the car and into the covered walkway. She hung onto Rick's outstretched arm, as steady and unwavering as an oak branch in a windstorm.

"Welcome to Ravenna Bible Chapel, Livy."

She eyed the familiar brick building she'd passed a thousand times, but never heeded. The original structure abutted a newer addition, twice as large. Vehicles packed the main parking lot. A finger of pavement curled around to the back lot, overflowing with more cars.

Chilly, rain-scented wind swept through the colonnade, but Livy stayed dry as she hobbled alongside Paula. She stopped, balancing on her good foot, and wrestled with her jacket hood, but couldn't make it work.

"Here, let me help." Paula rushed to assist, and Livy, her head covered, tried to see inside the white front door. She couldn't remember what real-life churches looked like inside. She'd never even attended a church wedding or funeral.

She was as out of place as Scott in Bath And Body Works, as Vienna in a convent.

Scott waited in the lobby, shifting back and forth on the balls of his feet. She forgot he'd be here, and her disappointment at Will for opting out turned to relief.

"Livy." A pleased smile transformed Scott's face. He made a move toward her, and she froze, thinking he meant to hug her. Will would hate it if she let another man hug her.

Instead of hugging her, Scott gestured inside. "I saved y'all some seats."

He led them to a row of padded chairs about halfway to the front. The place didn't look like the churches she'd seen on TV and in movies. It didn't display intricate, colorful mosaics or robed, sorrowful statues. No dark woodwork or lofty ceilings. This church held a bright and airy feel, its high, clear windows allowing cloudy light in. Most of the faces sported smiles and kind eyes. Like Paula and Rick. Ron and Melody, her hospital visitors.

Livy sat closest to the side aisle next to Paula and checked out the stage. A full band stood ready to perform, and three singers paced around the mike stands.

The hum of voices echoed as she leaned to Paula's ear. "You have a band here?"

"The worship team. They're very good."

A band playing in a church? For real? "I thought churches used pianos and organs."

Paula chuckled. "That's much less common these days. Most evangelical churches use worship bands, like ours."

The male singer boomed into the mike, and the hubbub died down. Folks hastened to their seats. Livy stayed in her chair as the others stood and the band launched into an unfamiliar upbeat song. A song she longed to dance to, if only she could.

A screen behind the stage displayed the words. The lyrics talked about overcoming by the blood of the Lamb. Livy's heart burned. The band sounded as good as any professionals. How sad she'd never known such talent existed within church walls. The crowd clapped along, not as lively as the crowd at Nils's service, but far more energetic than she expected.

They transitioned into a slower, more melodic song. Surprisingly beautiful. By the second go-round, she'd memorized the chorus. On the third verse, her voice soared with the singer's. Around her, arms waved in the air. Eyes closed, heads raised toward heaven. Scott and Rick's faces somber, their mouths forming words.

Paula shot a glance at her, eyes wide. Livy lowered her voice so as not to call attention to herself.

They sang several more songs before the band set down their instruments and left the stage. A polished gentleman, wearing olive-green khakis and a yellow polo shirt, got up from the front row and ascended to the stage.

"Good morning, folks." He panned the room in a slow

arc. "Have you all been learning a lot from our journey through Colossians?"

Shouts and amens popped up, nothing like the church experience she expected. "We'll be studying Colossians 2:6 today. Please turn in your Bibles and follow along. 'As ye have therefore received Christ Jesus the Lord, so walk ye in him, rooted and built up in him....'"

After the service, Paula helped Livy into the car. Rick stood nearby, talking with another man and watching the entire awkward production. Livy wished she had a curtain to hide behind. "Would you like to come over for lunch?" Paula asked.

Livy grunted, and then winced as she plunked to the seat like a hippo. "I would, but my grandma is coming over. She's probably waiting for me."

Paula climbed in back, and Rick started the car. The rain had stopped, but a blanket of industrial-gray clouds still hid the sun.

Paula's head emerged from between the front seats. "I enjoyed listening to you sing, Livy. You have a phenomenal voice."

"Thanks." Livy shifted to Paula. "I've been singing since I was a kid. DeeDee and I used to sing in a band. Are you familiar with Free The Defendants?"

"Oh, sure. You sang with them?"

"We did."

Rick swung a right. "The guy who died a few weeks ago?"

"Nils Nelsson. Yes, he did. His Celebration of Life service was packed out."

Paula's face twitched. Her eyes gleamed. "How did you come to know Nils Nelsson?"

"I've known him forever. He was my dad's best friend. He and my mom's best friend, Audria, had a love child together—my friend, Vienna."

"What an interesting life you've led."

"You could say so."

"Is your whole family musical?"

Livy stared out the window. Pavement flowed by like a black river. "Not exactly. My mom was a dancer, but Dad's the musician. He taught DeeDee and me to sing."

Something quivered in the sudden hush. A desire to confide in her kind new friends fought with her lifelong restraint.

She threw caution to the pavement and let it crush beneath the car's wheels. "My father is Declan Decker."

She eyed Paula, who raised a brow, but didn't seem overly surprised. "Oh, Livy."

Rick turned to her, brows at mid-forehead. "Unbelievable."

"But please, please don't tell anyone, okay? Only a few people know."

He braked at Green Lake Drive. "'Course we won't."

"What was it like growing up with Declan Decker?" Awe fluttered in Paula's voice.

"Let's say it's a pretty long story, Paula."

They crossed Green Lake Drive and meandered through neighborhood streets to Livy's cul-de-sac. Grandma's green Subaru, sporting Oregon plates and plastered with bumper stickers, sat at the curb.

"Someday I'll tell you all about my upbringing."

"I can't wait to hear."

Rick helped her out, and Paula walked her to the door, where they hugged.

"Thanks, Paula. It was a really nice service."

"May God make His face shine on you, Livy." Paula assisted Livy with the front door, helped her hobble inside, and then left.

Grandma and DeeDee lounged in the living room. Murf barked and danced around. Poor Murf must be wondering why she no longer knelt to pet him. DeeDee whistled for the dog, and he cocked his head at her, then at Livy with an uncertain swish of his tail.

Grandma watched, chuckling. Her unlined face shone with rosy good health. Her blue eyes radiated serenity. She had celebrated her sixty-seventh birthday last month but could still pass for fifty. She stood to hug Livy. "It's so good to see you, lamb."

Livy teetered on her crutches and plunked to the red corduroy recliner facing the sectional. Murf hopped next to her. "Good to see you too, Grandma."

"Tell me how you've been managing."

Kneading Murf's fur, she sighed and peeked at DeeDee. Her sister stared back, arms crossed, her face impassive lines, her eyes as hard as blue marbles.

Livy forced a smile. Time to lighten the atmosphere. "To paraphrase John Lennon, I get by with a little help from my twin."

Grandma laughed. "Kudos to you, DeeDee." She faced Livy. "You look good. I can tell you're adjusting. How many more weeks before your cast comes off?"

"Four."

"It will be here before you know it."

DeeDee cleared her throat. "How was chu-*urch*?"

"It was great. Did you know most churches these days have actual bands? The one I heard this morning could give Dad's band some good competition."

"Am I supposed to be impressed?"

Livy clicked her tongue. "You can think whatever you want, Deeds. You asked."

"Livy." Grandma extended a hand. "I'd like to hear about your new interest in church."

Livy studied Grandma's fingers as they pinched and released hers. "Today was my first time in church—ever. There's not much to tell yet."

"You asked me recently about Jesus. Are you still pursuing that?"

How to respond? "You mean, pursuing whether Jesus was God?"

Grandma nodded. "Yes."

"No, I'm no longer pursuing it." Grandma's face relaxed, and Livy took a breath. Might as well come out with it. "Because I've come to believe it. For me, the issue is settled."

DeeDee made a noise in the back of her throat.

Grandma's eyes widened. "Livy, I can't believe you'd fall for that lie. Jesus was a good man. A prophet—"

"No, Grandma. He was far more. Did Buddha claim to be God, and then prove it by dying and rising from the dead? Did Mohammed?"

Grandma merely crinkled her face. Lines of distress popped out on her forehead.

"In fact, Grandma, I'm curious why the possibility of Jesus as God bothers you so much. Why do you care what I believe about it, anyway?"

Her eyes hardened. "So much damage has been done in the name of Christ. People slaughtered. Wars waged—"

"No, Grandma, more damage has been done by godless atheists than by Christians. Christ-followers tried to repair the damage done by tyrants like Hitler and Lenin."

"Hitler was a Christian."

"If Hitler was a Christian, then I'm Lady Gaga."

DeeDee snorted. Livy offered a tiny smile, but DeeDee's eyes remained hard.

Livy turned again to Grandma. "You both have been seriously misinformed." Tension tightened her throat as she struggled to her feet and grappled the crutches. "I'm going to bring you a book I read, so you can look at it for yourself."

"Don't bother." An edge of steel sharpened Grandma's sweet tones. "I know you've been reading the Bible, and I hate seeing you get sucked into it. White men have used the Bible for centuries to keep their women and children in line. To justify oppressing women and minorities, especially in Western culture."

Livy jammed the crutches in a wide *V* and balanced on her good leg. "Show me where the Bible says it's okay to oppress women and children."

"Livy." Grandma leaned forward. "Even if the Bible doesn't come right out and say it, Christians *thinking* it does is enough for them to act on it."

"I find it hard to believe any of the Christian men I've met recently would mistreat their wives and kids, or think it's okay."

"But you don't actually know what goes on behind closed doors." Grandma's steely-blue gaze bored deep. "It happens all the time. You've seen the news stories. Some upstanding church deacon gets arrested for domestic violence. Or a priest accused of molestation. And on and on."

"What about Scott?" DeeDee's mocking voice cut in. "His wife divorced him for a *reason*. I wouldn't be surprised if he slapped her around."

Livy's chin jolted up. "Deeds, I can't believe you'd think that. Scott is a kind, good person, and he's crazy about his girls."

"Livy." Grandma's mouth flattened to a slit. "Not only are church men guilty of abuse, but they also threaten people with Hell if they don't toe the line. Is that a kind and loving thing to do?"

Livy rocked back. "You said a minute ago Jesus was a good man, yet he threatened people with Hell."

"Then he wasn't really so good, was he? Why would you

have anything to do with someone who threatened to throw you into a flaming pit for all eternity?"

"But if it were true, I'd want to be warned. Wouldn't you? If you had cancer and were told you would die if you didn't get treatment, would you be outraged at the doctor for insulting you? Or would you take the cure?"

"You're talking nonsense. It's hardly the same."

"So, Liv…" When DeeDee spoke, Livy tilted precariously. "Is Mom in Heaven or Hell?"

Livy's insides crumpled as she struggled to regain her balance. DeeDee somehow discerned the one question she didn't ever want to face. She stared at the floor, feeling two sets of hostile eyes.

She swallowed. "I don't know." Her voice came out soft, hesitant.

"But you have an opinion. So tell us."

Livy tightened her mouth to squelch a sob and hoisted herself toward her bedroom. "I don't know."

"What a copout answer."

"Livy, you believe in a God who would send your own mother to Hell." Grandma's soft tone thinly veiled her outrage.

Livy had to get out of there before they saw tears fall and had even more reason to mock her. In her haste, her right crutch knocked against the floor lamp and nearly toppled it. A swear word flew from her mouth before she could stop it.

Silent tears fell in earnest as she slowly righted herself.

"Copout." DeeDee's taunt reached Livy's ears, but she waited to release the sobs until she'd cloistered herself in her room. Huddling on her bed, clutching her favorite purple pillow to her chest, she sobbed until no tears were left.

Chapter Twenty-Nine

Scott parked on the sidewalk outside Shari's mother's house, noting the absence of Shari's car. He walked his daughters up the driveway and rang the bell. Nightfall was minutes away, and dusky gloom shrouded the house.

The porch light flicked on and bathed them in a yellow glow. The white front door, smeared and smudged, opened with a series of croaks. Amy, Shari's mother, peered through the screen.

"Come in, girls." She cracked the screen without looking at Scott.

He had grown accustomed to his former mother-in-law now ignoring him. Amy assumed he'd done something unforgivable to drive Shari from the marriage. Knowing Shari, she'd done nothing to set her mother straight.

"Hug, girls?" He knelt and grasped his daughters around their tiny waists, reluctant to let go, breathing in the familiar scent of their hair.

"Time to come in." Amy's voice slapped him.

He stood. "Where is Shari?"

Amy kept her eyes on the girls as they squeezed through the narrow opening. "Out and about with friends." Her gaze found his. "She has an active social life now."

"I'm not surprised."

"Hopefully you can develop one, too."

Scott ignored the dig and looked at his daughters' somber faces through the screen door. He waved and returned to his car, his heart as empty as his bed.

Develop a social life. Right. He could if he wanted to. But his one-year dating hiatus wasn't up yet. And it wasn't what his daughters wanted. Or what God wanted. A wave of frustration at Shari washed over him—Shari, whose selfish desires were more important to her than their daughters. Kinzie and Lacie didn't deserve parents who no longer lived together.

The sign for Laurel Court passed on his left. He couldn't help a quick glance at Livy's house. Golden light spilled from the windows, leaving the place warm and inviting. Like the Townsends' house. Like Livy herself.

Today had been her first Sunday in a church. Yet she sang along as though she'd been singing those songs for years. She probably hadn't known he could hear her incredible singing voice where he stood. His breath had caught when he'd seen her mouth open, her eyes closed, belting out the words in a voice like Martina McBride.

Considering her background, it shouldn't have been such a surprise.

A sudden urge to turn left into her driveway gripped him. He slowed, then thought better of it and sped up. How foolish he would look if Will were there.

He began to whistle a tune while he drove the curving streets toward Rosemary Drive. As he parked in his driveway, lyrics played through his mind. Then it struck him what he'd been whistling.

Bruno Mars's ode to an amazing woman. "Just the Way You Are."

He hit the remote, eased into the garage, and shut off the engine, reluctant to go inside. As he relaxed against the headrest, a thought pushed at his mind, wanting attention.

Bruno Mars could have been singing to Livy—an amazing and talented woman. Just the way she was.

No wonder he felt like a stammering middle schooler

whenever he was around her.

What a lucky dog Will was.

He shook the unwelcome thought away. The last thing he wanted was to move in on another man's woman, or even entertain the notion. Another flood of helpless resentment toward Shari swamped him. If she hadn't walked out on him, he wouldn't be so vulnerable to another woman's appeal.

He pounded the steering wheel once, then twice. "Lord, have mercy!" How could he explain this awkward dilemma to his accountability group? He was only six months into his one-year sentence and already losing his grip.

He wrenched open the door and forced himself through his kitchen door, snapping on lights as he went. NASCAR was the perfect cure for wayward thoughts. He picked up the remote and flipped the channels until the roar of racing engines swept away all other images.

***

Livy wiped the last of her tears, dropped into the rolling chair, and logged onto her laptop. Grandma and DeeDee's murmuring voices gravitated from the living room.

She opened her favorite social media sites to several new messages. After scrolling down, she stopped at a post from Vienna.

"Which Greek goddess are you?" asked the quiz. "Start here."

Livy recoiled. No way would she take the quiz. Yet a month ago, she'd have been all over it.

She hit Delete, and the quiz disappeared.

Didn't she own a reference book on all the gods and goddesses? She wheeled the chair to her crammed bookcase and scoured the titles. Books piled atop more books, some perching precariously. The slightest jostle could avalanche them.

She'd purchased a slew of New Age. Titles such as *Yoga Sutras, The Chakra System,* and *Vibrations for the New Age* filled her shelves, along with several popular fiction books.

She slowly eased one of her Chakra books from its tight quarters and turned to the cover. A human figure sat stiff and upright in the lotus position, silhouetted against a psychedelic backdrop.

She scanned the contents, growing more uneasy the longer she read. Her hand shot out, and the book thudded to the floor.

She yanked out books on crystals and tarot, dropping them to the floor. Next, her meditation and astrology books. But she could only reach the two middle shelves. The top and bottom shelves would require her to kneel or stand on tiptoe—both impossible.

Soon a two-foot high pile had sprung up on the floor. But now…how to get rid of them?

She rolled to the door, ready to summon Grandma.

A still, small voice impressed its message on her heart. "Call Paula."

She jerked to a stop.

"Call Paula."

Livy rolled over to the bed where she'd tossed her handbag and retrieved her phone. A new text message from Will awaited her. *What's your day look like?*

She told him she'd call him soon, and then called Paula.

"Hello?" Her friend's warmth sang over the line.

"Paula, it's Livy."

"How's your visit with your grandma going?"

"Not great. But I'm calling because I-I need a favor."

"I'm so glad you thought of me. I'll do whatever I can."

"Great. I've got a bunch of old books I want to get rid of, but I can't reach all of them or haul them away."

"Not a problem. Sounds like something Rick could help

with too. Do you mind if he comes along?"

"Not at all."

She ended the call after Paula promised to be right over. Then she called Will, who promised to drop by for dinner after he took his girls back home.

She hobbled into the living room. DeeDee and Grandma stopped chatting as she approached. Livy balanced on her crutches beside the souvenir shelves. "Some new friends of mine are coming over soon." She focused on the safari-themed throw draped over the armchair. Jungle animals zigzagged across the fuzzy fabric, silhouetted against a luminous apricot sky. "They're the couple I went to church with today. You'll get to meet them and see for yourself how sweet they are."

Grandma's mouth twitched, so subtly Livy almost missed it. "I'm sure they're very nice people."

Time to change the subject. "Deeds, do you mind putting Murf out back before they come over?"

DeeDee jerked her head side to side and got to her feet.

"Are you staying for a while, Grandma? My boyfriend's coming over later, and I want you to meet him."

"DeeDee already set up the guest room for me. I'm planning to stay for a couple days."

DeeDee stretched and yawned and whistled for Murf. "Nick's coming over tonight, too." She picked up the dog and carried him out of the room, returning moments later empty-handed. Livy smiled her thanks, but DeeDee still glowered.

Grandma's mouth relaxed. "I'm excited to meet both your boyfriends. This should be fun. How about I make some falafel wraps in tahini sauce? They'll never know it's vegan."

The conversation stayed in safe territory as Livy updated Grandma on her dealings with the insurance, and Grandma updated them on her involvement with Occupy Portland.

The doorbell rang. DeeDee stood. "I'll get it."

Rick and Paula walked in, beaming as Livy made introductions. DeeDee and Grandma greeted them with enthusiasm.

Rick winked at Livy. "We're ready to help you whenever you are."

DeeDee sat up straighter, toes pointed. "Help you what?"

Livy gulped. Would DeeDee feel hurt because she'd recruited someone else? "Help me simplify my bookshelf. I have way too many."

"I could have helped you."

"I know, Deeds." *But...?* "It was spur of the minute. And you've already done so much."

Paula rescued her. "We don't mind at all. This way, you get a break." She stopped, her mouth in an *O*, her gaze fixed on something near Livy's feet. Livy followed her gaze to the souvenir shelves, to the Asian statue collection. Hindu gods.

She recoiled. Why hadn't she ever noticed how sinister those things were? Especially the big one sprouting arms every which way like an octopus. And its wide, staring eyes...she shivered.

Livy lurched away from the creepy icons. She needed them out of here. But if she tossed them, DeeDee would throw a fit.

Paula's face had recovered its sweet expression. She rubbed her hands together. "Why don't we get started."

Livy led Paula down the hall while Rick made himself at home in the living room, ready to keep DeeDee and Grandma entertained.

Livy showed Paula where they stored extra boxes, and Paula carried a bundle to Livy's room. "What a cute room. So feminine. Look at all those pillows." Paula sniffed. "It smells good, too. What's the scent?"

"Today it's eucalyptus."

Paula stopped at the bookshelf. "You do have a lot of

books." She glanced at the pile. "And you're getting rid of a lot, too." Her mouth flew open as she picked up the top one. "Oh my. This looks like a New Age book."

"It is," Livy snapped and winced. "I'm getting rid of all of them. Which won't leave many books on my shelf."

Paula flashed her gap-toothed smile. "I'm proud of you. You decided this all on your own." She held her arms out. Livy leaned in and received her hug. Paula pulled back and met her eye. "You know what the early Christians did?"

"No, what?"

"They took all their sorcery books and threw them in the fire. You can read about it in the book of Acts."

Livy flinched. "I don't think I need to do anything so drastic. I just want them out of here."

"But what will you do with them?"

"I don't know. Keep them in the trunk of my car until I can drive them to a used bookstore, I suppose." She bit her lip. "I was going to see if my grandma wanted them. She's Wiccan, you know. But for some reason, I felt I was supposed to call you instead."

"I'm so glad you did. The dump is where they belong, if you want my honest opinion. They're not worth reselling or giving away."

"Right." Livy stared at the daunting array of worthless books she'd invested in over the years.

"But now you can replace them with good Christian books. I can recommend some authors you might like." The top shelf reached Paula's eye level, and she browsed the row of titles.

Livy navigated, and Paula removed. Soon the bookshelf was two-thirds empty. Three large boxes bulged. Rick carried them one by one to the garage and stowed them in Livy's car trunk. Livy followed, feeling helpless, Paula at her heels.

"Sure you don't want to build a fire under these?" Rick

chuckled as he stood next to the Jag's open trunk. "It's what the New Testament believers did."

"I know. Paula told me."

"On second thought." Rick propped a hand on the trunk's hood. "Why don't you let Paula and me haul them away? We'll take them to the dump for you."

"You'd do that? I owe you one, big time."

"Not at all. We're happy to do it."

"You're awesome." She pushed the garage door opener, and it rumbled up. Rick lugged the boxes one by one to the trunk of his car. Livy heaved a sigh. She wouldn't ever have to look at those books again.

She tapped Paula's arm. "Can we talk privately?"

"Of course. Honey," Paula said to Rick, "Livy and I need to talk. Can you come pick me up later? I'll text you."

"Yep." He kissed her goodbye and headed for home.

Voices and spicy aromas drifted from the kitchen. DeeDee and Grandma preparing falafel and tahini. Livy led Paula to the sunroom and closed the door. She flipped on lights and lowered herself to the couch. But with her cast tilting her off-balance, she came down crooked and toppled against Paula.

"Whoa." Paula grabbed her arm. "Careful."

Livy wiggled into an upright position and laughed. "That's the second time I've done that."

"The second time? When was the first?"

"I slipped and fell on Scott the night he brought the Bible over."

Paula laughed too then stopped, her chin tilted. "I didn't know you had such a close encounter with Scott." Paula's droll tone invoked Livy's fresh giggles, and Paula joined her. Livy bent over, allowing the day's tension to bubble out her mouth and dissipate in the air.

Her laughter spent, she sighed with glee. "Speaking of

Scott, he's sort of what I wanted to talk to you about."

Paula lifted her brows. "What about him?"

"I'm wondering what broke up his marriage." Livy laced her fingers. "Was there any abuse?"

"Not that I'm aware of." Paula angled away. "Why would you even think such a thing?"

Livy cringed. "Something DeeDee said." She glanced at the closed door and dropped her voice. "Trust me, I'd never believe it of him. But after church today, DeeDee and my grandma gave me flak about church and churchgoers. DeeDee suggested Scott slapped his wife around."

Paula's eyes rounded. "Wow." Her streaked bangs swished back and forth. "No, nothing like that. I got the impression Scott and Shari had fundamental differences of opinion on money. She enjoyed spending; he enjoyed saving—they argued a lot."

"I see."

"He did say some things to her he now regrets. But he promised the Lord if Shari came back home, he'd get it right the second time around. He learned his lesson." Paula tucked her legs underneath her. "I'm not saying Shari was justified in leaving. I believe most marriages can work if both people commit to it."

Livy heaved her cast-bound leg onto the ottoman and relayed the entire exchange.

Paula's nostrils flared. She rubbed her neck and fiddled with her cross necklace.

"I'm upset your grandma said those things to you." Paula reached over and placed her hand on Livy's. "True, some churchgoers are guilty of domestic violence. But you can ask yourself this question: Does it undo Christ's sacrifice on the Cross for you?"

"I guess not."

"The real issue is Christ, not Christians. Any of us are

capable of falling into sin. Your grandma is focusing on fallible human beings. She should be focusing on Christ."

Livy shuddered. "She won't go there, believe me."

"I got the impression she's closed to the gospel."

"About as tightly closed as you can get."

"As far as her remark about Hell…" Paula's eyes moistened. "It's hard when we realize our loved ones didn't make it to heaven. But it should give us reason to respond to God with reverent fear, not rejection. God has power over your grandma's soul, whether she believes it or not."

Chapter Thirty

Scott braked in his driveway, thankful to be home after a long day. Out of habit, he visualized a calendar in his head and marked a big red X across today's square—four blank squares before the weekend.

The deepening dusk and his growling stomach warned him Shari would soon arrive, and he needed to start dinner. He glanced at the driveway to his right and James McRabb Senior leaning against his pickup, one foot crossed over the other. In one hand, he held a glass with an inch of amber liquid. With the other, he beckoned Scott.

He got out and approached, his steps slowing.

"How's it going, Scott." Judging by James's tone, it wasn't a question.

"Not bad." Scott offered a hand, glad to see Jamie's car wasn't home.

James grasped his hand and shook. "Hey, can I ask a favor?"

What else was new? Scott moved into the arc of the porch light.

James sipped his whiskey. "I know you know a lot about electronics and whatnot. Well, Jamie's been having trouble lately with his car stereo. We were wondering if you wouldn't mind taking a look when he gets home from work tonight. 'Bout nine thirty or so."

Scott arranged a concerned expression. "What's it doing?"

"It dies at the oddest times. He says—"

"I can give you an educated guess." Scott clamped his teeth over his lower lip to stifle an incriminating smile.

"Yeah, please do."

"I suspect he's got the volume cranked too high. Those components can be pretty delicate, and he's likely overworking them. Like runnin' a car at eighty miles an hour in second gear. Tell him to see if it works better at half the volume. And it'll last longer for him, too."

"Thanks, bud. I'll tell him, but he probably won't like it. He takes after his old man. Likes to blast his music. I know it's been a nuisance for you, and I apologize."

Scott turned to go, but James said, "Oh, hey. Wait."

Ready to burst with thwarted laughter, Scott swung back around.

James jerked a thumb toward the house. "Since we're on the subject, the sound system in the house has been doing funny things. Would you mind taking a listen and telling me what you think?"

He didn't wait for an answer, but strolled along the front walkway to the door. Scott followed with heavy steps. A few minutes delay couldn't hurt. He allowed a grin to release while James had his back to him.

At the front door, James beckoned again. Scott mustered a somber expression and followed his neighbor into the dim living room.

"Want a beer?" asked his host.

"No, thanks." The same answer he gave every time. James still asked every time.

James lifted his glass. "Jim Beam?"

"No, but thanks."

The living room's cove ceiling created the illusion of height. Welcoming light shone through the archway to the kitchen. Pots and pans clanged, and chicken cooking tickled his nose. His stomach growled. Nancy McRabb truly earned her reputation as a topnotch cook. Which would explain the forty or so extra pounds around James's middle.

James led him to a dark corridor running the width of the house. Scott had never seen this section of the McRabb home. James stopped midway along the hall, opened a nondescript door, and glanced back. His lips stretched wide. "Welcome to my shrine." He flung the door wide, flipped the light switch, into another world.

Framed and mounted rock posters, many autographed, covered every inch of wall. Guitars of various colors and shapes propped along the edges. Red pillows scattered over the black leather sofa and armchair. Components of a surround sound system twinkled with LED lights on shelves stacked high with CDs and DVDs.

Scott gaped. "Nice."

"Thanks." James indicated the stereo, equipped with a subwoofer. "Want to take a listen? I think it's this speaker here. Keeps cuttin' out." He picked up a remote and pressed it. Pulsating rock music poured into the room.

Scott eyed the CDs—The FireAnts, Pearl Jam, Soundgarden, Free The Defendants, Nirvana. James must have owned most of these for twenty years or more. He checked out the posters, including Declan Decker in his FireAnts days. Behind Decker, Nils Nelsson grinned, his trademark coke-bottle glasses obscuring his eyes.

"You like all the local bands." Scott shouted over the music and moved closer to the poster. "Got any from outside Seattle?"

James leaned against the armchair. "Some, but we had the best bands right here in the Northwest back in the nineties." He swigged his whiskey. "Those were crazy days. Seattle's day in the sun. Never seen anything like it."

"I wasn't much of a grunge fan myself." Or of having to shout over a throbbing bass.

"Me and three other guys follow these bands around whenever we can. The ones still touring, that is. Mainly during summer when I'm not teaching. We're like old Deadheads. Except we call ourselves Grungeheads."

James fell silent and let the music reverberate around them. Scott couldn't move, couldn't speak. He'd had no idea something like this existed right next door.

He studied the Declan Decker poster. The rocker truly resembled Livy. James appeared at his side. "Shame about Nils Nelsson. You heard about him dying, didn't you?"

Scott nodded, his throat already going sore from yelling.

"Did you know Decker's twin daughters live a few blocks from here?"

He swung his head toward James, trying not to look too astounded. "Really? How do you know?"

"Oh, you know, word gets around. We Grungeheads make it our business to find out trivia about all the local bands."

How could James know a thing like that when Livy and DeeDee were so hush-hush? He was pretty sure Livy didn't even know he knew her father's identity.

"Pretty cool, dontcha think?" James's words slurred.

"Pretty cool. Do any other neighbors know?"

"Doubt it. Most people in this neighborhood don't give a diddley-squat about these bands anymore. It's not exactly a hippie hangout." James picked up the remote and adjusted the balance. "What do you think of the sound? Figured out why it's cutting out?"

"Not yet. Do you mind shutting it off for a sec?"

James obliged, and the noise ceased. Scott turned on the audio unit, then lowered the volume and put his ear next to each speaker. He fiddled with the balancer, and then flipped it off.

"I think there's a wiring problem in this speaker." He

pointed to the culprit. "If you don't mind, I can unhook it from the audio and work on it at home."

"That's fine. I owe ya, man."

Scott detached the speaker. "No, you don't. It's what neighbors are for."

"No, really. I'll have my wife bake you one of her wicked key lime pies. Don't want you to do it for free." James flipped off the light, and Scott followed him to the living room.

Something nagged at him. He wracked his brain, having wanted to ask James a question earlier, but the guy kept talking. Now he'd forgotten the question.

James slapped him on the back as they stood on the porch.

Scott nestled the speaker more snugly under his arm and glanced at his driveway. "I've got to get home and start dinner. The ex-wife is supposed to be here at seven, and I wanted to soften her up with homemade pasta."

James laughed. "Good luck, man. I don't envy you. Glad I don't have an ex in my life." He waved and went inside.

Had James really just rubbed his nose in his misfortune? Scott clenched his jaw and strode home to start the noodles. After he'd called Shari last night and told her he needed to talk, she promised to come over at seven. Without the girls.

"Father God." He stepped into his garage and set the speaker on the workbench. "I know the outcome is in Your hands." He took a deep breath. "Please move in Shari's heart. I need her home. I need my marriage back together."

If God restored his marriage, he could stop thinking about Livy.

In the kitchen, he frowned at the floor, praying and pleading. Minutes passed before a glimmer of hope lifted his spirits.

Letting out the breath he'd been holding, he retrieved pots and skillets and prepared his peace offering.

Just as he finished stirring green peppers into the marinara sauce, the doorbell rang. Shari stood there, a half-smile exposing one side of a perfect row of teeth. She wore the snug blue sweater he'd liked so much on her. Deliberate, maybe?

The familiar scent of Tabu emanated from her as she followed him into the dining room. They made small talk while they filled their plates, and then sat down across from each other, Shari gravitating to her old spot.

She wrapped a bundle of angel hair pasta around her fork and placed it in her mouth. "This is so good, Scott." Something about her hair looked different tonight. And she was in a good mood, for which he was thankful.

Scott felt like he'd sailed back in time to when the two of them ate dinner together every night, with their daughters' bright hair and happy smiles lighting the dining room. And his heart.

"Glad you like it." He dipped an asparagus spear in melted butter and bit down, savoring the succulent texture and taste. He hoped Shari appreciated the soft rock playing in the background.

"I have to admit, I miss your cooking. You spoiled me with authentic Italian pasta. Americans like their pasta too soft."

He swallowed. "Come back home, and I'll cook for you every night."

Shari shook her head as she chewed. "Is that what this is about?"

"What did you think it was about?"

"I hoped it was about child support, that you'd agree to increase it."

"Forget child support. Shari, we need to be a family again."

She said nothing, and Scott set his fork down and

watched her chew. She wouldn't meet his gaze.

Finally she looked up, an ocean of misery in her eyes. "Haven't we discussed this subject umpteen times already?"

"Every time I see the girls, they ask me when you and I are going to live together again. And I just don't know how to answer."

"The girls will be fine, if that's what you're worried about. Look at me. I survived my parents' divorce." She lifted another bite to her lips.

"No, they're not fine. They don't smile or laugh like they used to—"

"If you're trying to send me on a guilt trip, it won't work."

"Shari." Scott placed his palms on the table and leaned forward, no longer hungry. "I miss you. I miss us. I miss being together when the girls have special events at school—" He broke off when he saw her expression. Consternation fought with dismay and formed tears in her pale blue eyes.

"I'm sorry, Scott." She put her fork down and let the tears fall. "I didn't want to hurt you. You're a good man." She sniffed. The long, drawn-out sound grated his ears. "But I've moved on. I can't go back. My heart left a long time ago."

Her words pummeled him. "Why did your heart leave?" he choked out.

She picked up a napkin and caught a falling tear. "I met someone. He lives in Boise. We met online." Firm resolve set her face in grim lines and dissolved her tears. "Besides, I'd be crazy to come back. I get more money out of you now than I ever did while we were married."

A knife sliced into his gut, spilling his blood. "Are you saying you filed for divorce to get more money out of me?"

She twirled pasta on her fork, started to lift it, and then lowered it back to the plate, her shoulders sagging deeply. He stood, ignoring his unfinished dinner, his breath accelerating.

Shari rose, still avoiding his gaze. "I'd better go home now. Thanks for the dinner." She hurried toward the door and let herself out, while he grabbed the plates and dumped uneaten food into the garbage disposal.

He'd been naïve to hope Shari would reconcile. With grief pounding his heart, he picked up their wedding photo from the living room table and bashed it against the wood. Glass shattered with a gritty shroud of noise.

He flinched as pain ripped across his insides. Kneeling next to the woodstove, he lit some kindling and newspapers. Soon a warm glow wafted toward him. Still on his knees, he worked the photo out of its frame and crammed it into the stove. Grim satisfaction mocked him as the memento of his failed marriage curled up and burst into flames.

Chapter Thirty-One

Livy tottered into Paula's living room, bags of snacks in hand, to join the other Thursday night fellowshippers. Scott sat on a sofa conversing with Molly, the animated single mom she'd met last week. Scott, sporting a Marine buzz cut, glanced up when Livy waved at him. Instead of returning her greeting, he shifted back to Molly. Livy flinched at the uncharacteristic snub. She couldn't think of a thing she'd done to instigate it—Unless Paula told him she'd thought he beat his wife. Ouch. Surely, she wouldn't have.

Paula came toward her, arms open wide. "Livy. How'd you get here?"

"I persuaded Will to drop me off."

"Oh. He was okay with it?"

"As long as I don't say the word *church*, he just thinks I'm hanging out with my friend Paula."

Paula gave a wry chuckle and helped Livy dish up some food. "He's certainly welcome to come too. I'd love to meet him."

"I know." Livy glanced at Scott. Bringing Will here would never work. "I'll bring him over to meet you soon."

Paula searched her face. "Are things going well between you two?"

Livy shrugged, a frown tightening her face. "For the most part. Since DeeDee's been ice-grilling me all week, he's stepped up. He takes me to my doctor appointments, shopping, and so forth. But there's this wall between us. I feel reluctant to talk about Christ. And I can also tell he's antsy to, you know, pick up where we left off." Her tongue tripped, and her face heated.

Paula nodded. "Of course he is. He's a man. Have you decided how you'll handle it?"

"I think you and I need a private talk about that real soon."

Paula led the way to the living room with Livy's plate. "Look, there's some room next to Scott. Let's go sit." Paula set Livy's plate on the coffee table and helped her settle on the cushion. When Livy sat back with a sigh, Paula claimed a folding chair at a right angle to the sofa. Rick's laugh boomed from across the room.

Scott sat with his back to her. She tapped his shoulder blade. "Hi."

He offered a quick, over-the-shoulder nod. "Hey, Livy. Good to see you." Turning back to Molly, he resumed their conversation. A smug smile parted Molly's red lips.

"I'm ready for seconds," he told Molly. "How about you?"

Molly gave a silvery laugh. "I'm ready for pie, myself."

Scott grabbed his plate, still half-filled with food, and Molly followed him to the dining room. Livy pursed her lips, unsure what she'd witnessed. Maybe Scott just wanted to be alone with Molly and used a flimsy excuse.

A budding new romance could be happening under their noses. She grinned, picked up her plate, and forked a bite of potato salad into her mouth.

Paula laid her hand on Livy's shoulder. "Livy." She lowered her voice. "Before I forget, I have the name and number of the person I told you about. In fact, I talked to her yesterday and somewhat explained your situation. She said she has an opening tomorrow at noon. If you want it, call her in the morning. I can take you if you need a ride."

A host of emotions swirled inside Livy, and she tried to

grab at and make sense of them. Tightening her grip on her plate, she met Paula's eyes. "Sometimes I wonder if I really need to reopen the past." Her stomach twisted. "I mean, what's done is done. If her death wasn't an accident, wouldn't someone have figured it out?"

"No, not if involved only you. And it still affects you. It's floating around in your subconscious, demanding you take it out and look at it."

Her appetite fled. Still, Livy forced a bite of lettuce into her dry mouth to give herself something to concentrate on. She tried to chew, but it felt like chewing cardboard. Voices swirled around her, clamoring in her head.

Claire came over and sat on the cushion Scott vacated. "Hey," said Claire. "Good to see you again. Livy, right?"

"Yes." Livy gripped her plate tighter. "Not to chase you away, but I think Scott's sitting there."

Claire's smile vanished. "No, he's not. He and Molly are talking in the kitchen like they've forgotten the rest of us."

Livy snickered at Paula, whose face puckered. "I find that hard to believe."

"Why?" Claire's tone threw out a challenge.

"Well, because…" Paula opened her mouth then closed it.

"Molly's such a flirt." Claire's mouth clenched.

Livy covered her mouth to hide her grin, thinking of numerous times she and DeeDee fought over a man. Nothing beat a good chick fight for injecting drama into the evening.

But no chick fight erupted. Scott left early. Livy heard him near the front door saying goodbye to Paula and Rick. She hadn't had a chance to talk with him since last week, and she missed their discussions. She pulled herself up and hobbled over. He stood with his back to her as Paula and Rick took turns hugging him, and didn't see her until she moved next to him and laid a hand on his arm.

"Scott."

He turned a stoic face and stepped back.

"I like the ex-marine look you've got going on." He merely stared, and she chuckled. "You know, the new buzz cut." She widened her smile, hoping to lighten him up and encourage further conversation.

He ran a hand over his head, his eyes unreadable. "Oh. Right." He glanced at Paula, then waved, opened the door, and stepped out. "See y'all later." He shut the door with a thud.

Livy frowned at the closed door. What was going on with him? Not only would her own sister not talk to her anymore, but also the person responsible for helping her come to know God?

A now-familiar weepy feeling crept over her. She hoped Paula couldn't read it.

Chapter Thirty-Two

Livy's first session with a therapist felt as strange as her first time in church. She sunk into fat, black-vinyl couch cushions and appraised Paula's colleague. Maureen perched on the edge of her chair, tailored slacks perfectly falling to her crossed ankles, highlighting patent leather pumps. Her face reminded Livy of Paula's—chin lifted in calm detachment, mouth soft with compassion, eyes filled with caring. A face to inspire confidence and trust.

Maureen tipped her clipboard. "I understand you're here to talk about your mother's death."

"Yes."

"Tell me about her."

"It happened over twenty years ago."

Maureen's professional mask slipped, and surprise flashed across her face. "Twenty years? Then you would have been a small child."

"I was six. Going on seven."

"What brings you here to talk about it all these years later?"

"Paula Townsend thought I should."

Maureen smiled. "But there must have been a reason."

"Yes. She said you know of a therapy able to unlock old memories."

"I see." Maureen scribbled on the clipboard notepad. "You have locked memories from your mother's death?"

"My boyfriend thinks so."

Maureen set her clipboard on her lap and looked Livy in

the eye. "Are you uncomfortable about this?"

Livy threw up her hands and brought them down on her thighs. "I'm not sure I want to delve into this. Yet part of me does. I was thinking about my mother when I got hit by a car and ended up like this." She pointed to her cast-bound leg. "And I've been having dreams about her, which I haven't had for years."

"Something is eating at you, but you don't know what it is."

"I suppose."

"I think I can help you. But I can't make any guarantees. And you also need to know that, if we do discover anything, it might be very painful. But I can help you with that, too."

Livy nestled her hands in her lap and nodded.

"Now, tell me everything you know about the day your mother died."

"Before I do, I need to tell you who my father is."

"If you feel it's important, please do. Everything you tell me is confidential, other than those few exceptions listed on the paperwork I gave you."

Livy inhaled. "My father is Declan Decker." Her breath came out with a whoosh.

Maureen's brows rose to mid-forehead. "Really. How very interesting. I was a huge fan back in the day."

Livy offered a feeble smile.

"Is he still in the area?"

"No, he moved to LA years ago."

"So you don't see him much."

"About once or twice a year."

Maureen crossed one leg over the other and clasped her clipboard. "Okay. Thank you for the heads-up. Now I want to hear about your mother's death. Tell me everything you do know."

Livy stared at the wall of books behind Maureen. "One

day, when I was six, I was lying on the couch in the TV room. My sister and my nanny were in the room with me. I sat up and said, 'I'm hungry,' then went to find my mom. I don't remember why. My sister followed me and asked me where I was going. I said, 'I'm going to find Mommy.' She said, 'Don't you remember? Mommy's dead.'"

Livy burst into tears.

***

By the time Livy finished telling Maureen of the circumstances surrounding her mother's death, they were nearly out of time.

"Your story is a tragic one." Maureen set the clipboard face down on her lap. "I'm afraid I don't remember hearing about it at the time. Your father was pretty low-key about his personal life."

"Yes, he was. My sister and I liked it that way."

"And I have to agree with your boyfriend. He must be an insightful man. It's obvious you experienced a different version of events than your sister did." She held up the clipboard and squinted at it. "Your sister says you stood at the bedroom door, scared and hesitant to come in. Then when you saw your mother on the floor, you screamed and fainted." Maureen looked at Livy. "I can tell you what I think…if you'd like to hear."

"Yes, I would."

"I think you saw something right before your mother died that you weren't meant to see. And it rocked your world."

Livy's heart lurched. She dug her fingernails into her palms.

"And I'll do my best to help you figure out what it was."

"Thank you." Livy clenched her fingers together.

"Same time next week?"

"Sounds good."

Maureen helped Livy with her coat and assisted her to the elevator. From there, Livy only had to manage one city block to Ivar's Seafood Bar where she and Paula had agreed to meet for lunch.

"Wow." Livy, inhaling the savory odors of salmon mingled with clams, joined Paula at a window table overlooking Aurora Blvd. "That was intense."

Paula handed her a menu. "But helpful, I hope?"

Livy nodded and waved away the menu. "I'm going to have a chowder bowl. Anyway, I liked Maureen. Today all I did was fill her in on everything I knew about my mother's death. I'll go back next week."

Paula studied the menu while Livy scanned the popular, nautically themed restaurant. She shifted her tie-dyed skirt so it didn't bunch in back and sighed. "I'm getting tired of wearing skirts all the time."

A young waiter, scholarly in square black glasses, approached and took their orders. After he left, Livy leaned toward her friend.

"Maureen thinks I saw something I wasn't meant to see."

Paula nodded. "It would make sense."

"She said it could be something painful."

"I agree. When I take you home, why don't we have a prayer time about it? Even better, come over tonight and Rick and I will lay hands on you and pray. I'm betting Scott would be willing to pop over, too."

"Would he? I'm not so sure. He acted so standoffish last night. Just because he's interested in Molly doesn't mean he has to ignore his friends."

Paula's bangs swished as she shook her head. "Like I said last night, I find it hard to believe he's really interested in her."

"But why? He's a nice-looking man. She's a nice-looking

woman. Why wouldn't they be interested in each other?"

"A couple of reasons. First, he attends a men's accountability group, and they are holding him accountable to not date for a year after his divorce."

"A whole year? That seems too long."

"That's about how long the experts recommend people wait after a failed marriage to become involved with someone else. Too many people plunge into rebound relationships, which oftentimes don't work out because they didn't allow themselves to heal."

"Oh." Livy sipped her water. "What's the second reason?"

"He knows he can't be alone with attractive women. At least not yet."

"Because of the one-year thing?"

"Yes, and because it's too easy to get sucked into temptation."

"Hmm." Such foreign concepts. "Life is different for Christians, isn't it?"

"It is." Paula laughed. "We're aliens and strangers on this planet."

"I get the impression Scott is a man of integrity. I can't picture him getting sucked into temptation."

"He is a man of strong character."

"His wife must have been crazy to leave him."

"Not so much crazy as flaky. I worry about those little girls."

Livy shrugged. "Her loss." But how could someone walk away from a husband who was not only handsome, but also intelligent and kind? "If I had a husband like him, no way would I let him get away."

Paula cast her a look so penetrating, Livy wished she could unspeak the words. Paula probably thought she was interested in Scott.

When Paula spoke, her voice held a lilt. "Hopefully he'll find a wife who feels the same way."

***

Scott sat at his kitchen table, his laptop in front of him, and eyed the Bible lying next to it, trying to deflect the guilt darts shooting through him. He hadn't read it since Monday morning. Five days ago. He tapped his feet, waiting for Shari to drop by with his daughters. She'd better be here soon, because it was already nine and their dance class started in two hours.

Instead of picking up his Bible, he opened his social media.

The day had started sunny, and the weather forecast called for partly cloudy with a high of fifty-five. Not bad for a March morning. But not enough to thaw the deep freeze inside him.

The finality of his failed marriage had punched him upside the jaw Monday night when Shari walked out the door. Despite his numerous, fervent prayers, God had closed that door with an irreversible slam. A bleak chill sneaked into his heart and lingered in his chest all week, like a bad cold, rendering him incapable of smiling or laughing. Incapable of doing anything except grumble complaints at God.

God could have changed Shari's heart, but He'd chosen not to.

Scott barely managed to pull himself out of bed each morning and drag himself to work. Then come home, pop a frozen entrée into the microwave, and zone in front of the TV until he got too sleepy to stay awake. Most every night this week, he awakened in the wee hours of the morning on the couch. He heaved off the couch, and then crashed on top of his bed, fully clothed, tossing and turning for about an hour before finally falling asleep again. The alarm rang at six a.m., and the dreary routine began all over again.

Day after day, same old, same old.

He rested his elbows on the table, focused on the laptop, and clicked the friend requests. *Molly O'Connor wants to be your friend.* His mood amped up a notch. It wouldn't break any rules to accept Molly's friend request. In fact, he should take her out for coffee. She was available and interested. She deserved happiness after her cheating ex-husband abandoned her and their two children for another woman. Maybe in time, Scott could become interested in her, too. Forget the one-year rule. It was an arbitrary, legalistic measuring rod some guy dreamed up to sell books to poor suckers. Look what it got him—lonely evenings and an empty bed. Longing for an unavailable woman.

He had searched the Scriptures for a passage or verse to back up the one-year rule, but found nothing. He could ask Dan, but Dan would try to convince him the concept was in one of the Ten Commandments.

The second friend request came from someone named Vienna Inyoface Lenno. He didn't know anyone named Lenno, although it looked Italian. So where had he met this Vienna person?

He opened her profile—Aha. The cute dance teacher filling in for Livy. Miss Vee. The girl who'd made him laugh. The opera lover.

When he clicked her friends list and scrolled the names, his jaw dropped. Famous names. Musicians and actors. Local politicians.

Who was this girl, and how did she know these people?

He found Livy and DeeDee's names as well, and leaned closer to Livy's profile photo—a headshot of her and Will facing each other. Will's beaming face proclaimed he knew what a lucky man he was. Her Sofia Vergara smile glowed; her Jennifer Aniston hair reflected streaks of light. God blessed Livy with hair any man would want to run his fingers through. And a mouth any man would want to kiss.

Trying to pull his gaze away, he tightened his jaw at the unfairness of life. And love. And God.

He exited Livy's profile and returned to Vienna's. He ought to get to know her better before he decided whether to accept her friend request.

When the doorbell rang, he jumped up and raced to the door. Kinzie and Lacie stood on his porch alone, clutching miniature suitcases. He glanced toward the driveway and saw the edge of Shari's car, its exhaust clouding his front yard. No surprise she'd decided not to accompany the girls to the door this time.

Picking up his beautiful Lacie, he lifted her in the air and relished her gleeful squeals. Then he set her down, picked up sweet Kinzie, and hugged her to his chest.

Their warm smiles and laughter melted some of the winter ice in his heart.

Chapter Thirty-Three

DeeDee scrunched her legs under herself, struggling to concentrate on her least favorite task of running a business — marketing calls. The pungent scent of brewing coffee saturated the room as she dialed the next number.

"Hello, Ms. Swanson?"

"Ye-es?" came the cautious response.

"This is DeeDee calling from Saffire Dance."

"Oh. Hi."

"I wanted to thank you for your interest in our studio, and to let you know we offer a family discount of ten percent..." Her brain checked out as her mouth uttered the oft-repeated words. She refocused when Ms. Swanson promised to bring her three daughters in next week to observe.

On down the list she went. Despite her displeasure over the task, the growing level of interest in Saffire pleased her. This month, ten parents filled out their contact information on the website. Odds were, three to four of those would make the commitment and sign their children up.

Her cell phone chimed with an incoming text from Nick, bringing to mind memories of their date last night. She smiled and let her mind wander to more pleasant territory.

She glanced at the time. Class would be over in ten minutes. She logged off the computer and stretched her cramped legs. After scooping the coffee carafe under one arm and the packages of cookies in the other, she lugged her load into Studio A. When she finished setting out the snacks and beverages, she stopped and listened. Faint music from Studio C buzzed into the hallway. Vienna's Lyrical class didn't usually require music so upbeat. What was up?

She eased the studio door open wide enough to peek in, and her jaw dropped. Vienna, her newly-blonde hair falling out of its clip, was dancing with mad abandon, as were all the students, in a wild freeform, while The Black Eyed Peas blared through the speakers. Most of the parents laughed and applauded.

Vienna paused her dancing long enough to beckon the adults. "Hey, parents. Don't just sit there. Come join us!" Her hand swept through the air. "It's party time."

DeeDee stalked into the room, purpose in every stride. Vienna saw her coming and grinned. "Oh look, here comes the principal."

Snickers echoed from the parents' bench. Nearly choking with rage, DeeDee longed to slap her, and would if not for a roomful of eyes watching with anticipation. She spoke in an undertone, her face flaming. "Turn that off right now."

Vienna scowled, but complied. "Party pooper," she whispered and faced the kids, hands on hips. "The principal says, party's over, dudettes."

DeeDee stood inches away, her legs planted and arms crossed, her head feeling hot, stuffed with burning coals, their smoke spiraling out her ears. She took in a deep, cooling breath, letting it tame her fiery rage, and then perched on the edge of the spectator bench.

Vienna led the girls in a few minutes of cool-down exercises until class ended.

"Don't forget." Vienna smiled at the parents. "Cookies and coffee across the hall. Come on over."

DeeDee blocked Vienna's progress as the parents and kids filed out. When Vienna glared, but halted, DeeDee grabbed her arm. "What were you thinking?"

Vienna jerked her arm away. "I was thinking: let's lighten things up, man. Whatsa matter with that?"

"Did you clear it with me first?"

A distracted frown crossed Vienna's face. "Hey." She cupped her hand behind her ear. "Is that your office phone ringing?"

Sure enough, the faint ring of the portable phone drifted from the office. DeeDee spun on her heel and hurried along the hall, reaching the phone after the fourth ring. "Saffire, may I help you?" She crossed her fingers in case the caller proved to be one of the undecided parents she'd spoken to.

Nothing except buzzing and faint background voices greeted her.

"Hello? Who is this?"

She waited five more seconds, then clicked off and grasped the doorknob. The phone rang again. She caught it on the second ring.

"Yes? Who is this?"

Someone breathed in her ear. She counted to three, prepared to hang up again.

"DeeDee?" Her hand halted inches from her ear when the breathy male voice purred through.

"Yes?"

"Hi."

"Hi. Is this Qu—I mean, David?"

"It is."

"What can I do for you?" He'd better get to the point.

"How are you?"

"Fine." She nearly snapped the word. "How are you?"

"Fine."

"Didn't I see you last hour? Did you forget something?"

His plaintive sigh whispered into her ear. "I did."

"What did you forget?"

"Can you be a princess and see if I left my sweater in the

bathroom? I'll hold."

DeeDee rolled her eyes. "Hang on." She hurried to the bathroom. En route, she glanced over her shoulder toward Studio A, hoping for evidence Vienna was behaving herself and being a good hostess.

She checked both bathrooms, the towel dispensers, the backs of the doors, and then tucked the phone between her ear and shoulder. "No sweater, David."

He uttered an obscenity. "I know I left it there somewhere. Can you check the bench in the studio? Pretty please?"

She stifled a sigh and carried the phone to Studio B. Again, she peeked into Studio A where the parents and kids were socializing — everything calm and chaos free.

DeeDee reached the empty hip-hop studio, set the phone down, and checked the bench, behind the stereo, in the corners.

No sweater.

She put the phone to her ear. "Sorry, David. I don't see it." The phone's Low Battery indicator pulsed. She needed to get it on the charger soon. "But I'll keep my eyes open and let you know if I find it, okay?" She pivoted toward the office.

"Thanks, doll." His pause lingered.

"Is that all?"

"Hang on. A text is coming in."

Only his breathing came through for several seconds, and then a chuckle.

"Okay, that was all." He uttered a squeaky goodbye and clicked off.

DeeDee shook her head. Too bad she couldn't recover time wasted looking for a sweater. She plugged in the phone charger and headed toward Studio A, reaching the door as Scott and his daughters were leaving. She waved, and he smiled and waved back.

"How are you, DeeDee?"

She appraised him. His eyes sparkled, a rarity in Scott, and his mouth twitched. "I'm fine. And you?"

He opened his mouth, but she didn't hear his answer. The truth hit her like a tsunami.

The strange phone call. The fruitless search for a sweater. A nonexistent sweater, no doubt. The whole thing smelled of Vienna.

DeeDee hoofed it into Studio A. No Vienna. She approached Anna, Haley's mom. "Anna, glad you could stay."

Anna nodded. "This was a great idea."

"Did you see where Vienna went?"

She pointed to the door. "She just left."

"Thanks. Who was she talking to before she left?"

Forehead scrunched, Anna narrowed her lids at DeeDee. "Kinzie and Lacie's father, I believe."

DeeDee'd bet a million bucks Vienna promised Queen David backstage passes to Depeche Mode if he distracted her so Vienna could work her magic on Scott.

And DeeDee walked right into it.

How could she have been so gullible?

***

Scott's spirits got kick-started back to cruising when Miss Vee boasted she had two extra backstage passes for The Black Eyed Peas concert next weekend. When she played their song Boom Boom Pow and started dancing like a maniac, he couldn't decide if she was a hardcore rebel or a barrel of laughs.

From her dig when DeeDee walked in, he'd peg her as a rebel. But judging by her taste in music, a barrel of laughs.

She'd smiled at him when she mentioned the passes, as though she could see his dismal mood and knew he needed a lift. Yet Miss Vee couldn't possibly know The Black Eyed Peas had been his and Shari's favorite band during their early years. Although he'd rid himself of all his raunchy music after coming to know Christ, the band's songs still fascinated him.

Miss Vee couldn't know that.

After class, he checked out the corridor and office, half-hoping to see Livy, half-relieved when he didn't. He followed the others to Studio A and helped himself to coffee and cookies, watching his daughters hang on the bars with one hand and eat cookies with the other.

Somehow, Miss Vee ended up next to him.

"Dude." Her voice came out low and husky. "You were rockin' and rollin' in there. I saw those feet twitching."

He laughed. He couldn't seem to help it with the cute way she talked.

"I can tell you got a dancer in you, just waitin' to come out." She didn't look like a rebel at all, except the blue streaks in her hair. And those tattoos on her fingers and hands. The planes of her face were soft, like a child's, her eyes round and guileless behind thick pink lenses.

When she unclipped her hair, the blue-and-blonde mass fell like a thick curtain to her waist. He half-expected her to topple. Her small frame didn't look sturdy enough to support so much hair.

Shaking it out, she tilted her head at him. "Sent you a friend request. Did ya get it?"

He nodded. "I was surprised to see it."

"Why you be surprised? Us Italians gotta stick together."

He stepped back. "You are not Italian."

"Am so. On my mother's side. My dad's Swedish, like half the dudes in Seattle. I take after him." She cast a quick glance at the door then turned to him, her eyes asparkle. "Hey, you like The Black Eyed Peas, right?"

"My wife and I were huge fans. How'd you guess?"

"The way your face lit up in there. How would you like to meet 'em?"

He felt his mouth fall open. "No way."

"Way." She thrust her fingers into her red jacket pocket and pulled out a long rectangular ticket plastered end to end with Fergie's sultry pose. "I know these gangsters."

"But how?"

"I got connections." She leaned forward, dropping her voice. "Since nobody else wants 'em, they're yours."

Could he really *meet* Fergie and the rest of the band? Wouldn't Shari regret her words if she knew.

"Okay, I'll take them." He held out his hand.

She shook her head. The ticket disappeared behind her back. "Not yet. There's a catch."

"What catch?"

"Know where Uncle Herman's is?"

"That club in Edmonds?"

"Yeah. Meet me there tonight at seven."

"I can't." He gestured toward his daughters. "I have my girls tonight."

"Tomorrow night?"

"Why not now?"

"I left one of them at home." She returned the ticket to her pocket and took out her cell phone. "I gotta run. See you tomorrow night," she called over her shoulder. He hadn't even told her he'd go. She walked away, punching keys on her phone leaving his mind skimming through his list of friends, wondering who might want to go see The Black Eyed Peas with him.

***

"Daddy, aren't we going to Sunday school this morning?"

Scott groaned at Kinzie's question and glanced out the

kitchen window at the rain. He swallowed a pancake bite and met his daughter's questioning gaze.

"Not today, Kinzie."

"How come?"

Because the gloomy rain outside matched the gloom inside himself. Because seeing the happy married couples and their happy kids reminded him of his loss.

"Because I haven't taken y'all to Kidd Valley in a long time. Wouldn't that be fun?"

"But we can go after Sunday school."

"We could, but then we'd have to wait in a long line. If we skip church and go early, we'll get right in."

"Oh." Kinzie nodded at the plan's sensibility.

Besides, he and God weren't on the best of terms. And he'd been ignoring Dan's texts, asking why he hadn't shown up at the men's breakfast Friday morning and was everything okay? The last thing he needed was for Dan to find him at church and pin him down when he had nothing but feeble excuses.

He couldn't tell Dan everything was not okay, that God was forcing him to live a life he didn't want to live, and starting tonight, he'd be living the life *he* wanted. After all, some harmless fun wouldn't hurt God's feelings, nor would a sort-of date with cute Miss Vee.

He smiled in anticipation.

Chapter Thirty-Four

The parking lot at Uncle Herman's in downtown Edmonds was not crowded, and Scott found a spot five slots from the main door. Lucky for him, with the rain coming down in torrents. Rivulets freefell from roofs and streamed into gutters. Tiny rivers flowed along the sidewalk and twinkled under the streetlights. He pulled his fleece jacket hood over his head and shoved his hands in his pockets, keeping his head down as his strides carried him into the dim, smoky club.

He'd gone for casual tonight—jeans, Seahawks jersey—and he fit right in.

He spotted Vienna's bright hair and beelined to her corner booth. A mug of dark beer rested on the table in front of her. On a tiny stage next to the bar, a twenty-something singer strummed his guitar and crooned a folksy tune.

"Hey." He eased off his dripping jacket, draped it over the back of the booth, and slid in.

"Hey." Vienna grinned.

A big clip halfway fastened her hair, and hunks draped her shoulders. Clownish cosmetics caked her face beneath square black eyeglasses. Light sparkled on tiny rhinestones dotting the frames. He focused on them, not the shirt cut low enough to attract all kinds of male attention.

She obviously wasn't going for cute tonight.

He shifted, feeling an edge of discomfort. "Got the tickets?"

She eyed him with a lopsided smile. "So you're just

gonna waltz in here, grab the tickets, and bail?"

"Well, uh." He supposed he *had* assumed he would stop by, get the tickets, and leave, but he was picking up the vibe she considered this a real date. Her dress, her makeup, the way she ogled him…

Well, he didn't have to do anything he didn't want to do, and if she read more into this evening, it was her problem.

He needed a moment of space. "Where's the men's room?"

She pointed toward a hallway behind him.

"Can you excuse me a sec? Be right back."

She nodded, and he ventured along the corridor lined with closed doors. In the dark, he made out a Don't-Even-Think-Of-Coming-In-Here sign.

He shuddered, wondering what went on behind that particular closed door. Sensing something evil around him, he quickened his steps as though the darkness were seeping out from under the door and snaking through the corridor.

He pushed open the men's room door. Once inside, he whispered a prayer out of habit. "Lord, I ask You'll keep Your hand of protection over me."

As he returned to the table, a faint voice whispered to his spirit, reminding him his accountability group was God's hand of protection over him. Scott shook off the voice. It wouldn't hurt to humor her if it meant going home with two tickets to The Black Eyed Peas.

He smiled as he sat.

A waitress approached and placed a napkin before him. She balanced the tray against her middle and gave him an expectant look. "What can I get you?"

"May I see your beer menu?"

When she handed him a thick leather-lined menu, he perused the list. He hadn't indulged in a good dark beer in months. His mouth watered.

He placed his order then turned to Vienna and started with a safe subject. "I'm curious. How do you know Livy and DeeDee?"

Vienna lifted her beer mug. "There's a long story." Her voice sounded less husky and more heartfelt. "I've known them for, like, forever. Their mom and dad were best friends with my mom and dad."

"Interesting." Vee would have known Livy as a child then, possibly from before Declan Decker became famous.

An idea teased him. If her father was Declan Decker's best friend, then…

He visualized a grinning Nils Nelsson with his coke-bottle glasses and famous long blond hair. He eyed Vienna's equally long blonde hair. She claimed she took after her Swedish father…. Thick-lensed eyeglasses and all.

He was looking at Nils Nelsson's daughter. He'd wager his house on it.

It would explain so much — the famous friends, the carefree attitude. Enough clout to obtain backstage passes to The Black Eyed Peas.

She was still talking. "Livy and DeeDee and I, we were like the Three Musketeers, all the way through high school."

She must know Livy better than anyone besides DeeDee.

"Their mom called them Liv and Di."

Scott chuckled. "Serious?"

Her face had lost its playfulness. "She was, well, unique. She died when they were kids, and they started going by Livy and DeeDee." Her nose puckered. "Which makes me think of my dad, who died a few weeks ago." A sheen moistened her eyes. Her lips quivered, and when she clamped them together, her nostrils flared.

He said the first words that came to mind. "That's too bad."

"Yeah." She sniffed, and her shoulders slumped. "It was

really sad. He was only fifty-two."

The waitress returned with his bottle of beer and poured it into a chilled mug. He drank deep, smacking his lips. "Mmm, that's good." He smiled at the waitress. "Thanks."

"Welcome."

Vienna's face drooped. "I miss him a lot."

Scott tensed, waiting for a burst of emotion.

She heaved a deep breath and offered a half-smile edged with sadness. "Don't mind me. I'll be okay. I'm still getting over it."

"Understandable."

"It helps to know he's with God now, looking down on me and smiling."

Scott wasn't so sure Nils Nelsson made it to heaven, but he merely nodded, amazed and thankful the conversation strayed to spiritual matters.

Vienna straightened her shoulders and pointed a finger heavenward. "Sometimes I picture him saying to God, 'Can you send a couple of extra angels to watch over my daughter today, God? She's gonna need it.'" She gave a small giggle, which morphed into another puckered, watery-eyed smile. "Do you believe in God?"

His heart leaped. "I do."

"Me too." She sipped her beer with one hand and traced a crack in the table with the other. "I went to Sunday school as a child."

"You did?"

She met his eyes. "My mom took me every Sunday. It was fun with all the little stories and songs about Jesus and God. And making cute trinkets to take home to Mom."

"Ever thought about going back to church?"

She tilted her head. "Yeah, sometimes. Do you think it might help me deal with Dad's death? Like, help me heal faster?"

"I know it would. Some churches offer grief recovery ministries. I could get you information if you'd like."

Her eyes oozed gratitude as she leaned forward and placed a hand on his forearm. He averted his gaze from the front of her shirt. "I do want to know God better. Hanging out with you is probably the best thing I can do."

He smiled, feeling warm inside, having a good time, for the first time in more than six months. Vee proved to be a woman of depth after all. Whatever he could do to advance the Kingdom—

"I have a son." The abrupt subject change made his head reel. "Want to see his photo? His name's Fleming Michael."

"Unusual name."

"I named him after Renee Fleming, the opera singer. He usually lives with me, but he's with his dad for a few months so they can do father-son bonding." She held out her phone. A handsome blond boy, missing a front tooth, grinned at him.

"Cute kid. It's good he gets to spend time with his dad. That's important. I always wanted a son."

"I always wanted a daughter. Yours are so cute."

"They're great, aren't they?" He couldn't stop the goofy smile creasing his face.

"Your ex-wife seems nice. I talked to her at the Wednesday evening class."

Scott took a long sip of beer. "She's not exactly my favorite subject right now."

"I hear ya. My ex ain't my favorite topic either."

She stood, her beer mug empty. She gave him the same tilted-head, sincere gaze. "I don't know about you, but I'm still feeling a little down. I think I want to go home."

"Oh." His own beer mug was still half-full. "But I'm not done with my beer."

She shrugged. "Guess you'll want your tickets."

"That would be great." He'd run by the store and pick up

a six-pack. Stretching, he fumbled through his wallet and dropped a ten-spot.

"The tickets are in the car. Want to walk me out?"

"Of course." He retrieved his coat and helped her with hers, a long pink coat lined with fleece. A rich girl's coat.

Her face remained pensive, her lips pursed, as they left the club. Her steady strides displayed no hint of tipsiness.

He followed her through the deluge to the back of the parking lot, surprised two inches of standing water hadn't already pooled on the pavement.

She stopped next to a snazzy red Ferrari and dangled a key. The car beeped and flashed its lights.

A surge of awe swept him. What a sweet ride.

She winked as she stood in the streetlight's arc. Rain droplets beaded her coat hood and rolled down the side, splatting her shoulders. "Look at you. You be all, I wanna take a joyride in this thing. Am I right?"

His heart leaped for the third time that evening.

"How long has it been since you rode in a Ferrari?"

Well, never. He couldn't tell her so. "A long time."

She gestured to the passenger side. "Go ahead, climb on in. The tickets are in the door slot. I'll take you on a cruise while you grab them."

She didn't have to ask twice. He opened the door and folded his body into the low-slung bucket seat, lined with the softest leather he'd ever felt.

She climbed in, and the engine roared. "Yeah, baby. You da bomb." She swung into the parking lot and onto Edmonds's main drag. The wipers whipped back and forth, nearly wiping away the rain as fast as it fell.

She fiddled with some bells and whistles on the steering wheel. Soon his seat emitted warmth, and he was sitting on a leather-wrapped hot pad. A female opera singer warbled an aria, her voice thick with emotion, as if her world had collapsed around her.

He knew exactly how she felt.

Vienna glanced at him. "Where do you want to go?"

"You're the driver. Surprise me."

She grinned and revved the engine. Folks on the sidewalk swiveled their heads.

"Woot! I feel better already." She lowered the volume. "Ha, just think." The gravel pit was back. "Italian dude, Italian dudette, Italian wheels. Italian music! *Che figata*!"

Scott laughed, enthralled, as they zipped south along Edmonds Way. "What's that mean?"

"How cool is that!"

"When did you get this baby?" It probably cost as much as his house.

"Few months ago. It's a 2010 Italia." She laughed along with him. The tiny stones on her glasses flashed with each streetlight. "Zero to sixty in four seconds."

"Careful. You don't want to get pulled over for speeding."

"I know, dude. This baby's a cop magnet." She slowed and hooked a right, heading west toward the marina, and then hung a left.

He craned around to get his bearings. Dark, imposing shapes, partially hidden by trees, lined both sides of the residential road.

"Where are we?"

The narrow street wound left, then right. Like Rosemary Drive.

"Welcome to Woodway."

"Woodway? Really?" He couldn't help a quick intake of breath. The millionaires' hideaway, teeming with five-thousand square foot estates?

As they ventured farther along the winding street, the darkness deepened, but the rain seemed to let up. He no longer knew which direction they traveled. But he needn't worry; he wasn't in the drivers' seat. Plus, the God-built GPS system in his head never failed him yet.

Vienna hummed along to the music, and he leaned back, warmth seeping through him, dark shapes of trees flashing by. The comfortable silence stretched on.

She spun toward him. "Enjoying yourself?"

"Oh, yeah."

She uttered a raspy chuckle. "Just gotta stop by home, then I'll take you back. Aren't ya gonna get the tickets out of the slot over there?"

"Oh." He'd forgotten the tickets. "Right." He ran his fingers around the slot and grasped the contents.

"I found something here, but it's too dark to see."

"We'll be at my house soon."

"You live around here?"

"Mm. Hmm. Since last summer."

He couldn't think of an adequate reply. She jerked a sharp right, proceeded about a quarter mile along a skinny tree-lined road interspersed with gates. Then veered left onto a similar road, finally stopping at a driveway blocked by a pair of wrought-iron grandiose gates. The Ferrari's headlights illuminated a stone wall topped with barbed wire.

Vienna punched a button on the visor, and the gates swung upward in a slow arc. She slanted a gaze at him. "In case you're wonderin,' my daddy was rich."

Scott wondered why her wealth was so much showier than Livy and DeeDee's. After all, Decker's wealth must be at least comparable to Nelsson's.

A streetlight lit up the curved driveway and the thick trees lining either side. The Ferrari hummed along cobblestones and broke into a clearing, where a brick, multi-gabled house seemed to go on forever.

She stopped in front of the four-car garage and shut off

the engine.

"Welcome to Vee's Den." She switched on the dome light, and he looked at the tickets in his hand.

"Depeche Mode?" A swoop of disappointment hit him.

"Oops, those are for someone else." She snatched the tickets from his hand and frowned at them. "Now, what did I do with yours?" She screwed up her face, and Scott wrestled a tweak of annoyance.

She snapped her fingers. "I must have left yours on the kitchen counter." She shoved the tickets into the door slot beside her.

Scott fumbled in his jacket pocket to pull out his phone. He needed to see if anyone had tried to reach him. He managed to get the phone halfway out, but the seatbelt was clamped tight against his middle. He shifted and groped for the belt clasp.

Vienna sighed. "Gonna have to run in and grab them. Want to stay here or come in?"

"How long will you be?" He finally sprung the belt loose, which jolted his phone out of his pocket.

"Just a few."

He glanced at the dashboard clock. Eight thirty-five p.m. Plenty of time to get the tickets, ride back to his car, and get home before ten.

He felt around for his phone, but it had fallen on the floor. No matter. He'd get it later.

She gave a throaty laugh. "You be all, I wanna get the grand tour."

He chuckled. Was his awe factor so obvious? "I don't have time for a grand tour, but I don't mind a brief one."

She hit another button on the visor, and one of the four garage doors slid upward while a light flickered on inside. She swung her legs to the pavement and beckoned. "Follow me."

He tailed her through the lit garage, the size of a mini warehouse, empty other than a few boxes lining the shelves. He would have expected one or two more vehicles. So she wasn't a car collector.

Once inside the house, he sensed the vastness of it as she led him through room after room, flipping on lights with a remote. They entered a spacious kitchen so spotless he wondered if she ever used it. She stood in the middle of the room, her face puckered up, then walked around the center island and along each counter—marbled counters, finely crafted cabinets, shiny fixtures.

Impressive.

Vienna said nothing, but wandered into the next room. Mystified, Scott followed to a room displaying an 80-inch concave Smart TV and a state-of-the-art sound system. Shoes and clothes littered the tan carpet, and open snack bags spilled on a coffee table. A smoky mixture of cigarette and marijuana odors wrinkled his nose.

The plush sofa looked ready to turn an athlete into a couch potato. Vienna plopped onto the couch and crossed her legs.

"I think I found them." She removed her glasses, set them on a table, and squinted at him.

"Great." He held out his hand.

"But since you're here, you might as well stay for a few." She patted the cushion beside her.

He remained standing and heaved a breath. "I really shouldn't. I have to get up early for work."

Outside, a wind gust shook the multi-paned window, bringing a surge of pattering rain. Her face drooped. "Sunday nights can be hard, ever since my dad died." Her eyes misted over. "We used to talk on the phone about this time every Sunday evening." She clenched her lips, then, to his alarm, burst into tears.

"Oh." She sobbed, rocking back and forth, his discomfort growing by the second.

"Look." He tried for an assertive tone. "I really need to get back. Do you have a girlfriend you can talk to after you drop me off?"

She ignored his question and stood, wiping her eyes with her fingers. "I just need a hug." She approached, her eyes pleading, and grabbed him around the middle.

He jerked back and tried to extricate himself.

She let go and met his gaze. "I thought since you were a good Christian dude, you wouldn't mind giving a friend a hug."

He cast about for a response, finding none. Not liking the way her eyes glittered at him.

Beckoning to her, he said, "Let's go."

Smirking, she stayed rooted.

"Get the tickets and let's go," he repeated, firmer this time.

She fingered the buttons on her blouse as if preparing to remove it. Her voice dropped to a sultry whisper. "I like a man with backbone."

Bile churned in his gut. "Vienna, I didn't come here for this."

"You came for the tickets."

"Yes."

"Ha." She barked out a laugh. "Did you actually think I'd give away tickets worth four hundred dollars without something in it for me?"

Reality slammed into him like a wind shear. He lurched and spun, desperate to flee, then hotfooted his way to the other doorway, away from Vienna, and into a part of the house he hoped would lead to the front door.

"Hey," she shouted. "Good luck finding your way out of here." A series of distant beeps dinged, and the sheer depth of his predicament hit him. She'd turned on the burglar alarm. He had exactly sixty seconds to get out.

Panic threatened, and he breathed a prayer. Darkness still cloaked this section of the house. He paused to get his bearings. His sense of direction told him the front door was to his left, so he hurried down a short hall, shoulders loosening at the faint light shining through an archway at the end.

Follow the light.

He burst into the next room, his footsteps way too loud on the tile floor. A curving staircase wound to his right, and a double front door loomed to his left. Blessed light shone into the large windows, the streetlight revealing the way.

Hands trembling, he fumbled with the doorknob. Had Vienna followed him? Was she behind him right now, watching with those glittering eyes?

He didn't bother to turn his head. Prickles crept along his arms as he grappled with two deadbolts and a chain. Seconds ticked by. Any moment now, the alarm would screech in his ear.

His internal clock told him he had approximately fifteen seconds left. He wrenched at the locks, then the chain.

The chain caught, and he yanked on it. It gave, and he flung the door open with less than five seconds to spare. As he sprinted across the soaked lawn, even the persistent downpour couldn't slow him.

The gates were still open, so he ran as though flames licked his feet.

With a click and a squeak, the gates began to close. She was one determined woman.

He waved his arms as if he could stop them. "God. Help me!"

Dogs barked. He couldn't tell if they were after him.

The gears kept whirring, the gates closing. They were

about halfway down now. The barking dogs sounded closer.

Then the gates stopped. As Scott ran, something emitted a click and a groan as the mechanism malfunctioned.

His lungs heaved in deep breaths. "Praise God."

After another click, the gates continued their downward descent. A four-foot gap remained between the gates and the ground. Enough to squeeze under, but not if they kept closing. He could try to vault over them, but if they were hot-wired, he might not make it out in one piece.

He sprinted as though he were Usain Bolt, heart pounding, lungs aching. The gates stopped again with another groan.

A mere thirty feet to freedom. The dogs whined and barked again, louder and nearer.

In ten long strides, he reached the gates then rolled himself under just before they clicked and whirred into their final plunge. He hefted himself to his feet as they clanged shut with a decisive thud.

"Thank you, God." He was trembling so hard—from horror, from exertion, from cold—he could scarcely keep himself upright. He longed to lie down and curl up, but he needed to call a cab.

Two dogs barked and snarled on the other side of the gate. What a close shave. He patted his jacket pocket. No phone. He patted the other pocket. Still no phone. He checked his jeans pockets, his jersey pocket. Still no cell.

Then he remembered. It fell on the Ferrari floor.

He moaned. No phone, no cab. Thick, wet darkness robbing him of visibility. And no GPS to get out of here and back to Edmonds.

The rain soaked his face and mingled with repentant tears. He tugged his hood over his head and shuffled forward. Vienna had approached the house from the right. He headed the way they'd come in. But he didn't know if he was facing north, east, or south. If he was facing west, he was in deep yogurt. To the west lay the cliffs over Puget Sound.

He kept his feet moving and his mouth talking to God.

"I don't deserve Your favor right now." He wiped his face on his sleeve, leaving a moist smear. "But I can tell You're watching over me. Thank You for jamming the gates. Please help me find my way out of here, even if I have to walk all night."

As long as he felt hard pavement under his feet, he was still on the road. If he swerved off, crunching gravel warned him.

"I was wrong to think I could go my own way. Please forgive me." Headlights approached, and a shout of relief burst from his mouth. To see another human face right now would be a real blessing.

The car passed without stopping. He might even generate suspicion in these parts, a lone man walking along a deserted street in an upscale neighborhood.

A streetlight illuminated this section of the road. He was passing another gate on his right. To his left, the road forked.

Which fork to take?

He crossed the road, peering into thick darkness. Something protruded in front of him, and he extended his hand, encountering a hard, metallic object, rounded on top.

A mailbox.

So, he wouldn't take the fork into someone's driveway.

He stayed to the right, until he came to another streetlight showing the road still curving. For all he knew, he could be walking deeper into the neighborhood. Or heading in a circle. He shuddered at the thought of ending up back in front of Vienna's house.

He'd been so naïve. She'd seemed so sweet and innocent. But it had been a ruse. A scheme of the enemy's.

He groaned and poured out his confession to his

Heavenly Father. "I'll never stray again, Lord. Lesson learned. Please show me the way to go."

He stopped. The Lord was whispering to his spirit.

Follow the light.

Craning, he looked at the sky, unsure what light he was supposed to follow. Chilly rain drenched his face and startled him with its force.

He trudged several more yards, before a gap opened in the trees to his left. A faint, distant glow shone through. The lights of the nearest town. Edmonds.

And he knew which direction he was going.

Follow the Light.

"Yes, Lord. Always."

He was soaked, shivering, and cold. Yet the presence of the Lord came over him with such strength, he might as well be walking the streets of heaven.

Chapter Thirty-Five

Livy's Smartphone buzzed with an incoming e-mail as she sipped English Breakfast tea mixed with chamomile in the sunroom, her Bible spread open on her lap. Pulling her attention away from Psalm 23, she picked up the phone.

The message was from Scott. Need Your Help said the subject line. Why e-mail when he could simply text? Or call.

> Hi Livy,
> Hey, something came up that I might need yours and DeeDee's help with. Wondering if you all will be at the dance place tonight. I'd like to drop by and discuss. Blessings, Scott.

She tipped her head toward the back of the house. "Deeds!" Most likely, DeeDee was still in bed. Livy suspected Nick was in there with her. Last night, when she'd woken up in the wee hours of the morning, she'd heard faint voices in DeeDee's bedroom.

Hearing no response, she hit Reply.

> Hi Scott. I'm not sure of our schedule. You can always come to the house if you need to talk. I'll get back to you when I know more. Livy.

They worked out a plan for Scott to meet them at Saffire

that evening. Livy wished she didn't have to wait so long. He'd been so mysterious, giving not a hint as to what this was about. He didn't return her text, and her single phone call to him went straight to voice mail.

Finally. Time to find out what was going on. Scott's gaze kept shifting as he sat in Saffire's small office. His knee bounced nonstop, and sagging lines bagged under his eyes, giving him a deer-in-the-headlights look. Dark stubble sprouted on his chin and jaw.

She and DeeDee sat on the other side of the desk and waited. "What can we do for you, Scott?" DeeDee's businesslike tone cut the tension.

His eyes sought Livy. "I'm in a bind. I'm kind of embarrassed to tell you this, but I spent some time with your friend Vienna yesterday, and now I realize I shouldn't have."

DeeDee made a noise in her throat. "I knew that playette was up to something."

He lowered his chin, color mottling his thick neck. "Anyway, long story short, I dropped my phone in her car, and I was hoping y'all could try to get it for me."

"Oh, no." A pang of sympathy pierced Livy's surprise. Hadn't she just told Paula she couldn't picture him sucked into temptation?

"I think we can get your phone back." Righteous indignation brimmed in her twin's tone. "Can you tell us what happened?"

He squirmed and fidgeted. "She told me she had backstage passes for The Black Eyed Peas, and asked me to meet her at a place in Edmonds." The story tumbled out of his mouth, and Livy could picture every detail. Vampy Vee taking on the role of grieving daughter, playing on Scott's soft heart, luring him to her car, then to her house, intending to trap him into giving her what she wanted. She'd bet Vienna let the dogs loose in hopes they would track him and lure him to the house for safety. Instead, God had intervened.

Livy shuddered, impressed by the way he'd kept his wits and managed to escape, something very few men would consider once Vienna had her hooks in them. Livy had to admire him.

When he finished his story, he massaged the stubble on his jaw with quick, agitated strokes, his eyes pleading with Livy.

Livy clicked her tongue. "She has a long history of that kind of behavior." She glanced at DeeDee's glowering face, then at Scott. "What happened once you were out of the house?"

"I started walking, and eventually this young couple pulled over and offered me a ride. They seemed friendly, and they were wearing crosses, so I figured God sent them. I was about a quarter mile from the main road into Edmonds. They drove me to my car."

"Wow." Livy felt like cheering.

"I'm glad you told us." DeeDee swung one leg over the other. "I knew she had designs on you, and I told her not to mess with you. Now I wish I'd warned you. I apologize. I should have said something."

Livy searched her mind for something reassuring. "You don't need to feel embarrassed, Scott. Vienna is a trained actress."

DeeDee nodded. "She can make almost anyone believe almost anything."

"Except us."

"And her mother." DeeDee met Livy's eyes. "Time to fire the tramp."

"Indeed. Scott, we'll get your phone. And we'll see to it you never encounter Vienna again."

He smiled, looking years younger as he stood and strode to the door. He paused and waved. "Thanks. Just e-mail me when you have the phone."

The dark silence swallowed him up. The outside door clanged, then thudded closed.

DeeDee broke the silence first. "Think he's telling the truth?"

"Of course he is. I'd believe him over Vee any day."

DeeDee nudged her. "He likes you."

Livy whirled. "Wha—?"

"He likes you in *that* way." DeeDee grinned. "I can tell."

"No, he doesn't."

"Guys have always liked you." Her voice tightened. "Didn't you notice the way he looks at you?"

"No." Okay, maybe a little.

"Anyway, if things don't work out between you and Will, now you have a Plan B."

"Deeds." Livy snickered and elbowed her twin, enjoying the rekindled camaraderie. Their mutual disgust over Vienna's shenanigans had revived their bond.

She wasn't sure what to think about DeeDee's assertion. This wouldn't be the first time Deeds claimed someone liked her when he didn't.

Time to change the subject. "Deeds? About Vee? We need a plan."

***

DeeDee squealed the Jaguar to a halt within inches of Vienna's closed gates. Livy, in back, jerked forward. Audria, in front, grabbed the bird's-eye walnut dashboard.

"Oomph." Livy flinched as her teeth chomped on her tongue.

DeeDee lifted her coffee cup to her lips. "Think she'll still be in bed?" The dashboard clock read 8:13 a.m.

"I have no doubt." Audria lowered the window. "I'll punch in the gate code." Her fingers, barely reaching the keypad, made five quick jabs. The gates glided up, and DeeDee guided the car inside and stopped next to the garage. With the master bedroom on the other end of the house, Vienna wouldn't hear the engine hum.

Audria got out and went around the corner of the garage. Livy pictured Scott fleeing across this lawn. How furious Vienna must have been after he'd thwarted her.

Kudos to Scott.

Less than five minutes later, Audria sauntered over waving a black iPhone. "Got it. The car was unlocked, the phone under the seat. I doubt she even knew."

Livy drooped in relief. Good thing they'd recruited Audria. It hadn't been difficult convincing her to believe Scott's story.

"Lucky for him, she didn't know he dropped his phone." DeeDee coasted in reverse out the driveway and started the engine once she'd rolled onto the street. "She'd probably accuse him of something he didn't do, like she did with that guy last year."

Livy gasped. She had forgotten that. Last summer, one of Vienna's potential conquests refused her advances, but accidentally left his wallet at her house. The next day, she'd had him arrested for attempted rape. The poor guy spent a week in jail before police dropped the charges due to lack of evidence and Vienna's drug use history.

What a travesty of justice. Livy would rather see a guilty man go free than an innocent one thrown in jail.

***

"Hey, Vee." DeeDee motioned Vienna to the chair opposite her in Saffire's office. Vienna's heels clicked a staccato rhythm as she approached. "Thanks for coming in early."

Midafternoon sun, playing hide-and-seek with the

clouds, threw a dusty beam onto the ebony-stained wood floor. An air current floated through the open door.

"What'd ya need my help with?" Vienna, decked out in black, plopped down and flung one leg over the other. "Your text sounded mega-important."

"You could say so." DeeDee shrugged and removed an envelope from underneath Scott's cell phone, hidden away in the drawer. Holding it out, she faced Vee. "Here you go. Your final paycheck. We won't need you anymore."

Vienna gaped at the envelope like flames engulfed it. "Huh? You're firin' me?"

You bet your sweet grandmother I am. "Like I said, we won't need you anymore. You knew this was temporary, right?"

"Why you firin' me?"

DeeDee stretched her lips in the patient smile she used on her five-year-old students. "I won't need the extra help after all. I can manage six classes on my own." She thrust the envelope across the desk. "Here. Take it. If you have any stuff here, go ahead and gather it up and take it home."

"I don't have no stuff here." Vienna grasped the envelope gingerly between thumb and forefinger and flipped a blue tress over her shoulder. "Is this about Scott?"

DeeDee didn't flinch. "Why would it be about Scott?"

Vienna's eyes sparked. "You told me not to mess with--" Her mouth clamped shut.

"Vee? Did something happen between you and Scott?"

Instead of replying, Vienna opened the envelope, removed the check, and sneered. "Ain't hardly worth taking to the bank."

"You might like this one better, then." DeeDee removed a second check from the drawer. Instead of handing it over, she brandished it, the dollar amount clearly visible.

Vienna's eyes widened, and she opened her fingers, ready to snatch it.

DeeDee whisked it out of reach. "No, this is a severance check. You'll get it once you've signed a severance agreement."

"A say what?"

She dropped the check in the drawer and slid over a form. "Once you sign this, you get the check."

"What the h —"

"Sign, please."

"Why do I have to sign it?"

DeeDee clenched her teeth so hard they hurt. "To get your severance check."

Vienna gave the form a dirty look.

Folding her arms, DeeDee rocked back in her chair. "If you want to take a minute to read it, I'll wait."

Vienna scanned the legalese. "Just says I can't sue ya. Why would I?"

"Not saying you would. This is standard business practice." Although not typical for an employee after only two weeks. "Don't take it personal." Would Vienna notice the clause the attorney added, specifying the signer wouldn't seek legal action against any patrons or associates of the business?

DeeDee waited. She could imagine the war in Vee's head right now. Greed versus revenge. If she signed, she'd get money she didn't need and no revenge. If she refused, revenge against Scott remained a real possibility. DeeDee tapped her fingers on the desk.

Vienna's breathing slowed. Her fingers slid toward the pen.

DeeDee quietly expelled the breath she'd been holding. Greed won out. She nearly whooped as Vienna finished signing. After sending the signed agreement through the copier, she gave Vee the check and the photocopy, then stood and stepped to the door. "Thanks for helping us out, Vee. See you around."

Vienna stalked out, her high heels clacking down the hall and out the front door. Soon the Ferrari's roar faded in the distance.

DeeDee peered around the corner into the supply closet. Livy, who'd heard the entire exchange, had hidden there so Vienna couldn't accuse them of ganging up on her.

They exchanged a victorious thumbs-up. "Coolness," said Livy.

"Double coolness."

"No more Vee," they crowed, practically in unison.

Chapter Thirty-Six

Livy trembled as she sat in Maureen's waiting room. The words on her phone's screen blurred, made no sense. After five minutes of this, Maureen ushered her into her warm office and helped her settle in. They made small talk for a few minutes before Maureen got down to business.

"Today we're going to try something sometimes used on PTSD patients to help them sort through trauma."

Twisting her ring round and round, Livy took solace in Maureen's kindly expression. "Can you tell me more?"

"Sure." Maureen crossed her legs. "All you have to do is follow my moving finger with your eyes as we talk. You'll be fully conscious, so no need to worry that I'm going to put you under."

"How does it work?"

"It's supposed to simulate the rapid eye movement of the sleep state." Maureen stretched toward a glass-topped end table, where a pamphlet rested. "Here." She passed the pamphlet to Livy. "Take this home and read it."

Livy stuffed the EMDR pamphlet into her purse. "Thanks."

Maureen held up an index finger and moved it back and forth in a pendulum motion. "Just allow your eyes to follow my movements. I'll ask you some questions. Your job is to answer to the best of your knowledge."

Livy's gaze followed the pendulum back and forth.

"Let's start with the morning of June 5, 1993." A tense pause. "The morning of your mother's death."

Livy kept her eyes moving.

"Tell me what you would have done first thing that morning."

She better not get dizzy. "DeeDee and I would have gotten up and dressed—"

"What time?"

Livy pondered. "I have no clue. Nobody ever mentioned the actual time all this happened."

"Okay. Go on."

"We probably would have gone downstairs after dressing. Down the back stairs. But I don't remember."

"It was the day of your dance recital. What would you have worn?"

"A leotard and tights."

"Can you remember them?"

"I had so many. No, I'm sorry I don't remember."

"That's okay. So, let's say you and your sister went downstairs. Where would you have gone first?"

Livy wracked her brain, her eyes still undulating. "The kitchen?"

"The kitchen. That would be reasonable. Your grandma was in there, wasn't she?"

"She was in the kitchen making pancakes when she heard all the noise from the bedroom."

"Okay. So when you and DeeDee went down the stairs, you would've smelled pancakes cooking." Maureen kept her finger moving.

Livy sniffed the imaginary aroma of pancakes and shook her head. Her gaze flicked to Maureen's face. "I'm drawing a blank." She refocused on Maureen's moving finger.

"Has DeeDee ever told you in detail what the two of you were doing right before your mother died?"

"Not in detail. Her version is similar to everyone else's. She found my mother on the floor—"

"But you weren't with her."

"No. I came in later." Livy sighed. "Seems like we're covering old ground."

"I understand." Maureen stopped her movement and allowed Livy to compose herself. "Right now, we're trying to recreate the day, to see if we can trigger even the tiniest of memories. Don't worry if you're repeating yourself."

"Okay."

Maureen resumed her finger movement. "We know you weren't with DeeDee when she went into the bedroom and saw your mother on the floor. So the big mystery is, when did the two of you separate? And why?"

Livy followed the pendulum again. "I don't remember." She might as well be wearing a shirt with the words *I don't remember!* emblazoned on it. No other answer presented itself. No memories pierced the fog in her brain.

They continued for close to half an hour, Maureen asking questions she had no answer for. Frustration tore into Livy until she wanted to kick something.

Finally, Maureen stopped. "It may appear we're not getting anywhere, but often, if we're patient, the moment of epiphany will come at the most unexpected time." She folded her hands in her lap. "I have an idea."

Livy watched her, hope seeping away.

"Why don't you bring your sister in next time? She can walk us through that day in detail, and maybe it will awaken something in your mind."

Livy shrugged. "I'll ask her."

Maureen stood, assisted Livy to her feet, and escorted her to the elevator. "See you next week, same time. I'm looking forward to meeting your twin."

Livy waved as she hobbled into the elevator, and then made her way, as she had last week, to Ivar's, where Paula awaited her.

***

A crisp, fresh For Sale sign in the McRabbs' yard greeted Scott when he arrived home from work Friday evening.

Finally. He chuckled at the irony. A mere two weeks after he'd hit upon the solution to Jamie McRabb, the problem was going away on his own.

Instead of entering his house, Scott strolled to James's front door and knocked. Nancy answered within seconds.

"Scott." She held the door wide, her smile equally wide. "Come on in."

He stepped inside. A thrumming bass reverberated from the den. His head already hurt. How did Nancy put up with it?

"Did you want to talk to James? He's here."

No kidding. "No. Just curious why y'all are selling."

"Oh, James got wanderlust all of a sudden." Nancy closed the door, led him into the living room, and plopped on the sofa. Vibrations shuddered the floor. "He's decided he wants to move to Hawaii. He's tired of the gloom and doom here. Since Jamie's about to graduate high school, nothing's keeping us here."

"Did he get a job there?"

"Not yet, but he's heard good things about the construction industry."

"He's fixin' to quit teaching?"

"That's what he wants. I'm excited. Looking forward to sun and sand all day long." Her round face lit up. "I don't think I'll miss much here. I grew up here, so did James, and we both think it's time for a change of scene."

Scott nodded. "I feel like that myself, sometimes. Especially lately." He glanced toward the den. "I got his speaker fixed, and I've been meaning to bring it back. How about I run and get it? Can you tell him I'll be over with it?"

"I can."

Scott left, sped to his garage, and grabbed the speaker. When he returned, James waited for him near the front door.

"Scott, my man." He eyed the speaker under Scott's arm, then his wife. "Nancy, make sure you take him a key-lime pie tomorrow."

Scott's stomach clenched at images of pie.

James beckoned. "C'mon back and hook that baby up. Let's see how she sounds."

Scott entered the now-silent den, and James flipped on the light. Scott set the speaker in place, reattached the wires, and cranked on the audio unit.

He leaned his ear toward the repaired speaker. "Sounds like she's working just fine."

James slapped him on the back. "Can't thank you enough. Enjoy your pie."

"Heard you're fixin' to move to Hawaii."

"Yep." James nodded. "Gonna blow this town."

"Doggonit."

"We'll miss ya. You've been a good neighbor."

Scott couldn't echo the sentiment. "Just make sure you sell this place to good folks."

"Oh, I will. Got myself a great realtor. She said houses around here are selling like hotcakes."

Scott scanned the rock posters, irresistibly drawn to Livy's father. Now he remembered the question he'd meant to ask last time.

"Hey." He pointed at the poster. "How'd you get Declan Decker to autograph this?"

James scrutinized the poster. "I used to know him, sort of." His words slowed, his eyes tipped toward the ceiling, as if he were sifting through a haystack of memories. "Knew his daughters way back when, too. He gave me the poster one day and signed it right then and there."

Scott tried not to gape. "How did you know them?"

"Long story. And a long time ago." James opened the door, sniffed, and said, "I smell dinner. Must be time to eat." He pumped Scott's hand, said goodbye, then exited toward the kitchen. Scott went home, even more curious.

Chapter Thirty-Seven

After Livy had shared with her twin the frustrating details of last week's appointment, DeeDee agreed to join her at Maureen's. Still, the high tension between them had scraped Livy's nerves all week. Whenever DeeDee caught Livy reading her Bible, she made the irritating snorting sound Livy came to hate, the sound that filled her with an uncharacteristic desire to slap her sister. Yet at other times, lighthearted laughter broke up the tense moments. She sometimes caught herself meeting DeeDee's eyes, knowing what she was thinking. Just as in days of old.

Paula had gently suggested Livy pray every time DeeDee mocked her.

In the car on the way to Maureen's, she broke out in a cold sweat. What if today was epiphany day? And why did the thought of knowing the truth terrify her?

DeeDee's sturdy presence settled her anxiety. Maureen held out a hand to DeeDee as Livy made introductions. "Hello, DeeDee."

"Glad to meet you." DeeDee returned the shake and cast Livy a doubtful look as she and Livy took their seats on the vinyl sofa.

Livy refocused on Maureen, who finished explaining the therapy procedure to DeeDee.

"So, DeeDee, your job is to recreate the day in detail from the time you and Livy got up. Livy, go ahead and follow my finger like you did last week while DeeDee is talking. DeeDee, you don't need to watch my finger. It would be better if you looked at Livy. Let her feel a connection with you." Maureen swung her finger back and forth, and Livy's eyes followed.

"Go ahead, DeeDee. Let's start with the time. What time did the two of you get up?"

Livy felt DeeDee's eyes on her. "It was about eight, I think. I bounced on Livy's bed and told her to get up, said whatever Miss Joy was making smelled good." Livy sensed DeeDee turn toward Maureen. "Wait a minute. It was really Grandma, not Miss Joy, cooking breakfast."

Maureen frowned. "So where was Miss Joy?"

"I don't know. Anyway, Livy and I got dressed—"

"What did you wear?"

"My Nirvana tee-shirt, as I recall, and Livy put on a maroon leotard. The one she wore the most."

Livy's head spun. "I think I remember the maroon leotard. It was my favorite." She visualized herself donning the leotard. "And I probably wore my purple houndstooth tights, didn't I?"

"I'm not sure," DeeDee continued in a faraway tone. "Anyway, we got dressed and went downstairs—"

Livy clutched the sofa cushion. "The back stairs?"

"Yes."

Livy felt DeeDee stare and listened to her rhythmic narrative. "You and I were heading to Mom and Dad's bedroom. Then I went in to use the little bathroom in the back hall, you know, the one by the laundry room—"

"You never told me that."

"Is this important or something?"

"Livy," Maureen broke in. "You're trembling. Are you all right? Do you need to stop for a minute?"

"I'm good." Livy sucked in a breath and reached out her hand. "Deeds," she whimpered, never taking her eyes from Maureen's finger.

DeeDee clasped Livy's hand in both of hers and

squeezed. "I'm here, Liv."

"This is great," Maureen spoke. "We're getting somewhere. Go on, DeeDee."

"Anyway, I went into the bathroom, and you said you'd wait for me by Mom and Dad's bedroom door. You were going to practice our recital routine."

"Really?" An elusive fragment of memory teased her, and then floated away like a feather.

Maureen broke in again. "How long did you stay in the bathroom, DeeDee?"

"Awhile. I was trying to get my hair to curl."

"So it could have been ten minutes? Twenty?"

"Not twenty. Ten, probably."

Livy's limbs quaked like Jell-O. She gripped DeeDee's hand tighter.

"I came out of the bathroom and went to our parents' room, but Livy wasn't there. I remember feeling surprised, but I went on in to wake Mom. I wanted her to fix my hair. Then I saw her on the floor." DeeDee's voice cracked.

Maureen stopped. She placed her hands in her lap. "Livy, look at me." Livy slid her gaze to Maureen's eyes and caught her breath at the earnest compassion there. "Those ten minutes are, I believe, the missing piece. During this time, something you saw or heard sent you into shock."

Livy swallowed. The soothing cadence of Maureen's voice washed over her.

"We're going to explore those missing ten minutes, okay? Let me know if it gets to be too much for you."

Maureen swung her finger again. "Think back to the hallway. What was there besides the bathroom and the laundry room?"

"There was…" Livy gulped. "Another short hall leading to the back door, out onto the deck."

"Do you think you might have gone there while DeeDee

was in the bathroom?"

"I could have. Or I could have gone into my parents' bedroom. I could have gone back upstairs. I'm drawing a blank again."

"Okay." Maureen kept her finger wagging. "Let's pretend you looked in on your mom and dad while they were sleeping. What would you have seen?"

"Their heads on the pillows. Their bodies under the covers."

"If you'd gone back upstairs, what would you have seen?"

"Nothing. Well, actually, I would have seen our friend Vienna sleeping in one of the spare rooms. And Grandma's stuff in another."

"Where would Miss Joy be?"

"I don't know —"

"I don't think she'd arrived yet," DeeDee cut in. "I think she came later."

"Yet you thought she was fixing breakfast."

"I was assuming it, yes."

"Was it common for her to fix your breakfast?"

"Oh, sure. All the time. That's why I thought she was down there making pancakes — Is this important?"

"I'm trying to recreate everyone's whereabouts. Was anyone else there we haven't talked about?"

"I don't think so. Vienna's mother came over later, shortly after Mom had been found."

"Okay, let's move on. Livy, I've been watching your reaction as we've gone through these possible scenarios. So far nothing I've seen made my radar go off. So let's consider the possibility that you went out the back door while DeeDee was in the bathroom. What would you have seen?"

A fresh wave of trembling jolted Livy's limbs. "I would have seen the deck." Her voice wobbled. "…The gazebo."

"You saw something on the deck or in the gazebo that morning."

"I-I don't know—"

"Why would you have gone out the back door, instead of waiting for DeeDee at your parents' room?"

A vague picture formed in Livy's mind. Her eyes darted back and forth in sync with Maureen's finger. "Someone was there," she whispered.

"Who?"

"I don't know."

"DeeDee, if you were in the bathroom during this time, you might have heard something."

"I didn't hear anything. I had the water running because I was trying to curl my hair."

"Once you came out, what did you see as you passed the back door?"

"Noth—Wait a minute. I vaguely remember the back door being open and the screen door shut."

"Did it look like someone had just gone in or out?"

DeeDee shrugged. "Could have."

"Did you hear any voices?"

"No. It was completely silent. Eerily so."

"Eerily silent. And you didn't see Livy either outside or near the back door? Even out of the corner of your eye?"

"I don't think so."

"Livy? Are you seeing anything else?"

"Yes." Livy's voice rasped a crackling whisper. "Someone was there." She could see a vague outline of a person—no, three persons—but no faces. "There were three of them."

"Three of them where?" Maureen's voice stayed smooth and level, speaking to the spooked child inside Livy.

"In the gazebo."

"Was it unusual in your house for people to be in the

gazebo at that hour of the morning?"

DeeDee replied, "In the summertime? It wouldn't be terribly unusual."

"I'm thinking, then, either Livy happened to see the three people doing something unusual in the gazebo, or they somehow made her feel threatened."

Livy's heart thudded as she tried to clarify the images. She finally shook her head, every nerve jumping. "I can't tell who they were or what they were doing."

"Do you think they saw you and did something to frighten you?"

"I don't know—" Maureen must be as tired of hearing it as she was.

Maureen stopped and picked up her clipboard. "We're running out of time, but I'm really pleased with our progress. I expect we'll have a breakthrough next week." She offered Livy a broad smile. "Livy, sit and relax for a few minutes. You're going to be okay. Take deep breaths and visualize someplace peaceful." Livy forced herself to ease in slow breaths. Little by little, her tension evaporated, until she felt ready to let DeeDee lead her out of the office, down the elevator, to the Jag.

With her tension gone, a weary numbness gripped her while DeeDee kept up a running chatter.

"I'm dying to know who the three people were and what they were doing. I had no clue anyone was out there. If only I hadn't stayed in the bathroom so long. I could kick myself-"

The moment she got home Livy lay on the sunroom futon and huddled motionless. Nebulous images swirled through her mind. She hugged a pillow against herself and groped for the phone in her sweater pocket. She called Will, who answered on the second ring.

She squeezed the pillow. "Hi, baby. I know you're at work, but I need you."

"Hey, babe." His voice, brimming with love, comforted her. "I have one more hour. Then I'll be right over, okay?"

Livy's voice tightened. "I just need you to hold me."

"Sounds like you had a rough appointment with the therapist."

"Very rough. But productive. We're getting close, but I'm kind of weirded out. When you come over, I'll tell you everything."

"Okay. I love you."

"Love you, too."

***

Even though Liv was almost seven, she longed for her old blanket as she huddled in the alcove. She couldn't move. Couldn't breathe. Crushing fear left her frozen. The previous scene unfolded in her mind, a scene she didn't understand. It couldn't have been real. She must have been asleep and dreaming.

Screams and cries screeched from the master bedroom. She jumped and hugged her arms around herself. Daddy and Di were making a fierce racket. She slid out of her hiding place and tiptoed toward the room.

She stood at the doorway, her heart tripping over itself. Di and Daddy knelt on the floor near the walk-in closet. Di's face scrunched up as she wailed. Liv, moving in slow motion as though in a dream, crept closer. Mommy lay next to them, face-up, like she was sleeping. Daddy's head was reared back, his mouth twisted into a silent roar, as he shook his fist at the ceiling.

"What's wrong?" Horror, paralyzing horror, gripped her. "Is something wrong wif Mommy?"

Di looked at her. As pale as death. "Mommy's dead. She's dead."

The ground shifted under Liv, and she screamed, "*No!*"

Because that would mean she really—But she couldn't have....

Liv collapsed, her mouth whispering the same phrase over and over. "Mommy. No. Mommy. No." Then she knew no more.

***

With a cry, Livy awoke to a wall of darkness, intensified by the absence of moonlight streaming through the blinds. The dream lingered, made more frightening by its reality.

Clear images floated there, images from the day her mother died.

Whimpering like a scared child, she peered at the clock—5:21 a.m. Somehow, her session with Maureen had dislodged an avalanche of memories. Now they filled her mind like boulders and demanded her attention.

She snuggled tighter against Will's sleeping body, and draped her arms around his middle. He stirred, and she let out a shuddering sigh, thankful he was here. She couldn't hope to find solace with DeeDee this time, who was sharing her bed with Nick.

Still gripping Will, she lay there, her heart whirling with fear and shock. Countless minutes passed with prayers in nearly soundless whispers, begging the Lord to show her what to do with her newfound knowledge.

Uneasy feelings snaked into her heart. And she winced. "Lord, I know I was wrong to let Will stay with me tonight." She mouthed the words so Will wouldn't hear. "I was just so scared."

A voice whispered to her heart, "Yea, though I walk through the valley of the shadow of death, I will fear no evil."

The psalm, still fresh in her mind from yesterday's reading, she'd failed to put into practice. She'd turned to a man for comfort, not to God.

As six o'clock neared, she eased out of bed with a firm certainty.

Chapter Thirty-Eight

The Boeing 767 approached LAX late Sunday afternoon, sank into a wall of cloud cover, and broke through over the Pacific. Livy, her stiff left leg propped in the aisle, peered at the ocean below, and the haphazard layout of the San Fernando Valley to the east. DeeDee, next to her, held her phone to the window and snapped once, twice, three times, as though she hadn't already seen this view a thousand times.

Livy reviewed the script in her mind, the script she and DeeDee prepped for Dad and Joy.

She practiced again as they disembarked, as DeeDee wheeled her through the endless terminal to the pickup area where Dad's limousine waited.

Good thing he thought this was simply a pleasure visit. He'd seemed surprised, but pleased, they'd hop a plane to come see him. Livy allowed him to believe it.

Dusk deepened to darkness during the half-hour drive through the valley to Los Feliz. Livy and DeeDee talked very little, only occasionally reviewing one or two points of their speech. DeeDee grabbed a beer and swigged it, finished it off, and reached for a second before they left the Hollywood freeway. Livy chugged water in a vain attempt to hydrate her mouth and throat, dry with nerves.

Dad's home sat on a bluff amid other grand stucco homes. Most of his neighbors had some show business connection. His short driveway ascended the bluff at a forty-five-degree angle. The limo crawled up it, curved left, and halted outside the lit-up front door.

The driver came around, opened the door, and assisted Livy with her crutches. DeeDee rewarded him with a wad of cash and rang the doorbell. From her sister's somber expression, and no doubt her own as well, Dad would instantly surmise this was no pleasure visit.

Joy opened the door and greeted them with tight hugs. Dominic and August hovered in the background, waving. DeeDee stepped over the threshold, and then helped Livy ease into the high-ceilinged stucco foyer and under the arch. Joy kissed their cheeks as Livy balanced her crutches on the living room's maplewood floor, as glossy and flawless as an airbrushed photo.

"Where's Dad?"

"Downstairs." Joy stepped back and beamed. Her hair, freshly colored, took ten years off her face. Straight coppery strands framed her thin face and draped to her shoulders. "Come sit." Her forehead crinkled. "Is something wrong?"

Livy glanced at DeeDee for strength. "In a way. We wanted to talk to you and Dad in person."

Joy instructed the boys to get Dad, and they lumbered toward the back of the house.

Livy tried to chug more water into her dry throat, but couldn't manage it until she and DeeDee had plopped on the deep green leather sofa next to an oversized fireplace. She propped her crutches next to her and poured water into her mouth. Area rugs, as white and fluffy as Murf, dotted the spacious living room floor. High arched windows yawned to the south. A wide staircase led to a second-floor balcony, fenced in with wrought iron and running the length of the living room. The boys' bedrooms lay behind the upstairs doors.

Joy settled in one of the two matching armchairs. "Do you want dinner? I baked enough lasagna for the two of you, if you're hungry."

"I'm not, but thanks." Livy faced the tall windows, but only saw dark shapes of homes and cars. On clear evenings, from the bluff behind the house, one could see the buildings of downtown LA to the south, shimmering above a layer of smog.

Her eyes traced the outline of a bronzed guitar hanging above the fireplace. The clock etched into it read 6:50 p.m.

Dad burst into the room, a huge grin crinkling his face. The boys tailed him. DeeDee stood and gave him a hug, and he sat in the armchair to Livy's right. Dominic and August dropped to the loveseat, which angled the sofa.

"Kiddos. How was your trip?" Dad scrutinized her. "You look a lot better than the last time I saw you. You must be getting around pretty good now. How long till that thing comes off?"

"Two more weeks."

He bobbed his head. "It'll be the longest two weeks of your life, probably. Then what?"

"Then I start physical therapy. Hopefully in about eighteen months, I can start dancing again."

"I wonder," Joy interrupted, "whatever happened to the girl who ran you over."

Livy shrugged. "I don't know. The insurance company took care of everything." Her stifled yawn reminded her how weary she was of the subject. "I hope she won't be traumatized for the rest of her life."

"I hope she will be," DeeDee bit out.

Livy shook her head in vehement denial. "She didn't do anything wrong. Both of us were in the wrong place at the wrong time. The girl was only sixteen. Same age as August." She held her hand toward her brother. "Probably had her license as long as he has. Imagine if he accidentally hit someone. Wouldn't you want the victim's family to show him some grace?"

DeeDee scowled as though Livy had suddenly sprouted a third eye.

"I'm a good driver," August blurted. "Not gonna hit anybody."

Livy fastened her gaze on him until he met her eyes. "Do you think she was planning on hitting anybody?"

A pained expression scrunched his face.

Livy pushed her next words out, her heart shuddering. "I've been praying for her."

DeeDee scoffed. Dominic raised his brows as he and August shared raised-brow glances.

"Praying for her?" Dad's gaze bored into her. "You still into this God business?"

"Yes." She nodded. "I've been going to church. You should try it, Dad."

"Nah. I went to church as a kid. Believed in God, all that. For a while, seemed like God was giving me everything I asked for. Then—*bam*. He took my Luna." His lip curled. "After that, I was through. I thought, better quit asking God for things while I'm ahead. Or He'll start taking other things from me as well."

Livy's heart throbbed. "I didn't know that, Dad. I had no clue you'd ever spoken to God."

Bitter lines etched his eyes. "In my line of work, you don't talk about stuff like God."

Livy searched for the right words. "Losing Mom was a tragedy." She met DeeDee's eyes, seeking an ally, but DeeDee's expression told her nothing. She scooted closer to Dad's chair. "But you know what? You could have sought God for comfort. He would've been there for you."

Dad's scoff sounded exactly like DeeDee's.

"Please, Dad. At least try church sometime. It can't hurt."

His mouth contorted into a sneer. "You came all the way down here to try to get me into a church?"

"No. But we do have something else we need to talk to you about."

Perking up, he squinted at them. "What?"

DeeDee moved over and patted Livy's shoulder, her sister's scoffing giving way to reassurance, and Livy absorbed it, letting it flood her to the tips of her toes. Her brothers still sat on the sofa, their focus intent on her. She couldn't share the matter on her heart in their presence.

Joy motioned them upstairs. "Boys, go get your schoolwork done. You can visit more later."

They grunted, but stood and clambered up the stairs, slamming doors behind them.

With every eye on Livy, she studied the peaceful landscape paintings on the opposite wall and breathed a quick prayer. "I came to talk about the day Mom died."

Dad and Joy stiffened, but she went on. "I now know what sent me into shock." She met their eyes.

Dad and Joy simply stared at her.

Her heart skipping, she peeked at DeeDee, who gave her another it's-okay smile.

"At probably a little after eight that morning, DeeDee and I went downstairs the back way." Singsongy tones emerged from her mouth. She gripped the leather cushion, feeling as though she were floating and listening to herself from afar. "DeeDee went into the bathroom and told me to wait for her. So I wandered toward your bedroom, Dad. But I never got there. As I passed the hallway to the back door, I noticed the screen door closing as though someone just left. So I followed and got to the door before it closed all the way."

Joy's face began to resemble a mask. Dad's forehead creased, his intent gaze on Livy.

"And you know what I saw?" Livy reached for DeeDee's hand. "I saw my mother, in her white robe and flip-flops, walking toward the gazebo. You remember how it jutted against the back of the house?"

Livy paused and searched Joy's face. It remained impassive. Yet her quickened breathing hinted at deep emotion lurking below the mask.

"I stood and watched her enter the gazebo. And I saw you, Joy, in there. With your boyfriend."

"Jimmy," Joy whispered.

Livy nodded. She squeezed DeeDee's hand. "You guys sat down. You probably didn't realize a small child could see between the wood slats. And I saw what happened next.

"Jimmy handed Mom a needle. I could tell it was one of those needles she used for her 'bad medicine'." Livy made air quotes. "Mom stuck the needle in her arm while you and your boyfriend watched."

Livy's voice broke on a sob. "I didn't understand why you let Jimmy give my mother the bad medicine you knew could kill her."

Sobs wracked her. DeeDee scooted close and held her. "I ran into the house and hid in an alcove." She sniffed and rested her head on DeeDee's shoulder. "Someone came in the back door. Then I heard Mom's flip-flops heading to the bedroom. Next thing I knew, she was dead."

Her sobs subsided. She looked at Dad's face.

Stricken eyes stared back at her. Then he swiveled his head in Joy's direction.

"Your scumbag boyfriend killed my Luna Tunes?" His voice rose to a dangerous edge.

Fright shimmered in Joy's eyes. "N-no…No. It was an accident."

"An accident, my —"

"We came down here to find out why," DeeDee cut in.

Joy's mouth sagged as her tears dropped. "It was the worst day of my life." She paused and pinched the bridge of her nose. A tense silence pulsed. "The night before your mother begged me for one more hit. Your father and I had persuaded her to go back to rehab. She'd finally agreed, and I was planning to take her right after your recital." She focused on Dad. "You remember, don't you, honey?"

Splotchy red colored his face, and he glowered at Joy. She shrunk back, her face a mass of puffy pink. "But she said she wouldn't be able to get through your recital without one last hit. Her withdrawals were so bad, I reluctantly agreed."

"Why would she ask *you* for one last hit?"

"Jimmy…" Joy stared at the floor, her voice a near whisper. "Jimmy was her supplier."

Dad jumped to his feet. "That no-good son-of-a—" When Joy reached for his hand, he shook it off. "I was good to that kid. Let him sleep in my house, eat my food, play my guitars. And he was backstabbin' me."

He kicked the loveseat once, then twice, and stood with feet planted, arms crossed.

"When I found out Luna had died," Joy resumed her whispery narrative, "I was so freaked out. I told Jimmy to leave and never come back. I told him if he ever contacted me, I'd expose him. He really was bad news. I look back and shudder over getting mixed up with someone like him. I'll regret it until the day I die." She met Livy's eyes. "I was very fond of your mother. Please understand how agonizing it was for me."

"It was obstruction of justice," Dad growled. "You never said anything to anyone. He should've gone to jail, but you let him go free."

Loud wails convulsed Joy's body. Two bedroom doors cracked open.

Livy glanced up to see August and Dominic peering down. "Shh." One finger to her mouth, she pointed upward.

Joy's sobs dissolved into sniffles.

Dad dropped to the loveseat, away from Joy, still glaring

at her.

Seeming to shrink inside herself, she went on, "I never thought anyone would know. I had no clue anyone saw anything. I'm so sorry, sweet Livy. Sweet DeeDee. Words can't express..." She wept huge, heaving, gasping sobs. "I tried to make it up to you by being the best substitute mom I could be."

Dad, calmer now, watched Joy, his eyes slits. "Go pack up your stuff. I want you out of here by midnight."

Joy gasped. "You can't be serious."

"Dad!" Livy started to leap up, settled for waving jazz hands at Dad, until she had his attention. "That's kind of drastic. It happened twenty years ago. Hasn't Joy been punished enough? If anyone should be punished, it should be that Jimmy guy."

DeeDee shifted forward. "Joy. Joy."

Joy finally met DeeDee's eyes.

"What was Jimmy's full name? Maybe we can still find him."

Joy's voice sounded less tremulous. She sniffed and ran a finger along the underside of her eyes. "I'll never forget his name. His first name was Anthony, but he went by his middle name. James. Anthony James McRabb."

"Anthony James McRabb, huh?" Dad's sneer twisted, and he blinked back wetness. "I'm gonna hunt him down. And I'm gonna find him. And then I'm going to make him sorry he was ever born."

Chapter Thirty-Nine

The return flight to SeaTac was scheduled to touch down at three in the morning. Livy's eardrums popped as the jet shifted into its descent. She had gotten no more than an hour of sleep, and couldn't wait to reach her comfortable bed.

She'd never felt so drained in her life. The grueling confrontation had been nothing like she'd expected. Granted, she hadn't known what to expect. She'd half-feared Joy would deny it, would accuse Livy of making it up. Fortunately, Joy owned up to her catastrophic judgment error. Twenty years too late.

No wonder she had gone into shock. To her child's mind, Miss Joy meant stability, not chaos and death.

Livy's ears popped again, and she sighed. "Poor Joy. Dad loved Mom so much."

DeeDee nodded. "I don't think he's ever loved Joy the way he loved Mom."

"I want to be angry at her, or hate her, but I just can't. I'm sorry she carried that secret all those years."

"Wonder if Dad will ever forgive her." He'd made Joy leave despite hers and DeeDee's efforts to dissuade him. Joy had planted teary kisses on their cheeks and reassured them she'd be okay. She'd headed to a hotel, while they extracted Dad's promise to financially care for her and allow her to spend time with her sons.

Livy leaned against the headrest. "I keep wondering what's happened to Jimmy after all this time."

DeeDee glanced at the city lights below. "Dad needs to

find out what crime was committed. Manslaughter? And would the statute of limitations be expired?"

"Dad will work all that out with his attorney, I'm sure. And once he does, I feel sorry for Jimmy. He won't let it go until he's made Jimmy pay."

"Of course he won't, after what that monster did." She gestured at Livy's leg. "And after what it did to you. I don't see how you can rest until he's put away for life."

The words grated on Livy. Putting someone away for life for involuntary manslaughter seemed overly harsh. Jimmy hadn't meant to kill Mom. He was irresponsible, disastrously so, but not a murderer.

The more Livy thought about it, the more she wished Dad would just let it go and move on.

She and Paula recently talked about forgiveness, and the truth that God always dealt justly with wrongdoing. All a Christian had to do was to put the wrongdoer in God's hands and trust in His vengeance.

Peace flooded her. God would deal with Jimmy McRabb far more justly than Dad could.

***

Afternoon sun beamed on Livy as Will held her next to him on the futon. After she'd confided everything from the last two days, all he could say was, "Unbelievable."

"I know, right?"

He looked deep into her eyes. "Did it help you find closure?"

"I think so. At least I understand what happened and why."

"And now you can put it behind you and move on." He picked up his water bottle from the coffee table and lifted it. "To your future." He took a drink, eyed her, and grinned. "To our future."

"Will?" Her heart leaped. "Are you trying to tell me something?"

"Maybe." His grin widened. "Didn't we talk about moving in together not too long ago?"

"Moving in together?" She gave an embarrassed chuckle. "At first I thought you were talking about marriage. I thought you were trying to tell me your divorce was final."

His grin disappeared. "Are you kidding? It'll be a long time before I get married again. Been there, done that. No, I want us to be together. We don't need a piece of paper for that."

She nestled her head against his shoulder. How to explain? She feared his reaction if she told him living together was no longer an option. Her yo-yoing heart couldn't handle any more drama. Yet she needed to be honest. "I can't live with you, Will."

He leaned back, placed his finger under her chin, and forced her gaze to his.

"Why not?"

She searched his eyes, hoping to see understanding, compassion, kindness. Instead, what? Chagrin? Uneasiness?

"Because." She made herself hold his probing gaze. "You're still technically married. It wouldn't be right."

His face jolted, and creases furrowed his brow. "Wouldn't be right?" His eyes were too close, like a tropical fish in an aquarium peering at her through the glass. "Oh, I see what you're doing. This is your way of persuading me to hurry up my divorce so I'll marry you. Right?"

She shook her head.

He didn't seem to notice. "Next thing I know, you'll tell me you're pregnant and spring a kid on me, too."

Tears stung Livy's eyes. She tried to scramble away from him, but the cast impeded her. "I would never—"

"Oh wait, I know." His tone dripped sarcasm. His eyes

frightened her. "This is all about that God trip you're on, isn't it? You're planning to live in a convent, instead of with the man who's crazy about you."

With sobs ready to erupt, she shrunk against the futon's edge. "No, Will."

He slammed the water bottle on the table. "You know what." He stood and scowled at her. "Ever since the accident, something happened to the Livy I fell in love with. I don't know who *you* are, but I want my Livy back."

Her throat ached with unshed tears. "That Livy is gone."

His hazel eyes went dark as though someone had switched off a lamp inside him. "I know." He looked at her through a sheen of tears, then swallowed, pivoted toward the door, and stomped out.

"Will!" The fist-sized lump in her throat spread to her heart. "Don't leave." The front door slammed, and she gave in to the tears.

***

Livy pounded on Paula's door. "Paula, please be home."

The door swung open, and Rick stood there. "Livy. Something wrong?"

"Is Paula home?"

"Yeah, she's in the kitchen. Come on in."

He helped her over the threshold, and then disappeared. Paula came in wiping her hands on a towel. "Livy?" She eyed the crutches. "Did you walk all the way here on those?"

"It's only a few blocks. And I needed to let off some steam." Livy felt her face crumple. "I think Will just broke up with me." She gave in to wails, and Paula rushed to her.

"Oh, Livy." Paula pulled her into a hug. "You must have cried all the way here."

"I did." Livy sniffed and looked around for a tissue.

Paula, reading her mind, handed her the towel. "Here.

Use this."

"Are you sure?"

She eased it under Livy's nose. "I have a great washing machine."

Livy wiped her nose and sniffed again. "I didn't sign up for this."

"Sign up for what?"

"My boyfriend telling me he wants the old Livy back." Fresh tears fell down her cheeks.

Paula placed her hand on Livy's back. "Come sit down." She helped Livy to the sofa and grasped Livy's hands in hers. "That must have hurt you terribly."

Livy squeezed her eyes shut. "I know exactly how Joy felt."

"Joy, your nanny?"

She nodded. Paula braced her against her shoulder until her sobs were spent. Then she held Livy at arm's length. "What about Joy?"

Livy patted her wet eyes with a clean corner of the towel. "My dad kicked her out." She gave a shake of her head. Paula sat, unmoving, waiting.

"So much has happened in the last two days." She hoped sharing with Paula would help get her mind and heart off Will.

She wiped her eyes again and brought Paula up to date, from dream to confrontation. "At least I know Joy didn't have ill intentions. I'm sure her boyfriend didn't either. It was simply a tragic accident." Out of the corner of her eye, she noticed darkness had fallen. She would need a ride home. "If I ever see or hear the guy's name, I'll recognize it."

"Odds are, he moved on to a life of hardcore crime. He might be in jail. Or dead."

"But wait, there's more." She met Paula's curious gaze. "Something happened a few months ago that I haven't been able to forget."

She shared the graveyard incident and the groundskeeper's odd, yet prophetic, words. "I want to know how he knew."

Paula wrapped her arms around herself. "I'm getting goose bumps."

Livy laughed. "It was a little spooky when I realized he was right."

"He had to have been a servant of the Lord."

"You mean, an angel?"

Paula lifted her hands in a shrug. "Possibly, or he may have been someone the Lord used to get your attention."

"He got it, for sure. But how did the guy know?"

"Why not track him down and ask?"

Livy tilted her head. "You know what? I think I'm finally ready—"

The doorbell rang. Paula patted Livy's knee. "Excuse me a moment. It's probably Scott."

If she could get up and flee, she would. She didn't want Scott to see her with tear-splotched face and puffy eyes.

A startled expression crossed his face when he saw her. She smiled and waved.

He smiled back. "Hey, Livy." He stood motionless as if waiting for her to say something. She sat silent. *Awk*-ward.

"Livy," Paula rescued her, "we invited Scott for dinner. Do you want to stay, too?"

He had deer-in-the-headlights eyes again. A fleeting vision of her and Scott trying not to look at each other all through dinner crossed her mind.

Time to make a graceful exit. "I'd better get home." She gripped the armrest and pulled herself upright.

Paula reached out a hand, and Livy clasped it. "You're not walking back in the dark. Come on, I'll give you a ride."

Livy cast her friend a grateful nod. "Thanks." Feeling

Scott's eyes on her, she turned toward him, but he was already striding over to assist.

"Can I help?"

"Of course." Paula called to Rick in the next room, "Honey, I'll be back in a few."

Flanked by her two friends, she managed to get out the door and into Paula's car with a minimum of awkwardness. Scott didn't say much, but she felt safe with both him and Paula beside her. Then he told her to take care, said goodbye, and returned to the house.

Paula backed out, and Livy shifted to face her. "I haven't seen much of Scott lately. He wasn't at church Sunday."

Paula frowned. "Apparently he visited another church."

"Really?"

"That's what Rick said. He didn't know why." She turned toward Laurel Court. "He must be looking for another church. He's missed two Sundays in a row."

"That's too bad."

Paula glanced over. "I hope he finds what he's seeking."

Chapter Forty

Once the rainclouds finished dumping moisture on the city, the morning sun emerged and threw a mirror-like sheen on the pavement outside Livy's house. She squinted against the brightness as a black pickup filled with yard implements stopped at the curb. Agape Landscape Services lettered the side of the late-model truck.

A gray-haired man emerged from the driver's seat. Although she hadn't seen him for almost a year, she recognized him. Plaid shirt. Dirty jeans. Kind face. Sam Somebody.

She limped out to meet him. When she neared, his face lit. "So it was you who called."

"I can't believe you remember me."

His smile could melt ice. "I could never forget you. I've been praying for you every day."

"It took me a while to track you down. But I'm glad I did."

He searched her face. "I have a feeling you didn't really call for an estimate."

They still stood on the sidewalk, so she beckoned to him. "Come on up to the porch where we can talk." Once settled on her front steps, she turned to him. "You can give me an estimate if you want. After all, I went through several phone calls to find you. First the diocese, then the facilities office, then two or three landscapers since they couldn't exactly remember who was overseeing the cemetery in June." She stopped, out of breath.

Those compassionate eyes surveyed her. "You wanted to talk to me about the night you visited your mother's grave."

"Yes, I do. As it turns out, you were right. On the morning my mother died, I saw something I wasn't meant to see. And I want to know how you knew."

He pointed to the heavens. "The Lord knows everything. With Him, there are no secrets."

She crinkled her face. "You mean, He told you?"

"Not in so many words. I sensed a deep burden in you. While we were talking, the Lord impressed a message on my heart, and I knew He wanted me to tell you."

She interlaced her fingers. "How incredible."

"I get this feeling you've found the truth."

Livy chuckled. "If you mean Christ, you guessed right."

Tears sprung to his eyes. "You don't know how happy I am to hear you say so. The Lord has been seeking you."

"I realize it now. And I get what you meant when you said the truth would set me free." She told him everything she'd been through, then tapped the brace on her leg. "But I've been wondering something. Because of the accident, I may never dance again. Would God really take that from me for good?"

He shrugged. "I don't know."

"Would you ask Him for me?"

His voice was gentle. "He's your heavenly Father. You can ask Him as easily as I can."

She studied her hands, trying to find the words. "I do. Every day. So far, I haven't gotten an answer."

"But you will. I'm confident of it."

"How can you be?"

"He always answers His children's prayers. Sometimes the answer isn't what we want or expect. Have you read the story of Job?"

She nodded, recalling a Bible character who lost

everything before God replaced it all. The thought made her shudder. Surely God wouldn't...

"Do you remember what he said after he was left with nothing?"

She wasn't sure she wanted to know.

"He said, 'The Lord gave, and the Lord hath taken away; blessed be the name of the Lord.'"

"But he got it all back, and then some." She felt hope rise in her heart. "God restored Job's losses. He can restore mine."

"He sure can. But Job praised God even before he understood what God was up to."

"Seems way difficult."

"No one ever said the Christian way is easy. It can be hard to give praise to God when you don't feel like it." A smile stretched his face, deepening its crevasses.

She returned the smile. "By the way, what is your last name? And what church do you go to?"

"Baker. Sam Baker. My wife and I attend a nondenominational church up in Lynnwood."

She held out her hand. "Thank you for everything, Sam. You don't need to bother with an estimate. Consider yourself hired."

He stood, his lips twitching. "Very good, then. I can start today."

***

Livy limped alongside Dad and DeeDee into the cemetery, while Dad boomed out his annual Poe recitation.

"At midnight, in the month of June, I stand beneath the mystic moon—"

Livy leaned her head back and gazed at tonight's mystic moon, a pure, bright crescent pasted onto a cloudless background. Stars dotted the sky, bringing to mind a Psalm: "The heavens declare the glory of God." Her heart swelled, and she glanced at DeeDee, who appeared oblivious to the beauty overhead.

"Like ghosts the shadows rise and fall—"

She grinned at Dad's silliness and hugged a handful of flowers to her chest, taking in a refreshing breath of cool midnight air.

"The lady sleeps! Oh may her sleep, which is enduring, so be deep—"

Relishing her new phobia-free status, she would have skipped along beside Dad if not for her brace.

"Heaven have her in its sacred keep!"

Her spirits nosedived. Odds were slim that Mom was now in heaven's sacred keep.

They reached the massive stone and stopped. Dad spoke first, then DeeDee. Livy didn't pay heed to the words they spoke. Her mind and heart wrestled with a newfound awareness: Mom couldn't hear them. She never had.

When DeeDee gestured to her to take her turn, she took a reluctant step forward, ready to speak to the wind, but willing to for Dad and DeeDee.

"Hi, Mom." She tossed the flowers to the ground. "So much has happened since a year ago. After twenty-one years, I finally remembered what happened the day you died." She stopped, sensing Dad wouldn't appreciate a rehash. "Something else. I know God now. And I wish—" Again she stopped, unable to utter that she wished Mom had known God, too. DeeDee and Dad would hear her words as arrogant and self-righteous. She shook her head.

DeeDee peered into her face. "You're done already?"

She nodded, smiling. "Not that I don't have anything to say, but some things are best left unsaid."

DeeDee, as in sync as ever, nodded. Dad led the way toward the exit, where a different groundskeeper waited, a Hispanic man barely an inch taller than Livy. He greeted them in heavily accented English as he ushered them out the gate and relocked it.

They settled in the limo, where Livy lay on the seat and closed her eyes. The smooth ride nearly lulled her to sleep before Dad's voice jerked her into alertness.

"Livy."

She opened her eyes. DeeDee lay on the other seat, her eyes closed. Dad sat across from her, a beer in his hand, his gaze boring into her.

"What?"

"I've retained an attorney to press charges against Jimmy. If the prosecutor accepts the case, I need you to testify."

An eerie déjà vu spun her head. One year ago at this moment, he'd told them he was being sued. And now, he was the one bringing suit.

How could she make him understand she didn't want any more to do with this business? She started to shake her head, but he kept speaking. "Joy will testify, but only if she's granted immunity."

"Dad, please. You don't need my testimony. Joy's should be sufficient."

He continued as though she hadn't spoken. "My detective found him, and my attorney's drawing up the papers as we speak. He's still in Seattle, real close—"

"I don't want to testify." She couldn't bear to lay eyes on her mother's killer.

"Not even for your mother's sake?"

"You know they aren't going to believe me."

"If my attorney subpoenas you, you won't have a choice."

"Come on, Dad. Don't do this to me."

"You don't want to see justice done?"

She stayed silent, regretting she'd ever pursued this.

Would Dad really drag her kicking and screaming into a courtroom?

His head sagged. "A lifetime in prison isn't long enough to make up for what he and Joy did to your mother." She had to strain to hear over the hoarseness in his voice.

"It won't bring her back. Besides, isn't the statute of limitations up by now?"

"Murder has no statute of limitations."

"Are you serious? It wasn't murder. At least not in the eyes of the law."

"I suppose *you* think I oughta forgive the scumbag."

Did she? What an arduous task even for a believer, much less someone like Dad who'd never known God's forgiveness.

Dad stayed quiet for a long moment. Then, "That's what my grandma would've said. She knew God too."

"She did?"

"Yep." He chugged some beer, then swallowed. "Took me to church as a kid, prayed with me, helped me ask Jesus into my heart, all that good stuff."

"You're kidding."

"But I left all that behind, till the day I made a bargain with God."

DeeDee stirred and opened her eyes. Livy gaped at Dad, mystified over this decidedly uncharacteristic behavior.

"What kind of bargain?"

"The day I met your mother," words rushed out of him, "I got thrown in jail." He'd told them his jail story as a warning to always obey the law. "I promised God I'd live right if He'd let me out of there and help me win Luna."

"Sounds like He kept His end."

"Yeah, He did." His speech slowed, as though he was reluctant to admit the obvious. "Then after we were married, I promised Him I'd live right if He'd let me make it in the music business—"

"He kept His end again."

"You don't have to rub it in."

She flinched.

DeeDee sat up, swiping at her eyes. "Dad, you went on a religious kick, too?"

"I suppose you could call it that. But it didn't last."

Livy needed to hear the rest. "What happened?"

"Couldn't keep my end of the bargain, that's what. When's the last time you heard of a clean-livin' rocker?" He shook his head and poured more beer into his mouth. "It's an oxymoron. So God punished me by taking Luna. When that didn't work, He punished me again when Joy betrayed me." Bitterness soured his tone. "Although I didn't find out for twenty years."

"Oh, Dad."

"Now I'm thinking, if I don't ever keep my promise to God, He'll make sure my worst fear comes true."

"What worst fear?"

He squinted at her before he spoke. "To die alone."

She shuddered. A fear rich and poor alike shared. Even with all Dad's wealth, his fear was identical to a poor man's.

She knew what needed to be said, yet held back. After breathing a prayer for the right words, she opened her mouth. "I think God's telling you it's never too late to keep your end of the bargain. But He loves you whether you do or not."

"Yeah, right. That's why He took Luna. Because He loves me."

"But you were trying to live right on your own power. That's why you didn't succeed. You aren't supposed to strive to please Him. He gives us the ability to please Him."

"Yeah?"

"Yes. Through Christ who strengthens us." She glanced again at DeeDee, who was resting her head against the seat, her eyes closed. Maybe she was listening, but wanted to hide it.

"I think I remember my grandma saying that." Dad's voice dropped to a mutter. "But I didn't get it at the time."

Livy's heart rate accelerated. How amazing if Declan Decker came to know God too. "Can you have the driver take us home first? I have some books you may want to read. After you read them, we can talk about them."

Dad scooted forward and tapped the glass, then opened the window behind the driver. "Hey, change of plans. Get off at the next exit and head toward Green Lake, would you?"

Chapter Forty-One

By September, the McRabb house had transformed from slightly shabby ranch to blindingly white showpiece, decked out in red trim. Surprisingly, it had taken six months to sell. According to James, their first offer backed out due to "inspection issues." So he sank hundreds of dollars into repairs. Then the realtor's father died, and she'd temporarily left her business in a newbie's hands while she headed to Anacortes to deal with estate issues.

Here it was, six months later, moving day at last. The house was a beauty. Scott was thankful it was James, and not himself, having to move away.

He had refinanced and bought out Shari's half in June. It was all his now. He'd been rattling around alone in a house designed for a family of five for a year. It was time to get out into the real world and develop the social life Shari's mother had admonished him to.

His new church didn't offer much to singles, which was perfect during his dating hiatus. But he'd considered returning to his former church and its vibrant singles scene.

And Livy.

He wished he didn't still think about her. Since her cast came off in April, she'd spent more time at the dance school. DeeDee hired a new teacher, Miss Ella. According to Paula, Livy joined the church's worship team and spent time with a couple of men from the singles group. He sometimes caught a glimpse of her on Saturdays at the studio, and it took all his self-control not to seek her out for conversation.

Now, perhaps, it was time to fan that flame. He'd stayed accountable to his men's group, and they finally agreed he ought to stick his big toe into the dating pool, and see where God led.

As for Shari, she still resided at her mother's home with Kinzie and Lacie. And he suspected, happily spent his no-strings-attached alimony and child support checks. She'd broken covenant and abandoned the marriage, and clearly wasn't coming back.

In April, he'd requested joint custody, and the judge granted his wish — two additional days per week with his little girls. And he'd finally found the perfect puppy — a six-month-old Shepherd-Husky mix named Felix.

Life was looking up.

This time of year, daylight lingered until almost eight. As Scott drove through the neighborhood to the grocery store, he passed Laurel Court. Out of habit, he glanced toward Livy's house. Only one car occupied the driveway — Livy's black Jag. On Friday evening, she could be out on a date.

Or she could be home. He swung the wheel to the left. God probably wouldn't mind if he stopped by to say hello. He'd finished his year of grieving. It had been forever since they talked.

He parked at the curb, thrust trembling hands into his jeans pockets, and strode to the front door.

He heard halting footsteps a few seconds after he rang the doorbell. The door flew open, releasing telltale odors of dinner cooking. Livy looked at him, her mouth in a perfect *O*. "Scott?"

His heart skipped into overdrive. Skinny jeans and a white top accentuated her figure. Her hair, now longer, rippled around her shoulders and down her arms like a velvet shawl. Murf stood behind her, tail in motion, a glowing-white, full-grown beauty of a beast.

"Hi," he managed. "How are you, Livy?"

"I'm doing good." Her dazzling eyes widened. Still clutching the doorknob, she leaned back and glanced over her right shoulder. He heard a man's voice swell in the background. It could have been the TV.

She faced him. "I have company. Sorry," she said in an almost-whisper.

A man. He knew it.

Unable to speak, he pivoted and rushed to his car. Idiot. How he itched for the wide-open straightaways of Texas. He would fly down the highway at a hundred miles an hour with the windows down, letting the wind whip away all his foolishness.

***

Livy sipped a cinnamon latte at JavaJava Saturday morning while she waited for Paula. She scanned the familiar faces, until she saw A.J. carrying a four-pack of cups out the door. He nodded at her, but she looked away without returning his greeting.

Paula breezed through the door and headed her way. After exchanging hugs, they sat and Livy got right to the point. "I'm glad you could meet me. I wanted to talk to you about Scott."

A smile flickered across Paula's face. "Oh?"

"He came by my house last night while Ben was over, and when I told him I had company, he left without another word. It's been bugging me ever since."

"What's been bugging you?"

"Just the way he's been treating me. He's been less than friendly for months. Then he shows up at my door. Why?"

Paula's mouth stretched twice as wide.

Livy tilted her head. "What?"

Paula chuckled. "You haven't figured out he has a big fat

crush on you?"

Sputtering, Livy clapped her hand over her mouth as giggles shook her shoulders. Gulping in a breath, she pulled herself together. "How do you know?"

"His eyes every time you were around. He couldn't keep them off you. Even now, he asks about you often."

She couldn't stop the goofy grin. "My sister thought the same thing. But he sure has a funny way of showing it."

"Indeed he does."

"Why didn't he just tell me?"

"I'm sure he wanted to, but was trying to give himself time. The poor man has been womanless for a year. He's behaving like the guy in a song I remember from middle school."

"What song?"

"It came out long before you were born. 1979. Chuck E was his name. The female singer couldn't figure out why he was acting so strange all of a sudden. She'd look for him in their usual hangouts, like the pool hall, the drugstore, but he wouldn't be there. Finally, she figured out what was going on. He was in love. With her."

Livy's heart danced around in her chest.

"You can find the lyrics online."

She swirled the foam in her cup, silly grin still intact.

"How do you feel about Scott?"

"I—" Memories of their interactions whirled through her mind. "He's been a great friend to me. I'll always be grateful he helped me come to know God."

"How do you feel about Ben?"

"Ben? He's pretty nice. A strong Christian man. Loves to sing, like me. Isn't trying to rush me into bed."

"How about admiration? Respect?"

Livy stirred faster. "So far, so good."

"Does he make you feel the way Will made you feel?"

"Not at all."

"So it's platonic on your end."

"I suppose it is." A seismic shift was quaking inside her. As if from a distance, she heard herself say, "Scott is the smartest man I've ever known. I'm flattered he's crushing on me."

"You've heard the saying, smart is the new sexy?"

Livy laughed and leaned on her elbows.

"He needs a woman who sees him for the great guy he is."

"He is a great guy. While we were becoming friends, I kept discovering all these hidden depths—"

"I see."

"Not to mention his brilliant mind—"

"Of course."

"And a physique to die for—"

Now Paula was laughing.

Livy, vaguely aware she was gushing, slowed herself down. "You'd never guess how much we have in common."

"Like what?"

"He likes to mix coffees together; I like to mix teas. He likes sled dogs and so do I. We both like hip-hop." She shook her head and threw out a hand. "I can't believe Shari gave him up. But hey, her loss."

"Yes, her loss."

Livy blinked at the intensity in Paula's tone.

"And your gain, if you want it."

She swallowed hard and pressed her hand over her mouth. If she wanted it. Integrity, kindness, and smarts wrapped up in one gorgeous package. And hers for the taking, if she wanted him.

"I do." She looked Paula in the eye. "He was about to offer his heart last night, wasn't he?"

Paula nodded, her face somber.

The memory of his defeated retreat brought tears to Livy's eyes. "And I turned him away."

"You were in an awkward position."

"Now what do I do?"

Paula patted her hand. "I have an idea...."

Chapter Forty-Two

The smiling sun warmed Livy when she limped up Scott's driveway two hours later. Seizing a pigtail, she pulled her shaky fingers through it, checking for tangles. Her freshly polished red toenails peeked from the top of multicolored flip-flops.

An hour ago, first-date jitters rattled her. When she called Paula declaring she didn't know what to wear, her friend had laughed. "You could wear your rattiest old jeans, and Scott will still think you look stunning." Unconvinced, she'd grabbed and discarded several garments before opting for a boho-chic variation of last night's outfit: a mid-thigh denim skirt from Target, embroidered peasant shirt from Imports Plus.

She glanced at the house next door. The obnoxious blue car sat on the grass beside the garage, presumably to make way for the moving van. As people filed out of the house carrying furniture and boxes, a slight vibration emanated from the walls. Apparently, the whole family liked their subwoofers.

On Scott's front porch, she said a quick prayer. Peace flooded her. She raised her fist, poised to knock on the wooden front door, then changed her mind and rang the doorbell.

Undisguised surprise jolted his face when he opened the door. "Livy."

"Hi, Scott." She gave him a tilted-head smile. "I came by to apologize."

The way he regarded her transformed her knees to Jell-O. "Apologize for what?"

She tried to ignore her hammering heart as he opened the door wider. "Is this a good time?"

"Sure, come on in. Paula took the girls to a movie."

Livy stifled a grin. "How nice of her."

He led her into a living room lacking in scent or feminine frills. The flat-screen TV blared with a football game, but he picked up a remote and snapped it off before she could catch the score. He gestured her toward a rose-colored sofa, where she perched, and he settled his brawny frame into an armchair, his face taut.

Her hoop earrings brushed her skin like a gentle finger when she turned to him. "I want to apologize for last night."

His eyes flickered.

"I felt so bad afterward. I didn't mean to be rude—"

"You weren't rude. You had company. No apology needed." Despite the abrupt words, his mouth hinted at a smile.

"Thank you." She eyed her hands. "He was a friend from church. You probably know him. Ben?"

Scott ran his fingers through his inch-long hair, combing it in spiky clumps. "I know him."

"But we're just friends, so don't feel like you were interrupting anything."

"Oh. That's good to know."

Running her hand over her already-smooth skirt, she tilted her head. "It was so sweet of you to drop by."

He opened his mouth, and then shut it, eyeing her like a man on a diet might gaze at a dessert tray.

"I wish you could have stayed. We haven't talked in ages."

"No, we haven't. I was thinking the same thing as I drove by your street."

"I was starting to wonder if you were mad at me."

"Of course I wasn't mad at you." His eyes twinkled. "Why would I be mad at you?"

She shrugged, hands in the air. "Oh, I don't know. Maybe because of that bank I robbed last month?" She winked.

He laughed. His whole body relaxed. From ex-marine to skater dude in ten seconds flat.

Livy's laughter joined his. Then she eased in a calming breath. "After you left, I realized I've missed your friendship."

He inclined his head toward her. "I've missed yours." He exhaled. "It's why I dropped by."

The air crackled between them. Their eyes locked. She could lose herself in those eyes of his.

"If you want the truth," his voice tightened, "I've missed *you*."

She twisted to the side and rested her hands on the little table separating them. He reached over and covered her fingers with his.

"You're a special woman, Livy. I came by last night to tell you that."

She stayed perfectly still, afraid to move, to break the spell, relishing the weight of his fingers on hers.

He locked eyes with her again and caressed her palm. She savored their shared silence, their shared connection. The tingling sensations in her hands.

"Can I take you out for dinner and—"

The doorbell rang. Scott bolted upright. The spell shattered.

What terrible timing, said his expression. "Excuse me a minute." He rushed to the door in a huff of impatience. The door clicked open. "Hey, James."

"Came to say goodbye to my favorite neighbor." A man walked in. He saw her and stopped, mouth hung open.

Livy gaped. "A.J.?"

A.J. looked at Scott, his face scrunched, then at Livy. "You two know each other?" He waved his finger between them.

Scott stepped behind A.J., puzzled lines on his brow.

Livy stood, bracing herself on the sofa arm. "Yes. His daughters take lessons at our dance school. How do you two know each other?"

Scott crossed to her. "He's my next-door neighbor. Why did you call him A.J.?"

"Isn't it his name?"

He frowned at A.J. then her, his eyes cloudy with confusion. "This is James. James McRabb."

Livy reeled. Shock waves rippled through her, paralyzing her like a punch in the gut.

Anthony James "Call me A.J." McRabb.

Her mother's killer.

She waved her hand helplessly at Scott. Her expression must have alarmed him, because his eyes bugged and he bolted toward her as her knees buckled and she collapsed against the sofa.

"What's wrong?" He grasped her arms and pulled her upright. She breathed a desperate prayer and willed herself not to faint.

A.J. hovered to her left, his face a wary mask; Scott stayed anchored on her right, his eyes probing hers.

"Give me a minute." *And courage, please, God.*

A.J. leaned toward the door. "I can come back later."

Livy swiveled. "No, don't go."

He hesitated, his arm suspended halfway to the doorknob.

Courage flooded Livy like a warm ocean current. "I remember you now."

An uncertain smile broke over his face. His arm relaxed at his side. "You do?"

"You're Jimmy. My childhood nanny's boyfriend." She took a deep breath and let it float away, Scott's reassuring strength steadfast at her side.

A.J. edged closer to the sofa, eyes narrowing.

Scott gestured at the armchair. "Want to sit down?"

A.J. helped himself to the chair Scott vacated.

Livy scooted closer to Scott. "You used to hang around our house when my twin and I were little."

"You're Declan Decker's kid." A.J. nodded.

Scott's gaze stayed on A.J. She'd never told him who her father was, but he didn't appear fazed. He'd probably found out somehow.

She forced a light, friendly tone toward A.J. "But after our mother died, you disappeared. We never saw you again."

He plopped his elbows on his knees and threaded his fingers together. "Joy broke up with me." He turned his head, startling her with the grief and sorrow in his eyes. "She was real upset by your mother's passing."

"Yes, she was. So were DeeDee and I. My dad most of all." If A.J. only knew how close he'd come to the prison walls. If not for the prosecutor declining the case, he might be locked away right now.

"I was real sorry when I heard what happened." He studied his hands again. "I liked your mother."

"Did you know she OD'd?"

"I heard." He met her gaze, his eyes still anguished pools. Was he aware she could see into his heart?

Abruptly, he stood. "I better get back." His face wore its earlier impassive mask as he addressed Scott. "Need to get the rest of the loading done. We're driving down to Frisco and shipping everything to Hawaii."

Livy lurched. She couldn't let him leave.

"Sounds like a major production," Scott was saying.

She didn't hear the rest of the conversation. A.J. moved

closer to the door.

"Wait!" Livy rose and limped toward him. He watched her approach, standing frozen like a hunted animal.

She searched his eyes—remorse, regret, grief. She opened her mouth. Nothing came out.

They stared at each other.

Finally, words poured from Livy's mouth. "How have you been able to live with yourself all these years?"

A.J. staggered backward. "What do you mean?"

"I mean, I saw you give my mom her last hit of heroin. The hit that killed her."

He dodged for the doorknob. Livy tried to wrest his hand away, but he managed to open the door halfway before she thrust her foot in front of it, blocking him.

Scott came up beside A.J. and pulled the other man away from the door. "No, you can't leave yet. Sounds like you two have unfinished business to work out."

A.J. tried to shove Scott aside, but Scott planted his feet and stood firm. Livy nearly wept her gratitude. What a guy. Her hero.

Scott took the other man's arm. "Go sit down. Livy deserves some answers."

Instead of returning to the sofa, A.J. shook off Scott's grip and regarded her. Scott closed the door and slipped a comforting arm over her shoulders. She nestled closer and breathed in his clean scent.

"You want answers? Here's your answer." A.J.'s eyes flashed defiance. "I haven't been able to live with myself. Your mother's death was the worst thing ever happened to me. It woke me up, okay? I got out of drugs—never touched 'em again." He wrung his hands. "Been hoping for a chance to redeem myself with you and your sister. I hoped us being neighbors would give me the chance." His gaze shifted like a guilty child's and settled on the wall behind her.

The implication hit her. "You *moved* here because of us?"

He stared at the floor. "Like I said, I hoped it would allow me the chance to undo what I did."

A.J. stood there, wringing his hands, his face shrouded in guilt, and her heart twisted. So he'd suffered too, along with Joy, along with her and Dad, all these years.

He opened his mouth. "But y'know, I can't undo what I did. All I can do is ask your forgiveness."

Forgiveness. After years of phobia. The obsession that caused the ruin of her left leg, and the possibility she might never dance again. None of it would have happened. He'd kept his secret all these years. Bitterness chased away compassion. He didn't deserve her forgiveness.

She glanced up at Scott. He met her eyes and squeezed her shoulders.

She'd learned so much about forgiveness these last six months. Jesus had told a story of a king who'd forgiven a servant of an insurmountable debt. Then the servant turned around and demanded repayment of a small sum from another servant. The king heard about it and threw the unforgiving servant in prison.

She was that servant. And Christ was the king. He'd forgiven her a debt of sin she never could have repaid. Forgiveness she hadn't deserved.

A.J.'s careless actions twenty years ago wronged her and her family. Yet in comparison to the bushels of sins she'd been forgiven of, his wrongdoing amounted to a few shekels.

She leaned closer to Scott and soaked in his strength, then managed to whisper, "I don't know if I can. But I'll try. With God's help."

Gratitude flashed in A.J.'s eyes. Unshed tears burned in hers. She barely noticed Scott open the door for A.J., and their subdued words of farewell. She was only half-aware of returning to the sofa and collapsing.

Her breath was coming hard and fast. Scott sat beside her and cradled her hands in both of his. "Are you okay?"

She lifted her head in a weak nod.

He squeezed her hands. "That was unbelievable."

"It's so weird." She sought his eyes. "Since I know who he is, I can't believe I didn't recognize him. The man was Jimmy, twenty years older."

"You did the right thing. I was praying the whole time."

"Wait till I tell my dad." At Scott's questioning expression, she went on, "It's a long story. In a nutshell, he tried to bring charges against Jimmy, but the statute of limitations for manslaughter had expired. He was furious."

She could see on his face none of this made sense to him. "My dad is a long way from forgiveness. In fact, I still have so much to learn about it."

"It's one of the hardest things Christ asked us to do. Love our enemies, forgive those who wrong us."

"My dad won't even discuss God with me now. He's so bitter. It's like he's reliving the pain of Mom's death all over again. He keeps asking if God is so just, why'd he let Jimmy get away with murder?"

"God's justice doesn't always work the way we think it should."

"Why not?"

"He's also a merciful God. Unlike us. But aren't you glad He is? He chose not to give us wretched sinners what we deserve." Scott sat forward, elbows on his knees, his rough hands tight on hers. "Maybe this isn't about your dad. Maybe it's about James. I mean, A.J."

"How so?"

"I have a feeling God's working in James' heart right now. I've lived next door to him for years, never shared the Lord with him. I might be the only Christian he knows, and I failed him. But today, he got a taste of the Lord's forgiveness.

God's giving me a second chance to get it right."

Livy shuddered. What amazing insight. "We always think everything that happens to us is about us."

He nodded. "It's human nature. But sometimes God has a purpose we can't see because we're too close to the situation."

"God could have a purpose for my dad, too."

"He could. His purpose could come through you, when your dad sees you living out God's mercy and forgiveness."

Livy's heart welled up with tears. *Thank you, Lord, that I've found favor in this fine man's eyes.*

"In fact," Scott glanced out the window, "James hasn't left yet. There's still time to go tell him about God's forgiveness. What do you say? You feel up to it?"

She'd rather stay here with Scott. A pang of guilt pressed into her chest. *God, change my heart.*

"Sure, I'll go with you. But I feel so sad."

"Sad? Why?"

"Because after all this"—she nodded toward her ankle brace—"the years of wondering, I finally confronted the one thing from my past I'd been hiding from. But instead of relief, there's this huge sense of loss."

He rubbed his thumb along her palm. "Loss? Not freedom?"

"Yes, like I lost a best friend. My obsession is over. Just a big hole remains."

"And you have no animosity toward him?"

"Right now, I have mixed feelings toward him."

He squeezed her hands again. "Maybe a change of scenery will help you sort out those feelings."

"Like what?"

He smiled, his gaze burning with purpose. "First, let's go talk to James. Then how about we finish this conversation over dinner? I want to hear your story. Plus, we have some things to discuss."

She matched his smile. "What sort of things?"

"Dating things. Relationship things. Want to try that new seafood restaurant on the waterfront? With the Olympic mountains in the background?"

"You're such a romantic, Mr. Lorenzo."

He laughed softly and pulled her to him. "And I aim to prove it to you. Every chance I get."

The End

Author's Afterword

Dear Reader,

This is a work of fiction. Although many of the Seattle settings are real, places such as JavaJava and Saffire School of Dance are fictitious. Rosemary Drive and Laurel Court do not exist in the real-life Green Lake neighborhood. All the song lyrics and rhymes are, to the best of my knowledge, strictly original.

Eye Movement Desensitization and Reprocessing (EMDR) therapy is real. In my own life, it helped unlock a hidden childhood memory, just as it did for Livy. However, my use of it in this book should not be construed as endorsement. You can learn more about it here: http://www.emdr.com/.

Although this book ended before Livy learned whether God would restore her ability to dance, her story isn't finished. Life will move on, and so will her walk with God. Her story continues in Book 2 of the Seattle Trilogy. Stay tuned!

The primary non-fiction angle in this book is that of Christ's claim to be God in the flesh. Like Livy, you may wonder, did Jesus Christ really make such a claim? It's the most important question a person can ever ask. Because if it's true, our entire paradigm is turned upside down.

Many scholars--more learned than I--have sought the answer to that all-important question, and have produced an entire body of research. There are far too many sources to name, but I can recommend one online resource which can answer almost any question you may have about God, Christ, or the Bible: http://gotquestions.org/. Then you can decide for yourself whether the facts of Christianity that Scott shared with Livy are in fact true.

I also recommend Lee Strobel's website. He is a former journalist who used investigative tactics to uncover the truth of Christ's claims. You can find him at http://www.leestrobel.com/.

God's blessings on your journey to seek the truth.

~DVC~

Acknowledgements

This novel wouldn't have been possible without assistance from some wonderful folks offering their expertise.

Thanks to Deirdre Lockhart of Brilliant Cut Editing for her tough-yet-gentle critiques, for stretching me to the outer limits, and her endless patience. To Wendy Holley, critique partner and beta reader. I appreciated her listening ear and helpful suggestions. To Leanna Lindsey Hollis MD, Marcy Dyer, and Margaret Perry - a big thanks for clarifying the medical details. Any errors are unintentional, and are mine alone. To authors Gail Sattler and Misty Beller for their helpful insights. To Jim Dorothy, photographer extraordinaire, and Sierra Brownlow, for the use of her image on the cover. Many thanks to Pastor David Stevens, whose quote from a sermon on John 1 proved the perfect excerpt for the book Scott gave Livy.

Many other fellow authors from American Christian Fiction Writers (ACFW) and Christian Indie Authors lent their assistance in various ways. Thank you all for your roles in this exciting project.

Author Bio

Dawn V. Cahill, an indie author from the land of microbrews and coffee snobs, published her first book, *When Lyric Met Limerick*, in 2015. She blogs about puppies, substance abuse, and single parenting…sometimes all in the same day. She's going to finish that novel she started at age 11 called Mitch and the Martians…someday. She has written several newspaper articles and more limericks than she can count. *Sapphire Secrets* is her first full-length novel. Email her at dawn@dawnvcahill.com, or find her on Facebook, Twitter, and her website. She is a member of American Christian Fiction Writers (ACFW).

(If you enjoyed this novel, would you be so kind as to hop over to Amazon or Goodreads and let the world know what you thought of it?)